A SECOND KISS

"I think you're afraid to be alone with me," John said. He stared at Holly's lips, then his gaze slowly traveled down her body.

"I—I'm not afraid of you."

"Of course you are. You're afraid I'll kiss you."

"You said you wouldn't do that again."

"I find I cannot stay away from you." He stepped close to Holly and gazed down at her, his eyes hungry, devouring.

Holly knew that look. She'd seen it on his face when he'd kissed her before. Her pulse throbbed and her heart hammered. The anticipation frightened and thrilled her at the same time.

"You are so very beautiful," he whispered, smoothing back the hair along her face.

"I'm not." His fingertips brushed against her soft skin. The masculine scent of him, mixed with the spicy scent of his cologne, invaded all her senses.

"But you are. And you taste divine." He ran a thumb along her bottom lip while his free hand moved down her back and pulled her close. "Now that I've had a taste of you, I'm afraid I want another . . ."

He buried his fingers in the back of her thick hair and tipped her face up to his. "Kiss me, Holly."

The softly spoken plea melted over her. She didn't hesitate. She couldn't. She wrapped her arms around his neck, stood on her tiptoes and kissed him with all the ardor he'd aroused in her . . .

Books by Constance Hall

MY DARLING DUKE

MY DASHING EARL

Published by Zebra Books

MY DASHING EARL

Constance Hall

Zebra Books
Kensington Publishing Corp.

http://www.zebrabooks.com

To my best friend and critique partner, Sandra, a bright light in my life. To John, my editor, whom I will never be able to thank enough for making my dreams come true. And especially to all my readers who still believe in Christmas and its miracles.

Of all the nights within the year,
Oh, oh, the mistletoe!
That's the night to lovers dear,
Oh, oh, the mistletoe!

When blushing lips, that smile at folly,
As red as berries on the holly,
Kiss, and banish melancholy.
Oh, oh, the mistletoe!
—A Christmas song, author unknown

Chapter 1

Richmond, Virginia, October 1821

Holly Kimbel pulled at the ropes binding her wrists and watched a mouse scurry across the attic floor. It disappeared through a hole in a hat box. A lone lamp flickered in the corner. Dim shadows danced over crates, trunks, and pieces of old furniture around her.

How long had she been held prisoner? She glanced down at the marks she'd made on the dusty wooden floor and counted seven slashes. It seemed as if she'd been tied up for a year, not a week.

A gust of cold air seeped through the exposed eaves and wafted across her face and shoulders. She shivered, then jerked on the bindings, feeling the hemp cut into the chafed sores on her wrists. After days of tugging on the ropes, they were finally loosening. Thoughts of getting away drove her, and she yanked harder Another quarter-inch, and one hand would be free.

The heavy tread of footsteps on the stairs brought her head around toward the door. He'd be up any minute, probably with food. She tried to ease her wrist through a loop, but it caught at the wide base of her hand. She grimaced and tugged harder at the ropes.

The door creaked open. He maneuvered a tray through the small attic door. She froze and stared at him. He was handsome, with thick blond hair hanging down his collar. And he had searing blue eyes that could make a girl blush with one glance. He was like a lemon, beautiful on the outside, but once you took a bite, you knew how sour the inside could be.

He walked over to her, then gazed down at her, the ruthlessness of his soul radiating through his vivid blue eyes. "I see you're still here."

"Did you think I wouldn't be?" Holly gazed back at him, derision gleaming in her eyes.

"One never knows." He grinned at her. His teeth sparkled like the sharp white fangs of a wolf. "Have you changed your mind yet?"

"No." Holly tried to keep her shoulders straight while she twisted her wrists.

"That's too bad." He kneeled beside her and set the tray on her lap. His fingers dug into her chin, then he pulled her face around and made her look at him. "It looks like I'm going to have to keep you here until you do. Now you must eat and keep up your strength." He picked up a spoon and dipped it in a steaming bowl of soup.

"I don't need any strength to sit here and stare at bare walls." She kept her shoulders stiff so he wouldn't notice what she was doing, then contorted her hand and eased it through the rope. Almost there. The wide part of her hand slipped free. She bit her lip and fought a sigh of relief, then slipped the ropes off her other hand.

"Let's not have any more complaints. Open ..." He shoved the spoon toward her mouth.

He wasn't expecting her next move. His eyes widened as she jammed the spoon into his throat, then grabbed the tray and thrust it at him. Hot soup hit his face. He screamed and grabbed his eyes.

She scrambled to her feet and ran out the attic door and down the stairs, his curses ringing in her ears.

His footsteps were close behind her now.

She came to a dark, empty hallway and darted through a door, then gently eased it closed behind her. A sharp triangular beam of moonlight poured into the room through a window, throwing long shadows across a desk. She could see bookshelves lining the walls.

The lock turned on the door. Instinctively, she darted to the side, grabbed a heavy tome off the bookshelf, then raised it over her head.

He flung open the door and ran into the room.

Holly brought the book down, but he leaped to the side. The book grazed his shoulder, then tumbled to the floor.

"Damn you! Come here." He reached for her.

She jumped back and fell against the door, slamming it closed.

His hand snaked out toward her again. She darted to the left, barely able to avoid his hand, then ran around the desk.

Smiling, he advanced toward her. "It'll do you no good to run. I'll catch you."

"Not if I have anything to say about it." Holly circled the desk, matching him step for step. His tall, dark form looked like a specter in the moonlight. His eyes gleamed with a strange reddish glow that made her heart pound.

"You always had a stubborn streak in you." He caught her off guard and lunged across the desk. His arms clamped around her waist, then he jerked her back over the desk.

Her hip slammed against the mahogany wood. She yelped as he wrestled her shoulders down onto the desktop. A gold letter opener gleamed in the moonlight near her face. Before he could pin her hands down, she grabbed it and thrust it into his back.

"You little bitch . . ." he said in a croaked whisper before collapsing on top of her.

His head was near her ear. She heard him take one last rattling breath, then his breathing stopped. The dead weight of his upper body on top of her made her skin crawl. With trembling hands, she pushed him off her.

His limp body rolled off the desk. *Thud.* It hit the floor, the sound reverberating through the silence of the room.

Loud voices rose outside in the hallway. She glanced frantically at the window, ran to it, then pulled at the sash. She yanked on it, digging her fingernails into the wood. It wouldn't budge.

The voices were getting louder. Muffled footsteps pounded the hallway.

"Come on, open . . . please." She pounded on the wood with her fist, then put her whole weight behind her and shoved.

The sash creaked, then popped up.

She gasped with relief, gathered up the hem of her dress, and easily squeezed through the window. As luck would have it, she was on the first floor. She jumped to the ground.

The moment her feet hit the grass, she heard the door

to the study open. More loud shouts. Someone stuck their head out the window.

She crouched behind a hedge, her heart slamming against her chest, her pulse loud in her ears. She didn't dare look up, they might see her. Holding her breath, she waited until the voices left the room, then snatched up the hem of her dress and ran into the street. The din of her footsteps rang hollow on the cobblestones. Several lights burned in the windows of houses lining the street. It must be close to nine o'clock. She listened for footsteps behind her, but heard nothing except her own heavy breathing.

She sprinted down Nineteenth Street toward the dock, the cold night air burning her lungs. A breeze brushed her face, bringing with it the moldy, fishy scent of the James River.

Frowning, she remembered something and darted into a deserted alley. After a careful glance around her to make sure she was alone, she lifted the hem of her blue satin dress. She slid a still-trembling hand through a concealed opening in her petticoat, then beneath a false front. Her fingers connected with a small brooch near her thigh. She tugged it loose from where she'd sewn it.

She stood up straight, shook down the hem of her dress, then held up the large brooch, watching the diamonds shimmer around a fat ruby. Her fingers clamped around the brooch as if it were a talisman, then she rushed back into the street.

She strode downhill, increasing her strides, her suede shoes squishing through the mud. It had rained for three days straight. She had listened to it beating the attic roof. Piles of horse manure dotted the street and mixed with the mud, and she dodged them as best she could. When she reached the bottom of the hill, she turned left on Water Street.

The street looked alive with activity, even though it was late at night. Light glowed beneath the shutters that covered Union Tavern's windows. Several sailors mulled out front, propositioning harlots. Holly saw one of the men glance at her, but she kept her head down and almost ran toward the dock.

Stevedores lined the pier, loading a carriage onto a passenger ship. The captain stood on the bridge watching the progress, barking orders every now and then. He was an older, bearded man, swarthy in complexion. Deep wrinkles crossed a wide brow and gave him an aggressive bulldog expression, which was at odds with his vivid soft, gray eyes. An elderly couple stood next to the captain, eagerly watching the progress. By the intense expression on the gentleman's face, she guessed they must be the owners of the carriage. Three young ladies and several gentlemen stood next to them. They, too, observed the progress of the carriage as the men heaved it higher on the hoist.

Holly paused below the captain, cupped her hands, and called up to him on deck. "Can I gain passage on your ship?"

He stared down at her for a moment and took her measure, then the wrinkles in his brow deepened. In a thick Scottish brogue he said, "You don't even know where I'm going, lass."

"It doesn't matter, as long as I leave here right away."

A knowing gleam shown from his eyes. His bushy red beard parted in a grin. "Oh, you're wantin' that kind of passage." He waved his hand in a dismissive gesture, evidently not wanting to be bothered. "We're booked solid, all the cabins are full."

"I'll sleep anywhere," she said, pleading.

He paused a moment and pulled on his beard. "I do need a cook." He eyed her from beneath his bushy red brows. "Can you cook?"

"Oh, yes." Holly hoped the captain couldn't detect the lie in her voice, but in case he did, she held up the brooch in her hand so he could get a good look at it. "And I have this."

He narrowed his eyes at it a moment, pursed his lips, then pulled on his beard.

At his hesitation, she blurted, "It's genuine, Captain. I could buy a quarter of your ship with it."

The captain threw back his head and laughed, then waved at her. "Let it not be said that Captain McLain left a young damsel in distress. By all means come aboard, but you'll be working on the voyage over, brooch or not."

"Thank you, Captain." She noticed the elderly couple and the other passengers looking down their noses at her.

She avoided their gazes. Her present situation would no doubt label her as a lightskirt. She was a young woman, coming on board a ship at night, unescorted, without clothes or belongings, and working as a cook to boot. It just wasn't done by proper young ladies, but her properness had ended a week ago when she'd been snatched from her home and taken prisoner.

As she strode up the gangway, she inadvertently glanced over her shoulder. It was a mistake. Her gaze strayed back toward the dark hills of Richmond, toward the house that had been her prison for a week. She couldn't actually see the house for the trees, but she could feel it looming down on her. Memories of it would haunt her forever.

She touched the rope burns on her wrists. With vivid clarity, she remembered the daggerlike feel of the letter opener in her hand, the way it felt when it entered his back, the weight of his limp body on top of her. Her skin crawled. She rubbed her arms, then whipped back around and ran to the top of the gangway.

A queasy feeling churned up bile in her throat. She'd killed a man. How could she live with her conscience? Swallowing hard, she stumbled onto the deck. The ship's gentle rocking made her trembling legs more unsteady, and she grabbed the rail to keep from falling. She noticed the passengers and crew were watching her with a marked degree of suspicion and interest.

Don't fall apart. Not now. If she cried now, it would bring more attention to herself. Blinking back the tears that wanted so much to spill from her eyes, she stiffened her spine, then strode toward the starboard side of the ship, away from everyone. When she was far from the Virginia coastline, then she could cry.

London docks, December 15, 1821

John Bennington Holland Wentworth St. John, the Earl of Upton, sat at his desk, a ledger opened before him. He picked up another bill, frowned at it, then dipped quill in ink and posted the amount in the red column.

He stared at the amount in the blue column, then at the much larger figure in the red column. He shook his head, then mumbled a curse under his breath. His deep voice carried around the small, empty shipping office. He put down the quill, rubbed his burning eyes, then he pulled out his pocket watch. Ten minutes to midnight. He'd been working almost sixteen hours. Too long. He stood, stretched, then pulled his cape off the back of the chair and slipped it over his shoulders.

A knock sounded at the door.

He glanced up. Henry Thomas peered at him through

the glass in the door. John's eyes widened in surprise, then his brows furrowed. Thomas's appearance meant only one thing: bad news. He braced himself, then waved Thomas into his office.

Thomas was a short, stocky fellow. He normally wore a calm, placid mask of confidence, but right now his expression was that of a man who'd lost someone or something dear to him.

"Hello, my lord." Thomas executed a cursory bow and closed the door behind him.

"Please tell me that you've brought the family home for the holidays, Thomas," John said, with trepidation in his voice. "I hope nothing is wrong with the office in the Indies."

Thomas wet his lips, wrung his hands, then stared down at them.

"What is it?" John leaned across the desk.

"You'd better sit down, my lord."

"I don't want to sit down. Tell me at once what has happened."

Thomas looked up at him. "*Sea Challenger* and *Sin's Revenge* went down in a hurricane near Barbados. I thought I should come and tell you in person."

John rocked back on his heels, the words hitting him hard. It took him a moment to find his voice. "Both of them are destroyed?"

"Yes." Thomas looked down at his hands again. "It happened when they were both coming into the bay at the same time. They smashed into each other on the reefs. Damned queer bit of bad luck."

"The crew and the cargo?"

"All lost," Thomas said, his voice barely above a whisper.

John plopped down in his seat. "What about the office?"

"I knew you didn't have the money to buy more ships,

so I closed it and came here. I hope that was all right with you."

"Of course. What else could you have done?" A sharp pain stabbed his temple, and he grabbed his forehead.

"Let me get you a drink, my lord."

John nodded, then held his throbbing head and stared down at his desk. What was he going to do now?

Thomas walked over to the bookcase, found a decanter and two glasses on top of it, then poured three fingers into each glass. "Here you are, my lord. Drink it, it will do you good. I drank a whole bottle of port when I heard the news."

John took the glass and downed it in one gulp.

"What will happen to the company?" Thomas asked, taking a seat opposite the desk.

"I just don't know. I've got *The Saint Ann* left, but if word gets out, my investors might pull out."

"I'm sure word has reached the East India Trading Company. Your ships weren't the only ones to go down. They lost three of their own."

"I'm sure the wolves will be at my door."

"I wish it hadn't happened, my lord. I enjoyed managing the West Indies office for you."

John came out of his own despair for a moment and looked at Thomas. "I would like to keep you on here at this office, but I can't afford to pay you."

"I know that. I'll find work somewhere here in London, but thank you for thinking of me."

"You've been a good employee, Thomas." John stood up, walked over to a safe, opened it, then took out the last fifty pounds in it. He turned and handed it to Thomas. "Here. Back pay that I owe you. I know it's not all, but it might tide you over for a while."

"Thank you, my lord." Thomas stood. "If you need

anything—anything at all, please ask. You know I'll do anything for you."

"I know that." John tried to smile, but he couldn't.

"Will you be all right?"

"Yes, fine."

"Good night then, my lord."

John watched Thomas leave, then ran his hands through his hair and stared down at the ledger book. The company was ruined. He'd never raise enough money to buy two new ships.

In one angry swoop, John shoved everything off his desk. Papers flew up and sailed out into the office. The ledger careened through the air, hit the wall, and landed in a heap in the corner. John took one look at the mess around him, snuffed the candle with the tips of his fingers, then walked out of the office without looking back.

The bitter wind that had followed them all the way up the Thames stung Holly's face. Stray pieces of auburn hair had escaped the bun at the back of her neck and blew across her nose and mouth. She pushed them back from her face, then shoved her hands down into the pockets of the coat Captain McLain had lent her.

She leaned against the bulwark, narrowing her eyes along the dock. Ships, all shapes and sizes, bobbed in the yellow swirling fog, their tall masts moving up and down like dark ghosts hovering above the water. Lanterns winked along the bows, glowing in the fog. She heard footsteps and saw Captain McLain coming toward her.

He paused near her side and gently captured one of her hands, turned it upright, then placed a handful of bank notes in her palm. "This will tide you over, lass. Are you sure you won't come home with me for the holidays? Me wife would love to have you."

"No, I'll be all right, but thank you . . ." Holly stood on her tiptoes and pecked him on the cheek, feeling his thick beard tickling her chin.

A collective "Ooohhh" came from the crewmen, who were mooring the ship to the dock.

Captain McLain turned toward them, his cheeks still blushing. "Get to your business, gents, or you'll be swabbing the deck for the next six months without shore leave."

The men turned, half of them smiling, and continued to tie the heavy ropes.

Holly folded the bank notes, then stuck them in a secret pocket she'd sewn in the seam of her dress. She leaned over and whispered, "You're all bluster. You'd never deny them shore leave when Christmas is almost here."

"Wouldn't I?" Captain McLain tried to maintain a stern mein, but it melted beneath a smile. His smile faded as he said, "What will you do, lass?"

"The first thing I'll do is find suitable lodgings, then I'll buy some material to make new clothes." Holly glanced down at her only dress. It was once a deep royal color, but too many washings had faded the satin to light blue. The hem was frayed and torn in spots from wear, and grease stains spotted the skirt from her attempts at cooking. "When that is done, I suppose I'll look for employment somewhere. I don't know what I'll find to do. Perhaps someone will hire me as a cook." Holly cut her eyes at him.

The irony of her last statement made him throw back his head and chuckle. "I wish you luck there. Any more of that fine cooking of yours, lass, and we'd all be skin and bones."

"I know my culinary skills are lacking, but was it that bad?"

He patted her shoulder. "I'll make a confession to you, lass. I tried to feed the gulls those biscuits you made, and I'm sorry to say the poor buggers choked and coughed and died 'fore they could fly away."

"You're telling whoppers."

"I swear on me mother's grave. I've still got some. I thought I'd keep them and stuff them in the cannon the next time we're set upon by pirates." They both laughed, then all the teasing left his voice. "Sorry about you having to work on the voyage over."

"I didn't mind. It kept me busy trying to give you and the crew indigestion." She grinned at him.

"You're a good-natured lass, I'll give you that." The captain patted her on the arm. "Now, don't forget, you might find a nice boardinghouse with reasonable prices in Cheapside."

"You told me that." Holly smiled up at him for his thoughtfulness.

"You'll be careful. There are some who prey on young women all alone. And you being so young and only nineteen. It's like turning a rabbit loose in a wolves' den."

"I'll be fine, really. I can take care of myself." Holly said these last words with more confidence than she felt. London looked strange to her, even menacing, with the fog drifting along the dock, swirling between the many dark buildings and their shadows. The ship had been a comfortable haven for her and she really didn't want to leave it.

The gangway hit the dock, making a loud clunk.

Holly started at the sound, then she turned and said, "I should go. I want to be gone before the other passengers make their exit." She grabbed his hand. "I'll never forget your kindness."

Captain McLain blushed again. "It was nothing. You brightened the voyage for all of us, lass—even though you couldn't cook. Anyway, I owe you." He held up the brooch she'd given him and smiled.

"Yes, you do."

"I'll walk you down to the cab, a young girl shouldn't be alone on the docks."

"I'll go with her, Captain—that is, if you don't mind, Miss Holly."

Holly turned to see Kip, a sixteen-year-old with bright blond curls, behind her. His boyish face lit up with a shy grin. He stepped toward her, his peg leg tapping on the deck.

"That's very kind of you." Holly smiled at him. Since the other passengers considered her a lowly cook, beneath their notice, Kip, the captain, and the crew were her only companions. She had felt sorry for Kip during the voyage and gave him extra attention, teasing him out of his bashfulness. He had formed a boyish crush on her that she hoped would be of short duration.

She turned back to the captain. "I'll send your coat back to you when I buy one."

"Keep it, lass."

"Good-bye and Merry Christmas to all of you." She waved to the captain, then the crew.

They waved back, wishing her a Merry Christmas.

She walked down the gangway and onto the dock, unable to still a growing feeling of uneasiness. If only she could go back home where everything was familiar. But she'd never be able to go home again. The thought made her frown.

Kip was behind her, saying, "London ain't all that bad.

I grew up 'ere. Was a sweep for the better part of me life, that's how I lost me leg. I know London better than a body should. If you want to see the city, I'd be glad to show you the sights.''

"I would like that once I find a place to live." Holly listened to the *tap . . . tap . . . tap* of Kip's peg on the cobblestones.

"The cabbies will try to rob ya, if you let 'em. Better let me bargain the fare. I 'eard you and the captain talking. You going to Cheapside, that shouldn't cost more than six pence from 'ere. It's just north of 'ere."

"I don't know what I'd have done without your guidance. I'm sure they'd have charged me a pound, and I wouldn't have known I was being robbed blind.''

They walked down a deserted street. Gas streetlamps lit the sidewalk, casting a dim yellowish halo along the fronts of warehouses and shipping offices.

They turned the corner and strode along another street. It buzzed with activity. People bustled down the sidewalks. Lights shined from a tavern, the candles in the windows making frosty circles on the windowpanes. Holly noticed the cedar-and-pine garland hanging over the windows and the holly wreaths on the doors. Memories of the Christmases back at Kimbly, her grandmother's plantation, flooded back to her.

A sharp pang of homesickness gripped her. She ached for a glimpse of the swags made of magnolia leaves and evergreens dotting the thick oak mantels and doorways. If only she could smell the scent of her grandmother's gingerbread cookies and the apple cider brewing, all those spicy scents of cinnamon and nutmeg and ginger mixing with the clean scent of cedar. They always had a massive cedar tree for Christmas. Her grandmother liked the pungent aroma, which never failed to fill the large old Greek-columned plantation house. Holly had even been able to smell the odor up in her bedroom on the second floor.

Last Christmas was the happiest one she had ever shared with her grandmother. How she longed for her grandmother. Those thin frail arms holding her, the wrinkled cheek next to her own, the scent of the sweet rosewater perfume that always hovered about her. It was a scent Holly associated with comfort, strength, security, and love. She would do anything to hear her grandmother's steady, assured, prim voice say, "This will be our best Christmas ever, my dear." But she'd never hear that voice again, or feel those warm, caring arms around her. Her stolid grandmother, who bragged about never being sick a day in her life and who never complained unless it was about to rain and her rheumatism was acting up, came down with a high fever and died last January.

They walked near a small church. The doors stood ajar while a choir practiced. "O Come, All Ye Faithful" drifted from inside. Her lip trembled and a lump formed in her throat. She bit her lip to keep the tears at bay.

They strode past the church. Notes of the song drifted away, melting into the noises of the night. They came upon another tavern, smaller than the last. The sign out front swung in the wind, creaking on its chain. RILEY'S TAVERN was etched across it.

When Holly was about to glance away, the inn door swung open. A shaft of light cut through the darkness, then the silhouette of three burly men appeared. They stepped out of the tavern, the din of loud, drunken voices following them outside. They paused and looked at Holly and Kip, a cruel, unfeeling kind of stare, the way a butcher might look at a steer he's about to kill. Her skin crawled, and she glanced away.

"We'd better hurry," Kip said under his breath. He grabbed her arm and pulled her along.

Holly glanced over her shoulder at the three men. They were following them now. She turned back around, almost running to keep up with Kip. The steady thud of footsteps grew louder behind them.

"You can hire a cab around the corner," Kip said, snatching a nervous glance behind them. "The cabbies park their carriages there, while they go get a nip at Riley's Tavern." He lowered his voice and said, "Whatever you do, don't turn around, Miss Holly. Just keep walking to the cabbies. I'll have to handle the brutes behind us."

Kip pulled her around the corner. Cabs lined the street, their lanterns casting hazy yellowish circles in the foggy night. Most of the drivers were gone, save for one. He was huddled down in the seat, his head bowed, looking either drunk or asleep. Holly saw a tall man in a cape on the opposite side of the street, walking toward the cabs.

"You can't fight those men alone," she said, her voice tremulous.

"I know what I'm doin'," he said with more authority than she'd ever heard him use. "I've survived on the streets for most of me childhood. I'll be all right." He reached inside his coat and pulled out a dagger. "When I say run, you run."

Holly heard the footsteps closing in behind them, each muscle along her spine tensing. "I can't leave you."

"I know how to protect meself. You run to a cab and hop in, and no more about it. I can't be fighting these blokes and worryin' about you." Louder, he said, "Run!"

The authority and irritation in his voice galvanized Holly. She lifted up the hem of her dress and bolted. But she didn't get more than a few yards before her shoe hit a raised cobblestone. Her ankle twisted, then she lost her balance and tumbled forward, hitting the street. Barely aware of the pain in her scraped elbows and knees, she glanced behind her at Kip. He was jabbing his blade at two of the men, while the third one ran toward her.

Pain stabbed her ankle as she scrambled to get up. A pair of beefy hands grabbed her waist from behind, then she was lifted off the ground with a jerk. She landed in the arms of the third man.

"Hello, honey," he said, grinning, exposing his rotten teeth. "Got any spare change?"

"No!" Holly smelled the strong, sour odor of ale on his foul breath, while she balled up her fist and swung at his face.

"You're a mean little article, ain't you." Rotten Teeth grabbed her arms and clamped them down at her side.

"I can get a lot meaner," she hissed, trying to jerk her arms free of his steely grip.

She heard the sound of a scuffle and glanced over Rotten Teeth's massive shoulder toward Kip. One man held Kip's arms behind his back, while the other hit him in the stomach. Each blow to Kip's ribs made him hunch over and groan.

"Leave him alone! You'll kill him!" Holly screamed, then she noticed the tall stranger in the cape running toward the fray.

The caped man moved with lethal precision. He grabbed the man attacking Kip, jerked him around and hit him before the man had a chance to strike back. The brute stumbled backward, shaking his head, then came at the stranger again.

The stranger dodged the man's fist, feinted to the left, then struck three sharp blows to the brute's face, his fist moving with the deadly swiftness of a cobra. The man's legs crumpled beneath him, then he tumbled to the ground. Now that the odds were even, Kip held the other brute at bay, jabbing at the man with his knife.

Her gaze locked with the stranger's for a moment. The oddest golden eyes she'd ever seen stared back at her, so light they glowed bright yellow, like the eyes of a jaguar she'd once seen at a county fair. The rage on the stranger's face, coupled with the fierce V his brows made over his eyes, sent goosebumps down her arms. He looked vicious, more ruthless than the men attacking her. He strode toward her now.

Rotten Teeth noticed the gentleman's approach and tossed her aside. Her arms flailed at the air, then she landed on her side in the street, the stones gouging her palms and hip. She cried out from the pain.

"All right, you wharf dog, let's have a go at me, shall we." The deep, cultured voice sounded bored.

Holly glanced behind her. The gentleman stood in front of Rotten Teeth, his fists out in front of him in a boxing stance, enjoyment gleaming in his golden eyes.

Rotten Teeth was taller than the gentleman, with shoulders as broad as a bull and a neck the size of a tree trunk. He realized his advantage and smiled at the gentleman, then said, "I'll teach you a lesson you won't forget."

Rotten Teeth got off the first punch.

The gentleman was sleeker and faster than the brute, darting to the side with lithe grace. "Is that the best you can do? You're slow as a snail." He fist snaked out, striking Rotten Teeth's face before he knew what hit him.

Rotten Teeth stumbled backward, holding his nose. He growled, then charged at the gentleman.

The gentleman waited until the last minute, leaped to the side, and kicked the sailor on his rump with a booted foot.

Rotten Teeth pitched forward and landed on his face.

He rolled to the side, his face a mask of fury. "You think you're so quick. What will you do with this?" He pulled a pistol from his coat and pointed it at the gentleman.

Holly's breath caught. She watched the caped gentleman stand there, arms crossed over his chest, an air of open recklessness in his face and cynical humor on his lips. Why was he standing there asking to be shot? She couldn't believe the gentleman's stupidity. Why wasn't he doing something to defend himself?

Without another thought, she lunged for the brute holding the gun.

Chapter 2

Holly hit Rotten Teeth from the side and knocked the gun out of his hand. It discharged, sailed through the air, then hit the cobblestones.

Rotten Teeth reached for her, but strong arms clamped around her waist, then she was snatched off the brute's lap before he could touch her.

"Stay out of this," the gentleman growled, plopping her down on her bottom beside his long legs.

The gentleman whipped around, facing Rotten Teeth. A burly fist flew at the gentleman's face. He recoiled, dodged the punch, then his fist struck Rotten Teeth's chin.

Her attacker had a surprised expression on his face, then his eyes rolled back in his head, and he collapsed to the ground.

The gentleman swung around, facing her, his cape swirling around his long legs. He pointed a finger at her. "What did you think you were doing?"

"I thought that was obvious." Holly let the sharpness in her voice match his. "You stood there like a fly on a cow's behind. I thought you needed some help, or did you plan to let him shoot you?"

"I was close enough to kick the gun out of his hand. If you hadn't charged him like a Bedlamite, I would have done so."

"Bedlamite . . ." Holly paused, pondering his last insult, then said, "Let me assure you, if I were a loon, I would have let the man shoot you in the heart, then laughed about it afterward."

"You have a point," he said, his anger covered now by a derisive drawl.

"It is a pleasure to meet a gentleman who can admit when he's wrong."

"I don't do it willingly in front of young ladies, but I've made an exception in your case." His voice dropped to a rough velvety tone, though the irritation in his expression hadn't changed.

"I suppose there is something to be said for concessions."

"I agree wholeheartedly. Now that we've established the many facets of my character, and you haven't found it wanting, may I help you up?"

"Thank you." She placed her hands in his.

He pulled her to her feet, but didn't release her hands right away. He stared down at her for a long moment, looking directly in her eyes. She felt the suppressed strength in his large hands, the heat of his palms hot against her skin, warming her arms all the way to her shoulder blades. Her first reaction was to pull away. She was about to do just that, but he appeared to realize he was still holding her hands and dropped them.

"There you are, righted and ready," he said, stepping back from her.

Cold air hit her palms where his warmth had been. Inadvertently, her fingers clenched, trying to recapture the warmth. Without thinking, she put her full weight on her ankle. A sharp pain shot up her calf. She stumbled and tried to gain her balance.

"I've got you." He swept her up into his arms. "Why didn't you tell me you were hurt?"

Holly couldn't think to answer him. His face was inches from her, his breath hot against her face, his yellow eyes boring into hers. She grew aware of the warmth of his body penetrating her clothes and the hardness of his chest and arms encompassing her.

She hadn't noticed before, but he was handsome. His hair was cropped short, and brown, the color of expensive chocolate—it shined like chocolate, too. A straight strand of hair hung rakishly down over his forehead, meeting eyebrows darker than his hair. Deep worry lines etched his brow and the outside corners of his eyes. She guessed he was in his early thirties, but the permanent worry lines in his expression added a severeness to his face that made him look older. A dimple sat in the middle of his square, chiseled chin. Dark stubble covered his face and cheeks, defining the hollows of his high cheekbones.

"Well?" He cocked a brow at her.

"Well what?"

"What part of you is hurt?"

"Hurt?" Holly paused for a moment, still staring in his eyes, then said, "I twisted my ankle."

Kip strolled up to them, his wooden leg tapping on the cobblestones. "Are you hurt, Miss Holly?"

"No, just hurt my ankle from my own stupidity. And you?"

"Not a scratch," Kip said proudly. "I ran off the last of 'em. Don't think 'e'll be coming back." He looked at the gentleman. "Thanks for your 'elp, sir."

"My pleasure." The gentleman looked at Holly. "Is there someplace I can take you?"

"She ain't got no place to live," Kip answered for her. "She just got off the boat. I was going to 'elp her to a cab when those bruters happened upon us."

"You must come home with me then," the gentleman said with a finality that brooked no argument.

"I've been enough bother to you already. Just put me in a cab, and I'll find lodgings."

"That is utter nonsense. You will stay with me until your ankle is healed. We cannot have you limping about London."

"She don't know you, sir." Kip eyed him with a marked amount of suspicion.

"Her virtue is safe with me. I'm John St. John, the Earl of Upton."

Holly's eyes widened. "I never expected to meet royalty my first hour in London."

"Well, I hope that meets with your approval. Now, let's get you home. My valet has a wonderful cure for sprains."

"It must be nice to have a valet versed in the arts of healing."

"He comes in useful."

"Will you be all right, Miss Holly?" Kip asked, eyeing St. John with distrust.

"Oh, yes." Holly nodded, sensing she could trust this earl.

"I'll call on you tomorrow then." Kip looked at Lord Upton with a stubborn challenge in his eye, daring the earl to forbid him to see her.

"It's Fifteen Park Lane," Lord Upton drawled with acid

amusement, then he turned and carried Holly toward the cabs.

"I'm sorry I didn't pay more attention to my lessons on English etiquette," Holly said. "How should I address you?"

"Most of my acquaintances call me John. I expect you to do the same."

"Yes, Lord John."

"You can save the 'lord' for Prinny."

Holly smiled. "Now you're making fun of me. I do remember distinctly learning that," she reverted to a stuffy English accent, "one always calls the king Your Majesty."

"Very good. So you were listening half the time."

"When I wasn't falling asleep, though I do remember paying strict attention to the lesson on finger bowls."

"So you wouldn't embarrass yourself when you dined with the king?"

"No, because my inquisitiveness demanded to know why it was necessary to wash your hands at the table. It seemed like such a waste of clean bowls, when I always had to wash my hands before I was allowed anywhere near the table."

"And did you justify the use of them," he said, his voice laced with amusement.

"Not really, but I didn't care as long as I didn't have to wash them."

The harsh line of his mouth softened. "So you mind household chores."

"Not really, only washing dishes. My grandmother raised me and she didn't believe in slavery, nor did she believe in spending good money on servants. Consequently, we did all the work around the house."

"What part of the South do you call home? I don't recognize the accent."

Holly paused, realizing she'd already said too much

about her past. She said the first place that popped into her mind. "I'm from Charleston."

"And what is your last name?"

"Ki— Campbell," Holly said, recovering quickly. When she glanced up and saw they had reached a cab, she held back a sigh of relief.

He called the address up to the driver, then opened the cab door. With a gentleness that surprised Holly, he positioned her on a seat inside the carriage.

After closing the door, he sat opposite her, then stretched out his long legs, crossed his arms over his chest, and leaned his head back against the seat. He closed his eyes, a weary look etched in the deep hollows of his cheeks and across his brow.

Holly took that as a hint he might not be feeling gregarious, so she said no more to him and surveyed her surroundings. It was dark inside the cab, save for a dim beam of light that streamed through the small window. The air reeked of stale cigar smoke, body odor, and the musty filth that comes with age and overuse.

She heard the driver curse at the horses, then the carriage lurched unexpectedly backward. Holly wasn't expecting the sudden jolt. It pitched her forward and she landed on Lord Upton's hard thighs.

"Damn fool driver," he said under his breath.

Holly wished she could melt into the floor of the cab. Her cheeks burned as though her skin were peeling from her face. To make matters worse, she grew acutely aware of the clean, musky scent of him. She raised her head and stared at the waistband of his breeches as she managed a ragged whisper, "P-please forgive me."

She should move, but her hands were pinned beneath her, and she had to push on his thighs in order to right herself. When she made an effort to raise her head, his long, corded muscles hardened into knots beneath her fingertips.

"Don't move," he said, his voice strained as if a rope were around his neck. "Let me help you." He grabbed her waist and plopped her back on the opposite seat. "Are you all right?"

"Fine."

Unable to look him in the eye, she stared down at the floor. It was ludicrous to try for small talk, but she couldn't stand the silence, nor could she stand to feel his eyes on her. In a tone that was surprisingly calm, she said, "I see London has tipsy cabdrivers like the rest of the world."

"I'd like to wring this one's neck." After a moment of silence, he asked, "Which ankle is hurt?"

"My left one, but it's already feeling better." Holly mustered enough nerve to glance at him. He was staring down at the tips of her shoes poking out beneath her dress.

"I'd better see if you broke it. You could have injured it further when you fell just now."

"Really, I'm all right."

He ignored her and reached down, lifting up her left foot before she could protest further. "I won't hurt you." He pushed the hem of her dress several inches up her leg.

As if he sensed her discomfort, he said, "This will only take a moment." He held her foot while he took off her shoe. His fingers closed around her ankle.

Holly hoped he wouldn't notice the hole in the heel of her silk stocking. A few moments later, the pressure of his fingers on her leg made her forget all about the hole. She marveled at how gentle his touch was, and how wonderful his hands felt—until he hit a sore spot. To keep from crying out, she dug her nails into her hand.

"No broken bones." He slipped her shoe back on, then

gently replaced her foot on the carriage floor. "We won't need to fetch the doctor."

"I wouldn't let him look at me anyway."

"You do not like doctors?"

Holly stared down at her hands and said, "Ever since one bled my grandmother to death, I've had a fear of them."

"I'm sorry to hear it." He let the sensitive subject drop and didn't probe her further, only eyed her.

She hadn't noticed the lump of stuffing in the seat poking her bottom. Now the painful sensation bothered her, almost as much as his searching golden eyes. She pressed her hands into the seat and slid over. When she moved her right hand, her fingers caught inside a tear in the leather seat. Her gaze flicked in his direction, and she found him watching her with an impenetrable expression on his face. She surreptitiously eased her hand out of the tear, hoping he hadn't seen her blunder.

Instantly, the white wool flocking sprang out of the tear. A lump of it mounded near her thigh. Inwardly cursing the stuffing, the tear, and every shabby cab and cabbie in the world, she grabbed the coarse stuffing and made a feeble attempt to shove it back inside before he noticed.

"Do you need some help there?" he said in a deep drawl laced with amusement.

"No, no. It's just a matter of shoving it back inside." The more she pushed it in, the more it came out in her hand. The absurdity of the situation struck her appreciation for the ridiculous. She couldn't help but smile. Then she saw the sour expression on his face and she laughed out loud.

"Are you quite well?"

"Gracious, forgive me," she said, sobering. "I couldn't help my outburst. This night has been one disaster after another. First I'm set upon by thieves, then I twist my ankle. And we happened to have a drunken cabdriver. Now this . . ." She stared down at the stuffing. "I ask you, can anything else go wrong?"

"Let's hope not. Here, let me have a go at it." He leaned over and grabbed the stuffing out of her hand. With one smooth motion, he shoved it back under the torn seat.

"That was done like a master." She found herself grinning at him.

"You learn these things when you ride in hacks."

"I would have thought an earl would have his own carriage."

"This one doesn't." His words shot out like stinging barbs. He stared out the window, ignoring her.

In the tense silence, anger emanated from him. What had she said? She was only trying to make pleasant conversation. She stared at his profile for a moment, shrugged, then turned and looked out the window too. If all earls in England were sensitive and surly like this one, then she didn't want to meet another one.

Dunn took a puff off one of his master's cigars, then blew three smoke rings out of his mouth. He frowned at the inferior quality of the cigar. His master used to buy the best of everything, but for the past two years he'd been reduced to the cheapest tobacco available. Dunn would never have bought something so cheap for himself, but it was free, so he couldn't complain.

He watched the smoke rings float up to the ceiling and dissipate, then wiggled his toes in his boots that were propped up on the desk. He pulled the cheroot out of his mouth, then took a sip of port he'd also helped himself to. In the middle of swallowing, he heard a carriage pull up in front of the house and choked on the brandy. After a coughing spell that wracked his body for a good fifteen seconds, he finally caught his breath. He stuffed the cigar in his mouth, jerked his feet off the desk, and leaped from the chair.

He ran for the door, but paused midway, remembering the cheroot in his mouth. Frantic now, he darted back to the fireplace, tossed the cigar in the burning fire, then fanned the air, trying to clear the room of smoke. The glass he'd used on the desk was still there. He grabbed it, downing the contents in one gulp, then plopped it down next to the other clean ones on the table.

If his feet had wings, he couldn't have moved faster. He flew out of the study, slamming the door behind him, then sped down the hall and skidded to the front door. With his hand on the knob, he straightened his face, checked his cravat, then opened the door right as his master stepped up to it.

"Good evening, my lord," he said, his voice even, evidencing no hint he was out of breath. He noticed the young lady in his master's arms and his eyes widened.

The Earl of Upton did not look as a man should look with a young lady in his arms. He looked harassed enough to chew the oak legs off the desk in the study.

Dunn stared at the lady to see if she could be the cause of his lordship's ire. She was young, her skin too tan; she'd obviously been out of doors a great deal. Her face was oval shaped, her mouth wide but not too wide. A small, straight nose, not too pert, set off her best feature, large brown eyes veiled by long, thick, dark lashes. Her hair was auburn, but more red than brown. She wore the long wavy mass down and pulled back from her face. Unruly auburn strands framed the sides of her face. The only word to describe her was plain, but she wasn't ugly enough to cause his lordship to be cross as crabs.

"Hello," she said, smiling at Dunn, the dimples in her cheeks showing.

Dunn decided plain was too harsh a term to describe this young lady. She was charming. The dimples gave her face a winsome artless glow. "Hello, miss," he said, bowing.

His lordship brought her through the threshold. Dunn quickly jumped aside to keep from being run over, then frowned at his master's back.

"This is Miss Campbell, Dunn. She has a hurt ankle. Where shall I put her?"

Miss Campbell took in his master's sour countenance, then her dimples faded with her smile. "I don't want to be a bother to anyone."

"Perhaps the red room, my lord. It's the only one prepared for guests."

His lordship nodded, then strode up the steps, a deep frown on his face.

Dunn followed three steps behind him, a safe distance that he'd measured from previous dealings with his master's moods. He'd never seen his lordship in such a foul humor.

Dunn waited until they reached the top of the stairs, then hurried past them and opened the chamber door. He stepped aside and lit a candle. Light flooded the chamber, showing the dry-rotted curtains and the burgundy paper that had faded to pink and was peeling in the corners. The room held only a canopy bed and a small table, on which sat a wooden candlestick. It was the only other bedchamber, besides his room and the master's, that held any furniture. The rest had been sold off to pay debts. Dunn felt a moment of embarrassment for his master, then it quickly faded, for the young woman didn't appear to notice the shabby interior.

"Dunn will take care of your ankle and any other needs you might have. I don't have a maid, so you will have to attend to your own gowns." He laid her on the bed, then splayed his legs and jammed his fists on his hips. He stared down at her and asked, "Where can I find your luggage?"

"I don't have any."

"None?" he asked, his voice more irritated than incredulous.

"None." She avoided his gaze and looked down at her hands.

His lordship turned to Dunn. "Find her some clothes from the attic. And she's twisted her ankle. I expect you to take care of that as well."

"Yes, my lord." Dunn bowed, then watched his master's stiff strides as he left the room. He walked over and closed the chamber door.

She sighed loudly, then asked, "Is he always like that?"

Dunn smiled at her and walked over to the windows, then pulled the shutters. "He's normally very different, miss."

"He didn't speak to me the whole carriage ride home. All I said was, I thought all earls had carriages of their own. I guess I'm not used to the ways of the aristocracy around here. From now on, I'll watch every word I say."

Dunn turned and strode back across the room, slightly embarrassed by what he was about to say, but the young miss deserved an explanation. "His lordship is in Queer Street, miss. He ain't had the blunt to afford a carriage here in town for some months now. I guess you pricked his pride. It's been a source of embarrassment for him since he had to get rid of his stable."

"I'm very sorry. I didn't know."

"I wouldn't worry. He's quick to anger, but quick to get over it. Tomorrow he'll be back to his old self." Dunn paused by the bed. "Now which ankle is it, miss?"

"The left one."

"I'll just take a little feel." He took off her shoe, then probed her ankle. She had fine ankles.

She flinched.

"Hurts there does it, miss?"

She nodded, biting her lip.

"It feels a little swollen. I'll just go and get a poultice for it. You'll feel much better in the morning." He turned to leave, but her voice stopped him.

"How do you know so much about sprains?"

"In my youth I worked in a stable. One learns how to take care of sprains when dealing with horses."

"I trust one of your cures won't leave me with a mane and tail." She smiled, her white, even teeth gleaming in the candlelight.

He returned her smile and winked at her. "I've never had it happen before. I'll be right back, miss." He bowed, then closed the door behind him, thinking she was a ray of warm sunshine. And his master needed all the sunshine around him he could get.

Holly was dreaming about Christmas back home at Kimbly . . .

It was two days before Christmas. The aroma of her grandmother's rum-raisin cake, baked only an hour ago, still lingered in the air. Holly's mouth watered as she picked up a clove and stuffed it in the skin of an orange, then she glanced over at Kent. He was there helping make pomanders.

"That isn't how you do it," she said, while watching him

stick the cloves up his nose, being his normal irritating self. How she wished he'd didn't live on the plantation next to her.

"I know how to do it."

"You could have fooled me. The cloves go on the oranges."

"I'll put them where I want." He bent over and tried to stuff one in her ear.

"Now, Kent, you must behave," her grandmother said, her thin-veined hands pausing on a swag of running cedar she was hanging over the parlor doorway. Ella Kimbel was a small woman with gleaming silver hair and a placid face. Some of that placidity melted as she aimed a look at Kent over the rim of her glasses.

"I'll leave then." Kent jumped up from his seat, so quickly it knocked over the chair. He glowered at the chair, then stormed out of the room.

Holly listened to his footsteps stomping down the hall, then the slam of the front door.

"Mark my words," her grandmother said. "That child will cause trouble one day."

Holly glanced toward the doorway through which he had just exited and knew her grandmother was right . . .

She woke up when something heavy plopped onto the mattress and brushed against her bottom. For a moment she thought it was Kent and screamed.

"Good God!" A man's voice cut through the darkness.

Holly blinked the sleep out of her eyes and recalled where she was. With a surprising amount of speed for having just been awakened, she snatched the sheet up around her neck and scooted over to the far edge of the bed. "This bed is occupied, sir," she said, her heart thumping against her ribs.

"I surmised that when you screamed, madam." The

mattress dipped as he crawled out of bed, then he gave a tug and the counterpane slid off the bed.

"I couldn't help it."

The door to the bedroom burst open.

A shaft of light from the hallway filled the room. John stood in the doorway, wearing only a robe, his chest heaving. The light from the hall silhouetted his broad shoulders. They tapered down to a flat waist and slim hips. The robe met in the front near his navel, exposing the contoured muscles on his chest and the dark V of hair there. She couldn't take her eyes off his bare chest. It was the embodiment of male perfection.

"Hello, Brother." It was that man's voice again.

She turned to see a man standing near her bed. He'd carelessly wrapped the counterpane around his hips, but his naked chest was in full view. He was tall like John, but not as muscular. His chest was bare and white, and paled compared to the thick thatch of dark hair on John's broad chest. His hair was cropped short. Dirty blond curls hung down over his forehead, stark against the walnut-brown eyes that peered at her. He looked younger than John, perhaps twenty-four or -five.

John strode into the room. His robe parted slightly in the center, exposing his corded muscular calves with each long stride. Holly watched his progress, unable to draw her gaze from his legs and bare feet. The closer he moved to her bed, the warmer her body felt.

John paused near his brother and said, "What the hell are you doing in here, Teddy?"

"I always use this room when I'm in town."

"What are you doing home?"

"I finished my exams early so I came home for winter break."

"You could have given me some notice of your early arrival."

"I never had to before." Teddy turned to look at her.

Dunn had gone to the attic and found a silk nightgown for her. It had a plunging neckline that revealed far too much of her neck and chest. Teddy's gaze roamed over her. He stared at her like a tasty piece of cake, then a lazy smile turned up the corners of his mouth. "Who is this lovely madam?"

Holly realized she'd dropped the sheet and jerked it back up to her chin as she said, "I'm Miss Holly Ki—" She paused, catching herself, then added, "Campbell."

"Allow me to introduce myself Miss Ki-Campbell," he said, making fun of her forgetting her own name. "I'm Lord Theodore St. John, brother to that angry bear standing next to me. All my close friends call me Teddy." He executed a proper bow.

"Now is not the time for introductions." The bear grabbed his brother's arm and pulled him toward the door. "Let's let Miss Campbell go back to sleep."

"Wait, my clothes." Teddy jerked his arm free. He bent over to pick up his clothes. The counterpane slipped from his hand, giving her a clear view of his backside.

Holly squeezed her eyes shut and turned her head.

"Oops," Teddy said.

She heard the counterpane rustle as he pulled it up, then a soft whoosh, as if he were grabbing his clothes off the floor.

"Why even bother covering yourself? You might as well run through the house naked." John's voice was a low growl. "When did you start sleeping in the buff?"

"I've always slept this way and you know it."

"It might behoove you to check the bed before you go stripping down again . . ."

The door slammed.

Holly heard John's muffled tirade out in the hall. She'd held her laughter as long as she could. She fell over, buried her head in the pillow, and laughed until she cried.

John dragged Teddy down the hall. "How can you be so careless?"

"How was I supposed to know a woman would be in my bed? You've never brought a mistress home before." He paused, then frowned. "How come she's not in your bed?"

"She is not my mistress," John said through clenched teeth.

"Who the hell is she then?"

"An innocent I rescued from some thugs near the dock. If you had been more careful when you entered the room, you would have found that out. A bloody fine thing you did. I invite her into my home to protect her, and what do you do? You parade around in front of her naked. Will you always go through life blind and ignorant? I swear you'll never grow up."

Teddy jerked his arm out of John's grasp. "If I turn into an old curmudgeon like you, then I hope I never do."

"I wish you had the responsibilities I have, then you would see why I have to take life seriously."

"You've never trusted me with the responsibilities. You still treat me like a child."

"That's because you act like one sometimes."

"I'm no child," Teddy said, his voice defensive. "I'm twenty-four, but you fail to see that. You never confide in me." The harsh edge left his voice. He sounded hurt as he said, "I am your brother, but you're too damn proud to speak to me about anything. You may be eight years older than me, and feel like you have to shoulder every burden, but you don't. Give me a chance to share it with you."

"What good would it do to worry you with our money problems?" John said, the anger leaving his voice. He leaned back against the wall and rested his head there as his shoulders slumped.

Teddy was silent for a moment, then in a concerned voice asked, "Is the blunt situation worse?"

"I lost two ships. The second office is closed. I had to let Thomas go." John ground his teeth together.

"What rotten luck. What will happen now?"

"I don't know, but if my investors get wind of it, then I'm sure they'll pull out."

"Good God!" Teddy leaned against the wall, needing the support, too. "Will that end the company?"

"Yes. I can hardly make ends meet as it is. With one ship at sea, I won't be able to make enough profit to stay afloat." John's fist clenched at his sides.

"Can't we mortgage this house and buy more ships?"

"It's mortgaged to the hilt."

"And Brookhollow Hall?"

"I'm still paying the mortgage Father left on the place when he died." A pain stabbed John's right temple, and he reached up and rubbed it.

Teddy was silent a moment, then said, "There's always Matilda."

"Damn it, Teddy, I won't go begging her for money."

"Then I'll go."

"No, you won't." John narrowed his eyes at Teddy, a look that sent most people scurrying from his presence.

"All right, then I won't go back to school," Teddy said, his voice laced with stubbornness. "I'll find an heiress when the season starts, marry her, then all our money troubles will be over."

"You've only got the rest of the year before you get your degree. You are going back to school."

"Why? It just adds more of a burden on you. And if I marry an heiress, then our money troubles—"

"No, I did that once, remember? What good did it do? No. I won't have you marry because I can't support this family. You are going back to Cambridge and get your law degree." John waved his hand through the air. "I'll hear no more about it."

"All right, all right, it was just a suggestion." Teddy was silent for a moment, then said, "I guess I can try to conserve on my spending."

"You might try spending less at your tailor's and try not looking the part of a fop."

"All my college mates wear these kinds of clothes." He shook the vivid-colored clothes in his hand at John. "My tailor assures me what I wear is bang up to the mark."

"He's damn well color blind."

"You just want me to look frumpish like you. I won't do that. I'd rather give up food and have the money to buy fashionable clothes."

"You won't live long the way you eat."

"I suppose you're right there, but I can cut back somewhere else. We shall make do somehow. We are St. Johns, we'll get by . . ."

John didn't answer him, nor could he burden Teddy with his fear that he could end up in debtors' prison by year's end. He stared up at the ceiling, half expecting it to fall down on top of him at any moment.

"Speaking of getting by . . ." He glanced down the hall, toward Miss Campbell's chamber door. "What are you going to do with her?"

"I don't know." John jammed his fists down in the pockets on his robe.

"Can I have her? She's a delight, and her bottom felt very nice when it touched mine." Teddy's lips parted in a lusty grin.

"She's an innocent under my care," John said, "I mean it, stay away from her."

"I was merely admiring her. She has the most incredible hair. Did you see it falling over her shoulders?" Teddy grinned at her chamber door, his eyes twinkling.

John frowned, remembering seeing her in the bed. How could he forget it? Her hair flowed down to her waist in wild disarray, the silk gown she was wearing exposing the creamy flesh at her throat. And those doelike eyes. She looked so young, so innocent, and so bloody desirable.

Six months was too long to go without easing his body. The ache in his loins was unbearable. He'd long since given up his mistress, Cindra, because he couldn't afford to keep her, nor had he missed the convenience of having her body when he needed it. After working sometimes sixteen hours a day at the shipping office, he was so tired by the time he made it home that he fell into bed without thoughts of lust plaguing him. And it had worked fine until Miss Campbell came into his life. But she had ignited six months of pent-up desire in him that would surely burn him alive if he did not soon find relief.

John rubbed his right temple again, knowing it would be a long, sleepless night. "I'm going to bed."

Teddy put his arm around John's shoulders. "That's the thing to do. Papa always used to say, 'Things will look better in the morning.' I believe he was right."

"You don't believe that tripe. He always said that when he was foxed and had lost his shirt at a gaming hell." John glanced at Teddy, unable to believe his naiveté. Sometimes John felt more like Teddy's father than his brother.

"I believed it then, and I still do." Teddy's eyes gleamed

with the optimism that only came with youth, then grinned. "And let us not forget we have Miss Campbell to cheer us in the morning."

John frowned over at his brother. How could seeing the object of his lust in the morning do anything but make matters worse?

The next morning, Holly pulled back the cover, untied the poultice Dunn had wrapped around her ankle, then put her foot down on the floor. She eased her weight on it, felt no pain, then took a step. Dunn was a miracle worker. She'd thank him first thing.

She glanced around the room, noticing the sparseness of the decor and its dilapidated appearance. It once must have been a beautiful room. She could imagine what the faded burgundy paper and threadbare brocade curtains must have looked like new. Probably there would have been a burgundy rug on the floor and a covered lounge chair to match it. Just how deeply in debt was John?

The thought made her frown as she fixed her hair. She didn't have a comb, so she ran her fingers through the tangles, then twisted the long mass into a knot, using the pins she'd brought with her. Then she donned her petticoat, feeling it to make sure the jewels there were still securely sewn in place. Snatching up her old faded blue gown from the bed, she smoothed the wrinkles with her hand as best she could, then slipped it on.

She stepped into the hallway. Last night she hadn't noticed the walls, but now the empty picture hangers stood out. The discolored green-and-pink-striped wallpaper was stark below them, as if the pictures had hung there for a long time and were hastily taken down. John must have needed ready cash and sold them.

Loud voices met her at the stairs. She glanced down and saw John, nose to nose with a man in a dark suit. Two burly men stood behind them, looking mean and determined. Dunn was standing beside them, a deep frown on his face. He was a small man with thinning brown hair, and he looked like a child compared to the large men standing around him. Teddy was behind his brother, his arms crossed, glaring at the man arguing with John.

John squared his shoulders. "You'll get your money at the end of the month."

"I've held this bill for six months. I can't wait another day for the money."

"I can't give you what I don't have," John said, frustrated.

"You'll get your money," Teddy added.

"I want this bill paid now." The man thrust a paper at John.

John knocked it aside and stepped closer to the man. "I'll have it within the week. Now get out!" He pointed to the door.

Dunn darted to the door and opened it, looking expectantly at the intruders.

"If you can't pay us, then we'll find something of value to take in lieu of the money." The man crossed his arms over his chest, not moving.

"You'll have to wait for the money. You are not going through my house." John stood his ground, drawing himself up.

"We'll take what we want." The man made the mistake of pushing John in the chest.

Teddy leaped forward and shoved the man.

Chaos erupted. Fists flew.

Chapter 3

Holly ran down the steps and approached Dunn, who was cowering in a corner of the foyer. She grabbed his arm and asked, "Can you fetch two buckets of water?"

Dunn looked at her as if she'd lost her mind.

"I really am sane. Please hurry. And make sure it's cold enough to take your breath away."

"Very well, miss." Dunn hurried through a doorway off to the right.

Holly watched John hit one of the burly men, sending him stumbling backward right at her. She jumped out of the way. The man staggered back through the threshold and onto the front stoop. He teetered on the edge of the top step, while his arms groped at air. She reached out to catch him, but before she could grab his hand he again fell backward.

"Land sakes," Holly murmured, and watched the man land flat on his back. His eyes rolled back in his head, then he fainted. She turned and stepped back through the door.

At that very moment, the other muscle-bound clod hit Teddy and sent him careening toward her. She leaped aside again. Teddy slammed into the door, his shoulder barely missing her. The clod grabbed Teddy again, his fists flying. Each punch banged Teddy's body against the wood like a rag doll.

John dodged a blow from the man in the suit, feinted left, then drove his fist into the face of the clod hitting Teddy. He staggered back, shaking his head, stunned for a moment.

"Thanks, big brother," Teddy said to John, then dove at the clod again.

Dunn finally appeared, his arms laden with the buckets of water. Relieved at the sight of him, Holly skirted around John, who had both men hitting him now, and ran to Dunn.

"I'll take one of those, thank you." She grabbed a bucket from his hand, then threw the water on the fighting men. It stunned them for a moment, but they continued to pound on each other.

Holly narrowed her brows at them and said, "It sometimes takes two buckets."

"Here, miss." Dunn shoved the last pail at her.

This time she not only threw the contents on them, but the bucket, too.

The water hit John directly in the face. He paused, his fist about to slam into the clod's jaw. He shook his head, spewing water out of his mouth. The bucket hit the clod's head, then bounced, slamming into the man with the suit. It hit the side of his face, rolled down his chest, then banged against Teddy's shoulder and finally fell to the marble floor with a loud thud.

All four men turned in unison, their anger directed at her.

Holly gave them back look for look. "Now that I have your attention, gentlemen, don't move. We're out of water. Please, sir . . ." She waved her hand at the man standing near John. She watched him rubbing the back of his head and said, "I hope we can settle this without further violence. I can pay you."

"Stay out of this." John glared at her.

"No, no, I must insist. Consider it money rendered for saving my life last night. Now . . ." Holly bent over and picked up the bill that had fallen on the floor.

She shook the water off the corners, then scanned the wet page. The black ink had bled slightly from the water, but the figures were legible. She narrowed her brows and said, "Really, sir. No wonder Lord Upton didn't pay this. You're robbing him blind. Fifty pounds for 115 gallons of cheap port. Why, you can get better port in America for half that. The kind captain who brought me here showed me all about English money, so I know the exchange rate and I know this is just plain piracy." Holly shook her head at the man.

"It's the going rate, miss."

"Well, I really don't know how you stay in business. I'm sure I can speak for Lord Upton when I say he will never buy spirits from you again." Holly dug in her pocket, extracted the bank notes the captain had given her, counted out fifty pounds, then placed it in the man's hand. "There, all paid up. Good day to you, sir."

The man stared down at the money, disbelief mixing with the relief in his expression, then he nodded to her. "Thank you, miss." After casting John a sidelong look, he and the clod plodded out the door.

Holly stepped to the threshold and pointed at the prostrate man on the sidewalk. "Please see you take him with you, though you may have trouble lifting him." Abruptly, strong hands grabbed her from behind, then she landed in John's arms.

"I want a word with you," he growled, keeping his gaze straight ahead as though looking at her would make him lose control. The turbulence in the golden depths frightened her. More than frightened her.

"Put me down," she said, wiggling in his arms. "Why are you carrying me?"

"Your ankle is still tender, is it not?"

"It's fine thanks to Dunn's plaster. Now put me down." She glanced at Teddy for help, but he just shrugged and dabbed at a bleeding lip.

John entered a room off the hallway, then slammed the door closed with his foot. She glanced around at the massive mahogany desk in the room's center and at full bookshelves covering the walls. It must be his study, she concluded.

He plopped her on the floor, then stood and glared down at her. "What do you think you were doing back there?"

She bent back and peered up at him. He was well over six feet tall. She only came up to his shoulder, and she was getting a crick in her neck staring up at him. "I was repaying you for saving me from those men last night. I'm sure you've heard the old adage, one good turn deserves another."

"You may have thought you were doing a 'good turn,' but you had no right to pay that man."

"I'm sorry." His fingers dug into her flesh, and she said, "If you don't mind, you're hurting me."

He glanced down at his hands, then dropped them. "If you had stayed out of this, I would not have hurt you."

"I forgive you. Now let's forget the whole thing happened." Holly turned and opened the door to leave.

He knocked her hand away from the knob, then banged the door closed in her face. "Not so fast, we're not through with our chat," he said, bending close enough to her that she could feel the tips of his wet cravat brushing the back of her collar.

"What else is there to discuss?" His long arm was blocking her on the left side, so she tried to take a step to the right . . .

Bang! His other hand hit the door near her neck and shoulder.

She stood there, trapped by his arms, staring at the door. His hot breath caressed the side of her neck like hundreds of feathery fingertips brushing across her skin, sending shivers down her spine. He towered behind her, so close she could feel the heat emanating from his body. Inhaling deeply, she fought the light-headed, stimulating feeling he was causing in her.

"Are you afraid to turn around and speak to me?" His voice was deep and husky near her ear.

She bit her lip, then mustered enough courage to turn and face him. Those golden eyes bored into her as long as she could stand it, then she dropped her gaze and stared at his shirt sticking to his chest. The wrong thing to do, she realized. His shirt was wet, almost transparent, the dark patch of hair there visible. The memory of him last night, standing in her doorway in his robe, his bare chest exposed, flashed through her mind.

"I'm not afraid to speak to you." Her gaze stayed glued to the triangle of dark hair on his chest.

"Why is your voice trembling?"

She forced her gaze up to the dimple in his chin. "It's

not. And I don't understand why you're making such an issue over a few pounds.''

''I haven't begun to make an issue of it, but give me a few minutes.''

''Actually, I don't have a few minutes to spare,'' she said, trying desperately to keep the tremor from her voice and failing miserably. ''I must go and find lodgings.''

''Where did you get the money to pay my bill?'' He stared down at her faded dress. His gaze landed on her breasts, held for a moment, then moved back up to her eyes. ''You didn't even have a portmanteau when you got off the ship.''

''I can explain that.''

''Please do, madam.''

''I—I sailed without it.''

''Not very prudent.''

''Yes, well, I overpacked and couldn't lift my trunk.'' Holly stared at the wet strand of hair adhering stubbornly to his forehead while she lied. ''I had spent all afternoon packing and the time got away from me. The ship was sailing, so I had to run to the dock. I intend to send for my clothes.''

''And the money?''

''Oh, the money. The captain of the ship I boarded gave it to me.''

''For what reason?'' His gaze slid down her body again, but languidly this time, lingering over her breasts with frank impudence.

The lazy perusal peeled away every stitch of her clothing, and she felt naked beneath his gaze. A blush started in her cheeks and burned all the way to her collarbone. ''I don't owe you an explanation,'' she said, incensed by his frank action. ''And if you are thinking that I sold myself to the captain for money, let me tell you now, I'm no trollop."

"What are you then?" He cocked a dark brow at her.

"Just a visitor in a new country. Now, if you will step aside, I can leave."

"Let me make one more thing clear, madam—"

"Please, if you are going to insult me, the least you can do is call me by name."

"All right, Holly," he said, dragging the name through his teeth. "As I was saying, you will not look for a place to live. Since you took it upon yourself to be so generous and pay my bill, I insist you stay here until we are even."

Holly paused a moment, then said, "I suppose I could do that. Just how long am I to stay here."

"A month should do it."

"Very well. One month."

"Another thing," he said, his voice growing ominously low. "Don't ever humiliate me again by paying one of my creditors."

"I don't have to be trampled twice by a bull to learn to stay out of his pen."

"I'm glad you learn quickly." He dropped his hands and stepped back.

"It may surprise you to learn I do have," she raised her fingers, leaving an inch of air between them, "a little common sense. Now, if you'll excuse me . . ." She opened the door and left the room, feeling his eyes boring into her back.

The moment she stepped into the hall, she doubted the common sense she had so boldly touted. Why in the world had she just agreed to spend a whole month with a moody, disagreeable, overbearing earl? No doubt, she would regret it.

* * *

Holly heard John's footsteps behind her in the hall. She paused near Dunn, who was mopping the water up off the floor, and allowed John to walk past her.

The bright gold in his eyes pierced her for a long moment, then he pushed back the wet strand of hair hanging over his brow and strode up the steps. Over his shoulder, he said irritably, "I'll need some dry clothes, Dunn."

"Yes, my lord." Dunn leaned the mop against the wall, then hurried up the stairs.

She watched the sway of John's massive shoulders beneath his wet shirt as he climbed the stairs, the corded muscles in his back pulsing. He must have felt her looking at him, for he turned and glanced down at her.

There was a pregnant moment between them, then she averted her gaze and pretended to stare down at the floor. When she heard their footsteps die away, she grabbed the mop and began sopping up the water. As she pushed the mop along the floor, she noticed the thick film of dirt on the marble tiles.

A few moments later, she heard footsteps on the stairs and saw Dunn taking the steps two at a time. "I'll do that, miss."

"There's no reason why you should do it. I threw the water on the floor, I should clean it up."

"His lordship won't see it that way, miss." Dunn yanked on the mop.

Holly hung on, refusing to turn it loose. "Are you the only servant in this large house?"

"Yes, miss." Dunn pulled on the mop again.

"For heaven's sake, let me help you." She gave the mop a sharp tug and yanked it from his hands.

"Really, miss, you shouldn't." He reached for the mop again.

"Please don't." Holly raised her finger and wagged it at him. "If you touch this mop again, I might just be forced to hit you with it," she said, smiling. "Anyway, you have to see to his lordship's breakfast. I'll do this."

Hefting the awkward mop into the puddle of water, she began pushing it across the wet marble tiles. Every swipe of the mop made another streak through the thick film of dirt. She wrung out the mop and asked, "How long has it been since the floor was cleaned?"

"A while, miss. I only have two hands," he said, growing defensive. "Since the staff was let go over four months ago, I've been doing the job of the butler, the maids, the cook, and keeping his lordship looking proper."

"I'm sorry. I wasn't implying you didn't do your job. I'm sure it has been awfully hard on you."

The knocker sounded, and they both looked at the door, then at each other.

"I wonder who that could be," Dunn grumbled under his breath.

"If it's another creditor, don't let them in." She smiled at him and went back to mopping. "We'll have a river flowing through here if we do."

"I won't, miss. No one's getting through me again," Dunn vowed. With stiff, determined strides, he reached the door and opened it.

"Hello, Dunn. Is his lordship in?" A tall, beautiful woman with coal-black hair stepped through the threshold. She wore a royal-blue bombazine morning dress that was stunning against her pale complexion and black hair.

She paused and leveled her frosty blue eyes at Holly. "A new maid, I see." A smile spread across her face, but there was little warmth in it. Turning toward Dunn, she pulled off her gloves. "I didn't know Lord Upton hired a maid. When did this occur?"

"She's not a maid, my lady."

"No?" She stared at Holly, waiting for an explanation.

Holly stopped mopping, leaned against the handle, then said, "I'm a—"

"Guest," John finished for Holly as he strode down the stairs with Teddy behind him.

Teddy had changed his wet clothes and was buttoning the last button on a yellow-and-pink waistcoat. The colors clashed with his mulberry pantaloons and coat. Holly grinned. He looked like a strutting peacock in need of a good molting.

A magnetic force beyond her control drew her gaze back to John. His black Hessians gleamed with each step he took. Long, corded muscles pumped beneath a pair of cream breeches. A plain blue coat and white shirt covered his broad shoulders and chest. His linen cravat was tied in a Gordian knot. His clothes were not new. His velvet coat showed wear on the elbows, but he didn't need new clothes to look dashing. With his broad-shouldered, slim-hipped physique and proud aristocratic bearing, he could wear rags and look distinguished.

She had been leaning against the mop handle, watching him, and didn't realize it was moving until she began to fall. It was a quick recovery. Two stumbles to the right and she was upright again. She glanced around to see if anyone had noticed she'd made a fool of herself.

John was the only one who noticed. His eyes gleamed with amusement as he reached the bottom of the steps. "Hello, Lady Matilda," he said, speaking to the woman at the door without taking his eyes off Holly. The amusement faded from his expression as he glanced at the mop in her hand. His eyes narrowed at her, then he wrenched the

mop from her grasp. "Guests in my house do not mop
floors, Miss Campbell. Do I make myself clear?"

"Perfectly." Holly stared at the mop, wanting very much
to throw it in his face at the moment.

"Hello, Lady Matilda, you're looking ravishing as ever."
Teddy pecked the beautiful woman on the cheek.

"You coquette." The lady's face glowed from the attention. "When did you get home?"

"Last night." Teddy stared pointedly at Holly, and
grinned, obviously recalling when he'd jumped in her bed.

Holly felt her face redden, then glanced back at the
lady.

"Well, I'm glad you're home so early for the holidays."
The lady smiled at Teddy, then she looked at John and
her eyes glowed. "Please introduce your new guest to me."

John stared down at the mop in his hands, then scowled
at it as if he'd forgotten he was holding it. He thrust it
against the wall and said, "This is Miss Holly Campbell."

Matilda curtsied, taking in Holly's faded dress, then she
lowered her gaze out of politeness. "I'm pleased to meet
you."

"And I you." Holly glanced down at her own faded,
stained dress. Compared to this lady, the epitome of grace-
fulness, beauty, and elegance, she must have looked like
a street beggar.

"Miss Campbell, this is Lady Matilda," John said, contin-
uing with the introductions. "She was my wife's cousin."

Holly's jaw dropped open when she heard the words
"my wife's." She clamped her mouth closed, then said, "I
didn't know you had a wife, my lord." Holly kept her
expression indifferent, while she held her breath and
waited for his answer.

"My wife has been dead for two years now."

"I'm sorry." Holly felt relief wash over her.

"We were just sitting down to breakfast. You'll join us, of course." John smiled at Lady Matilda.

Holly had never seen him smile before. The transformation did wonders for his face. The permanent frown over his brow dissolved, along with the worry lines. He looked years younger and far too handsome. It must take a lady with a title to get a smile out of him. She watched John hold out his elbow for Lady Matilda. A pang of jealousy pricked her—which she had no right in the world to be feeling.

"Yes, I would love to dine with you. I did want to speak to you." Lady Matilda smiled and took his proffered arm.

John called over his shoulder, "You'll join us, too, Miss Campbell."

She had no intention of watching him smile at Lady Matilda for the next half hour, so she said, "No, thank you. I've got a full day planned now that I can walk on my ankle, and I want to get an early start. I'll bid both of you good day."

John turned, his gold eyes boring into her. After a moment, his frown deepened to a scowl. "As you wish, Miss Campbell."

"Don't feel you are intruding, my dear," Lady Matilda said in a polite but patronizing tone. "We'd love for you to join us." Her lips stretched in a wooden smile.

"Thank you very much, but I really have a lot of shopping to do."

"Shall we go then?" Lady Matilda pulled on John's arm.

After one more brooding glance at Holly, John turned and strode down the hall, arm in arm with Lady Matilda.

"Are you sure you won't join us?" Teddy looked hopefully at her.

"Very sure." Holly stared at Lady Matilda with her broomstick posture, and at John with his stiff wide shoulders and brooding good looks. They made a fine couple. For some reason the sight of them together made her frown at their backs.

Still frowning, she waited until Teddy followed them, then grabbed the mop again.

"No, miss, you can't," Dunn whispered, his voice dire.

"He won't find out. I'll be done before he's finished his breakfast," Holly said, then she defied the lord of the house by mopping up the rest of the water off the floor.

John escorted Matilda into the dining room. When his father was alive, he had always liked the room. It was a circular room, everything in it round. At one time, it had held a large round table, but John had to sell it recently to pay some of the more pressing past due bills. Now only a small square table sat in the middle that had once been used in the kitchen. It was a cheap table, swallowed by the massive room. A round worn Indian carpet blanketed the floor. Papered murals depicting rose gardens covered the walls. But like the old carpeting, the colors in the paper had dimmed and gave the room a dull, shabby look, a reminder of his own humiliating financial failures. He led Matilda across the carpet, his expression dour.

Teddy strode into the room and reached the sideboard before John or Matilda. He rubbed his hands together. "I wonder what delicacies Dunn has for us this morning." He picked up a plate, took the lid off the cover, then made a face as if he were staring down into a chamber pot. "I say, Miss Campbell may have had the right idea. I've suddenly lost my appetite. I'll forego breakfast this morning." He put the plate back down, then glanced at Matilda. "Very nice seeing you, Matilda." To John he said, "I'll try to join you in the office today, if I don't get waylaid."

Teddy glanced back toward the door, obviously thinking of using his charms on Holly.

John remembered the comment Teddy had made about Holly's bottom feeling good next to his. He had to quench an urge to strangle Teddy as he said, "I'll expect you."

Teddy looked at him, grinned, then strode out of the room.

"He seems preoccupied this morning," Matilda said.

"Yes, I believe he is." John scowled down at a plate, then picked it up off the sideboard and lifted the top off a chafing dish. He wrinkled his brows at the burned eggs. "Dunn's cooking leaves a lot to be desired."

"You needn't apologize for it." Matilda picked up a plate.

He turned to Matilda, really looking at her. She looked beautiful today. Matilda favored Elise in a lot of ways, but Elise had been much more cunning and self-centered than her cousin. He had often wondered what it would have been like if he had married Matilda instead of Elise.

"Wherever did you find Miss Campbell? She seems like a charming person."

"Three thatch-gallows attacked her down near the docks. She hurt her ankle, so I brought her here."

"She was down near the docks all alone?" Matilda pursed her brows in censure.

"She'd just gotten off the boat. She had an escort with her, but he was up against three men. Not very good odds."

"I should say not." She smiled at John, her eyes softening. "How nice of you to come to her aid, but you always were gallant."

"I did no more than any gentleman would have done under the same circumstances." John ladled several spoonfuls of charred eggs on his plate, then lifted the next cover and forked up a slice of ham. Scowling at the black edges, he flopped it on his plate. His palate had grown accustomed to Dunn's cooking since he'd had to let go of his French cook, though his stomach still protested furiously. He'd be tasting this breakfast all day and into the afternoon. But a little indigestion was better than starving.

"You said you had to see me," he said, glad to get off the subject of Holly.

"I hate to bring this up. I know it's such a delicate subject." She put a little spoonful of eggs on her plate.

"Come, we are cousins. You can tell me anything." John picked up a burned scone. He tapped it against the edge of his plate and decided it would make a good paperweight.

"Well . . . I read about your ships going down in this morning's *Ledger*. I feel terrible about it. I came right over to see if there was anything I could do."

"Thank you, but no, I can't think of anything you can do."

"Such a tragedy for you and the children. You know, if you need money—"

"We've been through this before. I won't take money from you or anyone else."

"I know, but I just thought—"

"I appreciate your concern, but I won't discuss it further." He stared hard at her for a moment, then plopped a dollop of clotted cream on the scone.

"I'm sorry if I upset you." She gazed down at her plate, looking hurt and troubled.

"I didn't mean to be so short with you." John softened his voice to a contrite level. He'd forgotten how sensitive Matilda was.

Her liquid blue eyes glanced up at him. A wistful smile turned up the corners of her lips. "It's all right. You know I would never have asked if your and the children's welfare were not at stake."

"I know. We'll get by. I've weathered other storms before, and I'll see this one through."

Silence settled between them. John waited until she finished filling her plate, then he seated her at the table and sat next to her.

She picked up her fork and stabbed at the eggs. "There is one other matter I needed to speak to you about."

He didn't like the tremulous tone in her voice and knew something was wrong. "What is it?" he asked, forking some eggs in his mouth.

"Well, I received a missive from Mrs. Pringle . . ." She paused, appearing uneasy, then went on. "She informs me the children need another nanny."

"What the devil is she doing writing you? They are my children."

"Please don't blame her. It was my fault. I felt it would take some of the burden off you, so I asked her to write me with any problems that might arise with the children. You know how I love them. I am their closest female relative—besides your grandmother, of course. And you know," she cleared her throat and lowered her voice, "she wouldn't be much help finding a new nanny."

"What is Mrs. Pringle doing—running them off? This will be the fourth nanny I've hired this year."

She sighed. "I don't like saying this, but with the low salary you are offering, you cannot expect to keep someone with qualifications in the position, not with the boys. You know how mischievous they can be."

"I'll punish them when I get home."

"You know that hasn't worked in the past. I believe we just need to find someone who needs a job." Her gaze lowered to her plate. "There is someone who might be able to handle the job."

"Who?"

"Miss Campbell seems like a perfect person for the position." Matilda stabbed a tiny piece of egg with her fork and put it in her mouth.

"Miss Campbell is a guest in my home. I can't very well ask her if she wants to be a nanny to my children."

She swallowed the eggs, trying nobly not to make a face. "Forgive me, but she looks in need of employment. You would only be helping her. I think she would be perfect. And the holidays are coming up. I'm sure she doesn't want to spend them alone in a strange city with no one she knows."

"She won't be alone, she's staying with me. And when I go to the country, I'll take her with me."

"What do you mean?" Her fingers strangled the handle of her fork, every knuckle whitened beneath her alabaster skin.

He stared at her hand. "We came to an arrangement. She is to rent a room from me."

"Surely you know the impropriety of her staying here, unchaperoned, with two bachelors." She stabbed her plate with her fork. It scraped across the fine china, sounding like a rusty nail on sandpaper. As if realizing what she was doing, she stared down at her fork, then plopped it on her plate.

"I hadn't thought of that."

"Of course you didn't, you're a man. Men do not think of these things." She sipped her tea and eyed him over the rim of the cup.

"It is fortuitous I have you to remind me."

She smiled and set her cup down. "You know I've tried to help you all I can since Elise's death."

"I know that, and I appreciate what you've done." John wondered now if she wasn't beginning to get too involved in his affairs.

Matilda's face glowed from the praise, then she straightened in her chair. "Getting back to Miss Campbell. I
believe the perfect solution to your dilemma is to hire her
as the children's nanny."

"It might be a solution to her housing problem, but I
don't know her well enough to ask her to mind the children," John said, voicing his thoughts aloud.

"She seems like a delightful enough person to me. But
if you are worried about her being with the children, I
shall ask Mrs. Pringle to send a weekly report to you."

"I'll have to think about it." He dipped the scone in
the clotted cream, tried to take a bite, but it was like granite
against his teeth. Frowning, he laid it down on his plate.

He stared down at the scone, the vision of Holly as he'd
seen her last night in bed rising up in his mind, her hair
down around her waist, the creamy flesh of her neck
exposed. Matilda was right, he shouldn't keep her here.
Perhaps it might be prudent if she did take the position.
He didn't like the idea of turning her loose in London
with no society and no place to stay as yet. She might have
a little money set aside, but not enough to live on her own.
Then there was the matter of the blunt he owed the little
minx. If she were safely installed in the country, he could
pay her back at his leisure. Also, if she were forty miles
away, he might be able to get her out of his mind.

Later that evening, John strode through the front door
of his townhouse, knowing he would never be able to get
Holly out of his mind. Earlier that morning, Matilda had
insisted she give him a ride in her carriage to the shipping
office, and he hadn't had time to speak to Holly about the
nanny position. He couldn't keep his mind on his work for
thinking about her. And when his brother never showed up

at the office, his mind had imagined all sorts of lurid things Teddy could be doing to her.

"Evening, my lord." Dunn greeted him at the door, his usual subservient expression tainted with worry. "You're home early."

"Yes." He didn't offer an explanation. He couldn't very well tell Dunn he'd come home to see Holly. Instead, he said, "Something is worrying you. What is it?"

"Nothing, my lord."

"What is that odor?" John sniffed the air, then handed Dunn his hat and took off his greatcoat.

"I believe you smell beeswax and lemon oil, my lord." Dunn closed the door.

He looked around the entrance hallway. The floor glistened, never looking so clean. The brass sconces gleamed from a good polishing. The oak wainscoting shined like it was new. All the cobwebs were out of the corners. "Been busy, Dunn?"

Dunn cleared his throat. "Actually, my lord, it was Miss Campbell."

"Miss Campbell?" John paused, one arm halfway out of his coat.

"Yes, my lord. She cleaned the whole house. She even had Lord Theodore cleaning."

"I thought I told her she was a guest in my house."

"I stressed that to her, my lord, but she insisted she be allowed to clean, and," Dunn braced his shoulders for a blow and added, "cook."

"The devil you say." He clamped his jaw closed to keep from bellowing her name. He could feel his neck muscles protruding beneath his cravat. His next words came out through clamped teeth. "Where is she?"

"In the kitchen, my lord."

John yanked his coat the rest of the way off, turned and

thrust it at Dunn. That's when he noticed the staircase. Pine roping spiraled around the railing. Bright red bows formed a neat line along the banister. He glanced down the hallway and saw bows and garlands over all the doorways. He pointed to the railing. "Is this her doing, too?"

"Um . . . yes, my lord," Dunn said, staring down at the floor. "She thought a bit of Christmas cheer would brighten up the place."

"Did she?" He strode toward the basement steps that would take him to the kitchen, his fists clenched in anger.

Chapter 4

"I love the way your eyes sparkle while you cook," Teddy said, standing beside Holly in the kitchen. He leaned close and gazed into her eyes. "Has anyone ever told you you're beautiful?"

"If they did, I would know they were lying. I'm plain as the day is long."

"I beg to differ. You're more beautiful than you know. Won't you grace me with just one little kiss?"

"No. Please stop making a nuisance of yourself . . . Ugh, what is that smell?" She sniffed the air, then glanced over at the stove. Smoke rolled out the sides of the lid covering the frying pan and curled up to the ceiling. "Oh, no, my chicken!"

She shoved Teddy away from the stove and pulled the lid off the frying pan. Burning grease spit at her as the smoke flew up into her face. Fanning the smoke out of her face, she coughed, then said, "You shouldn't have distracted me."

"It wasn't my fault. If you'd given me that kiss—"

"I'll give you something . . ." Holly thrust the platter at him. "Here, hold this." Avoiding the hissing grease as much as she could, she forked piece after piece of burned chicken onto the serving platter and frowned at it. "I hope this edible."

"I'm sure it is." He glanced down at the chicken, looking unsure of his statement.

His expression reminded her of Captain McLain's when she had placed food before him. It might not have bothered her. She might even have smiled and seen the humor in it as she had during Captain McLain's lighthearted teasing, but for some strange reason she had wanted to impress John with a perfect meal. Now it was ruined, and she felt like crying.

"No need to be polite," she said in a disheartened voice. "I'm terrible at cooking, but I thought I could do a better job than Dunn. I guess I was wrong. My grandmother tried to teach me to cook, but after she broke her tooth on a piece of steak, she banished me from the kitchen. I haven't given up trying, though."

"I'm sure you'll be excellent at anything you do."

"I'd rather you tease me than try to flatter my vanity with polite lies." Holly picked up a dishcloth and moved the spitting pan off the fire, then shoved the cover back on it.

"I would never do such a thing."

"You've been doing it all day. And you really shouldn't flirt with a woman who's seen your backside."

Instead of looking abashed as Holly hoped, he grinned. "Usually the women who have seen me naked don't mind that I flirt with them." He set the platter aside, then wrapped his arms around her waist.

"Well, this one does . . ." Holly used the dishcloth in her hand to give his forehead a few good whacks. "You must stop this!"

Abruptly, the door flew open, banging against the wall. Holly peeked over Teddy's shoulder and saw John striding across the kitchen, his gaze glued on them.

Without a word of warning, John grabbed Teddy and flung him across the room. He fell against a large china closet. Plates rattled. Two of them fell and crashed to the floor. Teddy stood, straightened the lapel of his mulberry-colored coat, then glared back at John.

"I told you to stay away from her." John approached Teddy as if he meant to attack him again.

"Why? So you can have her?" Teddy held up his fists and spread his feet.

Holly jumped in front of John before he reached Teddy. She was still holding the dishcloth and slammed it against John's hard chest. She could feel his heart hammering against her palms and the rounded contours of his muscles moving with each deep rapid breath.

He stared down at her hand on his chest, then, as if her touch burned him, he knocked her hands away. "Stay out of this."

"No. I'm not a mare to be fought over. Please, I don't want you two arguing over me." She turned and shot Teddy a reproachful glance, then glanced back at John. "Teddy didn't do anything wrong."

"Did you encourage him, then?" John turned his full gaze on her.

She flinched beneath his malignant gaze. "No, but—"

"Then stay out of this, Miss Campbell." He picked her up by her waist and set her aside.

She saw Teddy advancing and stepped in between them again. "All right," she said, holding up her arms. "Should I get a bucket of water, or do you two listen to reason?"

The two brothers glared at each other, then at her.

She didn't flinch under their gazes. "I'm glad you remember what it felt like this morning—thank the good Lord for water. Now, let me tell you, if either of you hits the other, I will walk out that front door and never speak to either one of you again. You needn't look so pleased, my lord." Holly cut her eyes at John. "I'll look for a place tomorrow. I won't come between two brothers, especially after they have been so kind to me." Holly took a step toward the door.

John grabbed her arm. "You needn't do that, Miss Campbell."

"You can't leave us," Teddy said, his voice pleading.

She looked at both of them. "Very well, but Teddy, you must promise to stop flirting with me and just be my friend."

"All right." He nodded, sulking.

"And you . . ." Holly shook the dishcloth at John. "You must try to have some control over your temper. I realize you have a lot of pressures on you at the moment, but that's no reason to go throwing your brother across the room. If anyone should throw him across the room, it should be me." She shook her finger at Teddy. "Don't think I won't do it, if you try to steal another kiss."

"I'll remember that." A grin pulled at the corners of Teddy's lips.

"Fine. Now, can we have dinner while it's still warm? Teddy, please tell Dunn dinner is ready."

Teddy nodded, cut his eyes at John, then left the kitchen.

When he was gone, John took a step toward her. "That

was the finest display of anger I think I've ever seen on a woman."

"Thank you, my lord." She wasn't sure if he was chiding her or teasing her about it. "I wasn't really angry," she explained. "No one should see me when I get really angry."

"Could you really throw him across the room?"

"Maybe not, but I would have tried."

"I have no doubt of it." A hint of a smile toyed with the corners of his mouth, then disappeared. "Now it is my turn to get angry. Why did you take it upon yourself to decorate my house for Christmas? Why are you in here cooking when I specifically told you guests do not work in this house?"

Holly didn't like the look in his golden eyes. She took a step back. "I tasted what Dunn fixed for lunch earlier. I don't like to see good food ruined, so I thought I'd try to cook dinner. And about the decorating, a peddler came to the door selling roping and ribbon. It was so reasonably priced, I couldn't turn him away. I thought you might like to have a little Christmas cheer in your home. I didn't think you'd mind."

"If I had wanted my house decorated, I would have ordered it done."

"Well, I'm sorry."

"Your apology doesn't sound convincing." He took another step toward her, his square jaw set with grim determination, those golden eyes flaring at her.

"It's the best I can do under the circumstances." She took another step back. It was odd. She wasn't afraid of Teddy, but John melted her mettle with one glance.

"It's not good enough. You defy me at every turn. You even went so far as to clean my house."

"I couldn't stand to see such a beautiful place so dirty.

Dunn is only one person. He can't keep this big house clean and wait on you hand and foot. So I thought I would help him. We all pitched in. It really didn't take long.'' Holly didn't tell John what sort of mess she'd cleaned up in the kitchen, or that she thought Dunn was a bit on the lazy side when it came to keeping the kitchen clean.

"It's up to me to worry about what Dunn does and does not do.'' He took another step toward her.

"I realize that, but surely you can't expect so much from him.'' She took a step back, and her bottom bumped against the counter.

He walked up to her and placed his hands on the counter, trapping her within his long, powerful arms. "Don't counsel me on how to handle my servants.''

"Someone needs to.'' She saw him staring at her lips and her heart pounded.

"But it won't be you.'' He leaned toward her.

Holly knew he was going to kiss her. Every womanly instinct in her body cried out that he would. He was so close, she could smell the musky scent of his aftershave. She squeezed her lips together, afraid of how his kiss would excite her, but more afraid he wouldn't kiss her at all and she'd never know what it felt like.

He paused, his lips inches from her mouth, then sniffed the air. "Is something burning?''

Overwhelmed by the anticipation of the kiss, Holly hadn't noticed anything else. Now she saw smoke coming out of the oven. "My bread!''

He stepped back as she ran to the oven and flung open the door. Smoke smothered her. She coughed, then fanned the air and pulled the four loaves from the oven. She set them on the counter, then plopped her fists on her hips and looked at the burned tops. Dinner was completely ruined now.

Holding back tears, she said, "I suppose we can cut off the crust." She was keenly aware he was watching her and probably smirking. Before he could see the disappointment and hurt on her face, she shoved the platter of chicken at him. "Here. Please take this into the dining room while I get the rest of the meal into serving bowls."

He scowled at her, opened his mouth to say something, then apparently decided not to and clamped his jaw closed. He turned and carried the platter out of the kitchen.

When he left, Holly sighed with relief. Every nerve in her body still pulsed at the thought of his kiss. There was no denying she had wanted that kiss. She couldn't understand why—he wasn't the slightest bit likable. And why did it bother her that she had ruined his dinner? Why should she want to impress him at all?

Dunn came through the door, his face ashen, his hands trembling.

"Something wrong?" Holly asked, then dumped out boiled potatoes into a bowl.

Dunn looked unable to speak, then he finally found his voice. "I saw his lordship carrying a tray to the dining room."

"And?" Holly asked, not thinking that was so unusual.

"He's never done that before, miss. Never. It just isn't done."

"Don't worry, I'm sure he'll survive it." Holly smiled at him, slapped a wad of butter on the overcooked potatoes, then chopped little bits of parsley over them, hoping to camouflage the fact they were so mushy. After that, she poured the glazed carrots into a chafing dish; half of the glaze stuck to the pan, and she had to scrape it out with a spoon. The green peas looked all right and she placed them artfully around the carrots. "There now, perhaps this meal won't be so bad after all. Should we call his lordship back to come and serve the vegetables?"

Dunn looked like he might faint, and Holly grinned at him.

John was unable to draw his gaze away from Holly, who sat next to him at the table. Her old faded blue gown was spotted with stains. A long streak of flour covered one side of her neck. Candlelight glistened in her auburn hair, setting the red highlights ablaze. Some of her hair had fallen down from the bun at the back of her head and hung in thin ringlets along her neck and face. She looked every bit the plebeian and utterly delectable.

Something about her candor and artless manner drew him. He had come close to kissing her in the kitchen. Even now, he wanted to lick the flour off her neck. He'd never met a young woman like her. Elise had been just the opposite. Never would Elise have appeared at the table with flour on her neck and in that old dress, nor would she have lifted a finger to clean his house or to cook for him— be it a burned meal or not. Holly's voice dragged him from his musings.

"You're not eating your chicken," she said, looking expectantly at him. "In Charleston, we eat fried chicken every Sunday. There's an art to getting the meat on the inside done without burning the outside and keeping it crispy. My grandmother made the best fried chicken in the county."

John stared down at the burned chicken breast on his plate, unsure whether he should eat it or slip it beneath the table.

"Have you always lived in Charleston?" Teddy asked, staring down at the mushy potatoes on his plate.

"Yes." She glanced down at a hole in the linen tablecloth near her plate.

John noticed she wouldn't look Teddy in the eye, a sure sign she was lying. He lifted his wine goblet, took a sip, then eyed her over it.

"I've heard it's beautiful there. I have a college mate from Charleston. Harry Renwick. Perhaps you know him?" Teddy raised a curious brow at her.

"No," she said, adding more emphasis to the word than was needed.

John studied her, watching her push the raw peas around on her plate, her dark lashes forming long crescents on her cheeks. Why was she lying about living in Charleston? It was odd in the extreme that she'd sailed without luggage. That story she had told him about running out of the house and leaving her clothes was a blatant lie. Holly Campbell might not even be her real name. He made a mental note to find the ship on which she had sailed and speak to the captain.

Her hand tightened around her fork, then she looked thoughtful and in a more nonchalant tone said, "I really don't recall the name Renwick."

"That's too bad. He grew up there, then moved here with his parents. They are railroad people, you know. I'll have to invite him over, so you can reminisce. Perhaps you might know some of the same acquaintances." Teddy grew bold and took a bite out of a chicken leg.

"I doubt it. Charleston is a large place."

Teddy didn't answer her, but his eyes widened as he chewed . . . and chewed . . . and chewed. He noticed her watching him, feigned a grin, then swallowed. "By Jove, this is delicious, John. Try it."

John wasn't sure about tasting it, but since Teddy had

made an issue of it, he pried off a piece with his fork, examined it closely, then ate it.

"I know it's a little overcooked. Do you like it?" She leaned toward him, anxiously awaiting his reply.

It was like eating burned shoe leather, but he couldn't look into those enormous brown eyes and tell her that. She had almost cried in the kitchen when she'd burned the bread. He made the mistake of swallowing the chicken. It stuck in his throat like a lump of coal. Before he choked, he grabbed his glass and drained it.

He noticed her eyes still on him and lied with ease. "Yes, it's tasty."

"I'm glad." She smiled, then ate a spoonful of peas.

John watched her gnawing on them as if they were the best tasting things in the world. He wondered if she liked raw peas.

"Dunn was telling me about Bond Street. He said if I liked to watch people—which I like very much—then I should go there."

"Yes, you should," Teddy said, excited. "The afternoon is better for it. I'll take you tomorrow."

A jealous knot tightened in John's throat. "I don't think Miss Campbell will be here tomorrow," he said with a marked amount of pleasure in his voice. "I have a position for her that will take her away from us."

"Thank you, but I prefer to find my own employment." Her enormous brown eyes gleamed at him and a stubborn firmness pulled at the corners of her rosy-red lips.

"You can suit yourself, madam." He eyed her, aggravated by her ungrateful attitude and still plagued by unbidden jealousy.

She was silent a moment and stared down at her plate as if pondering something. In a mellower tone, she said,

"I was ungracious a moment ago. I'm sorry. What position do you have for me?"

John stared hard at her, then said, "It would be working for me."

"Doing what?"

"My children are in need of a new nanny." He watched her eyes grow wide with surprise. She didn't look repulsed by the idea of children, so he continued. "I thought perhaps you would want the position—"

"Good God!" Teddy slammed his fork down on the table. "I wouldn't wish that on my worst enemy. You know Dryden and Brock are little monsters."

"Not if one knows how to handle them." John eyed Teddy, visions of choking him rising up in his mind. "I'm sure Miss Campbell will not have a problem."

"I don't think I shall. I adore children. I've never been a nanny before, but I'd like to give it a try." Holly smiled at John, her dimples winking at him as she ripped off a piece of chicken from a breast.

"You don't know what you're agreeing to. The boys are not children, they are little hellions," Teddy said, tapping his knife against a slice of the burned bread. It made an annoying pinging as if he were hitting porcelain. "Ann is a little darling, but those other two . . ." Teddy shook his head.

"Ann?" Holly raised a curious brow.

"That's my daughter. She is the youngest."

"A daughter. How nice." She set her fork down, looking pleased, then took a sip of port. "I'm sure the children and I will become great friends."

John had no expectations in that quarter, for he knew how devilish the boys could be. But Holly had bottom. He remembered the way she had jumped on the thug who had pointed a pistol at him. Perhaps if she could not befriend the boys, she could at least intimidate them enough to gain their respect.

"Well, then, that's all settled," John said, feeling a weight lifting from his chest. "I will escort you there tomorrow."

"You?" Teddy cried. "I thought you couldn't leave the shipping office at the moment. Why not let me escort her?"

"I haven't seen the children in two weeks. You can take my place at the office. I'll return within two days."

Teddy pursed his lips, then stared broodingly down at his plate.

"I should do a little shopping before I go. May we go the day after next?"

John frowned at her. "I suppose so." John wondered where she was getting the money with which to go shopping. He was sure she'd given him all her money this morning to pay his bill.

She didn't look concerned about it and grinned at Teddy. "Perhaps you'd like to go with me?"

Teddy brightened considerably. "Yes, I would love that, and I could take you to Bond Street."

John narrowed his brows at Teddy, then at Holly. She was smiling at Teddy, those maddening dimples deep hollows in her cheeks. Unbidden jealousy gnawed at him again. He had to conquer this overpowering lust for her. She was a penniless young woman under his care. "I'm going back to the office," he said, standing. "I won't be home until late. As a matter of fact, I might work all night."

"But what about your dinner?" Holly asked.

"I've suddenly lost my appetite." He strode out of the room, leaving Holly staring after him, her arched brows drawn together in a frown.

* * *

The next morning, frigid gusts whipped down Bond Street. Holly grabbed her hair and tried to keep the wind from blowing the pins out of it. Captain McLain's coat was too big on her. The bitter cold seeped beneath the loose wool, going right through her clothes, chilling her to the bone. She shivered, pulled the coat closer around her neck, and glanced around.

Rows of shops lined the street. Wreaths and garlands decorated the shop windows and doors. Some of the garlands had blown loose in the wind and dangled across the windows, banging against the glass. The street was bare, save for two gentlemen on the opposite side of the street. They were holding their hats on their heads and fighting the wind. She glanced at Teddy, who strode beside her.

He was whistling, his warm breath hitting the cold air, forming a white cloud around his mouth. The packages she'd bought filled his arms. The bitter cold didn't seem to bother him. He glanced at her. "I'm sorry there is no one on Bond today. I suppose the cold kept them home."

Holly shivered and glanced up at the thick grayish white clouds overhead. "It looks like snow."

"Yes, it does. Only fools would be shopping in weather like this." He shot Holly a pointed look, then they both laughed.

"I had hoped to find at least some fools on the streets," she said, smiling at him.

"I daresay, they will come out when the weather warms, then you will see all you like."

"I can't wait. I am curious about the fashionable young ladies and gentlemen in London."

"I'm sure they are no different than the society you have at home."

She was silent a moment, then said, "I had no society at home."

"You didn't?" Teddy looked incredulous.

"No. People shunned my grandmother for being an abolitionist. To make matters worse, she publicly condemned those who owned slaves. Consequently, the wealthy planters in our area snubbed my grandmother. We rarely went anywhere but to church and to market."

"I am sorry to hear that."

"Don't be. I don't feel as if I suffered from it. I was happy staying home with my grandmother." She pointed to a shop. "There's a modiste shop. Would you mind if we went in?"

"To be honest, I've looked at enough bolts of material to last me a lifetime." His white teeth flashed in a teasing grin. "There's a little tea shop across the street, I'll wait for you in there."

"All right," Holly said, watching him stride across the street, the hem of his black greatcoat stark against his bright yellow pantaloons. Perhaps it was better he wasn't going with her. She had felt rushed in every shop they had gone in—especially when he stood beside her, trying to look the gentleman and keep the impatience from his face. He must have been bored silly.

She waved to him, then strode into the store. A tiny bell on the door jangled when she closed the door behind her. The heat inside the shop engulfed her. Still shivering, she rubbed her numb hands together, feeling her new wool gloves rough against her palms. Even with the gloves, the icy wind outside had gone right through them.

Flexing her numb fingers, she strolled past the brightly colored bolts of material lining the shelves. The clean pleasant smell of new fabric filled her senses. A bolt of Forester's green crepe material caught her eye and she paused near it, then took off her gloves and stuffed them in her reticule. She touched the stiff material and rubbed it between her fingers.

She heard a throat being cleared near the back of the store.

Leaning past the bolt, Holly glimpsed a woman standing behind a counter. She had been adding up receipts and stopped calculating long enough to glare at Holly. The woman was middle-aged, with a small, pinched mouth and pointy chin.

"Good day," Holly said cheerfully.

The woman didn't answer her, but took in the oversize old navy-blue coat and Holly's worn blue dress, then her face screwed up. "I don't have anything you can afford. Perhaps you should try the East End," she said, setting down the receipts in her hand.

Holly had never been addressed so rudely. Her cheeks burned with a blush, then her embarrassment melted into righteous indignation. She dropped the edge of cloth she was feeling. "I have money to spend like anyone else."

"I don't sell fabric—that is, unless you wish to have a dress made. I'm sure you can't afford my labor." Her gaze snapped over Holly again with disapproval.

"How do you know that?" The perverse side of Holly was just getting activated.

She looked at Holly, then threw back her head and cackled. "You penniless gamines are all alike. You act like you can buy the world." Her smile faded and the pinched look returned to her mouth. "I'm through being trifled with. If you don't march out of here this instant, I'll send for a Charlie and you'll find yourself behind bars."

Holly opened her mouth with a retort, but the bell on

the door jangled. Cold air surged past her, whipping her skirt around her ankles. She clamped her mouth closed, turned, and saw Lady Matilda striding into the shop, her cheeks pink from the cold. She looked beautiful in a red dress and black mink coat and hat that exactly matched her hair color.

Her gaze landed on Holly right away, and her lips stretched in a tight smile. She pulled her dainty white hands out of a mink muff. "There you are. I saw Teddy going into a shop across the street. He told me you were here." She paused, surveying Holly's face. "Is something wrong, my dear?"

Holly glanced at the woman behind the counter. Her jaw dropped, then her eyes widened to the size of half-dollars. Someone could have blown the woman over with one breath.

Holly smiled at the clerk, a hint of triumph on her lips. "No, nothing is wrong." She turned back to Lady Matilda. "I suppose I should be going. Lord Theodore is probably tired of waiting. I'm afraid he's regretting accompanying me. I've kept him shopping all afternoon. It's terribly hard to find reasonably priced material in this town. I did see a reasonable shop near Piccadilly, where I found several nice pieces of material I can make into dresses. Perhaps I shouldn't keep him waiting." Holly eyed the saleswoman as she rushed around the counter and flounced toward them, waving her arms. She reminded Holly of a flustered hen.

"Don't leave on Theodore's account, my dear. You should always keep a gentleman waiting. It does them good to learn patience."

The saleswoman paused near Lady Matilda and curtsied. "Do you know this . . . this," she said her next words through her teeth, "person, Lady Matilda?"

"Indeed I do, Mrs. Dupree." Lady Matilda paused while she held the sides of her chafed cheeks. "She's a particular friend of mine."

"You're freezing, my lady. Let me get you some tea."

"And some for my friend here." Lady Matilda motioned toward Holly, then smiled graciously at Mrs. Dupree.

Mrs. Dupree gave Holly a sour look, then hurried into a back room.

"You really didn't have to do that." Holly watched Lady Matilda pull off her hat and spencer.

"It will not hurt her to be a little more accommodating." Lady Matilda pulled off her gloves. Her voice held a note of genuine conviction as she said, "If there is one thing I do not like it's rudeness. Just because you are not wealthy does not mean she should not wait upon you."

Holly glanced down at her dress, thinking of her petticoat beneath it and the fortune in jewels she had sewn there. She glanced back up at Lady Matilda, her expression giving away nothing. "Yes, well, I agree with you. She shouldn't have been insolent. I do have a little money." She held back a smile.

"She will bend over backward to please you now," Lady Matilda said in the superior tone of one who knows how to use her wealth to get what she wanted. "I'm one of her best customers."

"Well, thank you for championing me." She wondered why Lady Matilda was treating her as if they were friends. Yesterday when they'd met she had been no more than civil. But she supposed Lady Matilda's jealousy over John might have caused it.

Holly glanced at a bolt of green-and-red-plaid broadcloth. Where was the price tag? She lifted up the bolt and peered under it. When she found nothing, she asked, "Where are the prices?"

"If one shops in this store, my dear, you don't need to know the prices," Lady Matilda said, a hint of haughty amusement in her voice.

Holly made a face. "Even if I were wealthy, I wouldn't order a dress without knowing its cost. How would you know if you were being cheated?" Lady Matilda aimed a disdainful look at her, and Holly added, "My grandmother taught me to be a wise shopper."

"I'm sure that was prudent, since you most certainly had to live on a modest income." Lady Matilda smiled in a patronizing way, then ran her hand along a bolt of burgundy velvet. "Speaking of incomes. Did Lord Upton mention to you that his children need a nanny?"

"Yes, he did," Holly said, surprised Lady Matilda should know about the offer John made to her. "I already agreed to take the position. Are you the one I should thank for recommending me for the post, or was it Lord Upton's idea?"

"I admit it was my doing." Lady Matilda's blue eyes brightened.

"Ah, then I thank you." Holly had a feeling it had been Lady Matilda's idea. The lady seemed terribly anxious to get rid of her.

"If you would like, I can have my carriage at your disposal and you can leave this evening for the country."

"That is very kind of you, Lady Matilda, but Lord Upton already agreed to take me there."

"Did he?" Lady Matilda looked incredulous for a moment, then a hint of jealousy passed over her eyes. "Well, I'm sure he was just being kind. I'll speak to him and see if I can't take you. I have nothing on my calendar for the next couple of days."

"I believe he said he wanted to see the children."

"I thought he would wait until it was closer to Christmas."

Holly shrugged. "I suppose he wants to see them sooner."

Lady Matilda's brows furrowed for the slightest moment, then the polite opaque mask was back. "Well, I shall speak to him anyway." She paused, rubbing a piece of silk between her fingers. "I hope Teddy has not been bothering you. He can be the biggest flirt imaginable."

"No, he's been every bit the gentleman today."

Lady Matilda looked relieved. "I'm glad of it. He's so young. And young men don't know how to restrain their feelings." She lowered her voice, adding emphasis to what she was about to say. "And you know, dear, he has to marry an heiress, just as Lord Upton must."

"I don't think I like what you're implying." Holly looked pointedly at her.

"Oh, dear . . ." Lady Matilda grabbed her throat. "You mustn't think I was implying you were setting your cap for them, my dear. Of course you know your place and you would never do such a thing. I was just pointing out Theodore's failings." She took Holly's measure, then looked pleased Holly was plain and not beautiful enough to tempt Teddy or John.

"You've no need to point out his foibles to me, I have no desire to marry or become involved with anyone."

Mrs. Dupree strode through a door, carrying a tea tray. "Here you go, my lady." She set the tray on a little table near a sitting area in back of the shop.

"Excuse me, but I'm in a rush, I don't want to keep Teddy waiting."

"I insist you stay a moment," Lady Matilda said. "You will need a dress for your new position. Mrs. Dupree has some very serviceable ready-mades she can show you. I buy dresses here for my servants." She glanced at Mrs. Dupree. "Something in black, I believe. Yes, black, it will add authority to her address, she is so very young and plain. She's going to be a nanny to my niece and nephews, and we want her looking the part."

"Thank you, but I can't allow you to—"

"No, no, my dear, let me do this for you." Her eyes gleamed like two blue sparkling cubes of ice.

By the look in Lady Matilda's eyes, Holly knew the gesture didn't come from the kindness of her heart.

A block down the street, John entered number 9 Bond Street. He strode through Gentleman Jackson's boxing establishment and hoped going a few rounds might ease the lust plaguing him. Boxing had always helped in the past, and it was the only indulgence he could afford. Over a year ago, he had given up his membership at White's.

He thought of last night and how he'd worked most of it. But he hadn't been able to keep his mind on his work for remembering the image of Holly in bed.

Before he reached the ring, the sweaty stale odor in the building assailed him. It was a primal odor, similar to the lingering odor of sex. Fighting didn't come close to making love to a woman, but it ran a good second and gave him a kind of release. Thinking of releases brought Holly to mind again. He almost groaned aloud. His frown deepened as he reached the ring.

Four gentlemen stood near the ropes, yelling encouragement at two men in the ring. John noticed the Marquis of Waterton was one of the opponents. Waterton was solidly built, well over six feet like John himself, with sandy blond hair and bracing blue eyes. Waterton's income was more than one hundred thousand pounds a year; consequently, his wealth gave him power over the *beau monde*.

He could destroy a lady's reputations with a look, or ruin a man by a snub in the clubs, and he used that power with vicious deftness if someone dared cross him. He was known as "The Bear" of the *ton*. Those in society hated him, but were afraid not to socialize with him for fear of being cut by him. And so, the pernicious cycle continued, and he kept his domain in check through a phobia of insecurities that came with wealth and prestige and status in society. All except John. He was past caring what the *ton* thought of him and Waterton knew that.

Waterton saw John, drew back, then slammed his fist in his sparring partner's face. The young man staggered several steps, looked at Waterton cross-eyed, then fell to the mat.

A collective cheer from Waterton's toad-eating club went through the room.

His opponent was a young pup, who looked barely twenty-two. Blood trickled from his nose, and one of his eyes was swollen shut. He looked barely conscious. Several young boys who worked in the gym ran to help him up.

"So sorry, old boy." Waterton gazed down at his opponent with breezy indifference, then turned, not bothering helping him up. His gaze landed on John, amused contempt on his face, the kind of amusement that comes from condescension and a superiority of knowing his advantage over John was his wealth.

A young boy ran up to Waterton and handed him a towel. He took it, wiped the sweat off his face, then strode toward John. "Haven't seen you in an age, St. John," Waterton said, with polite derision. "Where have you been hiding yourself?"

"I spend most of my time at the shipping office."

"That's right. Sorry to hear the bad news about the ships." Waterton's voice was laced with exaggerated sympathy. "What bloody luck. Do you think you'll stay afloat?"

"I wonder that you have such a keen interest in my company." John leaned against the ropes, meeting Waterton's gaze. "I wouldn't think my sinking ships would give you a moment's notice."

Waterton smiled at him. For a moment, hatred crossed his expression, then it disappeared behind a cold, calculating mask. "They don't, but we're taking bets at White's on how long you'll stay afloat. I just wanted to get your opinion on the odds."

He strained to keep his hands from wrapping around Waterton's neck, feeling every muscle in his body straining. For more than a year now, when he was forced to give up his stable and sell off the paintings and furniture in the townhouse to make ends meet, he'd been the brunt of bets and jokes by the *ton*. He had a feeling Waterton was behind most of them. He had never figured out what he'd done to Waterton to instill his dislike, but for twelve years now Waterton had hated him.

John narrowed his eyes at him. "Don't you know that we make our own odds?"

"Some of us do, then again, some of us do not have the money to change the twist of fate." One corner of his lip lifted in a derisive snarl. "Are you up for a round? I daresay, I might get a bit more exercise beating you."

"It would be my pleasure," John said, taking off his coat, shirt, and cravat. He stretched, rippling the well-defined muscles in his chest and arms, then he stepped into the ring.

Waterton grabbed the towel off his shoulders and threw it in a corner. "As I recall, I felled you the last time we fought." He raised his fists and danced toward John.

"I believe you did." John hit out with his left.

Waterton dodged it and slammed his fist into John's ribs.

John fell back a step and caught his breath. He saw the grin on Waterton's face, then lunged toward him and faked a punch to Waterton's stomach. Waterton let down his guard, and John slammed his fist in his face.

Waterton looked surprised by the punch. His eyes rolled back in his head, then he collapsed in the ring.

"But it's my turn to win now," John said, staring down at the blood trickling from Waterton's nose. He stepped over his sprawled form, then bent to pick up his shirt. A sharp pain in his ribs made him grimace.

He noticed the gentlemen standing near the ropes, staring at him like he'd just committed murder, then they ran to help Waterton. John picked up his clothes from a chair, then put them on and left the gym. Holly's face rose up in his mind again and he cursed inwardly. It was useless, not even beating Waterton would get her out of his mind.

Chapter 5

Holly left Mrs. Dupree hovering around Lady Matilda as she measured her for a new ball gown. Clutching her packages, Holly stepped out of the shop. The wind whipped her skirt up around her ankles. Several drops of rain hit her face, then tiny particles of sleet bounced off her head and shoulders. She pulled her coat closer around her neck and hurried to the tea shop. A pinecone wreath flopped against the door as she opened it and stepped inside.

The heavenly scent of freshly baked pastries met her. She took a deep breath, shook the sleet off her coat and out of her hair, then surveyed the room. Ten small tables were scattered about in the front. Behind the tables, a long counter displayed colorful, tempting pastries of all shapes and varieties. The shop was empty, save for a nanny and a little girl who were sitting in the middle of the room.

She immediately noticed Teddy's bright yellow clothes and saw him waving to her from a table in the corner.

When she was seated across from him, she watched him slide down into the seat opposite her and stretch out his long legs. He was almost as large as John, and he dwarfed the small wrought-iron chair.

His gaze turned sultry as he reached across the table and pulled a piece of holly from a small Christmas arrangement on the table. He leaned forward and put it in the back of her bun. "There. You look truly in the Christmas spirit." He didn't move back right away and kept his face close to her.

Holly didn't like the I-want-to-kiss-you gleam in his eyes. She leaned back in her seat, and hoped to turn his mind in another direction as she said, "Do you think the children will like the Christmas presents I got them?"

"Of course they will, I helped you choose them." He slumped back against his chair and rested his elbows on the table. He studied her for a moment, then, with disappointment in his voice, "I've had a splendid day and I'm sorry it's about to end. I don't know when I've enjoyed such a felicitous afternoon with a woman." His lips parted in a charming smile.

"No need to lie about it, Teddy, I know you must have been bored stiff." She grinned at him. "You'll probably never volunteer to take me shopping again." She took a sip of the tea, feeling it warm her all the way down to the pit of her stomach.

"I would endure any amount of milliner shops to be near you."

"How gallant you are," she said in a teasing voice.

"Let me rephrase that." He grinned at her. "I'd fight dragons and demons to be near you."

"Why must you start this? You have been good all day."

The smile left her face. "Please don't start with your flummery now." She used her best reproachful tone on him.

"Flummery? I'll have you know, I'm no flummer," he said, pretending to sound indignant. "Flummers have big noses, buck teeth, and I have it on a good account that they drool when they are flirting with a young woman."

Holly laughed. "You are incorrigible."

"I hope so." He reached over to put his hand on hers.

Holly moved her hand before he could touch it and fingered a napkin on the table. A tense moment stood between them. Hurt drifted into Teddy's expression. She didn't know how to comfort him without giving him encouragement, so she remained silent.

He broke the silence, all the mirth gone from his voice. "Did you see Lady Matilda in the shop? I told her you were there."

"Yes, I saw her."

"She's a fine lady, always so amiable and generous. Since Elise died from consumption, she has gone out of her way to help John with the children. And she's been overly generous to me. I've never told John this, but she sends me an allowance for school."

"Why keep it a secret?"

"He's very proud. He'd jump down my throat if he knew."

"Your secret is safe with me."

Teddy grew pensive and stared down at the Christmas arrangement on the table. He said more to himself, "John and I used to have fun together, but it seems like such a long time ago. I remember when I turned ten and eight and he threw a hunting party to celebrate my birthday. We rode hell bent for leather all day. I was so tired and sore, but I wouldn't let him know it. I stayed up all night with him, playing cards and drinking until we were so foxed we couldn't make it to bed." He paused, a sad grin on his face. "He used to be so much fun to be with . . . but that was before Elise left him rolled up."

"Rolled up?" Holly asked, watching a little girl stuffing a monstrous-size piece of pastry in her mouth, the yellow custard filling oozing out the corners of her mouth.

"Penniless, to be more exact."

"Oh . . ." Holly glanced back at Teddy.

"The story goes back even further. When Father died and John came into the title, he found out that our father had gambled away everything we owned. By the time Father's debts were paid, there was nothing much left."

Teddy paused, then leaned back in his chair. "John knew we were in trouble, so he searched for an heiress and found Elise."

"Did he love her?"

"John would never marry someone just for money. I believe he cared for her very much at first."

"At first?"

"Yes, well, after she gave birth to their last child, she grew petulant. John couldn't seem to make her happy. He gave up trying when he found she had—um . . . other lovers." He scrutinized her expression. "I see I've offended you."

"No, no," Holly said, her face reddening. "I just can't understand how a woman could do that to her husband."

"It's par for polite society here. After a husband gets an heir off his wife, then she's free to take as many lovers as she likes, but she must remain discreet about it. And, of course, the man is expected to take a mistress as well."

"Oh, dear, I don't think I like your society here."

"It does take some getting used to." Teddy smiled at her, then the smile faded. "Elise got used to it fast enough. She loved the freedom marriage gave her. She threw lavish parties here in town and shopped any- and everywhere. She had credit with merchants all over town, and never stayed within the allowance John gave her. She hid the bills from him. He didn't know how much money she had spent until she died."

"How tragic, not to know economy in spending." Holly shook her head, unable to understand how anyone could spend money so frivolously.

"Yes, well, after he paid her debts he was practically broke again. Then he invested everything he owned in St. John Shipping in hopes that it would keep him afloat, but," Teddy sighed, "that looks like a hopeless venture."

"Why doesn't he just look for another rich wife?" Holly said in her usual practical tone.

"He's too proud. He swore after Elise died he'd never marry again for wealth."

"A man of principle," Holly said, pleased.

"Yes, perhaps too much." Teddy's dark brows came together and he stared pensively down at his hands.

Holly was silent for a moment, thinking how John had scolded her for paying the wine vendor that morning. Perhaps she had offended his sense of pride. She would have to be careful not to do it again. The nanny berated the little girl for stuffing her mouth so full, and it pulled her out of her thoughts. Watching the large woman wiping the child's face, she said, "Are all the ships gone?"

"No, not all. We have one left."

Holly furrowed her brows in thought.

"But John says if the investors pull out of the company, then he'll be ruined."

"Just out of curiosity, how does one go about investing in St. John Shipping?"

"It's on the exchange. All a person would have to do is buy stock. Why do you ask?"

"No reason," Holly said with a nonchalant air. She stared out the window, while a plan formed in her mind.

A tall, dark man in a cape strode past the window, his head down, trying to avoid the sleet. The broodingly handsome profile made her heart skip a beat.

John must have felt her eyes on him, for he turned and glanced in the window. His gaze locked on her, then on Teddy. His expression was already like an angry bear, but it turned even more menacing.

Holly wiggled nervously in her seat under his gaze. "Land sakes, something is dreadfully wrong with him."

"He doesn't look happy." Teddy kept a pasty smile on his face as he motioned John inside.

"Working all night probably didn't help his disposition." Holly watched John turn, his cape swirling around his body, then he prowled toward the shop's door. She frowned, remembering how he'd up and left the table last night. She had played cards with Teddy and Dunn until midnight, waiting for him to come home, then gave up and went to bed.

The bell rattled as the shop door was thrown open. Holly felt John's eyes piercing her back. The room grew smaller, engulfed by his presence. Her body warmed all over, her palms sweating as she heard his stiff footsteps getting closer. His nearness caused a frightened tingly feeling in the pit of her stomach.

He paused near the table, fists clenched, then stared down at her. "I hope you've finished all the shopping you need to do, because we are leaving for Brookhollow now."

"Now?"

"Yes, now," he said, his tone rapier sharp.

What had vexed him now? Grimacing at him, she stood, jammed her arms in her coatsleeves, then picked up her packages.

"You can't go now, John, it's sleeting." Teddy grabbed some of the packages off the chair, helping Holly. "There could be ice on the roads."

"I'm leaving now." John grabbed the packages out of Holly's hands. "I'll take these."

"Perhaps Teddy is right. I don't think we should leave, either," Holly said, growing incensed by his dictatorial behavior. Perversity made her add, "And I'm still not done shopping. I wanted to visit a haberdashery I saw down the street. You need not see I get home. I'm quite capable of taking care of myself. Good day."

John opened his mouth, but before he could get out another stinging command, she whipped around so quickly, the hem of her dress flared out, then she was hurrying out of the shop. The bell clattered loudly in her ears as she slammed the door and crossed the street. John really was insufferable at times. And she wasn't about to be around him when he was in one of his moods. He needed to realize that he couldn't order her about or growl at her whenever he felt like it.

Caught up in her desire to be far away from him, she wasn't paying attention and collided with Lady Matilda. Her eyes widened from the attack, and she stepped back and stared at Holly. "What is the matter, my dear?"

"Nothing." Holly glanced over her shoulder and saw John and Teddy coming out of the shop. Her gaze locked with John's. Fury and fire spewed from his eyes. Her shoulders flinched from the almost tangible impact of them and her gaze snapped back to Lady Matilda. "I really must be going." Frantic now, she hurried down the sidewalk, leaving a baffled Lady Matilda staring after her with her jaw open.

"But . . . but . . . would you like a ride, my dear?"

"No, thank you," Holly called over her shoulder. "I

have a bit more shopping to do, but maybe you could give his lordship a ride. It might help his disposition."

John watched Holly practically run past Matilda. He ground his teeth together, feeling his jaw aching from the pressure. "What does she think she's about, disobeying my order and roaming the city unescorted? Here . . ." He thrust the packages at Teddy. "I'm going to catch her."

John dashed across the street, leaving Teddy glowering at him, balancing all the packages in his arms.

"My lord, wait! I'll give you a ride," Matilda called to him.

"I'm going after Miss Campbell," John said, getting a glimpse of auburn hair and a faded blue dress as Holly disappeared around the corner.

He heard Matilda calling after him, but ignored her as he ran after Holly. The wind whipped sleet in his face, forcing him to blink. He turned the corner and called to her, "I order you to wait, Miss Campbell!"

She glanced over her shoulder, saw him, then, as if to defy him, she picked up her pace.

He cursed, wanting very much to grab her, wrestle her down to the ground, then ravish her. Yes, he wanted very much to ravish her.

Sleet came down harder now, bouncing off the ground like kernels of corn. He felt the soles of his boots slipping on icy patches on the sidewalk. Several times he had to stop and catch himself before he fell. The ice slowed her progress, too, and he was gaining on her. He passed a row of costermongers. One of them was selling hot cider and cinnamon, the wind whipping the enticing smell about in the air.

"Ready-made wreaths, six pence. Six pence . . ."

Another vendor's voice faded as he left him behind on the sidewalk.

A young girl was sitting near a fish booth, selling oranges, her crates stacked in rows of three. Holly darted around the crates. Her feet slid out beneath her. John felt his stomach tighten at the thought of her hitting the sidewalk. To his surprise, her arms groped at the air, then one hand connected with a lamppost. She slid against it. He saw the bottom of the lamppost sticking out between her legs as she hung on to it and felt some of the tension leave his chest.

Before she could bolt away again, he lunged for her. As he reached to grab her arm, he hit the same patch of ice on which she'd fallen. His legs flew out from under him. He cursed and hit the sidewalk flat on his back, then slid into a stack of orange crates.

The top crate fell and crashed against his chest. Oranges bombarded his face and neck, then rolled across the sidewalk and into the street.

A moment later, he felt the crate being lifted off his chest, then Holly was bending over him, her brown eyes wide and filled with fear.

"Land sakes! Are you all right?" She laid her hand on his chest and bent close to him. The pins had fallen out of her hair, and the thick mass hung over her shoulder, the tip of it touching his neck. "You should have let me gone shopping. I didn't want you to follow me. Why don't you answer me?" Tears welled up in her eyes. "Please tell me you're all right?"

Her warm breath brushed against his cold face, not only warming his mouth and chin, but every other part of him as well. He stared at her trembling red lips, at the sleet falling in her hair. Tiny drops of ice stuck to her long, dark eyelashes. He grew aware of her hand on his chest now, like a branding iron, burning through his clothes, straight down to the pit of his loins.

"I'll be all right momentarily," he said, his voice gruff as the desire he'd been trying so hard to rein exploded inside him. He grabbed her and pulled her down to his mouth for a kiss, burying his hands in her hair.

When their lips touched, she gasped. He drove his tongue into her open mouth, tasting her warm moist depths, feeling her soft, giving mouth against his. The taste of her was like manna, and he was sure he'd never get enough of it. He deepened the kiss, entwining his tongue with hers. The stiffness left her, and she relaxed against him. Her breasts pressed against his chest, their rounded softness tantalizing him. Then he felt her hands in his hair, and she was kissing him back with blinding ardor.

He forgot that his back was flat against a hard sidewalk, that sleet was hitting his head and face, that people were watching. All that encompassed him was Holly. Holly against him, Holly kissing him, her body pressed to his. His hands moved up her slender back, along her nape, then he buried his fingers in her hair. He reveled in the softness of the thick mass against his rough fingertips.

"Mighty fine, governor. You lay there kissing the wench while me oranges are scattered halfway across London. You could be grabbing some of me oranges, instead of hers!"

The young girl's voice broke into his lust-laden senses. His eyes opened, and he saw the crowd of vendors standing around them and realized he was making a spectacle. He broke the kiss.

Holly stared down at him, looking dazed by her own response to the kiss, then her face turned as red as her lips. She opened her mouth to say something, noticed the people standing around them, then lowered her head and began picking up the oranges.

John had no idea why he was grinning; he felt like a fool. He stared at her lips swollen from his kiss and his grin broadened.

"I've never seen the like," a man with no teeth said.

"The very idea. All these gentlemen think they can take advantage of anyone they like and right here in the street. You should've slapped 'im." This from the young, over-weight girl selling the oranges.

Every time someone spoke, Holly's shoulder cringed as if their words were a whip lashing her. She stared down at the sidewalk, throwing oranges into a crate like she meant to break it apart.

"All right, haven't you seen enough?" John asked the crowd. He flexed all his limbs to make sure nothing was broken, then carefully stood, feeling the pain in his bruised ribs from Waterton's lucky punch. "I'll pay you for the oranges." He pulled a leather pouch from his pocket, found a crown, then tossed it to the girl. "That should cover it."

The plump girl caught the money midair. Grimacing, she looked at the coin, then hurried to pick up the oranges that were scattered on the sidewalk.

"Brother, dear . . ."

He turned at the sound of Teddy's amused drawl and saw him sticking his head out of the window of Matilda's brougham. The carriage had stopped beside the curb.

"Need a ride?" Teddy grinned and raised a brow at him.

John frowned at Teddy, then at the driver for the amused look on his face. He glanced back at Teddy. "As a matter of fact, we do." He grabbed Holly's arm and pulled her to her feet.

"Unhand me," she hissed between her teeth, then tried to jerk her arm free. "Haven't you done enough to me today?"

"Not as much as I'd like. Now, you can either ride home with me, or cause a bigger scene," he whispered.

"If you ever humiliate me like that again, lord or not, I swear you'll live to regret it."

"Have no fear, I won't force my attentions on you again."

"Fine. See that you don't." She snatched her arm from his grasp, clasped her coat tighter around her neck, then marched over to the carriage.

A footman had jumped down and was letting down the stairs. John watched her flick her long hair over her back, then step up into the coach. He followed her, trying not to stare at her delicious little bottom as she gathered up her skirt and sat down.

"Here, Miss Campbell," Teddy said, shoving the packages near him into a corner, then patted the spot next to him.

"Thank you." Holly flopped down next to Teddy.

John was forced to sit on the opposite seat near Matilda. He crossed his arms over his chest and gazed ruefully at Teddy.

"Are you hurt?" Matilda asked, looking worried. "We came around the corner and saw Miss Campbell bending over your sprawled form."

"It was a comical sight," Teddy said, grinning. "Oranges all over the place. I wish I could have seen you go down."

"Lord Theodore, you are terrible," Matilda said, reaching to touch John's arm. "Are you sure you are all right?"

"Yes, yes. Nothing was hurt except my pride." John eyed Holly, who was staring out the window ignoring him.

"And Miss Campbell, it must have frightened you to see Lord Upton fall like that."

Holly turned her large brown eyes on Matilda, her lips in a tight, angry line. "Actually, I didn't notice until I saw the oranges rolling past me. But his lordship seems to be as sturdy as a gnarled oak." She added emphasis to the words "gnarled" as she eyed John. "I'm sure it would take much more than a fall to hurt him. Isn't that right, my lord?" She clenched her fists, clearly wanting to hurt him right now.

John didn't know why, but he grinned at her. "You are absolutely right, Miss Campbell."

Holly saw his grin, pursed her lips, then turned and stared out the window again. Some of the hair she'd thrown back over her shoulder fell forward. The thick, wavy mass hung down to her waist. John remembered the softness of it against his fingertips. His fingers curled into a fist as he curbed the overwhelming desire to run his fingers through it again.

"My lord, Miss Campbell told me you were taking her to the country. Forgive me, but that seems like an awful imposition, when I can take Miss Campbell. You'd have to rent a hack, and I have nothing on my calendar to keep me here in town." Matilda smiled at Holly, then glanced at him.

He remained silent and kept his gaze on Holly. She had glanced at Matilda and looked relieved by her suggestion. It gave him an inordinate amount of pleasure when he said, "I'll be escorting Miss Campbell. I had thought to do it this afternoon, but now that I have experienced firsthand how treacherous the streets can get in this sleet, I've decided to wait until morning." To get Holly's attention again, he said, "That is, if Miss Campbell is still working for me."

"Of course. She will be the children's nanny," Teddy said, answering for her, but then he observed Holly's mutinous expression and asked, "Won't you?"

Holly stared at Teddy, then at John for a long moment, her brows narrowed in serious contemplation. "Yes, I will take the position. And I don't really care how I get there." She turned and stared out the window again.

John glanced over at Matilda and saw the sullen look on her face. "What is the matter, Matilda?"

She sighed loudly. "I just wanted to see the children. It's been over three weeks since I've seen the little darlings. I had hoped to take Miss Campbell and see them tomorrow."

"If you'd care to go with us, you are welcome to do so." John tried to keep the annoyance from his voice, but a hint of it came through anyway. Politeness demanded he invite Matilda, but he wanted Holly all to himself.

"Everyone gets to go but me," Teddy said, his voice petulant. He saw John scowl at him and added, "I suppose someone needs to mind the shop."

"It won't hurt you," Matilda said. "Your brother needs to get away from the office for a few days. He works far too hard. And he hasn't seen the children in—how many weeks has it been, my lord?"

"Two," John said, hardly paying attention to Matilda while his gaze sought Holly's full red lips, remembering how hot and sweet her mouth had tasted when she'd given in to her passion. Perhaps it was a good thing Matilda was coming along. If he had Holly alone for hours in a carriage, he would definitely ravish the little termagant.

Sleet bounced off Holly's hand as she waved to Lady Matilda and watched the carriage pull away from the curb.

Lady Matilda waved back, all smiles.

Was Lady Matilda smiling because she would see the children, or because she had finagled a way to spend time with John? Either way, Holly was past caring. She was glad Lady Matilda was accompanying them on the journey. After tasting the passion in John's kiss, the idea of being alone with him terrified her. Lord, but the man could kiss. It had dissolved all her inhibitions. Like a lascivious little fool, she had kissed him back right there on the sidewalk in front of that crowd of people.

He did say he'd never kiss her again, but she didn't believe it, not with that smile he had bestowed on her. Oh, that smile. After the kiss, he had looked so satisfied with himself. It had angered her at first. Now that she'd thought it over, a wicked part of her wanted to taste his mouth again. But she couldn't. If she kissed him again, she'd begin to care about him. And she couldn't let that happen, wondering if she'd be transported and hanged for murder.

"Are you going to stand out here all day in the cold, Miss Campbell?" John's caustic voice bit into her thoughts.

She turned and saw him standing on the porch, scowling, his arms full of packages. Teddy was stepping through the threshold of the front door as Dunn held it open.

"I'm coming," she said, striding down the sidewalk and up the steps.

"What were you thinking about back there?" John whispered to her, his gold eyes glistening as though he had somehow read her mind.

"My thoughts are private."

"Not so private that I cannot tell what you're thinking." His lips stretched in a wicked grin.

"Perhaps then you should join the gypsies and make money with your mind-reading act."

"I'd like that if you held my crystal ball." His grin broadened, his handsome face a mask of sardonic amusement.

She had hoped to make him scowl. He wasn't likable when he scowled at her. Unnerved by his pointed gaze and this new affable mien of his, she didn't wait for his reply, but stepped around his broad shoulders and into the townhouse, feeling him watching her. "Hello, Dunn," she said, passing him.

"Hello, miss." He bowed, then spoke to John and Teddy. "My lord, my lord." Cold air whipped through the foyer as he closed the door. "Here, let me have those, my lord." He took the packages out of John's arms.

Holly shivered and began to take off Captain McLain's coat, but John stepped up behind her and touched her shoulders.

"Let me help you off with your wrap," he said, while his fingers caressed her shoulders.

Holly felt the pressure of his large hands. They covered almost all of her shoulders, and his fingertips were gently massaging her muscles. Each vertebra tightened as a shiver slid down her spine. She closed her eyes and felt her insides dissolving, just as they had when he had kissed her.

Finally, after what seemed like ages but had only been seconds, he moved his hands and slipped her coat off her shoulders. "There now." He eyed her with a self-satisfied grin, as if he knew what his touch had done to her, then whisked off his own cloak and hat and laid them on top of the boxes in Dunn's arms.

Dunn peeked over John's hat at Holly. "You have a visitor, miss."

"I do?" Holly's spine stiffened and her fingers inadvertently tightened around the sides of her dress. Had they found her already? Would they hang her now for murder?

"Yes, miss, a Mr. Kip."

Holly let out the breath she'd been holding. "Where is he?"

"In the drawing room, miss."

"Thank you, Dunn." Holly strode toward the drawing room.

"Well, well, young Kip was true to his word," John said, following on her heels.

"Yes, he was." Holly matched the derisiveness in his voice.

"Who is the fellow?" Teddy asked, annoyance coming through in his voice as he fell in step beside John.

"A young man who escorted Miss Campbell off the boat." John answered for Holly, sounding unusually pleased.

Why had John sounded so satisfied? She chanced a quick glance over her shoulder at him. He was still smiling and there was an odd look in his eyes she couldn't identify.

The doors to the drawing room were open. It wasn't one of the largest rooms Holly had cleaned yesterday, but in her opinion it was the prettiest. The walls were plain and painted royal blue. An Oriental carpet, worn from age, covered the floor. The rug might have added to the rooms run-down appearance, but the faded flower pattern offset the walls just enough to make it quaint. Two light-blue swags covered the windows. A bench-style sofa with a high wooden back, a table, and a small wooden chair that looked like it belonged in a schoolroom furnished the room with an uncluttered simplicity. The room reminded Holly of the parlor back at her grandmother's plantation.

Kip paced near the windows, the thud of his wooden leg dulled by the carpet. He noticed her right away. A blush tinted his cheeks as he walked across the room. "Miss Holly," he said, bowing.

"Kip, I'm so glad to see you." Holly smiled politely at him. "Won't you sit down?"

"Ah, nah, miss. I said I'd come and check on you." He eyed Teddy and John, then said in a low whisper, "I just wanted to see that you were all right." He stared at her hair hanging down her back, then at the wispy strands falling around her face in disarray. "You are all right, ain't you?"

"I'm fine, really." She tucked her hair behind her ears, aware she must look a fright. She hadn't noticed that her hair had come loose when John had kissed her on the sidewalk.

"Won't you have a glass of port? I'm sure we can find a bottle somewhere around here, since Miss Campbell has graciously paid the wine merchant." John cast Holly a sardonic look.

She rolled her eyes at him. "Please have a glass of port, Kip." She turned and sat on the sofa.

"No, no, I won't be no bother." Kip frowned, looking from Holly to John, then back to Holly, confusion on his face.

"No bother," John drawled, then eyed Holly with a cryptic expression as he strode over to the bellpull.

She didn't like the look on his face and fidgeted nervously with her dress, smoothing the faded satin over her knees, pulling it so taut, the worn material looked as if it would split at any moment. She realized what she was doing and was forced to turn it loose and sit back in her seat.

Before John pulled the cord, Dunn strode into the room, carrying a tray. "I took the liberty of bringing tea." He glanced at Holly, then his gaze swept the men in the room. "And port for the gentleman."

"Very good." Teddy's expression brightened.

"Tell me, Kip, how was your trip over?" John asked,

watching Dunn pour port from a decanter into three glasses.

"It weren't bad. Only ran into one storm. Ran off course a bit, lost a week or two, but we made it okay. Miss Holly 'eaved her guts out during the storm. Gave us all a fright."

"You don't say." John glanced over at Holly, his brows rising over his gleaming gold eyes.

"No need to bring all that up." She felt her cheeks redden at the memory of how she'd kept her face in a chamber pot. It was a nightmare she'd just as soon forget.

"Yes, we'd love to hear about it," Teddy said eagerly, as he accepted the glass of port Dunn offered him.

"I don't think so." She eyed Kip, but he was staring at John. What was John up to? Why was he asking questions about the voyage? "Let's talk about something much more pleasant," she said with a slight nervous tremor in her voice. "Where are you spending the holidays?" She rested her arms over her churning stomach.

"I'd really rather hear about the voyage over." John stared pointedly at her, watching her for a reaction. "How was your voyage out of Charleston?"

"Charleston?" Kip looked lost.

Holly cleared her throat, trying to get Kip's attention, but he wouldn't look at her. She would have thrown a pillow at his head if she had one handy. Kip opened his mouth to speak, and she knew she was knee-deep in trouble now.

"You must mean Richmond. We sailed outta there."

"Is that where Miss Campbell boarded your vessel?" John asked, glancing at her.

She shrank back against the sofa, feeling as if the floorboards were crumbling beneath her. Soon she'd be engulfed by lies.

"Aye, she boarded us right before we loaded."

"But I thought you said you were from Charleston?" Teddy looked at Holly for an explanation.

"W-well, I did live in Charleston." Holly prayed for a quick lie. "I was visiting . . . my aunt. Yes, my aunt." Dunn handed her a tea cup. Her hands trembled so badly the cup rattled on the saucer, and she had to grab it with her other hand.

"If you were visiting your aunt, why did you board a ship, madam?" John's scowl grew as he stared at the cup in her hands.

No doubt about it, she was going to hell. With a marked amount of calmness, under the circumstances, she said, "My aunt died, and after the funeral I felt I needed to get away. So I packed up my things and took the first ship out of port."

"Awfully sudden, wasn't it?" John cocked a suspicious brow at her.

"Yes, well, I was never a person to plan things."

Kip downed the glass of port in one gulp, then handed the glass back to Dunn. "I should be going. Got a few errands to run for the capt'n."

Holly saw the sphinxlike look in John's golden eyes, then jumped up from her seat. "I'll walk out with you." Relieved to be out of the room and away from John, she listened to the tap of Kip's wooden leg on the marble floor.

When they reached the door, Kip paused. "I just wanted to see how you was faring, Miss Holly. I'll tell the capt'n. He was worried about you, too. Maybe I'll stop by again."

"I won't be here. I took a position as a nanny to Lord Upton's children. I'll be in—"

"Near Brookthorpe, in Gloucestershire."

Holly jumped at the sound of John's voice at her back.

He was so close behind her, she could feel him breathing down her neck.

"Brookhollow Hall is the name of the estate," John added, his deep voice close to her ear, shooting tiny tingles down her spine.

"Do tell the captain I said hello and Merry Christmas." Her voice was strained, no merriment in it at all.

"Aye, I will. And if I don't see you again, have a Merry Christmas." Kip waved as he closed the door behind him.

She felt John's eyes on her back. "I probably should go and help Dunn in the kitchen," Holly said, and started toward the kitchen.

John grabbed her elbow. "A word first, madam." He guided her along the hallway.

"Can't this wait?" She tried to jerk her arm free. "I really should help Dunn."

"Dunn can wait." He tightened his grip on her and continued to lead her down the hall.

"Where are you taking me?"

"A place where I can get the truth out of you."

"Are you calling me a liar?" Holly attempted an indignant tone, but her voice wavered and only sounded frightened.

"If the kettle is black . . ." He stared at her, daring her to deny it, then pulled her into a small gallery that was bare of pictures. His gaze didn't stray from her as he locked the door. A maniacal grin twitched near the corner of his mouth.

"There's no need to lock the door." Holly nervously backed away from him.

"We're not leaving this room until you tell me what you are hiding. Why did you lie to me and tell me you sailed from Charleston? What are you hiding?"

Chapter 6

"I—I don't know what you're talking about. I told you the truth."

"You are not much of a liar."

"I'm not lying."

"If you're not lying, then why are your hands trembling?"

"It's a nervous condition."

He smiled at her, but it didn't touch his eyes. "I don't think you have a nervous condition at all. I think you're afraid to be alone with me and you might have to tell me the truth." He stared at her lips, then his gaze slowly combed her body.

"I—I'm not afraid of you."

"Of course you are. You're afraid I'll kiss you."

"You said you wouldn't ever do that again."

"I find I cannot stay away from you." He stepped close to her and gazed down at her, his eyes hungry, devouring.

Holly knew that look. She'd seen it on his face when he'd kissed her before. Her pulse throbbed in her temples, and her heart hammered in her chest. The anticipation frightened and thrilled her at the same time.

"You are so very beautiful." He smoothed back the hair along her face.

"I'm not." His rough fingertips brushed against her soft skin. She trembled as a quickening shot down her throat, her chest, and pooled in her stomach. The masculine scent of him, mixed with the spicy scent of his cologne, invaded all her senses. Every clear thought left her.

"But you are. And you taste divine." He ran a thumb along her bottom lip, while his free hand moved down her back and pulled her close. "Now that I've had a taste of you, I'm afraid I want another . . ."

He buried his fingers in the back of her thick hair and tipped her face up to his, but he didn't kiss her. Instead, he stared down at her. The self-control it cost him not to kiss her was evident in the rigid line of his mouth and the flexed tautness of his square jaw. His breathing grew heavy and rapid. She became aware of his hard thighs against her, and his powerful chest crushing her breasts. The movement of his muscles tantalized her nipples through her dress and petticoat and twisted waves of hot pleasure deep inside her. She was lost in his nearness and the feel of his strong arms around her.

"I won't force you to kiss me like I did before," he said, his hot breath searing her lips. "I want you to kiss me this time. I know you want to, I can feel you trembling." His voice grew husky and deep. "Kiss me, Holly . . ."

The softly spoken plea melted over her. She didn't hesitate. She couldn't. She wrapped her arms around his neck, stood on her tiptoes, and kissed him with all the ardor he'd aroused in her. His mouth covered hers, not hard like the last kiss, but meltingly soft, savoring the taste of her mouth. He nipped her bottom lip with his teeth, then traced her lips with his tongue.

He buried his hands in her hair, then pulled her head closer to his and deepened the kiss. Instinctively, Holly opened, and his tongue made a foray into her mouth. A deep, agonized groan escaped him, then his hands moved over her collarbone, down to her breasts, cupping, squeezing, rubbing her nipples with his thumbs. Any minute she was sure she'd die from the feel of him touching her breasts. His hips began to move against her. She could feel his male hardness, swollen, straining against the softness between her thighs. She was trembling and burning with a need that made her cry out his name. Her hips moved against his of their own accord.

"Oh, God," he said against her mouth. His breathing grew rapid and heavy. He pressed her back against the wall, while his hands moved down along her ribs, to her belly.

Holly felt each muscle flex and tighten beneath her petticoat and dress. She wanted to feel his hands on her bare skin. Trembling all over now, she clutched wildly to him, urging him to touch her. He moved his hands lower, along her abdomen, down her thighs. She felt his hand close over the soft flesh between her legs. Her head rolled back and she closed her eyes, arching against his hand, digging her fingers into the back of his coat. She would burn up inside any moment. He stroked her with one hand, while his thigh moved between her legs. Then he was yanking up the hem of her dress . . .

They didn't hear the knock at first, but the door rattled, then . . .

Bang. Bang. Bang.

"Open up, John, or I'll break the bloody door down. Holly, are you in there?"

John paused, his hand still between her thighs. He gazed down at her, desire raging in his eyes. "You'd better answer him." His voice was a rough whisper in her ear.

"I'm fine," she called to Teddy, trying to keep the tremor out of her voice.

"You don't sound fine." Teddy's voice was muffled behind the door.

When the pounding started again, John frowned. "I'd better go let him in." He kissed her hard, making her knees weak and sending a shiver through her. Finally, his fingers loosened from that throbbing, fleshy spot between her legs and he let the hem of her dress fall down her legs. He pulled back from her, then smiled, his eyes glowing with a fierce possessive light. "I promise we'll continue this later."

When his arms dropped from her waist and he stepped back, Holly's knees buckled. She leaned against the wall to keep from falling. Her body still throbbed all over from desire, and she sucked in air, trying to make the feeling go away. Had that been a threat? Would he continue to ravish her later? Clay couldn't be more pliant in his arms than she was. He could mold her any way he liked. From now on, she would stay well away from him.

As if he could read her thoughts, the corners of his lips turned up in a sardonic grin. It was obvious he knew exactly what he had done to her. She recalled her wanton exhibit of passion. A blush burned her cheeks as she watched John open the door, that grin still on his face.

Teddy tumbled through the threshold, his fists raised to pound on the door again. He took three stumbling steps into the room, caught himself before he fell, then stood. His gaze landed on Holly. Looking like the put-upon cavalier, he tried to assume an air of dignity as he adjusted his cravat, then he turned on John. "Damn you, what were you doing in here with Miss Campbell?"

"I was speaking privately to her." John cocked a brow at her. "I believe we understand each other."

"Perfectly." With a trembling hand, she pushed back a lock of hair that had fallen in her face. John watched her hands, and that maddening grin of his grew wider. Like a little girl who had been caught stealing, she shoved her hands behind her back and looked at Teddy.

"I don't think you should keep dragging Miss Campbell behind locked doors."

"How and when I speak to Miss Campbell is none of your concern."

"Please, I was perfectly all right." Holly stepped in between them, aware if she didn't, there might be another fight.

Dunn cleared his throat from the doorway.

"Yes?" John turned and shot him an impatient look.

"My lord, you have a visitor."

"Who is it?"

"A Mr. Jarvis." Dunn drawled the name as if he disapproved of the person.

"Where did you put him?"

"In the study." John turned to look at Holly. "Remember, we'll speak later." He turned and followed Dunn out of the room with stiff strides.

Holly could actually breathe fully again, now that he had left the room.

"I don't know why John is behaving like a grouser. He usually isn't this bad. He shouldn't have dragged you in here to berate you. I'm sorry. Did he upset you?" Teddy asked, his voice softening. He strode over to her and touched her arm.

"No, no, I think he was just venting his anger. And don't feel you have to apologize for him." Holly patted his hand and tried to sound nonchalant about the whole business. "I know he has a lot of pressures on him at the moment."

So did she. She would have to leave now that John was prying into her background. Why did he have to do that? If not for him, she could stay, but he would keep prying until he found out she was a murderess. Tonight she would have to sneak away and never see him again. Tears gathered in her eyes and she blinked them back, a hollow feeling growing in her chest.

John entered the study and eyed Mr. Jarvis, pacing in front of the desk clutching a black cap. His stocky build was hidden behind an old brown coat that was frayed from wear and dotted with stains. His thick red hair was stark against his white, freckled face. Long sideburns almost touched his mouth. The stale odor of ale hung about his person and permeated the room.

Jarvis saw him and paused. He bowed, a nervous tic twitching the left side of his mouth. "Sorry to bother you, me lord, but I had to see you."

"Sit, Mr. Jarvis."

"Thank you." Jarvis sat in the chair in front of the desk.

"Don't I know you?" John strode behind his desk and scrutinized the man.

"Aye, you might recognize me at that. I was one of the crew on the *Sea Challenger*. I met you when we came into port a few months back."

John raised his brows in surprise, then narrowed them at the man. "I thought all the crew members were lost at sea."

"By the grace of God, I made it to shore."

"How is that you escaped?"

"I'll tell you how it were." Jarvis shifted in his seat, rested his leg over his knee, then grasped his shin. "I was at the helm. The ship, she was arockin' in the storm, and I was havin' a devil of a time keepin' her on course. I didn't think nothin' of the storm, the *Sea Challenger* had brung us through worse squalls than the one we was in. Anyways, as I was saying, I was at the helm." He paused and made a face. The painful memory registered in his expression.

"What happened?" John leaned toward him and strangled the sides of his chair until his knuckles whitened.

"Someone hit me from behind. I went down like an anchor. Didn't know a thing until we crashed into the side of *Sin's Revenge* and both ships were pounding against the reef. They was all tore up . . ." Jarvis's voice drifted off. He stared down at his knee, his face growing solemn. He shook his head, then said, "I grabbed hold to a piece of her hull. It kept me from drowning with the rest of the crew. A few hours later, I made it to shore."

"Are you saying someone deliberately tried to destroy my ships?"

"That's what I'm saying."

"You're sure about this?" John leaned back in his chair and leveled his most intimidating gaze at Jarvis.

"Yes, me lord, it happen'd the way I said it."

"Did you see anyone who didn't belong on board?"

"There was only fifteen of us, me lord. The capt'n took on two new hands, but they were good sorts. No, I didn't see anyone."

"How did the saboteur get away then?" John drummed his fingers on top of his desk and noticed that the sound made Jarvis jam his hands in his coat pocket.

"I ain't rightly sure. Maybe he swam to shore. We weren't but a couple of miles out. Or a ship could have picked him up. I just don't know. All I know, it was a clever plan to wait until a squall blew up, then wreck both ships. I just want to see the bastard who did it put behind bars."

"So do I. Of course, you must realize how damning this looks for you, you being the only one to survive."

Jarvis bristled, the left side of his mouth twitching wildly now. "Do you think I'd be here if I was guilty? I came here thinkin' to do you a favor and tell you, but I see I've wasted me time. You're tryin' to pin this on me, but I won't stand for it." Jarvis jumped up from his seat and looked at the door as if he wanted to leave.

"We're not done yet." John leaped to his feet, ready to tackle the man should he make for the door.

"I realize it, but, by God, I ain't the one that took her down. And I won't have you accusing me—"

"I'm trying to get the truth here, Jarvis. So sit." John pointed to the chair.

Jarvis stared at it a moment, his expression unsure about being detained, then he slowly sat back down.

"I'm going to have to investigate this further. Where do you live?"

"East End, me lord. Barten's Boardinghouse. You can't miss it."

"I may need to speak to you again."

"Sure, I ain't signed on with another ship yet. I'll be in port until after the holidays."

"Very well then. Thank you for telling me about this. Good day."

Jarvis bowed, then slapped his cap on his head.

John leaned back in his chair, glancing at a large black stain on the back of Jarvis's old woolen coat as he strode out into the hall. He didn't trust Jarvis, nor did he believe he came to tell John the news out of the goodness of his heart. Jarvis could be the one who destroyed the ships, and John's only link to the person who paid him to do it.

Who was trying to destroy him? Who would profit from his loss? Not one single name came to mind. Waterton hated him, but if he had wanted to destroy John, he would have done it long ago. One thing of which he was certain: if he found the person responsible, he would enjoy the revenge he meant to reap on them.

Holly made her way toward John's room, her brows furrowed with worry. He had gone up to his room and refused to come to dinner. Teddy had tried to coax him down to the table, but John had growled at him to go away. Unsure of what to do now, she frowned down at the tray in her hands. Somehow she had to get him to eat something. She also wanted to see him one last time before she left. With her resolve firmly in place, she continued down the hall.

It was dark in the hallway, save for the dim light cast by a lone tallow candle that burned in a wall sconce. The pungent odor of the tallow lingered in the air. She wrinkled her nose as she reached his door, then balanced the tray on her hip and knocked.

"Go away, Teddy. I told you I need to be alone."

"It's not Teddy." Holly bit her lip and hoped she was doing the right thing. When he didn't answer her, she used a wheedling tone she had often used on her grandmother when she wanted to prevail upon her. "I brought you a tray. Please let me in."

When he didn't answer her, she took a step to leave, then heard the door open behind her. She glanced back and saw the door was ajar.

Not knowing what to expect, she eased the door open

with caution. It creaked on its hinges. She gingerly peeked around the edge.

A fire hissed in the grate. Dim, flickering shadows danced around the room. It was a large chamber, done in blue hues. Unlike the rest of the rooms, it had most of the furniture left in it. A large mahogany bed sat in the middle, with a French domed tester above it. A *secretaire* made of satinwood decorated with inlaid woods sat on the opposite wall.

He sat on a settee near the fireplace, a case opened before him. The silver handle of a dueling pistol gleamed from the box. He held the other pistol in his hand, while he ran an oiled cloth along the barrel. On a table near him, a lone candle burned. It threw shadows on the sharp angles of his cheekbones, outlining the deep frown lines around his eyes and between his brows. The stubble on his chin added to the unapproachable, menacing expression on his face. She had seen that fierce look on him once before, when he fought those men who had attacked her and Kip. She remembered his earlier promise to get the truth out of her. Perhaps it was a bad idea to try and get him to eat.

Her fingers tightened on the tray as she backed out of the room. She glanced furtively around her for a place to set it. Her gaze landed on a small mahogany table to her right. She set the tray down there, then turned to leave.

"Where are you going?"

The deep, barked words made her hand freeze on the doorknob. She sucked in her breath, the pressure in her chest growing. The room grew abruptly hot, even though the fire in the grate was low, the heat tenuous. "I thought I was disturbing you," she said, glancing at him.

"Stay. I need to speak to you." He raised the pistol in his hand and looked through the clean barrel at her.

"About what?" Even though she tried, she was unable to keep her voice steady while he stared at her through the barrel of the gun. What if he asked her about her past?

"I won't be able to escort you to my home in the country tomorrow." He lowered the pistol and rubbed his fingers over the hilt, his expression pensive.

"Oh." She let out the breath she'd been holding.

"No, I have something to do here that will require my utmost attention." He set down the dueling pistol and picked up the other one. His fingers caressed the barrel as he ran the cloth down the shiny, dark-gray metal, then he paused a moment. His expression softened, and he asked, "Will you do something for me?"

Holly nodded, unable to draw her gaze from his long, slender fingers, the memory of them on her breasts still vivid in her mind.

"Tell the children I'll see them when I can."

There was such tender entreaty in his voice, Holly found herself walking toward him. Her resolve to leave melted with each step she took. She couldn't leave him now, not when he needed her. She'd probably regret her next words, for they would somehow bond her to him and only cause her heartache when she had to go. But she couldn't help saying, "I will tell them, but won't you be able to see them soon, if not tomorrow?"

"I don't know when I'll be able to leave London."

"What is the matter?"

"You need not concern yourself with my troubles. You won't forget to give my message to the children as soon as you see them?" He stared at her as though he needed to hear her answer for peace of mind.

Holly hesitated, then said, "Yes, I'll tell them."

The tenseness left his shoulders. He nodded and continued cleaning the pistol. "I'll get word to Lady Matilda that I won't be able to go tomorrow."

"She will be disappointed."

"Lady Matilda is a very agreeable individual, I'm sure she will not be too disappointed."

"I hope not." She bit her lip, about to tell him he was blind when it came to Lady Matilda. The lady was anything but agreeable. *Calculating* more aptly described her.

"I hope the children will not be too much of a burden for you."

"I haven't met a child yet that was a burden."

"Have you had a great deal of experience with children?"

"You could say that. My grandmother and I used to visit the local orphanage. We even had the more troublesome children come and stay with us on holidays and weekends."

"It seems like you miss your home."

"I miss some things very much. I miss my grandmother most of all."

"And what about your deceased aunt in Richmond?" He raised a mocking brow at her.

"Yes, her, too." Holly frowned and hoped he wouldn't pry any further.

He stared at her from behind lowered brows for a long moment, but he didn't speak, then continued to clean the pistol.

The tension left her, and silence settled between them.

She watched the care with which he cleaned the pistol, then at the hard determined set of his lips. Inadvertently, her fingers tightened around the sides of her dress, and she crushed the material. "Are you going to use those?"

"Perhaps."

"Please tell me what is wrong."

"I don't need to burden you with my troubles."

"But I want to be burdened."

He studied her, weighing whether he could trust her or not. Finally, he set the pistol down in the case with the other one, then glanced up at her. "Someone destroyed two of my ships on purpose."

"But why would anyone do such a thing?"

"That is what I need to find out and why I can't leave London at the moment."

"How will you find this person?" Holly realized her dress was all the way up to her ankles from where she'd twisted the material. She opened her hands, then smoothed down the sides of her dress.

"I don't know. I have a feeling the person will be reveling in his success and he'll make a mistake."

"You should go to the authorities and let them handle the matter."

"No." He stared down at the pistols. "I'll see justice done."

By the firm tone in his voice, she knew arguing with him would be useless. She strode over to the tray and picked it up. "Please try to eat something now."

She crossed the room, then set the tray on the table near the pistols. "I'll be back in a little while to get the tray."

When she started to pull away, he grabbed her hand. "You won't repeat what I just told you. I need it to be kept confidential. I don't want my nemesis, whomever he might be, to know that I am aware of him."

"No, no, I won't," she said, relishing the feel of his large, powerful hand on top of hers, the heat of his palm seeping through her skin.

"Very well, then." He stared at her a moment, his gaze turning sultry. He eyed her lips. "You shouldn't be in my chamber."

Even as the words left his mouth, he pulled her down into his lap. Holly landed with her head pressed against his chest. She could hear the hammering of his heart next to her ear. It matched the rhythm of her own heart. He gazed down at her with those golden devouring eyes, then his mouth came down on hers. His lips slanted over hers in a desperate, blinding hunger, begging for a response from her. Unable to resist him, she answered his hunger with more of her own. She wrapped her arms around his neck and crushed him to her.

He slid his hand down the sensitive skin at her nape, then down her back, sending tingles down her spine. He moved around her waist, along her rib cage, molding his fingers to each rib, learning her body, then up . . . up to cup her breast.

Holly moaned, pleasure coursing through her, her senses filled with him. He teased her nipple with his fingers and ran his tongue along her lips, begging entrance. Holly opened for him, feeling his tongue slip into her mouth. She shouldn't be kissing him, letting him touch her, but she wouldn't—no, couldn't pull away. She sensed the urgent yearning in him. He needed to touch her, to lose his troubles in the momentary comfort she offered.

"You taste luscious . . ." he murmured, his voice thick with passion. He placed tiny kisses over her face, then down her white, slender neck, while his hand eased beneath the hem of her dress and petticoat. He caressed her ankle, calf, then her thigh, while he splayed his fingers and slid his hand slowly upward, wrinkling the material of her pantalettes against her skin, raising goose bumps along her flesh.

Lost in the onslaught of his hands and lips, Holly shivered and felt a slight tremor in him, too. When his hand touched the sensitive spot between her thighs, Holly's wits returned from the deep pleasure-induced languor he had created in her. She broke the kiss, then grabbed his hand and shoved it away.

A frustrated growl sounded deep in his throat, then he looked at her as if she'd slapped him.

"I can't do this." She jerked down the hem of her dress.

The passion in his eyes turned aloof and frighteningly icy. "You should never have come in here. I'm afraid I can't keep my hands off you. It's a good thing you are leaving on the morrow. Leave me now." He grabbed her waist and set her on the floor.

Holly's knees felt weak. She stumbled and clutched the arm of the settee. "I'm sorry," she said in a choked whisper, then ran from the room, slamming the door closed behind her.

She ran down the hallway. When she was safely away from his chamber, she fell back against the wall, chest heaving, her body still throbbing from the passion he'd awakened in her. How could he be so intensely passionate one moment, then so cold to her the next? Tears blurred her vision.

He had every right to be angry. She had kissed him back and practically begged him to touch her. It was a good thing she was leaving for his estate. A few more days with him and she'd be in his bed. The thought sent a shiver through her. She cared too much about him. There was no room in her life for a man. She was a murderess on the run.

She heard footsteps plodding down the hallway and saw Teddy striding toward her, his bright yellow britches blurring against the dark wainscoting.

She drew herself up, blinked back the tears in her eyes, and gained back some of her composure. She walked toward him and met him halfway in the hall.

He paused. "Are you all right? You look a little shaken."

"I'm fine, really." Holly feigned a smile.

"I say, did he upset you?"

"No, no, I was thinking about tomorrow. I guess I'm a little apprehensive about meeting the children."

"Remember to be firm and you can manage them. Carry a large switch with you." Teddy winked at her, then his expression sobered. He jerked his head toward John's chamber. "Did you get him to eat something?"

"Yes, I think he's eating now."

"I knew if anyone could get him out of his doldrums, you could. You're a marvel," he said, his gaze worshipful.

"It was nothing."

"I'll go and keep him company. See if I can cheer him up a bit."

"That would be nice of you." Holly touched his arm before he stepped away. "I have to ask you something."

"Ask me." He grinned at her, pleased he could be of service to her.

"This is purely hypothetical of course, but if one needed to locate a person, or . . . let's say, find someone who didn't want to be found, how would one go about it here?"

"Why?"

"No reason, I was just wondering," Holly said, sounding mildly interested.

"Well, a person could hire a Bow Street Runner."

"Can one trust these Bow Street Runners to keep the matter quiet?"

"Yes, that is why most people hire them for delicate matters. One of my mates at school has a father who's in the business."

"Really?"

"Scibner's the name. Julius, I believe—yes, that's his father's name. Julius Scibner. James—that's his son—said his father has done work for the Crown. I believe he's very trustworthy, if a person were looking to hire a runner." Teddy shot her a curious look. "You're not thinking of hiring one yourself? If you are in some sort of trouble—"

"Oh, no, I'm not in any trouble, but it's always good to know these things in case I might have need of a runner one day. One never knows what tomorrow will bring." Holly kept her voice breezy with indifference. He opened his mouth to question her further, but she said, "If you'll excuse me, I really should get downstairs and help Dunn with the dishes. He doesn't get them very clean." She hurried past him and left Teddy staring after her, a puzzled expression on his face.

Chapter 7

The next morning, Holly paused in the hallway of number 17 Bond Street and stared at the name, *Mr. Julius Scibner, Confidentiality at Its Best,* written in bold letters on the office door. She stuffed strands of her unruly hair beneath the forest-green Milan bonnet she had bought yesterday, then took off a pair of new gloves and a cape that matched her bonnet. They were made of heavy serviceable wool.

She folded the cape over her arm, then patted out the wrinkles in the new black, ready-made servant dress Lady Matilda had bought for her. It did nothing to enhance Holly's coloring and made her look sallow as old mustard, but she couldn't very well hire a runner in her old faded blue dress. Squaring her shoulders, she knocked on the door.

"Enter," a man barked.

Holly opened the door and stepped into the office. The

smell of cigar smoke met her at the door. She wrinkled her nose and glanced around the small office. A large mahogany desk filled one end of the room. Two wooden chairs sat opposite it.

A distinguished-looking gentleman with keen gray eyes peered at her from behind one of the desks. A pair of square wire-rimmed glasses were perched on top of his balding head. He lowered them and looked her over. He stared at her for a moment, then in an annoyed tone asked, "Are you lost, madam?"

"No, I believe I'm in the proper place. I need to hire a runner."

"You, madam?" He peered at her over the rim of his spectacles.

"You are a runner, aren't you?"

"Yes."

"Then I suppose you are for hire?"

He appeared amused by her irritation. "Please sit." He motioned toward a chair.

Holly strode over and sat in a chair opposite his desk. She straightened her skirt and set her reticule down in her lap, then looked expectantly at him.

He clasped his hands on the edge of his desk. "What can I do for you, Miss . . ."

"Campbell," Holly finished for him.

"I'm Mr. Julius Scibner." He bowed his head slightly.

"Pleased to meet you, sir. You came highly recommended."

"Really. By whom?"

"That's really not important. What is important is why I need to engage you."

Mr. Scibner grimaced, moving his glasses on the bridge of his nose. "What may I do for you?"

Holly glanced around the room, then lowered her voice.

"Everything I'm about to say must be kept in the strictest confidence."

Mr. Scibner drew himself up and looked offended. "That goes without saying, madam."

"Yes, well, I had to make sure. You understand."

"Completely."

"Good." Her fingers tightened around her reticule as she continued. "Anyway, Lord Upton—he owns St. John Shipping—recently found out someone sabotaged two of his ships. Now he has taken it upon himself to go and find that person and confront them. I'm worried something will happen to him."

"Are you related to this Lord Upton?"

"No. He hired me to be a nanny to his children."

Mr. Scibner cleared his throat, then his keen eyes narrowed at her over the rim of his glasses. "Forgive me, Miss Campbell, but most nannies could care less about their employer's welfare. I feel you might be more involved with Lord Upton than you are saying. You must be completely honest with me—"

"All right." Holly waved her hands through the air. "I do care about him."

"Are you his mistress?"

"I don't think that is any of your business."

"Just getting the facts straight, madam."

"The fact is, I'm not his mistress. There. Now, will you take this case or not?"

He stared at her simple dress. "My fees are very expensive, Miss Campbell."

"Yes, well, I thought you'd say that." She opened up her reticule and pulled out a handkerchief.

She opened the white linen and set it down on his desk. Diamonds and sapphires lit up the room. Mr. Scibner's

eyes popped open as he stared down at the pendant, bracelet, and matching necklace.

"You can close your jaw, Mr. Scibner." She grinned at
his reaction.

"These belong to you?" he asked incredulously, then
picked up the diamond pendant and gazed at it.

"Yes, they are mine, sir. And I know their value." Holly
remembered how shrewd her grandmother had been
when it came to trusting people with valuables and she
added, "Now, I'll require a receipt, and then I'd like for
you to sell them to a jewelry dealer who will give me what
they are worth. And if you will, open an account at a bank
in my name."

He glanced at her. "Of course, Miss Campbell," he said,
with a deference in his voice that had not been there thus
far. He pulled out a piece of paper, described the jewels
and that he had received them, dated it, then signed it
and handed it back to her.

"And Mr. Scibner, I don't want anything to happen to
Lord Upton. You will have someone watch him and keep
him from harm."

"Yes, madam. I have several men I can rely upon."

"Good." She remembered Lady Matilda was supposed
to pick her up at the townhouse and asked, "Do you have
the time?"

Mr. Scibner pulled out his pocket watch and looked at
it. "It's early, yet, madam. It's only nine o'clock."

"I should be going. You can reach me at this address."
She stood, extracted a piece of paper from her reticule,
then placed it in his hand. "Please be discreet when you
contact me there."

"But, madam, you will be a rich woman when I transact
this business for you. Won't you be staying in town?"

She pulled on her heavy wool gloves. "No, I intend to

use most of that money to make an investment in St. John Shipping."

Mr. Scibner shot her a knowing look. "So that is how it is."

"Yes," she said, then pulled her cape over her shoulders and fastened the black frog on the front. "Could you do that bit of business for me also? I trust you can handle it."

"Your servant, madam." Mr. Scibner stood, bowed, then clicked his heels together.

"Good day." Holly smiled at him, then hurried out the office, the distress that had bothered her all night finally gone.

John paced down the length of the parlor, turned, then snapped a glance out the window. Soft morning light streamed down on the street's cobblestones. The frost had not yet melted and glistened on the irregular stones like thousands of pieces of cut glass. His gaze strayed to the sidewalk, where a lady herded three small children down the sidewalk. A black lacquered cab crept past the sidewalk but didn't stop. Where was the little minx? She'd left the house without a word to anyone this morning.

He recalled how nervous she'd been when he questioned her yesterday about her past. What if she'd run away? And last night, she hadn't come to get the tray in his room but sent Dunn to do it. That had irritated him, too. He supposed she stayed away because he'd shocked her last night by touching that sweet place between her legs, but still, it grated against him that she could be so hot in his arms one minute and so cold and aloof the next. Then he couldn't sleep all night, for lurid recollections of how she had wrapped her arms around him and kissed him, the feel of her breasts in his palms, the supple warmth of her thigh, the taste of her mouth, and the softness of her lips. Lurid dreams of making love to her kept him up most of the night. What was she doing to him?

"All this vexation really isn't necessary, my lord." At the sound of Matilda's voice, John turned from the window and glanced at her sitting next to Teddy on the couch.

She folded her hands in her lap and shot him a severe look. "I'm sure there is an explanation for her absence. And really, she seems capricious, and, I might add, a little scatterbrained. It probably slipped her mind that we were going this morning."

"I don't find Miss Campbell scatterbrained at all," Teddy said, growing defensive.

"Forgive me. I was just pointing out some things I've observed in her character. I didn't mean to disparage her behind her back."

Teddy was sitting on the sofa next to her. He leaned over and touched her arm. "I'm sure you didn't."

John saw something move out of the corner of his eye. He turned toward the window and saw Holly step out of a cab. He didn't recognize her at first. She had on a new black dress and a green cape with a hat and gloves to match. The new clothes were in no way fashionable. On any other person they would have looked dowdy, but on Holly they added to her artless charm. Her cheeks glowed with a rosy tint from the cold, her large brown eyes sparkled. She was grinning, too, her dimples beaming.

"Is she finally here?" Matilda asked.

Before John could answer her, Teddy jumped up and stood beside him at the window. "By Jove, it is Miss Campbell." A wide grin split his lips and his white teeth gleamed.

In four long strides John stood at the parlor door, arms crossed, waiting for her. He wasn't sure if he should rant at her or kiss her.

Dunn opened the door. She graced him with a smile. "Hello, Dunn. What a wonderful morning."

"I don't know, miss."

She looked at John and the smile left her face. "I see what you mean," she whispered, then stepped past Dunn and paused before John. "I can tell by the look on your face that you are angry, so let me apologize right off. I needed something that I forgot to purchase yesterday, so I went shopping early this morning."

"Where are your packages?"

"Here . . ." She patted her reticule. "And I hope you don't ask me what it is, for it would embarrass us both." She lowered her voice. "It's something for a woman's toilet."

"Are you ready to leave, Miss Campbell?" Matilda appeared from behind John's wide shoulder, pulling on her gloves.

"I'm so sorry for keeping you waiting. My packages . . ." Holly glanced in the hall, looking for them.

"Dunn already put them on Lady Matilda's carriage," John said with asperity.

"Then I guess this is good-bye for a while." Holly's animated brown eyes gleamed at him.

John fought an overpowering urge to grab her and kiss her, though he would much rather take her to his chamber and thoroughly ravish her.

Teddy strode into the hallway. He bent over Holly's gloved hand, then kissed it. "I hope to be seeing you in a few days."

Holly graced him with a wide, dimpled smile. "That is a pleasure I look forward to."

"All right, then, let us take our leave." Matilda smiled and looked up at John with her long-lashed blue eyes. "Good-bye, my lord. And I'll tell the children how disap-

pointed you were at not being able to accompany us. I'm
sure they'll understand you have to work."

"Yes, good-bye." John waved to her, but then his gaze
sought Holly. He watched her stroll down the steps.

"Well, there is one consolation at Miss Campbell leaving
us." Teddy stepped near John's side and waved.

"What's that?"

"We won't have to eat any more of her cooking."

"You have a point there," John said, grinning, as he
thought of the burned chicken he'd been forced to choke
down. He'd make sure she never entered the kitchen
again—unless, of course, Waterton came to dinner.

Before Holly climbed inside the carriage, she turned
and glanced at John. She smiled at him, her large eyes
softening and gleaming like two pieces of polished silken
rosewood. He found himself smiling back at her, aching
for the feel of her next to him.

He noticed Matilda had turned around and was staring
at him, too. For a moment, her eyes turned icy blue, then
the emotion melted behind a tight-lipped smile. He had
never seen Matilda miffed over anything. What had he
done to anger her? Right now, he had other more pressing
things to worry about, like who wanted to ruin him.

Holly sat next to Lady Matilda. The steady sway of the
carriage rocked her back and forth. Outside, carriage after
carriage passed them, some already decked out for Christmas, with red rosettes and holly on the horses' collars.
One gig had mistletoe all along the edge of it, with wide
bows on the front. People scurried down the sidewalks,
packages filling their arms, the anticipation of Christmas
bright on their faces.

"It is a shame John could not come with us, but he says

he's too busy to leave London." Lady Matilda spoke for the first time since leaving the townhouse.

"Yes." Holly turned to look at her and noticed the brooding pout still on her pretty face. She supposed Lady Matilda was still angry that she had been kept waiting this morning, so Holly added, "I'm sorry for the inconvenience I caused you this morning."

"Think nothing of it. I'm just glad we are on our way. I asked James to drive us through Hyde Park on the way out of town. Have you seen it yet?"

"No, but Lord Theodore told me about Rotten Row and how every sort of young lady could be seen in the morning riding there. He told me he goes there when he's in town to ogle the cattle, but I suspect he's ogling the ladies."

A pasty smile stretched across Lady Matilda's face. "Yes, well, he's no different from the young bucks who go there to eye the debutantes who will be out this season."

"When does the season start?"

"The height of the season starts in spring and lasts through the summer. Parliament will convene in January, and people are trickling back to town now. I'm sure there are plenty of sights to be seen today. You'd be surprised the number of ladies one can spy on a sunny morning like this—especially after that horrid weather we had yesterday."

The carriage swung left and they entered Hyde Park. Holly craned her neck out the window as far as she dared. She saw several young ladies riding together with their grooms following behind. Their beautiful sea-green riding habits and spencers matched, stark against their black mares. They made a striking pair. She guessed it was a tactic to attract all the eligible young lords in the park. It seemed to be working. Three young men rode some distance across from them, watching every toss of the young ladies' heads, and every attempt to hide their coquettish smiles. Another young lady walked a terrier, accompanied by a large woman who was twice her companion's size.

Holly's gaze moved past a stand of oak trees, and a tall gentleman galloping across the park caught her eye. He rode a huge gray stallion, hardly moving in the saddle, his posture as stiff as a stone statue. He reined in near a gravel path, then glanced around him, looking for someone. His gaze locked with Holly's, then he turned his horse toward Lady Matilda's carriage.

Holly fell back in her seat. Her fingers twisted nervously in the sides of her dress. Did the gentleman think she was flirting with him? To her mortification, she heard thundering hooves slowing, then he appeared beside the carriage window and tipped his hat.

"Why, good morning, Lady Matilda." His lips parted in a white-toothed grin.

Lady Matilda leaned past Holly. "Lord Waterton. I had not expected to see you so early." She didn't sound the least surprised to see him.

Holly had a feeling the gentleman didn't come to flirt with her. It seemed more like a clandestine tête-à-tête with Lady Matilda. She summoned enough nerve to lean near the window and look at Lord Waterton. His nose looked swollen and slightly bent, but other than that he was a handsome man, with embracing blue eyes and blond hair that was unusually long, curling past his beaver hat to his collar. His broad shoulders were covered by a dark greatcoat with eight capes. She could see why Lady Matilda wanted to meet him in the park.

Lord Waterton must have felt Holly's gaze on him, for he turned and gazed at her, the blue in his eyes brightening several shades lighter. "Ah! I see you are not alone. So this is the illustrious Miss Campbell?"

"Have we met, my lord?" Holly asked, surprised he knew her name.

"Well, in a way." His eyes glazed over and she saw a hint of cruelty behind them that had not been there before. "You could say I know you from reputation."

"I don't know what you could mean?" Holly eyed him suspiciously.

He tapped his riding crop across his thigh. "Word has it that you were seen kissing St. John near Bond Street. He was flat on his back and you were on top of him. It has caused quite a stir." He raised his brows at Holly, then a cruel, triumphant grin turned up the corners of his lips. He glanced over at Lady Matilda to see her reaction.

Blood rushed into Lady Matilda's cheeks, and her jaw clenched. In a voice that could melt ice, she said, "I would thank you not to offend my friend with unsubstantiated rumors."

"If it is rumor, then it was in the society page of the paper. Obviously you have not read your *Post* this morning."

"No, and if you know what is good for you, you won't read gossip columns, either. Good day, Lord Waterton." Lady Matilda leaned past Holly and snapped the leather curtain over the window.

Lord Waterton's loud guffaw went through Holly like needles, then he rode away, the sound of his horse's hooves thudding away on the frozen ground.

"Insufferable, vulgar lout." Lady Matilda plopped back in her seat and clenched her shaking fists in her lap. "Spreading such lies. He should be drawn and quartered."

"I take it he is not your friend," Holly said, melting back against her seat, glad Lord Waterton was gone.

"Heavens, no! Cannot stand the man. Whatever gave you that idea?"

"He looked as if he were waiting for your carriage."

"Hah! He was only waiting to rub my nose in the gossip. He thrives on cruelty. He's the worst kind of knave, and no gentleman."

Holly's respect for Lady Matilda increased. At least she had enough taste not to like someone like Waterton. Perhaps Holly had judged the lady too harshly.

Lady Matilda drummed her fingers on her reticule. "I wouldn't let what Lord Waterton said upset you, but . . ." She paused, pursed her lips, then went on. "If, indeed, Lord Upton did kiss you, you should be on your guard."

"My guard?"

"Yes, my dear. Titled gentleman like Lord Upton find mistresses from among women," Lady Matilda lowered her voice, "who are not of their class. So beware. I happen to know Lord Upton has not had a mistress for six months. He may be on the lookout for one, and since you are from America, he may think he can keep you cheaply."

Heat rushed into Holly's cheeks. She narrowed her brows at Lady Matilda and twisted her fingers around the handle of her reticule until the green cord ripped out of one side.

At Holly's silence, Lady Matilda continued. "I see I've offended you, but you should be aware of these matters. You are so young you probably haven't considered these things, but let me tell you, gentlemen are well aware of them. They know the benefits of finding a mistress from the unrefined classes. They do not require jewels, a townhouse, a carriage, or the like. A gentleman can sequester someone like you in the country, in a small little cottage, and visit you when the whim hits him with little expense out of his own coffers."

Holly found her voice. "I can safely promise you, ma'am,

I have no intentions of being Lord Upton's mistress—now or any other time. And I resent you implying it."

"I see I have trod upon your feelings. Please forgive me if I hurt you, but I was just trying to warn you." Lady Matilda touched Holly's arm.

"Thank you, but it was not necessary." Holly wanted to shake off her touch, but suffered it.

"Please don't be angry. It was kindly meant." Lady Matilda smiled all too sweetly, then said, "I should tell you how excited I am."

"About what?" Holly wondered what she would say next that was cutting.

"John and I shall marry soon. It is inevitable. Why, I'm practically his wife now. And, of course, I am of his own rank and have a large dowry he desperately needs. Yes, I feel sure he will propose any day now."

Jealousy rose unbidden in Holly, but she kept her voice composed. "Please let me know when the happy day is so I can attend the wedding."

"To be sure, I shall."

Holly rested her head back on the seat and wondered if there was any truth in what Lady Matilda had just said. The lady would probably say anything out of jealousy. But still, John had kissed her on the street and humiliated her. It didn't matter that she had kissed him back like a little fool. He should never have done it. Then the second time he had ordered her to kiss him, knowing just how to use that velvety deep voice of his, how to look at her and make her insides melt. She should never have kissed him. He knew exactly how to manipulate her.

And he had touched her breasts and that other place. Even now, she could feel his hands on her, her insides tingling from the memory. He had used her. The bad part was, she didn't know if she was strong enough not to let him do it again.

Later that afternoon, the carriage took the ruts in the drive like it had no springs at all. Lady Matilda grabbed Holly's arm to keep her from falling off the seat. "I didn't know Lord Upton had let the drive get in such a state."

Holly shoved Lady Matilda back in the seat. The wheels passed over another dip. The carriage rocked again. "I believe it would have been better had we walked to the house," Holly said, clutching the seat.

"I'll have to speak to him about it. He is so very stubborn when it comes to taking money from me, but I'll insist that he allow me to fix this drive. We've had such a damp fall, it must have ruined the road."

"Yes." Holly hung on and glanced out the window.

A forest edged the drive, the trees bare of leaves, adding to the gloomy, forbidding look. Abruptly the trees gave way to an open lawn, the grass overgrown and grayed by its winter dormancy. The house stood in the center of the lawn, a huge rectangular Baroque structure. A swirl of smoke rose from several of the eight chimneys that towered above the roof. The windows and doors were void of Christmas decorations and the gray stone facade added to the stark look of the place.

The carriage finally rocked to a halt.

Holly unclenched her fingers from the seat and flexed them, wondering if they still worked after gripping the leather so tightly.

Lady Matilda sighed. "Well, I never thought we'd arrive safely. Let me warn you, the staff here has been reduced to almost nothing, but you will notice the furnishings are not sparse like the townhouse in London. I believe Lord

Upton didn't want to sell off anything from the hall because he didn't want the children to know what sort of financial distress he was facing. Which brings me to another matter. You may not get paid right away, but I'll pay your wages."

"I'm not worried." Holly smiled at her. "But thank you."

A hard thud sounded outside as the doormen hopped down onto the frozen ground, then they opened the door. Holly stepped out and noticed the footmen were boys a far cry from twenty. Their faces were chafed, their lips blue from the cold. One of the boys was shivering.

Lady Matilda stepped down and turned to stare up at the driver. "James, you should have driven slower over those ruts. Were you trying to kill us? If I feel one bump going out, you'll be out of a job. Do you understand?"

"Aye, me lady." James bobbed his cap, then huddled down inside his coat. Lady Matilda turned in a haughty huff and headed for the door, not even bothering to glance at the footmen.

Holly turned back to them, then looked at the driver. She quelled the urge to apologize for Lady Matilda's ungracious dressing down. "I'm sure you should come in out of the cold."

"Oh, no, miss." One of the boys wiped his red nose on his sleeve. "It's our job to stand out here and wait for the mistress."

Lady Matilda turned back toward the carriage. "Are you coming, Miss Campbell?"

"I'm trying to persuade your servants to get out of the cold, but I think they need a word from you."

Lady Matilda made a moue with her lips. In an irritated tone, she said, "After you tend to the horses, you may go to the kitchen and have a cup of tea. Then one of you will have to get Miss Campbell's things, but I'm sure she would rather you get warm first, so off with you."

The three men looked at each other, unable to believe their boon, then the driver scrambled down off the box.

The young man who had been shivering whispered to her, "Thank you, miss."

Holly smiled at him, then watched them hurry around the back of the house. She strode up the steps, Lady Matilda's stiff back in front of her.

"That was very considerate of you to think of my servants," Lady Matilda said, her voice tight. "I tend to forget about their comfort in the winter."

"They looked so cold."

"I suppose one has to be from an indigent background to realize the discomfort of servants." Even though Holly couldn't see her face, she knew Lady Matilda was wearing a haughty smile.

Holly grinned at her back, not offended in the least by her affront, nor would she set the lady straight. Let her think what she liked. If the news of her wealth circulated, then surely everyone would ask questions about her identity. It was better to play the role of a pauper.

Before she reached the door, it opened and a tall, thin man with thick silver hair and gentle eyes answered the door. He graced Lady Matilda with a smile and bowed. "Good afternoon, my lady." He glanced at Holly and studied her for a moment. "Miss."

"Hello." Holly rubbed her gloved hands to get them warm. She followed Lady Matilda into the house, feeling the sudden warmth hitting her cold cheeks.

"Pringle, this is the new nanny, Miss Campbell," Lady Matilda said with airy indifference. "Where is Mrs. Pringle?"

He made a face as if the mention of the name had

bothered him. "I believe she's in the game room with Lady Upton."

"How is Lady Upton?" Lady Matilda didn't wait for a reply, but pulled off her gloves and looked preoccupied with the movement, as if Pringle's answer didn't much matter to her.

"She has been behaving herself, my lady."

"Well, I suppose that is all we can expect." By way of explanation, Lady Matilda turned to Holly. "Lady Upton is Lord Upton's rather eccentric grandmother." Before Holly could comment, Lady Matilda turned back to Pringle, pulled off her coat and bonnet and handed them to him. "And the boys, how are they?"

"Miss Withers has them secured in the schoolroom. No mishaps this morning." Pringle looked relieved by his report.

"Ah, very good. Perhaps you should show Miss Campbell to her room and I'll go and find Mrs. Pringle."

"Very well."

Holly watched Lady Matilda walk through the entrance hall and go through a door. It was a beautiful entranceway with wide, curved steps on either side that led to a balcony on the top floor. The furniture in the house looked intact, not like John's townhouse in London. Several busts stood in deep recesses in the walls and two high-backed benches were placed on either side of the foyer.

"This is a lovely house," Holly said, and glanced around her.

"Yes, miss, we try to keep it so."

"But where are the Christmas decorations?" Holly glanced around for any sign of them.

Pringle lowered his voice. "We haven't decorated for Christmas here since the death of the countess two years ago."

"What about the children?" Holly said, appalled.

"Year before last, the family was in mourning, miss. The countess died on Christmas Eve. And this year, the master hasn't ordered it done, so we figured since his lordship's funds are so tight . . ." Pringle paused, swallowed hard, his Adam's apple bobbing up and down in his throat with embarrassment. "We thought it best not to even bring up Christmas to the children."

"Who thought this would be best?" Holly was ready to give the person a piece of her mind.

"My wife." Pringle's voice held an unmistakable sadness. He stared down at Lady Matilda's coat in his arms.

"I see." She would contrive a way to decorate for the season. A house with children living in it should be festive and bright this time of year. She was not daunted by the frown on Pringle's face and added, "Now, how do I find my room?"

"Your chamber is on the top floor, miss. If you wait for me to put these in the cloakroom, I'll show you the way."

"Thank you." Holly watched his coattail flapping against his long, thin legs as he moved through the entrance hall and slipped behind a small door off to the side.

She heard loud voices behind the door Lady Matilda had gone through, then . . .

Bang! The door burst open and slammed against the wall.

"I said I'm going to kill those damned pigeons!" An elderly woman stood in the threshold, trying to wrench a shotgun from the hands of a large buxom woman with three double chins.

The elderly woman's white wig listed to the side of her head. The belt on her burgundy dressing gown hung loose at her sides, exposing the front of her faded muslin nightgown. She was much smaller and frailer than the larger woman, but seemed bent on getting the gun.

"Now, listen to me, Lady St. John, you can't go shooting this thing," the larger woman said, while she pulled on the barrel with both hands.

"If you don't get out of my way, I'll shoot *you*." Lady Upton kicked the fat woman in the knee, then snatched the gun out of her hands. The movement sent the elderly lady stumbling backward, still clutching the gun.

Holly looked down the barrel pointed straight at her, then Lady Upton's finger must have hit the trigger. The loud report pounded against Holly's eardrums like a cannon blast.

Chapter 8

After a moment, Holly realized she was still alive and opened her eyes. Her heartbeat felt like it would never stop hammering her ribs and her legs trembled.

Lady Upton clutched the gun and looked at Holly, confusion clouding her eyes. "Anoria," she said, her eyes widening. Her mouth opened, stretching the deep wrinkles over her hollow cheekbones. Her bottom lip quivered. She stared down at the shotgun in her hand, then back up at Holly. Tears glistened in her faded brown eyes. "I could have killed you." Her hand opened and the shotgun fell from her fingertips, clanking against the marble floor.

Holly flinched, half expecting the gun to discharge again.

Lady Upton opened her arms, smiling now, tears streaming down her cheeks. "Come here, child, don't you even know your own mother?"

Holly didn't know what to do. Lady Upton looked so

happy to see her. What harm could it do to humor her? She strode toward the elderly lady, then hugged her, feeling Lady Upton's petite, but sturdy frame in her arms.

"Where have you been? You naughty girl. We have your come-out ball tonight. You have to get ready for it and stop this shilly-shallying around. That is why I was trying to kill those damned pigeons. You should see the droppings they left on the sills. We can't have people seeing those droppings." Lady Upton patted Holly's back. "Do you not agree?"

"Yes, Mama." Holly glanced over her shoulder toward the large woman, who jammed her hands down on her hips and scowled back at Holly. Lady Matilda was behind her, looking relieved the ordeal was over.

"I'm so glad I found you." Lady Upton stood back and gazed into Holly's face. The affection she was feeling for Anoria beamed through the glazed confusion in her eyes.

"Me, too, Mama." Holly reached into her reticule and pulled out a handkerchief. She dabbed at the tears streaming down Lady Upton's cheeks, then pushed her wig back to the middle of her head. "There now. I'm found and I promise you, I'll take care of those pigeons."

"All right."

"Mrs. Pringle, show Miss Campbell to her room. I'll escort Lady Upton abovestairs to her chamber," Lady Matilda said, grasping Lady Upton's hand. "Shall we go up, madam?"

"I suppose so." She narrowed her gray brows at Lady Matilda. "Who are you?"

"I'm Lord Upton's cousin by marriage. Surely you remember me. I'm Lady Matilda."

Lady Upton wrinkled her nose. "Who is John?"

"Your grandson, madam."

"Well, I don't remember him or you, but I'll let you

escort me to my room," Lady Upton said, jerking her robe together with a dignified snap, then turned to Holly. "You shall come and visit me, Anoria."

"Yes, Mama."

"Very well. And wear your new gown, I want to see it."

"Yes, Mama."

Holly watched Lady Matilda escort the elderly lady up the stairs.

Mrs. Pringle came toward her, her round face crimson and swollen with rage. She straightened her white cap where it had fallen almost over one eye in the scuffle, then said, "How dare you insinuate yourself into the good graces of that confused old woman! You will learn your place here, missy. Lady Matilda told me all about you and how you came to England unescorted. Your type doesn't fool me." She shook a plump finger in Holly's face. "I'll be watching you. If you try anything around here, you'll be out that door so fast your hair will curl."

Holly squared her shoulders, not backing down from the attack. "I wasn't trying to do anything, I was just being kind to her."

Holly heard footsteps pounding the marble and turned to see Pringle rush into the foyer. He grimaced when he saw his wife, then paused. "What was that noise I heard?"

Mrs. Pringle turned and glared at him. "You stupid fool. I thought I told you to keep the gun case locked."

The sharp, piercing reproach deflated Pringle's shoulders. He slouched, and in a timid voice, said, "I did lock it."

"Well, you didn't or it wouldn't have been opened."

Holly heard a snicker from abovestairs. She glanced up. Two young boys were peeking over the rail, impish gleams in their eyes. One of them looked two and ten with dark-brown hair like John's and the same golden eyes, the other looked several years younger, with sandy-blond hair and green eyes. The older one saw her looking at him. He stuck out his tongue and wagged his fingers on either side of his head.

She glanced at the Pringles to make sure they didn't see her, then crossed her eyes and stuck out her tongue at him. Just as quickly, she straightened her face and glanced back at the Pringles. She heard the boys' repressed laughter.

"I'm sure I locked the case," Pringle said, his tone abruptly lacking any certainty under his wife's crushing gaze. "It must have been one of the boys."

"Well, she could have killed someone today. See that you check it every hour." Mrs. Pringle's gaze cut back to Holly. The mere sight of Holly made Mrs. Pringle's bosom swell. The keys, suspended on a chain around her neck, jingled in protest, then she resumed her tirade.

"Now, missy, you'd better learn that I am the final word in this house. Is that clear? You are only the children's nanny. You answer to me. And you'll not be pretending to be Lady Upton's daughter again. It could only do her harm to think she is still alive."

"I don't see the harm in humoring her," Holly said, crossing her arms over her chest.

"I won't have an upstart in this house."

"I'm only here to take care of the children, Mrs. Pringle. This will not be a permanent position for me—that should ease your mind. So you see, you need not worry that I'll invade the household. I only want to do my job."

This assuaged some of the anger from Mrs. Pringle's face. "See that you do." As another threat, she added, "Mind, I'll be writing weekly reports to his lordship about you." She leveled her gaze at Pringle. "Show her to her room and see she gets to work." With that, she turned and stomped out of the room, slamming the door behind her.

Pringle turned toward Holly, wearing a beaten-dog expression. "This way, miss."

"Is your wife . . ." Holly paused, unsure if she should ask what was on her mind for fear of offending him.

"You mean is she always that way?"

"Well, yes."

"I'm afraid so," Pringle said, his tone flat, as if he were used to answering the question.

"I'm sorry."

"No need to apologize. I know she's a hard woman."

Holly followed Pringle up the stairs, casting a sympathetic glance at his back. Hard didn't come close to describing that woman. Tiger, now that was close. She knew as long as Mrs. Pringle saw her as a threat that life in the house would not be pleasant. Thinking of threats made her look down a long hallway for the boys, but they had completely disappeared. All she could see was the dark wainscoting covering the walls and several brass wall sconces. They continued down the hallway, their footsteps thudding on the Persian carpet. It was worn and looked ancient. The deep blue and red hues in the flowers had turned pink and light blue. Pringle paused before a door at the end of the hallway.

"These are the servants' stairs, miss. You'll be expected to use them." Pringle held the door for her.

"Of course." Holly stepped through into the stairwell. She heard a bird chirping and glanced up, catching sight of a cinnamon-colored canary flying above her head.

"One of his lordship's birds has escaped the aviary," Pringle exclaimed.

"His birds?" Holly asked, still staring at the delicate

feathered creature as it landed on the side of the stair railing and peeped down at them.

"His lordship raises canaries. The profit he makes from it keeps food on the table here and clothes on our backs."

"I'd love to see the aviary."

"I'll show it to you when you get settled in, miss." Pringle reached for the bird, but right before his fingers touched its wings, it took flight, fluttering past Holly's face. "I'll have to catch that one later and put it back. I told his lordship he should clip their wings, but he won't hear of it."

Holly listened to the delicate beat of the canary's wings fading away into the still hollowness of the stairwell and thought it would be a shame to clip their wings. It was surprising to her that John cared enough about the birds to leave them as nature intended.

Pringle continued up the stairs, his footsteps like thunder compared to the whisper of the canary's flight. Holly followed after him. When they reached the third floor, they stepped through a door and stood in a hallway, where the walls were dingy white, looking in need of a good coat of whitewash, and dotted with the children's dirty fingerprints. Four doors lined the hall.

"The schoolroom is there, miss." He motioned to the first door on the left. "Master Dryden and Master Brock's room is here," he said, then nodded toward a door opposite the schoolroom.

"Which one of the boys is the oldest?"

"That would be Master Dryden."

"Ah," Holly said, remembering the sight of Master Dryden's tongue sticking out at her. She grinned.

"There's a parlor here, you'll be sharing it with the governess, Miss Withers," he said, nodding to a door next to the boys' room. "Miss Withers's room is there next to the parlor."

"Where is Miss Withers?"

"Teaching the boys, I'm sure." He paused before a door at the end of the hall and opened it. "And this is your room here, miss."

Holly strode past Pringle and into the chamber. It was a small room, with only a bed, an old armoire, and a washstand. She took off her cape, hat, and gloves and hung them in the armoire. Chill bumps ran down her arms. She rubbed them, glancing over at the empty brazier in the room.

As if Pringle had read her mind, he said, "I'll get some coal for you, miss. We try to conserve on it."

"I understand."

"I'll bring your luggage up, too."

"There isn't much of it, just a few boxes, but thank you. One more thing, Pringle. Where is Miss Ann?"

"She'll be in her chamber." Sadness crossed Pringle's face. "It's on the second floor, across the hall from Lady Upton's chamber."

Before Holly could ask him why he had looked so sad at the mention of Miss Ann, he closed the door. She frowned, then smoothed back the hair that had come loose from the bun at her nape. With the intention of finding Ann, she turned toward the door, but a thumping noise and a muffled cry coming from the next room made her pause.

She listened for a moment, then strode out into the hall. Pausing before the door Pringle said led to the school-room, she gingerly opened the door, not knowing what to expect. She gasped when she saw a woman trussed to a chair, a rag stuck in her mouth.

The woman glanced at Holly. Relief flooded her face and her shoulders slumped against the ropes.

"We had better see about getting you untied." Holly worked the knots, sure Dryden and Brock had been busy little boys.

The ropes finally fell away and the woman pulled the gag out of her mouth. "My lord." She grabbed her chest. "I didn't think anyone could hear me up here. You must be the new nanny. Take my advice and leave while you still can. If I had another position to go to, I would leave here instantly."

Holly held back a smile. "Hello, I'm Holly Campbell." She didn't hesitate over the false last name now.

"I'm Miss Withers, the governess." She nodded, bobbing her head like a turkey. Actually, she favored a turkey, with her pointed nose and long, thin neck. Her hair was a nondescript brown, her eyes small, with a hint of cruelty. By the hollows in her cheekbones and the light frown lines around her mouth, Holly guessed she was in her early forties.

"It's a pleasure to meet you."

Miss Withers stood and patted out the wrinkles in her gray dress, then glanced toward the door. "When I get my hands on Dryden, he will regret this little coup d'état. I told Lord Upton he should be sent away to school now that he is older, but I think because his coffers are low, he refuses to send the boy away. He'll be the ruination of the other children. He is a terrible influence on Master Brock and his sister."

"I've met quite a few little boys like Dryden."

"Have you? Where?"

"My grandmother was quite active in the local orphanage, and we always had one or two children staying with us."

"But I'll bet you've never come across a child like Master Dryden."

"I'm sure he's a challenge. I look forward to meeting him," Holly said with genuine enthusiasm.

"I pity you." Miss Withers looked at Holly as if she couldn't believe anyone could possibly look forward to meeting Dryden.

"How did they tie you up like that?"

"I nodded off just for a second while they were supposed to be doing their sums. The rapscallions got the rope around me before I knew it. When I get my hands on those two, it will be the last trick they play on me." Her cheeks flushed with anger. "Please excuse me, I have to go and find the little darlings and drag them back to this room." She stiffened her spine, then turned in a huff and marched from the room.

"Good luck!" Holly called to her back, aware Miss Withers wouldn't find the boys until they wanted to be found. It was probably better she didn't find them. With that furious look on Miss Withers's face, Holly wasn't sure what she'd do to them.

She thought of Ann again, then went in search of her. Pringle had sounded so melancholy at the mention of Ann's name, it had caused a spark of anxiety in her that hadn't died away.

Holly stepped out of the stairwell onto the second floor, her footsteps echoing off the dark mahogany wainscoting. She glanced down the hall and saw Lady Matilda speaking to Miss Withers.

"Miss Campbell, I was just asking Lady Matilda if she'd seen the boys," Miss Withers said. "Since she hasn't, I suppose I'd better go and find them. If you see them, please let me know."

"I will," Holly said, pausing near Lady Matilda.

"Fine. Good day, madam." Miss Withers curtsied to Lady Matilda, then hurried down the hallway.

"I hope you found your accommodations to your liking?" Lady Matilda's voice was congenial, but there was a slight tightness in her lips that never seemed to soften unless she was with John.

"Yes, I did. The room is very nice."

"I must apologize for that spectacle this morning. It should never have happened. Lady Upton does have a nurse, but Wednesday is her day off. You may be required to attend her on that day and look after the children. Do you think you can do that?"

"Yes," Holly said confidently.

Lady Matilda smiled, belying the frosty look in her blue eyes. "I hope you get along here. And if you have any problems I would appreciate you coming to me instead of Lord Upton, since I'm sure he has enough trouble dealing with his financial losses. I have been overseeing the staff here since my cousin died. And I'm sure Mrs. Pringle will be of help to you."

"Of course," Holly said flatly, aware Mrs. Pringle would rather grind her bones and serve them for dinner rather than help her.

"I will take my leave of you now." She appeared to add her next words for Holly's benefit. "I'm sure John cannot do without me in town." Lady Matilda turned to leave.

"What about the children? Don't you want to see them before you go?"

Lady Matilda paused. "I visited Ann before I took Lady Upton to her room, and Miss Withers is searching for the boys. I'm sure I cannot wait around until she finds them.

I must get back to town in case Lord Upton needs me. They will understand. Tell the boys I'll come for a long visit when Lord Upton decides to leave London. That should please them.''

"I'm sure," Holly said, wondering if the boys would be disappointed at all. It was obvious all Lady Matilda cared about was getting back to John.

"Another thing, you might find it odd the house is not decorated for Christmas, but we are still in mourning for my poor cousin. Such a terrible twist of fate leaving the children motherless, and on Christmas Eve. It was tragic." Lady Matilda shook her head, setting her long black curls bobbing near the sides of her face. She paused a moment, a flash of genuine feeling in her eyes, then said, "It's been terribly hard for Lord Upton. And I don't think he's ever really gotten over Elise's death. This time of year surely must bring back horrible memories for him. You understand."

"I do, but what about the children? They must need something to brighten their lives."

"I offered to decorate the hall for John, but he specifically told me he doesn't wish to bother with Christmas." She frowned, her expression growing pensive. "I was surprised to see he had decorated his townhouse."

"I'm afraid that was my doing," Holly said, frowning.

"You?" Lady Matilda looked as if Holly had smacked her. She clamped her mouth closed and straightened her shoulders, then said, "Well, you should have asked me for direction before you took it upon yourself. From now on, you will come to me and ask permission before you do something like that again. Is that understood?"

"Perfectly." Holly nodded, a stiff motion that flipped several flyaway strands of auburn hair over her eyes. She pushed them behind her ear and felt them spring back out again.

"Well, that is all. I trust you will remember your place here. Good day." Lady Matilda turned in a huff, then strolled down the hall, her expensive silk gown rustling beneath the exaggerated sway of her hips.

Holly watched Lady Matilda turn the corner and disappear down the steps, aware she had no intentions of answering to this haughty lady. John was the master here. He must have some say in the running of his own home. Lady Matilda acted like she was already John's wife. How could he be in love with such an arrogant, overbearing woman and go around kissing Holly—in the open and on public sidewalks? Perhaps Lady Matilda was right. Perhaps he was only interested in Holly as a possible mistress. She'd have to keep her guard up around him.

After Holly had dashed John and Lady Matilda from her mind, she remembered why she had come to the second floor. She stood in front of Ann's chamber door now, listening for any sounds coming from the room. An odd heavy silence emanated from inside. Her hand trembled slightly as she rapped on the door.

"Come in," a barely audible voice said.

She opened the door slowly, afraid of what she might find on the other side. The hinges creaked. The room was dark, save for a lone candle burning on a small table. A little girl, about seven, sat on the bed, a cloud of pillows behind her. Her long straight blond hair hung down over her shoulders. Candlelight flickered off her small heart-shaped face. She stared down at a doll in her hands as if nothing else she could possibly look at would interest her. Her long brown lashes cast half-moon shadows on her cheeks. The pasty, unhealthy whiteness of her complexion made Holly suck in her breath.

Holly bit her lip, then forced a cheerful note into her voice. "Hello."

The little girl glanced up at her with large green eyes that held no light, not a spark, the flame of childhood snuffed out of them long ago. "Who are you?" she asked, her soft voice tremulous and leery.

"I am the new nanny." Holly strode into the room. "You must be Lady Ann."

"I've had a lot of nannies," Ann said indifferently. "Just when I get used to them, they leave. Are you going to stay for a while?"

"Absolutely. Just try to get rid of me."

"I think they leave because when Nurse—she takes care of Great-grandmama and me—is not around, the nanny has to care for me, and it requires an awful lot of time." She sighed and hugged her doll close to her.

"I don't think it has anything to do with you. More than likely, it probably has something to do with your brothers. What do you think?"

She pursed her brows, weighing the question. "Well, you might be right there. They can be beastly."

"Your father asked me to give you and your brothers a special message."

"Did he?" Ann asked, a hint of excitement in her voice.

"Yes. He said to tell you he missed you and that he would be home soon."

The corners of Ann's mouth drooped and she stared down at her doll again. "He always says that. I don't see him very often."

"It's not because he doesn't want to see you. He works very hard when he is not here."

"Yes, I know that is what Pringle tells me, but I wish he could work here." Ann glanced toward the door.

Holly didn't know what to say to comfort the child, so she glanced over at the drawn drapes. "Did you know there are certain fairies who live only in the sunshine, and when you don't let the sun in your room, the fairies stay away?"

"Mrs. Pringle said the sun was not good for me, but she didn't tell me fairies live in it," Ann said, her voice skeptical.

"Fairies only show themselves to people who believe in them. I don't think Mrs. Pringle believes in them, so naturally she wouldn't know about them." Holly waved her hand toward the window. "Shall we invite the fairies inside?"

Ann nodded, her long blond hair falling over the doll's face.

Holly walked over and pulled back the heavy burgundy brocade curtains. The afternoon sun shot through the windowpanes and across the foot of the bed, engulfing Ann's legs in a shaft of triangular light.

Holly pointed to the dust motes floating in the air. "See those tiny little things."

"Yes," Ann said, staring at the motes with open curiosity.

"They're food for fairies. If you look closely, you can see them grab a handful."

"I don't see them," Ann said, staring, her gaze intent.

"Fairies are shy, you can't expect them to pop right out any old time you want to see one. When you least expect it, you'll see one." Holly walked through the beam of light, swirled dust motes around her like drifting snowflakes, then sat on the bed.

"I don't blame them for hiding from me." Ann stared down at her legs.

"Why do you say that?" She reached out to touch Ann's

hand, but Ann drew it back. Holly dropped her own hand back in her lap and grimaced.

"Because no one wants to be around me."

"That isn't true. I like being around you."

"Do you?" Ann glanced up at her, her blue eyes searching Holly's face to see if she was telling the truth.

"Yes, very much."

Ann was silent a moment, absorbing Holly's words, then she asked, "Do you think the fairies will like me?"

"I haven't met a child yet they disliked."

Ann's expression lightened for a moment, then she bit her bottom lip. "I wish they could make me walk again."

Holly knew something was wrong with the child, but she hadn't expected it to be her legs. She kept the surprise from her face. "Have you never been able to walk?"

"I used to, but I stopped walking when Mama died." Ann grimaced, pain glowing in her eyes at the memory.

"Did you hurt your legs? Is that why you stopped walking?"

"I just woke up and couldn't walk. The doctor put these braces on my legs. I do not like them much, and I have to take this medicine which tastes like horse pee . . ." She saw the skeptical look on Holly's face and added, "Least that is what Dryden said when he tasted my medicine." She pursed her lips. "I don't believe he ever tasted horse pee. Do you?"

"I doubt it," Holly said, smiling.

"You speak funny. You're not from around here? Are you from Brussels? Miss Withers said people speak strange when they are from Brussels."

"I'm from America."

"Do they have fairies in America?"

"Of course they do, but they live under toadstools. I used to hunt for them in the woods with my grandmother."

"My grandmother died before my mother," Ann said with a wistful sigh. "All I have is Great-grandmama and I don't think she knows about fairies. Did you find any fairies with your grandmother?"

"Actually not a one, but I could see their lanterns come on at night when I'd peek out my window. My grandmother didn't know it, but I spent hours staring out my window at night when I was supposed to be sleeping."

"Those were just fireflies."

"No, I'm sure they were fairies, because when I looked real hard at the lights I could see their wings and little people bodies."

Ann's thin brows drew together. She became silent, coiling the doll's hair around her fingers.

Holly glanced at the doll and noticed it was almost bald from where Ann had twisted away most of the hair. She broke the silence. "I was thinking of going outside for a walk. Would you like to go with me?"

"I'm not allowed out in the air. The doctor says it's bad for me."

"Then perhaps we can go and look at the aviary together?"

"No, no." Ann shook her head, fear glowing in her eyes. "They frighten me, and Papa doesn't allow us in there unless he's home. He says it disturbs their breeding habits."

"Well, I suppose I shouldn't disturb them, either. Perhaps I'll see them later. I'll come back in a little while and check to see if you need anything."

She cast a compassionate glance at Ann and left her hugging her doll, a melancholy look on her small, pale face. Back home in the Charles City Orphanage, Holly had seen overly sensitive children struck hard by the death of one parent, or both. Some couldn't speak, others went inward and lost all touch with reality. Ann had just given up walking when her mother died. The sad thing was those children in the orphanage rarely recovered, but sunk deeper into themselves, their spirit consumed by an inner abyss of bleakness. She prayed that had not already happened to Ann.

That little girl needed something to brighten her existence. Celebrating Christmas might help, but Holly had to think of a way to do it without getting Mrs. Pringle's dander up—and then there was John. Lady Matilda said that his wife had died at Christmas. Ann had just mentioned she'd stopped walking on Christmas Day. Poor John. It must have been terrible for him. She understood why he didn't want to celebrate the holidays, but the children needed some gaiety in their lives. She would have to find a way to give it to them.

She thought of John again and the added burden he had with someone trying to ruin his company. Mr. Scibner's face rose up in her mind. Was he keeping John safe without being discovered? If John found out what she had done, he'd never forgive her. She hoped Mr. Scibner was competent enough to keep a vigilant eye without John finding out about it.

John paused before a thatch-roofed cottage on Whitechapel Road. Icicles hung from the eaves, dripping in the sunlight. Shafts of light beamed through the frozen water, shooting rays of rainbow colors into his face. He raised his hand and shielded his eyes, then noticed the windows in the cottage were fogged over. He raised his cane and rapped on the door, watching the condensation drip down the panes.

The oddest feeling someone's eyes were on him made

him turn and glance over his shoulder. A dray loaded with ale kegs rattled past him. A chimney sweep strode down the opposite side of the street, whistling, his back to John, a set of long brushes slung over his shoulder.

The cottage door creaked open. He stared into the surprised face of Henry Thomas and the strange feeling dissolved.

Thomas smiled hospitably. "My lord, what an honor."

"I had hoped you still owned this cottage and took a chance coming to see you. May I have a word?"

"Of course. Please come in out of the cold."

John stepped through the door, the delicious aroma of baking mincemeat pie wafting beneath his nose. The cottage was small. The room in which he was standing no bigger than the parlor in his townhouse. It held a small oak table and four chairs. The back opened up into a kitchen area.

Thomas's wife stood near a counter, holding a baby on her hip, staring at John with a pleasantly surprised smile on her face. She was not a beautiful woman, but plain and tall, everything about her sturdy looking, even her square jaw. But she had a gentle, unpretentious air about her that made her seem pretty and comfortable to be around. Yes, *comfortable* described Thomas's wife. John had always liked being in her company, the few times he had met her. She was similar to Holly, straightforward, unassuming, guileless. He stared at the fat-cheeked baby on her hip, and the vision of Holly with a baby in her arms rose up in his mind to taunt him.

He blinked and willed the vision to fade, then saw Thomas's little daughter standing beside his wife. She held a cookie cutter in her hand, still poised over a rolled-out piece of dough, while she stared, wide-eyed, at him.

"You know my wife," Thomas said, motioning toward her.

"Yes, Mrs. Thomas, a pleasure to see you again." John bowed. "How have you been?"

"Well, my lord, we cannot complain, though I preferred the West Indies to this cold climate. I'd forgotten just how cold it could be here, but I'd follow Henry to Siberia if he asked me to." She glanced at Thomas, love glowing in her eyes.

A pang of jealousy gnawed at John. He had never had a woman look at him that way. Elise was too self-centered to love anyone. When he had courted her, she had been infatuated with him, but that soon wore off after they wed. Later in the marriage, they grew so far apart he could barely stand to be in the same room with her. And she never let him forget it was her money that had saved his family from ruin. He thought of how unbearable his own marriage had been.

Thomas was still sharing a glance with his wife as if no one else were in the room, then finally he said, "You know my daughter, Allie."

"Yes, nice to see you again." John stared at the brown-haired child and thought of Ann. He felt an emptiness inside him that wouldn't be filled until he saw Ann and the boys again.

"Please, my lord, sit over here by the fire." Thomas pulled out two chairs from beneath the table and set them near the hearth. "Let me take your coat."

John handed him his cane, cape, and hat, then sat down in a hard-backed chair near the fire. The chair creaked beneath his weight and he was afraid it might break if he moved too suddenly.

Thomas hung up John's belongings on a peg by the door, then crossed the room and sat in a chair near him.

"I'll make tea," Teresa said, bouncing the baby, who had started to whine.

"No need to bother, I'll only be staying a few moments." John glanced over at Thomas and lowered his voice. "The reason I'm here is, a Mr. Jarvis, one of the sailors on board the *Sea Challenger*, came to see me yesterday—"

"There was a survivor?" Thomas's eyes grew wide with surprise and shock.

"Apparently. He informed me someone knocked him unconscious and deliberately steered the ship into *Sin's Revenge* during the storm." John watched Thomas closely for his reaction.

"My God! I don't believe it. Why? Why would anyone do such a thing?" The color drained from his face. He shook his head, leaning forward, then rested his elbows on his knees, his wrists hanging limp between his legs.

Either Thomas was a superb actor or the news had given him a genuine blow. John wanted to believe the latter. "I'm not sure. That's why I came to you."

"But you don't think that I—that I could possibly know anything about this," Thomas said, sounding indignant and hurt.

"No, I'm sure you don't. I just wanted to know about the crew on board the *Challenger*."

"I don't know much about them. Captain Burgess hired his own men. I couldn't tell you anything about the crew. It was a damn shrewd plan to have *Sin's Revenge* also sabotaged at the same time."

"What better time than in a hurricane? The West Indies Company lost two ships of their own in the storm. I would never have known about this if Jarvis hadn't come forward. Whoever did it must have waited for just the right moment so it would look like an accident." John rubbed his throbbing temples.

"What about this Jarvis fellow? The fact he survived and didn't come to me when the office was still open makes me wonder if he could have been the one who sunk the ships."

John leaned back in his chair, clasped his hands, and steepled his fingers. "I thought of that, but I doubt I could prove it unless I can find the man who hired him and tie the two together. He certainly wouldn't be stupid enough to go to this man anytime soon."

"If you like, I'll watch the bastard for you." Thomas's eyes took on a furious gleam that surprised John. "He should pay for this."

"No, I think I'll handle this myself, but thank you." John touched Thomas's shoulder, sure now he hadn't had anything to do with the sinking.

John stood. "I'll leave you then. Take care." Mrs. Thomas paused from helping her daughter cut out cookies. "Leaving so soon, my lord? I wish you could stay and sample some of our Christmas pies."

"Perhaps another time. I really must take my leave." It was the first time John had given Christmas a second thought. Christmas only held painful memories for him. Two Christmas Eves ago, Elise had died, and the next morning Ann had stopped walking. Since then, John had tried to put Christmas out of his mind.

Thomas hurried over and handed John his cape, hat, and cane. "You'll let me know when you catch the bastard."

"Yes, I shall."

This seemed to appease Thomas's anger and he managed a smile. "Good-bye, my lord."

John walked out the door, then turned and strode down the street. There was that feeling again that someone was watching him. He glanced over his shoulder. The sweep he'd seen earlier was behind him. Their eyes met for a second, then the man darted into an alley.

John swung around and started running toward the alley. A tall boardinghouse loomed to his right, its shadow blocking the sidewalk from the sun. A patch of ice was left over from yesterday's sleet storm, and he didn't know it until the soles of his boots hit it. Cursing, he slipped, groped the air, then slid all the way to the alley on unsteady legs.

He grabbed a corner of the building and gained his balance, then glanced down the alley. It was bare, no sign of the sweep. The only thing he saw was a cat prowling near a fence in search of a rat or mouse. Just like him! John hoped he had better luck than the cat. Whoever was following him was apt at it. He wondered if his nemesis was having him followed.

A plan began to form in his mind to catch the man shadowing him.

Chapter 9

John finished paying the cabdriver, then headed toward St. John Shipping. He glanced over his shoulder, a movement that had become habitual over the past hour, and couldn't find anyone following him. He saw only an empty sidewalk and a cab with no driver. Turning back around, he listened to his boots thudding on the cobblestones, feeling his cape coiling around his legs as he walked. Before he reached the office, he heard Teddy's raised voice. He paused with his hand on the door and peeked through the window.

Sir Joseph Romley and Teddy stood nose-to-nose, Romley's large belly almost touching Teddy's waist, his bloated face glowing red with rage. Teddy's complexion was pink from the neck up, stark against his canary-yellow coat.

John stepped inside, then slammed the door behind him, the bell over the door protesting. Teddy and Romley turned in his direction. John scowled at them. "What is going on here?"

"Tell him." Teddy glared at Romley.

"Well, I—I . . ." Romley paused and stepped back from Teddy.

John didn't like the nervous tone in Romley's voice. He shot Romley such a pointed look that it made him clutch the lapel of his coat and take another step back. "Well?" John said curtly, losing his patience.

"I—I . . ." Romley paused from his stammering, while his red-veined face turned even redder. He ran his hand around the top of his cravat, then squared his shoulders in a feeble attempt to gather his courage, which only thrust out his protruding stomach even more. "Hell!" he said, flustered. "Might as well say what I came to say. I already told your brother. The investors want out." Romley took another step back, afraid of John's response. He bumped into the desk, groped at the edge, and eyed John.

"Do you speak for all the investors?" John asked, his voice menacingly soft.

"Yes." Romley ran his hand around his cravat again like it was a noose. "Believe me, I don't like giving you the news above half, but I thought you should hear it from me. After all, I was the one who found the investors for your company."

"This will ruin me." John clutched his cane with both hands. The wood snapped beneath his grip.

Romley eyed the broken pieces of ash in John's hands, his eyes widening with fear. "You can't expect us to stay in your company when you've lost two ships."

"I have another, I'll just need time to recoup my losses."

"They don't want to wait. I tried speaking to them."

"Who are they? I'll speak to them."

"You know I can't divulge that information. As their

investment banker, it is my duty to keep their identities concealed. I could lose my bank if I told you who backed you. You've had a nasty run of bad luck, St. John. And with the rumors going round about your own financial status, you really cannot expect them to keep backing you. It wouldn't be a practical investment, and I honestly can't advise them to keep their money in your company." Romley's last word came out like a squeak.

"You needn't say more. I wouldn't want you compromising your business on my account." John clenched the halves of his broken cane, fighting the urge to wrap them around Romley's neck. When John started the company, Romley had acted like John's best friend, now he wouldn't even persuade the investors to stay with him.

"They want their money by the end of the month."

"They'll get it when I can give it to you."

"They want it at month's end, or they're prepared to take you to court. The scandal will destroy what's left of your company. No one will want to do business with you. You'd better find a way to come up with the money. Perhaps you'd better look for an heiress at Almack's."

John pointed to the door. "Get the hell out!"

"Just a suggestion, St. John," Romley said, backing toward the door, clutching his cane with trembling hands.

"Get out!" John took another step toward him.

Romley cast him a sidelong glance, then, as if a hornet was after him, he darted out of the office.

"Damnation! We're on Queer Street now. What shall we do?" Teddy crossed his arms over his chest, chagrin marring his expression.

"I don't bloody know." John threw the ends of the cane across the room. They crashed into the side of the desk, bounced off the wood, then one slid to a corner and struck the wall, while the other rolled across the floor and hit the heel of Teddy's boot.

Teddy glanced down at it and frowned. "I can't blame you for being vexed. What a bloody spineless worm that Romley character is. He didn't act like he wanted to help us at all."

John turned to look at Teddy, but someone walking across the street caught his eye. He glanced out the window and glimpsed a man, loitering near a cab stand reading a paper. He wore a dark, inconspicuous suit and a heavy black coat.

The man's next movement was done with blithe, swift precision that John might have missed had he blinked. The man turned a page of the paper, snapped a surreptitious glance around the side of it at the shipping office, then raised the paper with a lightning flick of his wrist. In the fleeting glance of the man's face, John noticed he was a gray-haired man with gold wire-rimmed glasses. He didn't look like the chimney sweep John had seen earlier, but there could be more than one man following him.

John watched the man hide his face behind the paper. He turned another page and attempted another glance at the office. But this time John stared directly into the man's eyes. Surprise and bewilderment registered on his face, then he flicked the paper back up again in a flustered, nervous motion. Something about the little gentleman reminded John of a nervous chihuahua.

John stepped away from the window and turned toward Teddy. "Unless I'm very much mistaken, someone's having me followed. Come on, we're closing up shop early today."

"Why would anyone have you followed?" Teddy asked, incredulous.

John hesitated a moment, doubting if he should take

Teddy into his confidence, then he finally said, "I think it's the same person who wrecked our ships."

Teddy looked confused, and John informed him of the story Jarvis had told. When he finished, he looked at Teddy's stricken face. "I think the man following me could be connected somehow. We have to catch him."

"How do you propose we do that?"

"I have a plan. Just follow my lead." John walked toward the door. He'd catch the nervous little bastard and then he'd get the truth out of him.

"Is he still following us?" Teddy asked, snorting a pinch of snuff.

"On our left." Out the corner of his eye, John could see the cab following at a sedate pace, then noticed the snuff box in Teddy's hand. "Where did you get the blunt to buy that rot?"

Teddy gulped, looking abruptly uncomfortable. "I bought it out of the allowance you gave me."

"I gave you only enough money for school expenses and clothes. How could you afford to buy snuff?"

"Actually, I borrowed some blunt from a friend." To explain away his careless spending, he said, "It's all the crack, and this is the cheapest brand." Teddy made a face at the brown powder, then said, "It's not very pleasant."

"I'm not surprised." John grimaced at Teddy, taking in his bright yellow coat and breeches. He really was a town fop, into every trifling craze imaginable. Would he ever grow up? With a marked amount of mockery, he said, "Perhaps you should get a quizzing glass to go with your snuff box."

Not in the least touched by the slight, Teddy said in all earnestness, "I looked at some, but the one I want is made of gold and too expensive, and I won't be caught with a cheap imitation."

John shook his head, feeling the cab slow, then stop. He glanced over at Teddy. "All right, you know what you're to do."

"Yes. I start a fight with the driver of the cab, then you're going to pounce on the man." Teddy snapped his snuff box closed with his thumb in a practiced motion, then put the box back inside his coat pocket.

"I'll go first . . ." John opened the cab door and paused when he heard Dunn's voice booming down the sidewalk.

"You can't do that. Lord Upton will have you strung up by your ballocks— Good God! What am I saying? He'll have *me* strung up for letting you get away with this."

John glanced past the side of the gig and glimpsed Dunn following two men down the walk as they carried the sitting-room sofa. Two burly guards stood at the door to his townhouse, holding pistols. A crowd of onlookers clustered together on the sidewalk, their eyes glued to the tragedy unfolding before them.

"Pay the driver, Teddy," John said, then sprang from the cab in one leap and headed toward the townhouse.

In four long strides, John stood in front of the guards. One of them was a bullet-headed man with a brown muffler around his neck, the other looked like a fox, with bright orange hair and a pointy nose.

"What is the meaning of this?" John addressed Fox-face.

"Foreclosing, gov." Fox-face pulled a cigar out the side of his mouth and spat on the stoop, missing the toe of John's boot by inches. "You're six months late on your payment." He took in John's murderous expression, then raised his pistol like he wanted to use it. "Everything in the house belongs to the bank now."

John glared at him, then at the people standing on the street. If he threw these knaves off the porch, it would just cause more of a scandal, but he was sorely tempted. As it was, his humiliation would probably be the lead story in *The Morning Post.* Far better not to feed the scandalmongers, he decided. He swallowed what was left of his pride and turned. Every tense muscle in his body protested as he strode down the steps.

Teddy paused next to him. "What the bloody hell is happening?"

"The bank has foreclosed," John said through his teeth.

Two men thrust them aside and carried out a trunk.

"Hey, those are my clothes!" Teddy exclaimed, jerking on the arm of one of the men.

Fox-face leaped down the steps and shoved Teddy back from the trunk. He smiled arrogantly. "Not anymore."

Teddy looked ready to pounce on the man, but John grabbed his arm. "Not here. We have an audience."

Teddy glanced over his shoulder and noticed the people gaping at them. "Hell and bedamned!"

"Go and get Dunn," John said, glancing at Dunn still arguing with the men while they loaded the sofa on a dray.

John noticed the cab that had followed them parked across the street, near where the people had gathered. The gray-haired man was in the carriage, trying to look inconspicuous as he watched the proceedings as he peeped from behind a newspaper. John had forgotten about the man in all the chaos.

He strode across the street now, his steps stiff and determined. The little man didn't notice him; he was watching Teddy pulling Dunn away from the dray.

John reached the cab without detection. He threw open the door, shoved his large hand inside the gig, grabbed hold of the man's cravat, and yanked. The man fell down the steps, his eyes wide with fear. John held the gentleman up by his cravat and glared at him.

John tightened his hold on the cravat. The wily little man blinked at him from behind his spectacles, his face growing redder by the moment. "N-now, y-you don't understand, my lord," the man stammered, his voice strangled behind the tight cravat.

"You have two seconds to help me to understand." John drew the cravat tighter.

"A-all right, but please don't resort to violence. A young woman paid me to follow you."

"Who the bloody hell are you?"

"The name's Julius Scibner, I—I am a Bow Street Runner."

"Who hired you?"

"I can't tell you that."

John lifted the cravat.

Scibner made a choking sound, then croaked out the words, "All right . . . I'll tell you."

"I'm glad you saw it my way." John loosened his hold on Scibner's cravat, but didn't drop his hand from around his neck.

Scibner squeezed his eyes shut, relieved that his life had been spared, then opened them again. "A young woman hired me to find out who sabotaged your ship, and she asked me to follow you because she was concerned about your welfare."

"What young woman?"

He paused, grimaced, then, as if it pained him to speak, he said, "A Miss Campbell. I believe you know her."

Inadvertently, John's hand tightened around Scibner's Adam's apple.

He coughed, then his voice grew raspy and barely audible. "My lord, you're killing me."

John realized he might have exerted more pressure than he should have. He dropped his hand.

Scibner stumbled backward and fell against the cab. "Please don't be angry with her. She was just concerned about your well-being."

"I told her I would handle this my way."

"You had better let me deal with this matter, my lord. I'm a bit more inconspicuous than you, and I have men everywhere. I've already done some investigating and found Mr. Jarvis survived the shipwreck. I have men watching. And with a bit more poking around, I can find who is trying to ruin you."

John weighed Scibner's suggestion, then noticed some of the onlookers were now watching him and Scibner. He lowered his voice. "Perhaps you're right, you're a little more inconspicuous, but I won't be able to pay you right away."

"Miss Campbell has seen to that."

"Where the devil did she get that kind of money?"

"You will have to ask her that yourself." Scibner looked determined on that matter.

After a long heavy pause, John finally said, "I want updates on your progress every day. And I have another task for you as well."

Mr. Scibner nodded. "At your service."

"I want you to investigate Miss Campbell's past. She is from Richmond, Virginia, and left her home in a hurry. I want to know why."

"I can handle that," Mr. Scibner said, having no compunction when it came to changing client loyalties in this case. His eyes gleamed. "It might take a few weeks, or maybe even a month."

"I care not how long it takes. Miss Campbell is not going anywhere, I'll see to that. Just find out the information.

You'll excuse me now, I have something important that needs my attention." John strode away from him.

"What is that, my lord?" Scibner asked behind John's back.

"I have to speak to Miss Campbell." John headed for the other side of the street, with every intention of doing more than just speaking to her.

At that same moment forty miles away, Holly stood on a stool and leaned further over into a holly bush. Prickly leaves stabbed the back and sides of her neck. For some reason, unbeknown to her, an image of John rose up in her mind, the usual scowl on his face darker than she remembered. The image faded. She shrugged, then shoved the offending limb aside and clipped it with a pair of pruning shears. She had decided to start gathering some greenery for Christmas decorations. Where she was going to put it, she wasn't sure.

Turning, she tossed the branch behind her to the ground. It landed on top of the pile of boxwood and pine limbs she had spent two hours gathering. She glanced up at the sky. Dusk was creeping across the edge of the horizon, painting stripes of deep pink, indigo, and purple across the clouds. Only half an hour of sunlight was left, which was probably good, for her fingers and toes were growing numb from the cold. She had hoped the boys would be curious about what she was doing and perhaps make themselves known to her, but she hadn't seen them. Miss Withers was still looking for them, so Holly supposed they would stay hidden at least until suppertime.

As she raised the shears, she heard giggles behind her, then someone kicked the stool out from under her. Groping at the air, she tumbled down through the branches.

Spiny leaves tore at her face, pricking her arms and legs through her clothes. She heard her dress rip.

Thud. She landed flat on her back. Lying there on the ground, her eyes closed, holly leaves digging into the back of her scalp, she forced the air back into her lungs and heard voices.

"Now look what you did, Dryden. You've killed her."

"I might have pushed her, but you watched." Dryden's voice was deeper than Brock's.

"I didn't want to, but you made me." Brock sounded close to tears. "Now what are we going to do? We'll hang."

Intrigued and amused by their conversation, Holly kept her eyes closed and played dead, while she listened to their footsteps draw near.

"We don't know if she's dead yet. Go ahead and see," Dryden urged.

"I ain't touching her. You do it. You're the one that kicked the stool from under her," Brock said.

"I didn't kill her alone. You helped. Maybe we can just leave her out here. Even if she ain't dead, the cold will finish her off, then the ravens will pick her flesh clean, and if anyone does find the body, it will look like she just fell off the stool. No one will know we killed her."

"But what if they call out a search?"

"You heard Mrs. P. yelling at her. She won't care if our new nanny is never found."

"I was starting to like her better than the rest," Brock said. "You got to admit, none of our other nannies ever stuck out their tongues at us."

"She doesn't know her place," Dryden said with a superior air in his voice.

"I think she would have been fun. We haven't had any fun since Mama died at Christmas."

"That's all you whine about. Can't you think of anything

but Christmas and Mama dying? I hate Christmas. It's a stupid holiday."

"I can't help it if I want to celebrate Christmas," Brock said, sounding hurt.

"You can help whining about it. You might as well forget it. Papa will take us to church like he did last year, but that is all. You know what he said. He doesn't have the blunt to celebrate Christmas properly, and if he can't give the servants and his tenants a gift, then he wants to avoid the whole affair. I don't blame him. And if you cared about Mama, you wouldn't want to celebrate the day she died."

"I just thought—"

"No, you never think."

"Sometimes I hate you, Dryden." Brock paused, and silence hung between the two brothers.

The wistful dismalness in Brock's voice bored directly into Holly's heart. These poor children. She would find a way to give them a Christmas with all the trimmings. They needed the healing love Christmas brought, and desperately.

Brock broke the silence. "What are we going to do about her body? We'll hang if anyone knows what we did."

"We're not doing anything. They won't know we killed her, so stop your sniveling."

"I didn't kill her."

"All right so I killed her, but you watched. Anyway, I didn't like her."

"You never like anyone," Brock said.

"That's right. Now, are you going to blow off at the mouth, or be a man of honor and keep your lips sealed?"

There was a pause while Brock thought this over. "All right, but I'm sick of hiding from the Withers. I'm turning myself in. 'Course that was your show, too. Shouldn't never have listened to you when you wanted to tie her up. I've gotten more beatings because of you."

"Quit whining, will you?"

"I'm not whining."

"Are, too."

"Am not . . ."

Holly waited until their voices faded before she opened her eyes. She tried all her parts to make sure they were still in working order, then rose. She groaned and rubbed her backside. A plan of revenge was already forming in her mind. Teaching the children a lesson was going to be fun. Perhaps they would think twice before kicking a stool out from underneath someone else!

Later that night, Holly sat in an abandoned hunting lodge. It was about a mile from the house and almost hidden by the forest. It was a small stone structure, with a small kitchen in one corner and a sitting area in the other. The only furniture was a wobbly table, two oak chairs with spokes missing in the back, and a rickety elm settle near the fireplace. She'd accidentally found the lodge when she was walking to keep warm. For hours, she had hidden inside it, aware if she went anywhere near the house the boys would find her.

She had found some wood in a woodshed out back and started a fire in the hearth. Not one for remaining idle, she had spent her time cleaning the interior of the cottage as best she could with an old broom she had found by the hearth. What had started out as a dirty cobweb-infested place turned into a quaint little cottage. With some curtains, a tablecloth, and a little more furniture, it could be adorable.

She glanced at the dying fire, which threw flickering

shadows around the room and across the shutters that had been nailed closed. A thin beam of moonlight poured through a wide, jagged crack between the shutters and cut a dim, hazy path through a dark corner of the cottage. It must be close to ten now. The boys would certainly be in bed. She grinned, thinking of what she had in store for them.

She rose from the settle, leaned over, dipped her hand in some ashes from the edge of the fireplace, then rubbed the black soot beneath each eye and in the hollows of her cheeks. She stared at her reflection in a broken mirror on the wall, smiled at her grotesque appearance, then pulled her cape around her and left the hunting lodge.

The moon hung like a huge ball in the sky and beamed a soft blue glow along the path in the woods. Naked limbs from oaks, elms, and ash trees loomed over the path. She ducked several low-lying boughs and made her way to the end of the path and onto the grounds. The frigid air was redolent with a crisp frost that already touched the dormant grass with a glistening sheen. It twinkled in the moonlight like a carpet of silver icicles.

The house loomed in the distance, a giant gray ghost. A massive greenhouse jutted from one side, which Holly supposed was where John kept the aviary. Behind it stood an unkempt garden, overgrown with weeds and untrimmed hedges, which she had walked through earlier in the daylight. It might have been a lovely place at one time and could be lovely again with someone to care for it. It saddened her to know John didn't have the money to keep a staff of gardeners.

Her shoes crunched in the frozen grass, her brittle footsteps sounding like grinding teeth. Before she knew it, she was pausing at the servants' stairwell. She hoped Pringle hadn't closed up the house for the night. When she tried the knob, it made a sharp click, then opened.

Smiling, she stepped inside, then closed the door behind her.

"Is that you, Miss Campbell?"

Pringle's voice echoed down the stairwell and made Holly jump. She clutched her pounding heart, then glanced up the stairs and saw him making his way down the steps.

"Land sakes!" Holly said when she could speak. "You scared the daylights out of me."

"I've been worried about you, miss. I was just locking up the house. Mrs. Pringle seemed to think you'd left us already and didn't want me to send for the magistrate. I was sure you wouldn't leave the house without a word to anyone. If I had not found you by midnight, I meant to go for help." Pringle came down the steps, a candle held high, his thin, cranelike body bathed in candlelight. It darkened the hollows in his cheeks and gave his face a cadaverous look.

"Thank you, Pringle. I believe it was wishful thinking on your wife's part." Holly smiled up at him.

He paused in front of her, studied her face, then her torn dress, and cried, "What has happened to you?"

"It's a little prank I intend to play on the boys. Do I look like I've come back from the dead?"

"They didn't try to kill you?" Pringle blinked at her, his expression full of disbelief and chagrin.

"They thought they did. That's why it's so important I play this little prank on them. Hopefully, Dryden will think twice about his actions in the future. Nothing like getting your drawers shocked off your backside to turn a body around."

"If you say so, miss, but I doubt our Dryden will ever change."

"We can only hope." The smile melted from her face. "Did Ann ask for me while I was gone?"

"No, miss, not as far as I know."

"Oh," Holly said, the disappointment coming through in her voice.

"It takes a while for her to warm to anyone." Pringle touched her shoulder.

"I know, I just thought perhaps she would have wondered where I was. Well, Rome was not conquered in a day."

"No, miss." Pringle smiled at her.

"I'm going to go on up and have a little fun. If you should see Dryden or Brock running through the house, you'll know why."

Pringle shot her a conspiratorial smile. "I won't try to help them. I left a candle burning in the hall, miss. If you hold it, they can see you better."

"A fantastic idea. Thank you, Pringle." Holly smiled at him, then hiked up her dress and cape and trudged up the stairs.

Holly paused near the boys' room. A dim light flickered beneath the door. She pressed her ear against the oak and heard their muffled voices chatting away. Smiling, she tiptoed over to her room. The door creaked, and she deliberately opened the door slowly several times, hoping the boys heard it.

She darted into her room, flung her cape and gloves on the bed, then grabbed a water pitcher that happened to be empty. She hurried back into the hallway, shutting the door with a loud bang. Her room was only three doors from the boys. She could see the shaft of light beneath their door suddenly go out.

She yanked the candle off the wall sconce. "Ooohhhhh!" She groaned as loud as she could, her voice echoing eerily in the hall. "Ooohhhhh!"

"It's her, I tell you!" She heard Brock's tremulous voice from behind the door.

"There's no such thing as bloody ghosts, you twit!"

She smiled and bumped the pitcher against the wall a few times. She groaned again. When she reached their door, she plopped the pitcher down with a loud thump, then flung their door open. She paused, scanning the room for them.

Two small beds stood on either side of the room. The boys were together in one bed, huddled in a corner, the fear on their faces priceless.

"Did you think you could get away with killing me," Holly said in a low unearthly growl.

Brock pointed to Dryden. "He did it! He did it!"

Dryden looked too scared to speak, his eyes wide open, his jaw agape.

Holly crept further into the room and closed the door behind her.

Dryden pressed his back against the wall like he wanted to dissolve into it. For all his bravado, he appeared more frightened than his brother.

"Please don't hurt us," Brock said. "Dryden is sorry he killed you."

"Is that true?" Holly looked at Dryden.

He opened his mouth to speak. His jaw moved, but no words would come.

"I'll take that as a yes. I hope you know what you did was cruel and uncalled for. Will you mend your ways, Dryden?"

Dryden shook his head, an errant strand of dark, straight hair falling down over his forehead. With the dimple in his chin, and those golden eyes, he looked just like a terrified miniature of John.

Abruptly, a door hit a wall down the hall, then, "Miss Campbell, where are you?"

Holly cringed at John's bellow.

"Was that Papa?" Brock glanced toward the door, then started yelling, "Papa! Papa! Help us!"

"Shhhhh! Don't call for help. Do you want him to find me?" Both boys cocked their heads at her, not understanding the fear in her voice. "Listen, you have to hide me. One word and I'll really be mincemeat." Holly saw relief break out on Dryden's face, then a knowing grin twisted the corners of his lips. After one more glance at him, she blew out the candle and dove beneath the bed. "Remember, Dryden, one wor—"

The door burst open. Light exploded in the room from the candle in John's hand. Holly noticed a piece of her dress sticking out from beneath the bed and jerked it back, hitting her hand on a bed slat. She bit her lip to keep from crying out.

"What's the matter?" Some of the anger left John's voice. "Why were you calling for help?" He strode into the room.

She held her breath and watched his boots getting closer to the bed, the black leather on them glistening with a spit shine.

Dryden spoke first. "It was nothing, Papa."

Holly quietly let out the breath she'd been holding. A dust ball flew up and stuck to her wet lips. She spat it out, certain Dryden would be blackmailing her the rest of her life for what he just told his father. She frowned at the dust bunnies near her face and wondered who cleaned under the beds.

"You should be asleep. Why are you still up?"

"Your bellowing woke us, Papa," Dryden said, an obsequious quality in his voice Holly hadn't heard thus far. "Are you angry at the nanny?"

"That is none of your concern." John paused, then in a voice as brittle as winter straw, he asked, "How do you like her so far?"

"I think she's a . . ." Holly pushed on the mattress, hitting Dryden in the back and making him pause.

"She's a what?"

"She's a very good nanny."

"Yes, I like her very much, Papa," Brock said.

Holly smiled beneath the bed.

"I'm glad you both like her," John said, with no gladness in his voice. "Now, what are you doing in the same bed? Brock, get in your own bed. Now."

Holly saw Brock's bare feet hit the floor then walk over to the opposite side of the room. The bed creaked, then his feet left the floor as he crawled in it.

John's voice grew indulgent. "Now, go back to sleep. I'm sorry I woke you."

She couldn't see him, but she was sure he was tucking Dryden in his bed, then walking over to Brock's bed. "By the way, have you seen Miss Campbell?"

"No, Papa," both boys spoke in unison.

"Very well. Now to sleep with you. I shall see you both in the morning."

She watched John's boots as he headed toward the door. Then it closed and the room was in darkness. His footsteps died away. The tension finally left Holly's body. She crawled out from beneath the bed, then stretched a cramp out of her shoulder and arm. Moonlight streamed in through the small window, bathing the room in soft, dull light. She couldn't see the boys' faces clearly, but she felt their eyes on her.

As she shook the dust off her dress, it galled her to say, "Thank you for saving my hide."

"We are even now, Miss Campbell."

Holly didn't like the devilish tone in Dryden's voice. "All right, we are even, but I don't expect any more pranks from you, either."

"We'll be good," Brock said.

"I know you will. You'll be so busy you'll have to be good."

"Doing what?" Dryden asked.

"I found this lovely little lodge in the forest. I thought we could decorate it for Christmas. It would be our own secret. Maybe you could help me make pine roping for Christmas decorations. Then there are the bows to tie and we can bake cookies. I thought it would be fun."

"It sounds like fu—"

Dryden interrupted Brock. "For your information, we're not celebrating Christmas." Dryden cut his eyes at his brother.

"Perhaps not here in the hall, but what about the lodge? I don't think it would hurt to fix it up a bit."

"I'll help," Brock said, growing bold and avoiding Dryden's gaze.

"Good. We'll have to keep it a secret—especially from your father and Mrs. Pringle. And we'll bake goodies in the lodge. There is a hearth there that we can use."

"Can we eat them?" Brock's excitement slipped into his voice.

"Of course, half the pleasure of Christmas is eating the goodies," Holly said. "I always got a stomachache when Christmas came, because I ate so much of Grandmother's rum-raisin cake. It never failed, every Christmas Eve I spent

the evening over a chamber pot. You would think I'd have
learned after a while not to eat so many sweets, but I never
did."

Brock laughed at this, but Dryden remained silent. His
face was in a shadow, but Holly was sure he was scowling
at her like his father.

"I'm not eating any," Dryden said.

"I'll eat your share," Brock said.

"I don't care."

"We'll save you some just the same," Holly said, pulling
the dust bunnies out of her hair.

"Don't. I won't eat it. And I won't help you decorate. I
hate Christmas," Dryden said, clenching his fists and hitting them on the mattress.

"No one will force you to join us." Holly walked over
to Brock and pulled up the covers around his neck. "There
you are. Are you too big for a good-night hug?"

"I don't think so," Brock said, sounding shy.

"Very well." Holly hugged him, then rustled his hair.
"Good night."

She turned to do the same for Dryden, but his voice
stopped her.

"I don't want to be tucked in—especially by you."

"All right. Good night then, and don't let the bedbugs
bite." Holly smiled at them, then opened the door, peeked
down the hall to make sure it was safe, then tiptoed from
the room. She recalled what Dryden had said about Christmas and hoped he would change his mind. He was a lonely
little boy. She wanted to give him the love and attention
he craved—if he would only let her.

After easing the door closed, she turned to go to her
room, but long, steely fingers clamped around her arm.
She flinched as her heart skipped a beat.

"Did you think I couldn't see you hiding under the bed?"

"J-John." It was the only word she could get out before he pulled her down the hallway.

Chapter 10

"I know you must have spoken to Mr. Scibner. I can explain," Holly said, feeling his fingers tighten like steel jaws around her wrist.

"I intend to give you every chance to do just that." His voice was menacingly low, a barbed edge in every word.

A door swung open and Miss Withers poked out her head, a sleepy look on her face. She watched John drag Holly past her door, then said, "Miss Campbell, there you are. I was so worried when you disappeared. Is there something wrong—"

"Nothing, Miss Withers," John answered for Holly. "Go back to bed."

Miss Withers shot Holly a commiserating look, then closed her door.

"You don't have to pull me, I can walk."

His fingers locked tighter around her wrist and he remained silent. With an angry twist of his hand, he opened her chamber door, pulled her inside, then slammed it. As though remaining close to her would make him lose control, he dropped his hold on her and stepped back in front of the door. He crossed his arms over his chest, blocking the door like an immovable sentry. His anger was a tangible thing that filled the whole room.

"Why did you take it upon yourself to hire a Bow Street Runner?"

The barked words made Holly jump. "I did it because the person trying to ruin you might want to harm you. I thought you could use some assistance." Holly backed away from him until her bottom hit the foot of her bed. Her fingers dug into the coverlet, strangling the material.

"How very considerate of you, especially after I told you I preferred to find the person on my own. The next time you want to interfere, you will allow me the courtesy of telling me about it."

Lady Matilda's words about John proposing to her soon flashed back in Holly's mind. Then a vision of him kissing her on the sidewalk blazed in her memory, along with Lady Matilda's warning that he only wanted her for a mistress. Indignation abruptly replaced her fear.

"Believe me," she said, "I'll never interfere in your life again. Now, if you don't mind, this happens to be my room. It is improper for you to be here. If you wish to berate me further, please do it elsewhere. Now, please leave."

For a long moment, he stared at her and looked surprised by her abrupt coldness, then the dark centers of his eyes grew piercing and the scowl was back in place. "I'm not leaving until you tell me how you could afford to hire Mr. Scibner." His lips thinned to a mulish line. "Bow Street Runners do not come cheaply."

"I'm sure they don't, but since I engaged Mr. Scibner

and he's working for me, I don't think the cost of his fee should bother you."

"Where did you get this money to pay him?" His gaze swept over her once, his eyes lingering, devouring her all the way down to her toes, then he glanced back at her face.

"That is none of your concern, my lord." Holly raised her chin to a haughty angle, feeling her body growing hot from his deliberate perusal.

"It is my concern when you spend it on me, and you obviously need the money." He stared at her again, but this time his gaze flicked over the bottom of her dress.

Holly glanced down at the black ready-made dress Lady Matilda had bought her. The hem was frayed and the seam on the right side torn open, showing her petticoat. She raised her head and met him stare for stare. "I don't need the money. You've given me a job here and a roof over my head. What else do I need?"

"You could start with a dress that doesn't look like you've been attacked by wolves." Some of the raw edge left his voice as he asked, "What happened to you?"

"I fell into a holly bush."

"What the devil were you doing in a holly bush?"

"I tripped."

"How does one trip into a holly bush?"

"It wasn't easy, believe me," Holly said with derision.

"Perhaps you should stay out of the woods if you cannot refrain from falling into trees."

"I'll remember your advice. Now will you please leave my room?" Holly pointed to the door.

"I'll leave as soon as I make myself clear. You'll never again pay one of my bills, or hire someone behind my back. Do you understand?"

"Perfectly."

"And one more thing. Mr. Scibner now works for me. You will have no further contact with him." He left the room without another word, rattling the door on its hinges.

Holly walked over and turned the key in the lock, then beat on the door, punctuating each angry word she uttered. "Ohhhh! Hateful man."

She stepped away, then tore at the hook and eyes at the back of her dress, hearing the seam rip. All he wanted was her body. That was as plain as clear glass. Why hadn't she seen that? She was more angry with herself for acting like a fool and letting him touch her. Well, he wouldn't get another chance.

She should just walk away and forget him. But it was too late, she had embroiled herself in his life, investing in his company, caring for his children, feeling sorry for him. She was in too deep. She had to keep him afloat until he recouped his losses, then she would take what profit she'd made from his company and leave him before he married Lady Matilda.

She recalled Teddy saying John would never marry again for wealth. He must love Lady Matilda, since she obviously was wealthy. The thought made her tear at her dress. She jerked the material off her shoulders, then let it fall to the floor in a torn heap around her feet. The sight of the ugly black dress taunted her. A tear fell from a long, dark lash and landed on the black chintz, rolling down the shiny material to the floor.

Snatching up the dress with an angry swipe, she walked over to the small window in her room. She threw open the sash. A wall of cold air hit her. Sucking in her breath, she balled up the material and sent it flying out the window. It sailed over the roof. The material flapped like the ragged wings of a turkey buzzard, then it disappeared below the eaves. It was a rag now and she was glad of it. The moment

Lady Matilda picked it out, Holly had hated it. She slammed the window closed, then ran over to her bed and hopped into the cold sheets. She shivered and hoped John's sheets were like ice cubes.

" 'Tis my job to warm the master's bed. Now give it to me." Dunn shook his finger at the brass bed warmer in Pringle's hand.

"I always warm his bed when he is here." Pringle looked determined and clutched the handle of the bed warmer.

"You don't, I do it."

"You only do it if I have something else to see to. Now, I'm warming the master's—"

Abruptly, the chamber door flew open. It banged against the wall, making Dunn and Pringle jump. Pringle lost his grip on the warming pan. It fell against the sheets with a loud thud.

Dunn looked at his master standing in the doorway, angry as a demon from hell.

"What the devil is going on here? I could hear you two outside in the hallway."

"Nothing, my lord." Pringle fired Dunn a look, daring him to contradict him, then said, "I was just warming your sheets, my lord."

"Leave it, and be gone."

Pringle set the warmer inside the sheets, then cast Dunn an annoyed glance and left the room.

"Is my bath ready?" His lordship yanked his arms out of his coat, throwing it carelessly on the floor.

Dunn winced when it hit the floor. He ran over and picked it up, smoothing the wrinkles with his hand. "Aye, my lord." Thinking he would be brave, he asked, "How did you find Miss Holly?"

"Hard-headed, willful, shrewish and," he paused and added, "beautiful." He yanked open the buttons on his vest.

Dunn watched him, wincing with each yank on the silk. "Yes, she is that, my lord." Lord Upton heedlessly tossed his vest to the floor. Dunn snatched it up. "I didn't think so at first, but I've decided she is one of the loveliest young women I've ever known."

His master's dark eyes grew darker and he looked through Dunn instead of at him. Some of the anger left his face as he said, "She is lovely, isn't she? There is something so artless and fresh about her, but she wasn't herself. She was cold to me a moment ago. I know not what has gotten into her, but she is not the same woman who left me a day ago."

"Could it be, my lord, you were abrupt with her?"

His master stopped pulling on his cravat and pinned Dunn with one of his scathing glances. "I only pointed out my feelings to her. No, I sensed a coldness in her that had nothing to do with the way I approached her."

"Perhaps I could question her, my lord."

He began jerking at the cravat again. "Can you do it without her finding out I sent you?"

"You know me, my lord, I can get milk out of a bull if need be." Dunn grabbed the cravat before it hit the ground.

His master raised a dark incredulous brow at him. "Very well, see what has come over our Miss Campbell." He unbuttoned his shirt. "I'd be most interested to find out."

"I shall have the news for you tomorrow, my lord." Dunn helped his master off with his shirt, not giving him a chance to throw it on the floor. He folded it and hoped Miss Campbell would be forthcoming with her feelings. If not, he would be in for some grueling days ahead.

He'd never forget the quarrels his master had with Lady Upton before she died about her spending and indiscreet affairs. Lady Upton had loved to rile his master by flaunting her lovers in his face and bringing up the fortune she had brought him. His master had been irritable back then—more than irritable. A frustrated stallion in mating season better described him. Dunn wasn't about to go through that hell again. If the master wanted Miss Campbell, and he must care for her, Dunn would hurry things along.

Early the next morning, Holly saw that the boys ate their breakfast and dressed—in spite of Dryden's protests that he didn't have to wash his face and hands. After a small battle with a washcloth, she sent him to the schoolroom, clean but not very happy.

Now she stepped out of the servants' entrance and headed down the hall toward Ann's chamber.

"Miss Campbell!"

Holly turned at the sound of Dunn's voice and saw him hurrying toward her. He was out of breath by the time he reached her side.

"Good morning, Miss Holly." He smiled at her, his gray eyes twinkling.

"Good morning."

He took in her faded blue dress, then his smile faded.

Holly nervously ran her hands over the front of her old dress, aware she looked like a beggar. "It's all I have," she said, offering an explanation. "I bought material for new dresses, but I haven't had the time to sit down and sew."

"Would you like for me to sew them up for you?"

"You can sew?"

"Yes, miss, I grew up with four sisters. My mother took in sewing to keep food on the table, and she commandeered all of us to help. I was forced to learn to sew. I make all his lordship's clothes. If I may say so, I'm pretty handy with a needle.''

"I thought you said you worked in a stable.''

"Yes, miss, I did when I turned ten and three.''

"So you escaped sewing for horses.''

"You could say that, miss,'' Dunn said with a smile in his voice.

"Well, if you truly don't mind. I could cut out the fabric and leave the pieces with you. I really don't have time to sew, there are so many other things I should be doing.'' Holly thought of the little lodge and the plans she had for it.

"Very well, miss, it would be my pleasure. I should be going now. You can drop the material off for me in his lordship's chamber.''

"But I don't wish to go anywhere near his chamber.'' Holly bit her lip and frowned at Dunn.

"He won't be there, miss. Even if he was, he wouldn't bite your head off.''

"I don't know about that. He chewed my ears off last night.'' Holly pursed her lips and frowned, the image of John's harsh, scowling face rising up to haunt her.

"I'm sure he didn't mean it.''

"I know he has reason to be upset, but he needn't take it out—''

"You don't know, miss, but the bank foreclosed on the townhouse in London.''

"When?''

Dunn clasped his hands in front of him and shook his head. "Yesterday. They swooped down like vultures. Took everything, even Lord Theodore's clothes. I managed to sneak his lordship's clothes out the back.''

"How horrible it must have been,'' Holly said, feeling

those strings that tied her to John growing tighter. She'd have to write Mr. Scibner and tell him to use some of her money to get it back.

"Yes, and humiliating for his lordship." A frown furrowed Dunn's brown brows.

"I'm sure it was. Who is minding the shipping office?"

"Lord Theodore."

"But where is he staying in London?"

"I believe with acquaintances from college."

"Things really are in a muddle," Holly said, more to herself. "Can anything else go wrong?"

"Well, it could. He was upset last night after he came from your room." Dunn watched her closely.

"I'm sure he was. He was like a grizzly bear last night. I probably shouldn't have treated him so rudely, but I won't be his mis—" Holly paused, realizing she'd said too much, then added, "I suppose I should congratulate his lordship on his upcoming wedding."

Dunn looked as if Holly had hit him with a piece of lumber. His mouth fell open, then he closed it and asked, "And who is he supposed to marry?"

"Lady Matilda."

"That's news to my ears."

"Perhaps he's failed to mention it. She told me Lord Upton was in love with her and would ask for her hand any day."

Dunn shook his head. "No, miss, I'd know it if he were thinking of such a thing."

"But she said—"

"Begging your pardon, but don't believe a word that lady says. She's been chasing after him since Lady Upton died, but his lordship has shown no interest in her at all. And if I know my lady, she probably told you he was only showing attentions toward you in hopes of making you his mistress. That's what you were going to say a moment ago, isn't it?''

She nodded, too embarrassed to speak.

He was silent a moment, his expression going from angry to pensive, then he spoke. "I can't set your mind totally at ease on that matter, but I can tell you Lord Upton has a high regard for you. I've been his valet for fifteen years, and I can vouch for his character. He is a man of principle and honor. He would never take an innocent woman— no matter how much he wanted her—and turn her into a mistress. Other noblemen might, but not him.''

A heavy, oppressive feeling lifted from her chest. She grinned at him and said, "Nothing you could have told me could have made me happier. All the while I've been believing what Lady Matilda told me. I should have known better. How can I thank you?'' She bent over and pecked Dunn on the cheek. He was so short she didn't have to stand on her tiptoes to reach his cheek like she did with most men.

His face reddened, then he looked happy about something as he said, "A kiss is thanks enough. I'd better go, miss.''

"Wait!''

"Yes, miss?'' He turned and looked at her.

"I could use your help on something.'' Holly told him about her plans for the lodge, then said, "I hope I can count on you to keep him distracted for a few days. I'll see if Pringle would like to help also, but we must hide the truth from Mrs. Pringle.''

"We can do that. She's all bluster with very little up top.'' Dunn pointed to his temple.

Holly laughed and shook her head. "I feel so sorry for Mr. Pringle. How does he stand her?''

"I've often wondered about that, myself. I believe

women like Mrs. Pringle are all sweet-natured when they're
courting, then once they're married, their true character
emerges. Then their poor husbands are stuck with them,
pining for the sweet-natured girl they fell in love with.''

"Why, Dunn, you have a romantic heart," Holly said,
grinning at him and watching his face turn red again.

"No, miss, just stating plain old facts." He turned and
strolled down the hall.

Holly watched his short, cocky stride. He seemed
delighted about something. Holly hoped she could trust
him to remain quiet about her Christmas plans. She was
sure John would be furious if he found out. Then again,
perhaps it wouldn't be so bad. He could scowl at her all
he wanted, now that she knew he at least respected her
enough not to ask her to be his mistress. She turned and
headed for Ann's room.

She found Ann on the bed, in the exact spot she'd left
her in yesterday. But she was dressed in a lime-green frock.
Her hair was braided back from her face and secured with
a green bow that matched her dress. She was reading,
holding a book in one hand and her doll in the other.

A young girl with bright red hair and freckles pulled a
crocheted throw over Ann's legs with a quick, precise snap.
She glanced over at Holly. "Hello. I'm Sarah Chapman,
Ann's nurse. You must be Miss Campbell."

"Yes."

"Glad to meet you," she said in a harried tone. "I've
been waiting for you. You don't mind if I go and check
on Lady Upton? I can't leave her for a wink. After that
episode with the gun, Mrs. Pringle threatened to fire me
if I didn't keep a closer eye on her. It takes two to do this
job."

"I don't mind."

She nodded, then hurried from the room, her starched bombazine dress rustling as she left.

Ann had glanced up from her book. "I hope Great-grandmama doesn't get into the gun case again."

"I hope not, either." Holly frowned, remembering how she had almost been shot, then changed the subject. "I would like to ask you something."

"What?"

Holly walked over and stood by her bed. "I found a little lodge out in the woods. Would you like to help Brock and me decorate it for Christmas?"

"Christmas . . ." Ann paused, frowned, then said, "We haven't celebrated Christmas since Mama died. I don't want to celebrate Christmas. You won't make me, will you?"

Holly shook her head. "I won't force you to do anything you don't want to do. Will it bother you if *I* celebrate Christmas? You see, my grandmother loved the holidays. If you could have seen our house! My grandmother wouldn't stop until the whole house was trimmed out in greenery and bows." Holly paused and smiled sadly. "But she died, too, and I'm going to miss our Christmases together. I don't think I can go through the holidays without doing something. She would want me to celebrate the holidays."

Ann slowly shook her head, gently stirring long strands of blond hair around her shoulders. Her fingers inadvertently clamped around the doll's waist, her knuckles whitening under the pressure. As if the words were being pulled out of her, she said, "I know what it feels like to miss someone. If it makes you feel better, I'll help you decorate the lodge."

She knew it had cost Ann an awful lot to make the concession. Ann was afraid of Christmas for fear someone else close to her might die. All she needed was one joyful

Christmas to melt her fears. Holly was determined to give it to her.

"I thought you would feel that way," Holly said, then inadvertently leaned over to kiss Ann's forehead.

Ann stiffened and drew away. "My mama used to kiss me like that."

"I'm sorry, I won't do it again if you don't like it."

"Please don't. It doesn't feel right. Papa is the only one who does it now. It feels right when he does it."

Holly hoped one day Ann wouldn't pull away from her. "Would you like to go to the cottage now?" Holly asked hopefully.

Ann hesitated a moment, then said, "I suppose it might be all right."

Holly smiled at her and knew Ann had just crossed a great hurdle in her life. Perhaps with a little encouragement, she'd cross another.

John was on his way to Ann's chamber, when Dunn called behind him, "My lord! My lord!"

John turned to see him running down the hall. He was out of breath when he paused in front of John. It took a moment of panting before he whispered, "I know what upset Miss Holly, my lord."

"What?" John kept his voice low.

"She thought you were interested in her only to make her your mistress."

John paused, thinking the thought had crossed his mind when he'd first met Holly. But after he'd kissed her and found out she didn't know how to kiss a man, he knew just how innocent she was and dashed the idea away. He voiced his thoughts aloud now. "Where the devil did she get such an idea?"

Dunn appeared to take great pleasure in his next words. "Lady Matilda, my lord."

"Why would she tell Miss Campbell such a thing?"

"Jealousy, my lord."

John raked back the errant strand of hair on his forehead. "Lady Matilda is no more jealous of me than she would be of Teddy."

"Forgive me, my lord, but you have been too busy to notice, but Lady Matilda is in love with you."

"Stuff and nonsense. Do you not think I wouldn't notice if a woman was in love with me?"

Dunn paused and weighed what he was about to say. Finally, he said, "In this case, I don't think you have."

John was silent a moment. Could he have misinterpreted Matilda's signals? Could the kindness she'd shown the children been done out of some misplaced affection for him? It still seemed preposterous. But he wasn't concerned about Matilda at the moment, which prompted him to say, "I hope you set Miss Campbell's mind at ease."

"Yes, my lord, I did."

"Very good then, Dunn." John turned to go into Ann's chamber, but Dunn's voice stopped him.

"One more thing, my lord. Later, if you have time, I need you to try on some clothes I believe are getting too small for you."

"Too small?" John stared down at his flat waist, wondering if he'd gained weight and didn't know it.

"Just a few things, my lord—when you can spare the time."

"All right." John dismissed him with a wave of his hand, then he opened Ann's chamber door.

Holly was tying a bonnet on Ann's head. She saw him and smiled, her dimples beaming, her large brown eyes glowing with a liquid softness that melted over him like butter. Whatever Dunn had said to her did the trick. She was smiling at him again. His body responded immediately to the ravishing, disheveled sight of her. She wore the same old blue dress in which he'd found her, but it displayed her full breasts enticingly. Her hair was pulled back in a bun. Wisps of curly auburn hair had escaped and framed her oval face with windblown perfection. She looked artlessly beautiful, and tempting enough to drive a man to lust.

Ann saw him. She shoved the bonnet and Holly's hands aside, crying, "Papa! Papa! You're home!"

Every time he saw his little girl's eyes light up for him, a knot grew in the back of his throat. He swallowed hard, then in two long strides, he was at her side, snatching her up in his arms.

She wrapped her tiny arms around his neck, then she was kissing his cheek. "I'm so glad you're home."

"Me too, puss." He returned the kiss and felt her thin, useless legs pressing against his forearm. Forcing a smile, he said, "Have you missed me as much as I missed you?"

"More." She kissed him again, then she drew back, her expression serious. "Have you met the new nanny, Papa? This is Miss Campbell."

"We've met." John smiled at Holly. "I hired Miss Campbell. So, how do you like her?"

"Oh, Papa, I can't tell you now." Ann glanced over at Holly, looking sheepish.

"And why not? I think Miss Campbell should know how you feel about her."

"I'll leave if it bothers you." Holly turned toward the door.

"No, stay. It is all right," Ann said. "I don't mind telling him with you here." She turned back to John. "Miss Campbell is different than the rest. She's not afraid of me like the rest of them were."

"They were afraid of you?"

"Not of me, exactly." She paused, made a moue with her lips, then said, "Of my legs, you know."

"Oh."

"You know what else she told me?"

"I'm almost afraid to ask." John grinned at Holly again.

"She said there were fairies in the sunlight, so I've been keeping my curtains open during the day. Mrs. Pringle doesn't like it, but I told Sarah to keep them open anyway. You know what else, Papa?"

"What?"

"Miss Campbell even tried to kiss me, but I told her I only let you kiss me."

"I'm honored." John nuzzled her cheek again.

"Your whiskers hurt when you do that. Miss Campbell doesn't have whiskers like you." Ann rubbed her hand over the stubble on his chin.

"I hope not." John's grin widened as he stared at Holly's rosy lips.

Holly laughed and brought Ann's attention back to her.

"Oh, Miss Campbell, I forgot to tell you," Ann said, her voice laced with an unusual enthusiasm. "Guess what I saw?"

"Let me think . . ." Holly tapped the side of her temple, then her voice grew excited. "Could it be that a fire-breathing dragon flew right past your window and singed your eyebrows?"

"There are no such things as dragons."

"Then a giant walked past your window, barely missing the side of the house. And the ground shook when he walked, and when he breathed on the house, smoke came down the chimney."

"No," Ann giggled. "You're being silly again, Miss Campbell. I saw a fairy."

"Just a fairy?" Holly feigned a look of disappointment.

"I bet you've never seen the kind of fairy I saw," Ann said, bragging. "It had white transparent wings and glowed all over."

"It sounds lovely. You're right. I've never seen one so beautiful."

"Tina saw it, too." She motioned with her head toward her doll.

"Well, if she saw it, too, then I'm glad both of you saw it at the same time," Holly said. "That never happens. Usually fairies only appear to one person. We should celebrate the occasion."

John smiled at Holly. Her influence on Ann was amazing. Since Ann had stopped walking, the only thing that cheered her were his visits. He'd despaired that her illness had smothered all her youthful zeal for life and the ability to believe in fantasy, the kind of fantasy so much a part of childhood dreams. But it appeared that Holly had begun to give that back to Ann.

He gently placed Ann on the bed, then dragged his gaze from Holly. "I suppose I should come back later to see you so you can speak to Miss Campbell about fairies and the like."

"Please don't leave on my account. I just came to see if Ann would go for a walk with me. I intend to ask her brothers to go with us, too—if I can drag them from the schoolroom."

"Papa, will you go with us?"

Before John could answer, Holly said, "I'm sure your papa has better things to do. I thought this could just be the four of us."

John glanced at Holly. She stared back at him, smiling,

her lips tight. He wondered why she didn't want him along. Perversity made him say, "Yes, I think I shall go with you. You'll let me know when you are ready, won't you, Miss Campbell?"

A taut smile hid Holly's disappointment. "Yes, of course. I should go to the schoolroom and tell the boys then." She curtsied, then turned and strode to the door.

John watched the sway of her hips beneath her dress, and didn't think he'd mind at all keeping an eye on Holly. It would be prudent if the children were along, then he might be able to control his desire for her. Even now, his loins pained him for want of her nearness. He watched her disappear through the threshold and into the hall and felt a sense of loss at her absence.

"Do you like Miss Campbell, Papa?"

He turned and stroked the top of her small head. "Yes, I like her."

"So do I." Ann snuggled next to him, nestling her head in the crux of his arm.

John hugged her and knew his feelings for Holly ran much deeper than mere fondness.

As Holly walked up the servants' stairs, she grumbled under her breath, "Why did he have to decide to go with us? He's spoiling everything."

When she reached the top floor, she stepped out of the stairwell and ran into Mrs. Pringle.

She bristled, hitched up her ample bosom with the inside of her arms, then narrowed her eyes at Holly. "There you are. I've been looking the house over for you."

Holly braced herself for another verbal attack. "What is the matter?"

"How dare you tell Lady Ann that she should open her

drapes. And that silly nonsense about fairies. That's all the child can talk about."

"I'm sorry, but I thought the sunlight would cheer her up."

"The doctor left strict orders that she should stay out of the air."

"I'm convinced doctors know very little. One bled my grandmother to death, so you see I'm not sure listening to everything they say is such a good idea. My grandmother always said, 'There's nothing that a walk in the fresh air and bright sunlight can't cure.' It always worked for me."

"It might work for you, but around here, we do what the doctor says. I won't have you putting such notions in her head. And that business about the fairies is just plain nonsense."

"I didn't see any harm in stimulating her imagination. It might get her mind off her legs."

Mrs. Pringle's cheeks blew out and she shook her finger in Holly's face. "From now on, mind your own business and stop putting silly notions in the child's head. She's lame, she has to learn to live with it."

"Yes, she does." Holly was silent a moment, then said, "That's why I don't see any harm in giving her a little joy in her life."

"Then you intend to encourage such nonsense?"

Holly nodded.

"We shall see about that. I'll tell the master." Mrs. Pringle turned to leave.

"I'm not your enemy, Mrs. Pringle, even though you believe it," Holly said, watching Mrs. Pringle turn around and glare at her.

"No, but you forget who's in charge here. I've been taking care of Lady Ann since she was born, and I won't have the likes of you telling me how to care for her."

Mrs. Pringle's back straightened, hefting out her bosom, rattling the keys on her necklace.

"I'm not trying to take your place, Mrs. Pringle. I only want what is best for Ann." Holly gritted her teeth to keep from saying more, then turned and strode toward the schoolroom.

Mrs. Pringle huffed under her breath. Then the door slammed and heavy footsteps pounded the stairs in the stairwell.

Holly shook her head and paused in front of the schoolroom door. It took several deep, calming breaths to compose herself, then she quietly opened it. The sight that greeted her made her fingers tighten around the doorknob and her jaw clamp together so hard her teeth ached.

Chapter 11

Brock sat at a table, quill poised over paper. In spite of the tight, white-knuckled grasp he had on the feather, his hand trembled. His bottom lip protruded and quivered. He glanced up at Miss Withers with terror in his eyes.

She stood beside him, glaring down at him, then slammed a cane down on the table. "That is all wrong. Do you not know that four times six is twenty-four? Do it again."

Whack. The rod hit the table again.

Brock cringed, the cane inches from his hand.

Holly saw his hands now and the black-and-blue marks on his fingers. A dark figure in the corner drew her gaze. Dryden stood, facing the wall. His arms were pulled back behind him, his fingers laced in a fingerstock, a wooden device with holes drilled into it to hold a child's fingers in place.

After a moment of blinking in disbelief, Holly flung the

door back. It banged against the wall. Miss Withers jumped at the loud noise, turned, then saw Holly, the cruelty hiding in her eyes earlier blatant now.

Without taking her eyes off Miss Withers, Holly marched into the room and stepped up to the woman. She was five inches taller than Holly and probably outweighed her by twenty pounds. But that did not stop Holly from glaring up at her and jerking the cane from her hand.

Miss Withers narrowed her beady eyes at Holly. "How dare you! What are you doing in here, Miss Campbell?"

Holly shook the cane in Miss Withers's face, punctuating each word. "How could you use this on the children?"

"Now, see here." Miss Withers bristled, her turkey neck elongating, the thin waddlelike skin beneath her chin stretching. "That is the only way I can keep order in this schoolroom. I have to discipline them somehow."

"There are ways to discipline children. This is not one of them." Holly brought the cane up and broke it over her knee. The crack sounded like the strike of a lightning bolt in the silence. She stomped over to Dryden, who turned to look at her with amused wonder and awe in his eyes.

"Are you hurt?" Holly helped him ease his fingers out of the stock, then flung it in a wastebasket in the room.

He shook his head.

"Are you sure?" She wasn't convinced and touched his shoulder.

He winced and backed away. "I'm all right."

Holly stared at him a moment. "Let me see your back."

"No." He pulled away from her.

"The child is fine," Miss Withers said, angling her pointed jaw. "I only punished him for what he did yesterday. He knows he deserved every whack."

Through gritted teeth, she hissed, "You don't want to

speak to me at the moment." Holly jabbed her finger at the window. "For two cents, I'd toss you out there and not look back." She grabbed Dryden's hand and pulled him toward the door and called over her shoulder, "Brock, come with me."

"Where are we going? I don't want to go." Dryden was fighting her in the hallway, trying to wrench her hand from around his wrist.

"We are going to see your father." Holly held on with both hands and jerked him toward the door to the steps. He tried to kick her, but Holly was too quick and jumped aside. She grabbed his shoulder, deliberately putting pressure on his sore back.

He froze, his face contorted in pain.

"Now listen to me, young man, we are going down those steps to Ann's room and find your father, then you are going to show your back to him, since you wouldn't let me see it. What that woman did to you was wrong, and I won't have her doing it again. Now, get moving."

"Why do you care?" Dryden said through his teeth. "Just leave me alone."

"No, I won't. And I do care about you, whether you like it or not. Now, get down those steps and act like the gentleman I know you can be." She dropped her hold on him, afraid she was hurting him.

He cut his golden eyes at her, looking just like his father.

"Ah, go on," Brock urged Dryden, and stepped up to Holly's side.

"You're with her, aren't you?" Dryden sounded like he'd lost faith in his brother.

"She's right. Miss Withers should never have beat you this morning."

Dryden looked askance at Brock, then at Holly. "All

right, maybe I can convince him to get rid of you, too."
With that, he stomped down the steps.

"He'll get over it, Miss Campbell," Brock said, sounding
apologetic while he started down the steps with Holly.

"I know he will." Holly listened to Dryden's stiff footsteps echoing below her and wasn't sure of her words.

"I heard that, and I won't ever like you!" Dryden bel-
lowed up the stairwell.

"But I'll still like you." Holly heard his footsteps almost
running now. He'd run from anyone willing to care about
him, but she was determined to break that calloused facade
and reach that part of him crying out to be loved.

John heard a noise in the hallway, then Ann's chamber
door burst open. Dryden stood in the threshold, heaving.
He glanced at John, then over his shoulder, an expression
on his face as if Satan were chasing him.

A moment later, Holly appeared behind him, her large
expressive brown eyes filled with anxiety, her face flushed
with it. Brock emerged and stood in front of her.

Little of Brock's timid air came through the mask of
fear on his face. His youngest son was a follower, not a
leader like Dryden. John wished Dryden would start to
lead his brother in the right direction for once.

He looked at both boys, then tried to keep the impatience out of his voice. "Are you here for a reason?" John
addressed Brock, since he knew his youngest son would
tell the truth.

Both boys stood there like stone statues.

Holly stepped past them. "I believe the boys have something to tell you, my lord," she said, an undercurrent in
her voice. "I'll get Ann ready to go for our walk while you
speak to them." She glanced toward the door anxiously,

a silent appeal for him to speak to the boys out in the hallway.

"You can speak to them here," Ann piped up, hugging her doll.

"No, I believe this matter requires some privacy." John stood, glanced at Holly one last time and saw the distress on her face, then guided both boys out the door.

He closed the door behind him, then asked, "Now, what is the matter?" He looked into Dryden's stubborn mien, then turned to Brock.

Brock punched his brother's arm. "Tell him."

"I will." Dryden punched him back.

"Tell me what?" John stepped between them and grabbed their arms.

"It's about Miss Withers, Papa," Brock spoke up.

"What about her?"

As if summoned by her name, the woman came hurrying down the hallway. She clutched her chest and took a moment to catch her breath, then said, "I demand to be heard on this issue, my lord."

"What issue?"

"This . . ." Brock grabbed Dryden's shirt, then yanked it out of his pants and up to the top of Dryden's shoulder blades.

John's jaw slackened when he looked at Dryden's back. Three raised whelps slashed across his back and shoulders. The skin was swollen and had turned purple and red.

He clenched his fists and glared at Miss Withers, his temper barely checked. Through his teeth, he said, "Did you do this?"

"He tied me up yesterday. I thought I would never get loose. I've taken all the abuse from him I can stand. He deserved a good punishment and I gave it to him."

"She did this, too, Papa." Brock held out his hands, the bruises evident on his fingers and palms.

John held back the urge to wring her thin neck. "If there is punishment to be given in this household, I will do it, Miss Withers. Now, get your things and get out of my house."

"I'll get out all right," she spat at him. "They're brats, the both of them. And that little monster will end up killing someone one day, you mark my words. He should be put away in a school where they can handle problem children like him. They would do worse to him than I did."

"That is quite enough. If you don't get out of my house this very minute, I'll throw you out." John took a step toward her and saw her bolt down the hall. She flounced through the door to the stairwell and slammed it behind her.

He turned back to Dryden, who wore a devilish grin as he watched Miss Withers's exit.

Dryden saw his father watching him and the grin faded.

"You, young man, know better than to tie someone up. You are supposed to be setting the example for your brother. I'm disappointed in you, Dryden. Very disappointed."

"She deserved—" One sharp glance from John and Dryden clamped his mouth shut.

"I should punish you, but Miss Withers has seen to that." He saw a gloating smile tug at the corners of Dryden's lips and added, "This doesn't mean we are done with this incident. Tomorrow I want a written dissertation on why you must respect your elders and those of authority over you."

"What about Brock? He helped."

"You, too, young man." John pointed to Brock.

Brock cut his eyes at Dryden, shooting him a thanks-a-lot look.

"Dryden, you will have Dunn look at your back," John said. "Then you will go for a walk with your sister and Miss Campbell so your back does not get stiff and sore."

"But I hate Miss Campbell—"

John silenced Dryden with another look. "Why do you hate Miss Campbell?"

"I just do. I wish she'd never come here."

"I like her," Brock added stubbornly.

"Who asked you?" Dryden hit his brother's arm.

"That is enough. Dryden, you will go for this walk and you will be pleasant company for your sister and Miss Campbell."

"Yes, Papa." Dryden poked out his bottom lip, turned, then headed for the door. Brock followed him down the hall.

"See what trouble she got us into," Dryden said, stomping down the hall. "I don't know why you listened to her. I didn't want to show him to begin with."

"Shut up," Brock said. "I like her better than you. At least we're rid of the Withers . . ."

"Yeah, but now *she's* here."

"I hope she stays."

"Well, I don't. She's too nice. There's always something wrong with chits who are too nice."

"I don't care what you think, I like her. And she's pretty, too. I wish she were our mother."

"Don't even think it . . ."

Dryden's voice faded as the boys disappeared behind the stairwell door. In spite of his anger, John found himself smiling.

He heard Holly laughing behind the chamber door, and Brock's words came back to haunt him. "I wish she were our mother." Holly would make a good mother for his children. They needed a mother. He couldn't be with them and run the shipping company, too. He hated to think what Miss Withers would have done to the children had Holly not been here. Holly was a godsend.

Then again, she was a curse. Her youth and artless candor had awakened a longing in him that could consume him. He'd never wanted a woman like he wanted her. Not even Elise had stirred such desire in him. If she'd had Holly's warmth, or even a small portion of it, she might have, but there was a frosty aloofness about Elise that didn't allow him, or anyone, to get close to her. Holly would give herself to him, heart and soul. He knew it the first time he kissed her. And he wanted that warmth, needed it in his life.

But he couldn't have her. That was the torture of it. Until his finances were in a better state, he couldn't marry her. It was humiliating enough to put his own family through such disgrace. Then there was her past over in the Colonies that troubled him. She was definitely hiding something. But what? Hopefully, Scibner would provide some answers, and soon. His frown deepened.

He knocked on the door, then poked his head in the room. Holly was tucking Ann in her push chair. She turned and smiled at him. He tried not to look at her dimples. "I've decided I should stay here and see that our Miss Withers is escorted where she needs to go," he said, "so I shall have to decline the walk. Perhaps another time."

"Oh, Papa, we'll miss you." Ann paused and looked confused about something, then said, "Is Miss Withers going somewhere?"

"She'll be leaving her position here," John said, glancing at Holly.

Holly met his gaze and looked relieved.

"Oh." Ann stared down at her doll.

John's whole body strained as he asked his next question. "Did Miss Withers ever hurt you, Ann?"

"No, she was very nice to me. Did she hurt someone else?"

The tension in his chest eased as he said, "Yes, she punished Dryden severely."

"I did hear her say Dryden needed punishing, and he was always upsetting Miss Withers. Dryden behaves badly."

"Yes, well, he'll behave now that I am here."

"Are you sure you won't come with us, Papa? We shall miss you on our walk." Ann stared up at him, her eyes pleading.

"Yes, we shall." Holly glanced at him with sincere regret glistening in her large brown eyes.

It took every ounce of John's willpower to say, "I promise to go another time."

"Will you send Dunn to look at Dryden's back?" Holly asked. "I'd go to him, but I know he won't let me near him."

"I already sent him to Dunn. I'd like to speak to you later about Dryden."

"I've been meaning to talk to you, too."

"Very well, when you finish with your outing, we shall talk."

Holly nodded. John's gaze fell to her full breasts pulling against the bodice of her dress, and remembered the way they filled his palms. He looked at her ripe red lips and wanted to taste them again. A vision of stripping off her clothes rose up to torture him. Damnation, but he knew he had made the right decision not to go on the walk. The less time he spent with her, the better.

Lady Upton appeared in the doorway, a cane in her hand, which she carried like a club instead of using it to steady herself. She wore a faded green satin gown, with wide sleeves. It had been the height of fashion in the last century. Her face was powdered, but some of the white powder had fallen on the collar of her gown and made it look like she had a terrible case of dandruff. But even in her state of disorder, there was something regal in her bearing that not even her lapses of memory could diminish.

She lifted her quizzing glass and peered at John. "Well, I thought I heard your voice, John John. I suppose you've made love to everyone in the room, but now that your grandmama is here, you stand there like a stump in need of a good boot in the bottom."

John smiled at her, then went to her side, placing a kiss on her wrinkled cheek. He stepped back from her. "How are you, madam?"

"I've never felt better. The pigeons are still on the roof. Would you see to shooting them? They really are a nuisance."

"Yes, madam, right away."

She looked from Holly to John. "Who is this person?"

"This is Miss Campbell," John said, smiling indulgently at Holly. "Miss Campbell meet my grandmother, the Dowager Countess of Upton."

Holly grinned at her and curtsied. "Pleased to make your acquaintance, Lady Upton. Ann and I were about to go for a walk. Would you like to walk out with us?"

Lady Upton smiled down at Ann, then touched the bottom of Ann's chin. "What a beautiful child you are."

Ann smiled timidly. "You remember me don't you, Great-grandmama? I'm Ann."

"Of course I remember you," she said, indignant, then turned to Holly. "I should like to take the air with you— I'd prefer a gallop. I always took a morning ride when my

Alistair was alive, but John John hasn't kept a stable for some time." She raised her quizzing glass and leveled it at him. "All he's got in there is that stud of his, and no one in their right mind would ride him. I believe John John is in Dunn Territory, though he rarely discusses such things with me. We St. Johns have never been without horses in our stables. What is the trouble, John John?"

"Nothing you need worry over, madam," he said, humiliation burning his cheeks.

"See, what did I tell you? Stubborn he is, just like my son for the world, though he is not plagued with the vices my Rupert had—gambling, a nasty pastime. He's handsome like his father, though. Rotten luck, my Rupert should leave him in such debt. I'd hoped he could pull us out of it, but he doesn't have the knack for making money like my husband, Alistair—though, believe me, he used enough of my dowry to make his fortune." She chuckled at Holly, her wrinkles stretching across her face.

"I don't see why John John doesn't marry a rich widow, but he's one for procrastination, and he's got that damnable pride like Rupert had. But money doesn't grow on trees, you know. Are you rich, my dear?" She gave Holly a once-over look.

Before Holly could answer, John said derisively, "If you are done bragging me up, madam, should you not think about your outing now? I'll expect a full report when you get back." He hoped that would change the subject.

He headed for the door, avoiding Holly's gaze. She was grinning at him, he could feel it, the way he could sense her presence in a room. He closed the door behind him, then walked down the hall, wondering how much longer he could stand being near Holly without touching her.

* * *

John sat at his desk, separating the bills from the personal letters. His hand paused over a letter from Mr. Scibner. He broke open the seal and read:

> *Greetings, Lord Upton,*
> *Our friend Jarvis has yet to contact anyone, but I'm still having him watched. I wrote about the other matter and expect to hear back in six weeks or so.*
>
> > *My best regards,*
> > *J.S.*

John frowned down at the letter, then heard a knock on the door. "Enter," he said, folding the letter and tucking it into his drawer.

Pringle walked into his office, a black dress slung over his arm. It looked like the dress Holly had on last night.

Pringle paused, then said, "My lord, I have safely escorted Miss Withers to the gates. May I say how sorry I am to learn that she was cruel to the children. Had I known I would have tossed her out on her ear."

John knew if any tossing were to be done, Mrs. Pringle would probably do it. "I know that, Pringle. What is that slung over your arm?"

Pringle frowned down at the shredded material. "I believe it is a dress that belongs to Miss Holly, my lord."

"What the deuce are you doing with it?" John eyed him, perplexed and bitten by a mild pang of jealousy.

Pringle glanced at him. In an uneasy voice he said, "I was just returning it, my lord."

"Returning it?" Every muscle in John's body grew taut. This jealousy was ridiculous. Pringle would never seduce

Holly, but still he couldn't help this possessive feeling where she was concerned.

"Yes, I found it on the terrace."

"What the bloody hell was it doing on the terrace?"

"Not exactly on the terrace, my lord."

"Where then?"

"Stuck on a drain pipe, my lord. I saw it waving up there like a flag and had to get a ladder to get it down."

"Give me the dress, I'll return it to her." John relaxed back in his chair.

He handed John the dress, his hands trembling slightly. "Will there be anything else?"

"Yes. Would you tell Dunn I'll need my riding clothes. I believe Whisper is in need of exercising." He couldn't bear to part with his last stallion and kept him in the country, for it was too expensive to keep him in London. He rubbed his fingers against the black chintz dress and added, "Lawrence still works in the stable and takes care of the aviary, does he not?"

"Aye, my lord, he's staying on with us, though he hasn't received a wage in over two months."

"I know," John said, his fingers tightening around the material. "I also realize I owe you and Mrs. Pringle back pay. You will get it."

"I have no doubt of it, my lord," Pringle said with confidence. "We're in no rush. We worked for your father when he was late on wages, and we'll work for you, no matter what."

"I appreciate your loyalty." John felt his face reddening.

Pringle must have sensed John's embarrassment, for he bowed and said, "I'll go and inform Dunn, my lord."

John watched Pringle leave the room and unconsciously twisted Holly's dress in his hands. He frowned, and then looked toward the door, hearing footsteps.

Mrs. Pringle's wide body filled the doorway. "My lord, may I have a word?" she asked.

"What is it?"

"It's about Miss Campbell. I think you should fire her."

"Fire Miss Campbell." John leaned back in his seat and rested the dress over his knees. He rubbed his thumb over the crisp fabric and asked, "Whatever for?"

"She is poisoning poor Lady Ann's mind. She is only a child. And she opened her curtains so the draft would get to her. Now I have just learned she has taken the child for a walk after I told her what the doctor said. She is insolent to me and refuses to submit to my authority. I can't run this hall without—"

John raised his hand, cutting her off. "She stays, Mrs. Pringle."

"But—"

"But nothing. My daughter is the happiest I've seen her in a long time, and I believe Miss Campbell is the reason. Now, we will not speak of this again. And you will allow Miss Campbell to take Ann out. Is that clear?"

"Yes, my lord," Mrs. Pringle said through her teeth, then curtsied and left the room, her keys jingling around her neck.

John glanced down at the dress laying across his thighs. A sudden desire to see Holly, to hold her, clawed at him. He had used the excuse of exercising his horse as a pretense for leaving the hall, but what he really wanted was to be near her. He stood and strode toward the stable.

"Look, Miss Campbell," Ann whispered, "there's a deer."

Holly stopped pushing the chair. A deer stood on the

path, seventy feet in front of them, sharpening his horns on the side of a thick ash.

Brock, Dryden, and Lady Upton had been walking behind Holly and Ann. They strode up behind Holly and stared at the deer.

The buck caught a whiff of their scent and turned to look at them. A cloud of white condensation blew out from his glistening black nose. His large dark eyes locked with Holly's for a brief moment. He dipped his horns as if to say "How do you do," then darted off the path.

Holly watched him leap through the woods, his hooves barely touching the ground, sailing over fallen logs and past leafless shrubs and trees as if he were weightless.

"Wasn't he beautiful?" Ann's voice still held excitement and awe in it.

"One of the largest I've ever seen at Brookhollow," Lady Upton said, staring at the spot the deer had just left.

"It was just a buck," Dryden said tonelessly.

"He was a beautiful creature," Ann said passionately. "Dryden, you never see any beauty in anything. Can you not for once look at something and admire it for what it is?"

"A deer is not for admiring, it's for sport and eating."

"You wouldn't kill that deer," Ann said, on the verge of tears.

"I will when Papa takes me shooting."

Holly was about to call Dryden down, but Brock said, "Stop teasing her."

"I'll do what I—" Dryden paused at the cadence of hooves pounding the ground behind them.

Holly saw John galloping toward them on a huge chestnut stallion. Never slowing once, he dodged low-lying limbs like an Indian trick rider Holly had seen at a circus in

Richmond, leaning from side to side, gracefully keeping his balance. He looked very determined to join them.

"Look," Lady Upton said, still staring at the spot where they'd seen the deer, "there's a person hunting on our land. They have a rifle."

Holly glanced through the woods and saw someone sitting on a horse. A hood covered the person's face, only the eyes were exposed. She couldn't see the color, the person was too far away. But she did see the rifle clutched at their side.

"They're not going to shoot the deer!" Ann cried.

"No, child, you need not worry," Lady Upton said in a nonchalant voice. "He's pointing the sights this way. We had better get down."

Before Holly could scream, Lady Upton shoved Ann out of the chair, then knocked Brock and Dryden to the ground. Moving with the lightning reflexes of a young woman, she whipped around and tackled Holly. They hit the ground with a hard thud. But the sound was absorbed by the ear-splitting blast from the gun.

Chapter 12

Holly's ears still rang from the loud report of the gun, but she could hear the hammering of hooves behind her. John. He could be shot! She raised her head and frantically looked for him. He was galloping across the path, not ten feet from her. She felt a moment of relief. But it was short-lived as he rode right past her, his horse's hooves churning up clods of earth.

Their eyes met for a moment, and his eyes burned with a ruthless determination as he yelled, "Take the children back to the house!"

Why didn't he stop? She sat up on her knees, cupped her hands, and screamed, "Wait! Wait!" He acted as if he didn't hear her and galloped toward the man who had shot at them.

Another shot.

John ducked to the side. Her heart leaped into her

throat. She half expected him to fall from the saddle, but he sat up and continued straight for the shooter.

When John didn't stop, the hooded rider must have decided John was a madman, for he whipped his horse around and galloped off through the woods. John rode after him the way a crazed soldier would, yelling expletives at the person like a battle cry. Holly watched John's black cape flowing out behind him, flapping over his horse's glistening coal-black rump. Her gaze stayed glued to him until horse and rider became one dark, blurred entity among the trees.

"Geminy! Did you see Papa? He rode right for that man," Brock said, raising his head off the ground.

"Sure he did. He's no chicken heart," Dryden said.

Holly turned and helped Ann back up into her chair, then grabbed Lady Upton's arm. "Let me help you, madam," Holly said.

"My word! I didn't know my heart could still tick like that." Lady Upton smiled as she took Holly's hand.

"You saved our lives." Holly straightened Lady Upton's wig, which had fallen over her right ear.

"What else is an old lady good for?" Lady Upton beat the dried leaves and dirt off her burgundy wool coat.

"I think we should all go back to the house now and wait for Papa," Ann said, her bottom lip trembling with fear.

"I think so, too." Holly found that her hands were trembling so, she could hardly push Ann's chair.

"Will Papa be all right?" Tears glistened in Ann's eyes.

"Yes, he will," Holly said, forcing a confidence in her voice that she didn't feel. She glanced back at the woods and bit her lip. What if he were killed? The person bent on destroying him might be trying to kill him now. Tears burned her own eyes.

* * *

Four hours later, Holly paced in the foyer and watched candlelight flicker along the walls. A hall clock chimed seven times. Each bong pounded against Holly's eardrums like a massive church bell. She glanced at the door, something she'd done more times than she could count. Where was John? Pringle and Dunn had gone out looking for him. Holly had wanted to go, but they refused to let her. She wasn't good at waiting. She'd rather be out doing something than waiting and envisioning terrible things.

Her mind had conjured up all sorts of images of him, laying on the ground bleeding to death. Or worse yet, having fallen from his horse and broken his neck. And then she'd seen him tackle the man, only to be shot . . .

A sound from outside made her glance again at the door.

The door opened. A blast of frigid air blew through the foyer, then John appeared. His face was chafed from the cold, his lips blue. His teeth chattered as he glanced up at her.

Without thinking, Holly ran to him, then threw her arms around him. "I was so worried." She buried her face in his cape. The black wool felt cold and rough against her cheek. The brisk smell of the forest and fresh air lingered on him and mixed with the odor of horse, leather, and his own clean scent. She breathed deeply, unable to believe he was home.

He slammed the door with his foot, then his strong arm encompassed her. "I wondered what I would have to do to get you in my arms again. Did you miss me?" He tipped her chin up and made her look at him, then grinned down at her, his eyes searching her face.

"I thought you were dead."

"Would you cry at my funeral?"

"That's a horrible thing to ask me." Holly raised her hand to hit him on the chest.

He grabbed her wrist. "You give me hope, my sweet. At least I know you care."

He tilted her face higher, then brought his lips down to hers. The force of his kiss stole her breath. She reveled in the feel of him holding her, his cold lips moving across hers, his tongue urging her mouth open. She opened for him, allowing him access.

Her knees grew weak and she leaned against him. Holly heard her grandmother's voice in the back of her mind, saying, "Stay away from a man who can make your knees weak with a kiss, honey, or you'll regret it." Her grandmother had been a wise lady. Holly knew she'd regret giving in to this passion, but she possessed no defenses against it. She wanted him to touch her, needed to feel that he was still alive and close to her.

"I want you, Holly. All I could think about was coming home to you . . ." He kissed a line down her throat, the stubble on his chin brushing against her soft skin. Then his hands were on her breasts.

Holly moaned, ready to give him anything he wanted. Surrendering to the heat of his hands and lips, she arched her back.

She didn't realize someone had opened the door until John broke the kiss and stepped back from her. She felt the cold air brush against her as Dunn came through the threshold. Pringle was hard on his heels.

"My lord, you are home," Pringle said, trying to sound as if he hadn't caught them kissing, but the shock on his face was plain.

Dunn was blatantly smiling. "We combed the countryside, my lord. We'd given up hope."

"The bastard knew this area. I tracked him for miles, but he kept just out of my reach, then I lost him."

"Do you think it is the same man who is trying to ruin your company?" Holly asked, her voice still tremulous from the kiss.

"I don't know. He had ample chances to shoot me, but he shot over my head to scare me away." John was pensive for a beat, then said, "It looked to me like the person he was aiming for was you, Holly."

"That is utter nonsense. Why would someone be shooting at me?"

"I don't know." John looked at her from behind lowered brows. "I was hoping maybe you could tell me that."

"I've done nothing to make anyone want to kill me."

"No? Suppose it was someone who followed you over here from the Colonies?"

"No one knows I'm here." Holly glanced down at the dimple in his chin, unable to look him in the eye.

"Who doesn't know?"

"No one."

"You're bound to have some family members wondering where you are."

"I don't. I'm all alone."

He grabbed Holly's arms and stared down at her, all the desire gone from his eyes. They were cold, hard, determined. "Tell me if you are in trouble," he urged.

"I'm not in trouble." Holly flinched, then knocked his hands away. "It's you who's in trouble. That man was trying to kill you, not me, but you are too stubborn to see that. Now, I'm going to my room." Holly knew if she didn't leave, she'd burst into tears. She hurried down the hall toward the servants' stairs and didn't stop running until she reached her room and slammed the door closed.

Why couldn't he stop badgering her about her past? He

would never stop until she left. But she couldn't leave, not knowing that someone was trying to kill him. Holly sat on her bed and had a good cry.

The next morning, Holly knocked on John's study door.

"Come." His voice sounded deeper and sharper behind the closed door.

Holly straightened her shoulders, steeling her courage. She prayed he wouldn't question her again about her past. Gingerly, she opened the door and stepped inside. "You needed to see me," she said, watching him as he stood before a gun case.

His back was to her. When he reached for a gun, his broad shoulders stretched against a white linen shirt, every rippling muscle along his broad back outlined. The chiseled V of his chest tapered down to a thin waist and slim hips. Crisp dark-brown hair hung down to the bottom of his collar. She noticed how long and graceful his fingers were as they closed around the gun and he pulled it from the case. He looked devastatingly handsome. In spite of her grandmother's warning, she longed to run her fingers through his thick hair and to feel his lips on her mouth.

"I did want to see you." He turned and his gaze flicked down her body, then back up to her face. "I see you have on a new dress."

"Yes. Dunn made it for me." Holly nervously smoothed out nonexistent wrinkles in the yellow gingham dress.

"It becomes you," he said, his tone velvety soft.

"Thank you." Holly blushed and wrung her hands.

"Please sit down." He glanced down at the rifle in his hands, then motioned to a chair in the room. "There's something I wish to discuss with you."

"What is it?"

"It's Dryden. He is not a gregarious child and a bit hard to get to know. He wasn't always like that. Since his mother died he's turned into a different child. I hope he does not frighten you away."

"I'm not afraid of Dryden."

"I know he resents you for some reason." He laid the rifle across his desk, then sat. The old leather chair creaked under his weight; the sound was like a hiss in the silence.

Holly's brows came together, then she said, "I'm afraid he does."

"I can't imagine why."

"I'm not quite sure myself." She chewed on her lip while she thought, then said, "I did try to show him extra attention. Perhaps he resented that. He might have thought I was trying to take his mother's place, but I was only trying to be his friend. He seemed like such a lonely little boy. I thought perhaps he'd respond to a little affection. But he only pushed me away. I've seen quite a few little boys like him in the orphanage my grandmother supported. They did naughty things to get attention. When someone tried to give them the love and affection they craved, they acted like Dryden and pushed them away."

"Are you implying that I don't give Dryden enough affection?"

"I'm not accusing you of anything, but have you stopped to consider all the time you are forced to spend away from the children?"

After a long, pensive moment, he said with growing frustration, "I have not stopped to consider it, but I cannot be both places at once."

"I know. You're a good father, but I think since Ann's sickness and the death of your wife, Dryden feels neglected. He needs to feel special in your life again."

John stared absently down at the ink blotter on his desk

and shoved back the strand of hair on his forehead. He said his next words more to himself. "I admit I have been spending an awful lot of time with Ann when I'm home. I might have neglected both the boys."

"May I make a suggestion?"

"Of course." He looked at her as if he had forgotten she was there.

"Perhaps you could take them to the office with you sometime."

"Yes, that might work." He paused, gritted his teeth, then added, "But I'll have to find the person trying to destroy me first, and then there is the town—" He clamped his mouth closed.

"I'm sure you'll get the townhouse back." She realized she'd made a blunder when his dark brows met over his nose again and irritation crept into his expression.

"How did you know about the townhouse?"

"I—I . . ." Holly tried to think of a lie so that he wouldn't know she had been gossiping with Dunn. Finally, it came to her and she blurted, "I read about it in the paper."

"I'm sure all the tongues are wagging in town, but what do I live for but to feed the scandal-broth."

"I'm sorry." She stared down at her hands as she twisted them in her lap.

"No need to apologize. I'm used to it." His fist clenched the edge of the desk, his knuckles whitening beneath the pressure. He remained broodingly silent, staring past her at something only he could see.

At the uncomfortable silence, she glanced at the rifle on his desk. "Every time I see you, you have a gun in your hands. I hope you're not going to use that on someone?"

A wry smile turned up one side of his mouth. "Actually, I'm going out to look for our little friend with the gun.

After the way I chased him, he's probably in Scotland by now, but I want to make sure. I think I'll take the boys with me and spend some time with them while I try to pick up his trail.''

"I was thinking of taking Ann out for a walk this afternoon. Would that be all right, do you think? We won't stray far from the house.''

"I don't see why not. I'll comb the grounds to make sure that bastard is not hiding anywhere. Still, make sure you don't stay out too long.''

"We won't, and you must be careful, too.''

"Will you be worried about me again?''

"You know I will.'' Holly stared straight into his eyes.

"I'm not sure of anything about you, Holly, least of all how you feel about me. You melt in my arms, but when it comes to telling me the truth about your past, you run away from me. I'm growing very tired of you running away.'' His gaze slowly perused her curves, devouring her body.

"Don't you see, our relationship must not go any further,'' Holly said, still wringing her hands, which were trembling now.

"I know you don't feel that way. It is that secret you are harboring that makes you say this.'' He glanced at her, his expression rueful.

"It's not.'' Holly stamped her foot at him.

"Of course it is,'' he said, his voice growing sharp with frustration. "You feel the attraction between us. I've heard you moan with pleasure when my hands touch your breasts. And I've felt you shudder in my arms when I touched that sweet place between your thighs. You can deny it, but you'd be lying.'' He stood and took a step toward her.

"Leave me alone! Just please leave me alone!'' She stole a glance at him, then ran out of the room.

* * *

That afternoon, Holly strolled along the path to the lodge, pushing Ann in her chair, feeling the wheels jostling over the roots on the path. The sun peeked around the edge of a scudding cloud and shot bright rays through the leafless limbs that hung over the path. Thick from the night before, frost still blanketed parts of the forest floor. Fallen leaves glistened in the shadows of tall trunks, their burnished wet hues vibrantly alive with oranges and browns. Silence hung over the forest, heavy and dense in the air, the only sound Holly's footsteps and the rattle-bump of Ann's chair.

She saw Ann shiver. "Are you getting cold?"

"No. I'm very comfortable, and I can't wait to see our secret place."

"I think your brothers will like it, too."

Ann tilted her head in thought. "I suppose so, but I like having it all to ourselves." She sighed and added, "But I suppose it is only proper that we invite them."

Holly grinned. "Yes, we wouldn't want them to miss the fun. I promised Brock this morning that I'd take him to see it tonight."

"Can I come, too?" Ann hugged her doll, then rode in silence.

"Of course."

The gray stone walls of the small lodge rose up before them. A pair of doves were roosting on the top of the chimney. They took flight when Holly and Ann approached, their white wings stark against the slate roof.

"Look at them, Miss Campbell. Did you know it's good luck to see a pair of doves together?"

"I've never heard that."

"Yes. They mate for life. It's believed if you see them

roosting together that you'll find the true love of your life."

"Is that so?"

"Sharon told me that, but I do not believe her. She's awful superst—what is that word?"

"Superstitious?"

"That's it."

Holly grinned down at Ann's small blond head and wondered if somewhere inside there was a ninety-year-old woman hiding. She longed to find the carefree little girl buried within her.

"Perhaps Papa is your mate. Do you love him?"

"That is a very personal question," Holly said, biting her lip.

"I only asked because he smiles at you a lot. He only smiles at people he likes."

"He probably has a toothache and looks like he's smiling."

"No, I'm sure he likes you. So, do you?"

"Do I what?"

"Do you like Papa? It's all right to tell me."

Holly hedged, then said, "As men go, he's very nice. Yes, I suppose I like him."

"That is good news. Maybe I'll have a new mama, and I think I'd like you to be my mama. You're funny."

Holly stared down at Ann, watching her twist her doll's hair. It was flattering to know Ann approved of her, but she couldn't admit to this innocent, guileless child that she would never be her mother because she had murdered a man. How could she ever begin to explain such a horrible thing to Ann—or John? She was glad they'd reached the lodge.

"Here we are." Holly opened the door, then turned the

push chair around and pulled it up the two steps on the stoop and into the house.

The strong scent of pine filled her senses. She remembered the holly and pine branches she had cut and glanced toward the corner. The green mass had somehow multiplied overnight and not only filled the corner, but jutted out into the middle of the floor. Had she cut so much?

Ann pointed to it. "Look, someone left a pile of brush in here."

"I did. It's for Christmas decorations. You still want to help me, don't you?" Holly came around to the side of the chair and squatted, waiting for Ann's response.

Her golden brows furrowed, then she looked over at Holly. She gnawed on her bottom lip and hugged her doll.

When Ann didn't answer her, Holly said, "I really could use your help."

Ann paused, twisting the doll's hair now. "I suppose if you need me."

"Of course I need you." Holly hugged her and caught herself before she kissed Ann's cheek.

"It's all right this time." Ann nodded her approval.

Holly grinned, then pecked Ann's pink cheek. "Well, shall we get started? I bought an awful lot of material in London before I came here, and I thought you could help me make curtains, too. I hope your stitches are straighter than mine."

"Of course they are," Ann said, sounding indignant. "My mama taught me to sew. She was very good at it."

"I'm sure she was."

"We used to sew together, when Mama didn't have a headache. And when she got sick, she would sew with me until I got on her nerves . . . then I had to leave the sickroom." She clutched her doll and sighed loudly, staring down at her legs. "I tried not to get on her nerves. Papa said the least little thing disturbed people when they were sick. I usually went to my room and Papa read to me. He doesn't read much to me anymore—only when he's home."

A lump formed in Holly's throat. She swallowed hard and forced a cheerful note into her voice. "We'll have to see what we can do about that. Would you like for me to read to you when he's away working?"

"I think that would be nice."

She pushed the chair near the fireplace, then rubbed her hands. "We need a fire in here."

"Yes, we do."

Holly grabbed several logs she had left near the fireplace, then knelt, placed them in the grate and lit them. Out of the corner of her eye, she saw Ann moving around in her push chair trying to get comfortable.

"Would you like to sit down here with me on the rug?"

"Could I?"

"Of course." Holly lifted Ann's thin body with ease and helped her down on the floor.

Ann leaned her head on Holly's shoulder. Holly smiled and put her arm around Ann. They stared into the fire for a moment, then Ann reached down and scratched her leg.

Holly looked at Ann for a moment, unable to believe what she'd just seen. "Can you feel your legs?" she asked, her voice incredulous.

Ann nodded. "I can feel them. My legs aren't numb like a lot of people who can't walk. I just can't make them work. The doctor said it is a good sign I can feel them. Sarah moves my legs to keep the muscles in shape, but I don't know what good it does."

"An awful lot of good. You never know, you might walk again and you'll need strong muscles in your legs."

"I'll never walk again." Ann shook her head, adamantly, while apprehension gleamed in her blue eyes.

"I know it's hard not to grow discouraged. I used to think I couldn't do a lot of things."

"You did? What couldn't you do?"

"I could never get over my fear of the dark—I never really conquered that fear." Holly cocked a brow at her. "You won't tell anyone?"

Ann shook her head. "I'm even afraid of the dark, that's nothing to be ashamed of. What else?"

"At one time I was desperately afraid of dogs, which was sort of silly because I was raised on a plantation. My grandmother loved dogs and was always bringing home strays. We must have had twenty or so, but they knew I was afraid of them and they stayed away from me."

"Did you ever get over your fear?"

"Yes, I did, and I have Kent to thank for it." Holly paused, then frowned as the memory of thrusting the letter opener in Kent's back rushed back to torment her.

At Holly's silence, Ann asked, "Who was Kent?"

"Kent was our neighbor's son." Holly cleared her throat, trying to get control of the tremor in her voice. "He was about the meanest imp in the world. He always teased me because he knew I was afraid of dogs. He had this one big old hound dog that he used to set loose on me all the time when I'd come down the road from school. Every time, I'd run to the house, screaming for my grandmother. I could hear Kent laughing at me all the way home. He really was hateful."

"Like Dryden."

"Much worse." Holly thought of the torment Kent had caused her as a child—and as a grown woman. She grew aware of her nails digging into her palm and relaxed her hand. "Anyway, when I'd get home, Grandmother would say, 'If you'd face your fear and make friends with that dog, he wouldn't chase you.' I knew she was right. Finally, one day, I took a bone with me to school. And sure enough, Kent set his dog loose on me like he always did. And I had to tell myself I could make friends with him. I kept repeating it, watching that old dog bare his teeth and snarl. I remember the saliva foaming on his big yellow fangs."

"What did you do?" Ann asked, horrified.

"I told myself I could do it. I was going to pet that dog or die of dog bites. I took out the bone and let him sniff it. He stopped snarling at me and jerked it out of my hand."

"Did you pet him?"

"The next day I brought him a piece of pie. And I made him let me pet him before he snatched it away. He never chased me after that. We became quite good friends. It nearly killed Kent."

Ann hugged her doll and giggled.

It was the first time Holly had heard her really laugh. The light tinkling sound brought a smile to Holly's lips. It was a wonderful carefree sound, and Holly vowed to hear more of it.

Two hours later, Holly pushed a giggling Ann through the terrace doors. They opened into a massive parlor done in the French style. Gilded scrollwork covered the walls. A vast oval cove in the ceiling was filled with beautiful allegorical paintings of fruits and foliage. More gilded scrollwork graced the ceiling. Crushed red velvet covered the sofas scattered about the room and the floor was fashioned of light oak planking. The red swags over the windows looked in need of replacing, but other than that, the room didn't appear bare, like the rooms in the London townhouse.

"Show me how Father Christmas walks again," Ann begged.

Holly surveyed the room to make sure they were alone. "Well, if you promise not to laugh again."

"I won't." Ann straightened her face like a soldier on patrol.

Holly stuffed her arms beneath her cape, creating a massive stomach, then blew up her cheeks and bent her neck to make it look as if she had three chins. She waddled across the room like a duck. "How is this? Do I look like him?"

Ann giggled.

"You promised not to giggle." Holly shot Ann such an offended look, it made Ann laugh even louder.

"I didn't know you were a clown, Miss Campbell." John's deep voice echoed through the room.

Holly glanced toward the doorway and saw him striding toward her. Mesmerized by the handsome sight of him, she watched his long-legged strides, the stiff sway of his wide shoulders, the long muscles in his legs working beneath the tight tan buckskin breeches. That stubborn piece of dark-brown hair hung down over his forehead.

She realized her hands were still under her cape and jerked them back at her sides, a blush searing her cheeks. How long had he been standing there?

He shot her a hooded glance, looking none too happy about her antics. "Where have you been?"

"Papa, you should have seen . . ." Ann paused when Holly squeezed her shoulder to remind her about their secret place.

"Seen what?" John crossed his arms over his chest and stared down at her.

"Seen the beautiful deer," Holly answered for Ann. "Magnificent creature. Must have had sixteen points. Wouldn't you agree, Ann?"

Ann pursed her lips and feigned serious contemplation. "Yes, all of that."

"You have been looking at this deer all afternoon?" John cast his gaze at Holly for an answer.

"Of course not, Papa." Ann's tone was that of a mother scolding her son. "We have been taking the air. It was lovely."

"I'm glad you enjoyed yourself while I've been searching the grounds for you. I was just going out again. Don't ever leave this house again, Miss Campbell."

"But I asked you earlier if it was all right."

"I said not to stray far from the house. You have been gone for hours."

"I'm sorry."

"There you go apologizing again," he said, smirking at her. His gaze scrutinized her body beneath her woolen cape, then snapped back to her face.

"I suppose it's a habit of mine." Holly bent over and began pulling off Ann's gloves and bonnet.

"An annoying one." He didn't sound annoyed as he stepped back and took in every detail of her behind.

At his frank perusal, her heart hammered in her chest and that familiar warmth melted her insides like butter.

Holly heard the brisk tread of footsteps, then Sarah hurried into the room. She bobbed a curtsey at John, the sides of her mobcap bouncing around her thin face. "My lord, Pringle sent me down. He said he saw Lady Ann and Miss Campbell coming into the house." She grabbed the push chair. "We'll get you abovestairs straight away, my lady. I've been keeping your bath warm for thirty minutes. Did you have a good time?"

"Yes, and we saw a deer . . ." Ann turned to share a look with Holly, then Sarah pushed her into the hall and their voices faded.

The look wasn't lost on John. He stared long and hard at Holly. "Where have you really been?"

Holly pulled off her gloves and tried to sound nonchalant. "Walking! my lord. We stopped by the gardens, not that they were very pretty with all those weeds growing in them. Perhaps I could weed them for you."

"You will not weed my garden."

"You needn't bark at me. You really are overly sensitive. Now you've ruined the wonderful glow I had from my walk with Ann. Sometimes I wonder why I stay employed here. If you'll excuse me, I had better go and check on the boys." Holly turned to leave.

"I'm not done with you yet."

With those final words, John grabbed her arm and pulled her into his embrace.

Chapter 13

John held her so close she could hardly breathe. She tried to pull away, but he tightened his arms around her waist. "You are more than an employee to me, Holly. If you think you can leave here when you like, then you had better think again," he drawled.

Her body warmed all over. She felt his broad chest pressing against her breasts, his hard thighs tangled in her skirt, his hips so close she could feel his arousal. She knew she would be a lost woman if she didn't get free.

"If I want to leave, you can't hold me," she said, shoving at his chest.

Promptly, Mrs. Pringle entered the room and gasped. "Well, I never." She shoved her hands on her large hips and glared at Holly.

Holly sucked in her breath, knocked John's hands away, and stepped back from him. Without a mirror she couldn't be sure, but her face must be the color of cooked beets.

"Did you want something, Mrs. Pringle?" John's voice cut through the silence in the room like a dagger.

"I came to see if Miss Ann was back yet." She rounded on Holly. "How dare you keep that child out in this cold all afternoon. If she doesn't catch her death—"

"She was quite warm, I assure you," Holly said, feeling Mrs. Pringle's beady eyes boring down on her.

Mrs. Pringle kept her gaze locked on Holly, not appearing to notice John at all. "You are quite the one. I know how someone like you wags. You're nothing but a lightskirt. I should have known you'd be trying to wiggle your way into the master's bed. Pack your things this instant and leave this house."

"That is quite enough." John's deep voice echoed around the room.

Mrs. Pringle stared at John as if noticing him for the first time. She pointed at Holly. "But she is—"

"If I hear you utter one more word, you will be the one to leave this house. Do I make myself clear, Mrs. Pringle?"

Mrs. Pringle shot Holly a look that could flay the skin off her body. "Quite clear, my lord. If that is all . . ." She exaggerated a curtsey that had no deference in it, then stomped from the room.

"That woman will push me too far one day."

"What was she supposed to think?" Holly dug her fingers into her cape. "She found me in your arms like any cheap harlot. Just stay away from me."

"I cannot do that." His gaze flicked over her, then he reached for her.

Holly jumped back. "Don't." She held up her hands to ward him off. "There are things about me—wicked things—you don't know. You are making matters worse by trying to seduce me. Please don't do it again." Holly hiked up her skirt and ran from the room.

"Wait, Holly!"

His voice echoed behind her and made her run faster. The dark paneling in the hallway blurred behind her tears. The servants' stairs were at the end of the hallway. She took them two at a time, listening for his footsteps. When she didn't hear them, she sighed with relief.

Tears ran down her cheeks by the time she reached her chamber. Trying to hold back the sobs, she fumbled with the knob, then stumbled into her room, slamming the door behind her. She threw her cape and gloves across the foot of her bed, then pulled off her bonnet with trembling hands. Sobs wracked her now. She fell onto her bed and buried her face in the pillow.

Something was wrong. Her face didn't meet down feathers, but something squashy and thick. It oozed over her face, in her eyes, and into her mouth. She raised her head, spit the goo out of her mouth, then wiped whatever it was out of her eyes. She blinked down at the pillow.

Thick mushy red mud oozed from a long cut in the pillowcase and pillow. Someone had taken out the feathers and filled the inside with mud. That someone she could hear laughing now.

She glanced over her shoulder and noticed Dryden staring at her through a crack in the door. He was guffawing so hard, he was bent over. If she showed her anger now, she would be giving Dryden what he wanted. With calm, deliberate movements that were jerky from the self-control it was costing her, she rose from the bed.

Dryden sobered too quickly, his convulsive display of laughter plainly done to further her anger.

"You can come in now," Holly said, a tight, controlled edge in her voice. She walked over to the washstand in her room, picked up the pitcher, and poured water into the bowl. She heard the door squeak open as she sluiced her face.

"Aren't you going to scream at me? I know you want to. You must hate me for what I did."

Holly grabbed the towel on the edge of the dresser and wiped her face. "This may surprise you, but I don't think there is anything you could do to me to make me hate you."

"You have to."

"Well, I don't hate you. As a matter of fact, this stunt you pulled makes me feel very sorry for you." Holly brought the towel down from her face so she could look into his golden eyes.

"Why should you do that?"

"Because I'm aware why you do these hateful things."

"I do them because I like doing them." He crossed his arms over his chest and glowered at her.

"I don't think you like doing these things at all."

"I do."

"You'll never convince me of it." Holly laid the towel down on the washstand, then strode across the room toward him. When she was several feet away, she put her hands on his shoulders. "I know something is bothering you. Let me help you."

"No. I don't need you or anyone." He knocked her hands off his shoulders and raised his square jaw to a stubborn angle, giving her a better view of the dimple in his chin.

"People are not made that way. Everyone needs somebody—especially after they lose someone dear to them."

He stomped his foot. "That's not true. I don't need anyone! Especially you!"

"You can hate me, but I'll still want to be your friend."

Dryden squeezed his fists together and held his breath,

his face turning red. "I don't care. I'll never let you be my friend. I'll hate you until I'm old and gray and whither up and die." He turned and ran out of the room, slamming the door back against the wall.

Holly didn't go after him. He needed time alone. She was about to turn around when something caught her eye near the door. She turned and saw Brock standing in the doorway, his left eye almost swollen shut.

"What happened to you?" she asked in horror.

"Dryden and I had a disagreement. I tried to stop him, but he hit me. I'm sorry. I told him not to do it, but he did it anyway."

Holly held out her arms to him. "You needn't apologize for Dryden."

"Someone should." He didn't hesitate, but stepped into the circle of her arms.

Holly hugged him to her breast. "You are such a brave young man." She kissed the top of his head and felt his arms go around her waist, then he was hugging her back with a fierce tightness.

He stepped back and glanced up into her face, his green eyes pleading. "You won't let Dryden run you away, will you? You'll stay with us, won't you?"

Holly smoothed back the hair on his brow. "Dryden will not run me away. And since you were with your father this morning and missed the walk Ann and I took to the lodge, I thought we could go tonight. You should see how pretty it looks. Ann and I accomplished a lot today."

"I want to see it. Dryden won't come, but I'll be ready."

"You can't tell your father we're going. We'll have to sneak out of the house."

"I know how to keep a secret." Brock drew his finger across his lips, pretending to lock them.

Holly heard a throat clear behind her. She turned and

saw Pringle standing in the doorway, his hands clasping and unclasping in front of him. When he noticed the mud stuck to her hair and collar, his eyes widened. "What happened to you, miss?"

"You don't want to know." Holly waved her hand through the air. "What is it, Pringle?"

"His lordship requests you dine with him tonight."

"Tell his lordship I'm not feeling well," Holly said.

"I don't think he'll be very happy, miss," Pringle said in an apprehensive tone.

"I'm sorry, but that is how I feel. I just want to lie down and rest." Holly rubbed her throbbing temples and stared at him. The ache in her head was sudden. She was sure the thought of eating alone with John had caused it.

Pringle pursed his lips and stared at the mud covering the front of her new dress. He hesitated a moment before he said, "Do you have something else to wear, miss?"

"Not really. I washed my blue dress, but it's still wet. Dunn might have something for me to wear, though."

"Dunn?" Jealousy gleamed in Pringle's eyes. "Why should he have clothing for you?"

"He is doing a bit of sewing for me. I gave him some material this morning, though he might not have had time to sew another whole dress."

"If you'll allow me, I can see if Lady Upton has something you can wear. Her clothes are a little outdated," he paused and uttered his next words with disgust, "but I'm sure they are much better than anything Dunn can sew."

"That would be very nice of you." Holly glanced at him, suspecting she might be getting involved in a rivalry between Dunn and Pringle. She scowled down at the large mud stain on the top of her dress. "I suppose anything would be better than this."

"Very well, I'll go and find something for you. And I'll have a bath sent up."

"Thank you, Pringle."

Pringle looked satisfied and awfully smug about something as he left the room.

"I'd better go and find Dryden," Brock said.

"That might be a good idea." Holly ruffled Brock's blond curls. "He might need someone to talk to."

"What time are we going to go tonight?"

"We'll have to wait until your father is asleep."

With the air of an excited spy, Brock said, "I'll keep a close eye on him."

"I know you will."

Brock turned then and ran from the room, wearing a satisfied grin, his blond curls bobbing near his face. Holly closed the door, then began to strip the muddy sheets off her bed. She thought of John's invitation to dinner. It was too dangerous to accept. She just couldn't be alone with him. She should be making plans to leave, but she couldn't leave until after Christmas. The children needed some joy in their lives. Then there was that person who had tried to kill John. She could never leave until she knew John was out of danger.

John was in the library, nursing a snifter of cheap brandy. He took another swallow. The bitter taste burned all the way down his throat. He grimaced, then stretched out his long legs and stared at the fire's reflection leaping along the tips of his boots.

What was he going to do? He couldn't pick up the trail of that person who had shot at him. He would never admit it to Holly, but he thought she was right. That person might have been trying to kill him. They had tried again to fire at him when he'd gone after them. If not for his quick reflexes, he would have been shot. But he didn't tell her that, for he needed a way to pry the truth out of her, and he thought he could use her fear. But damn her, she was stubborn. Why wouldn't she trust him?

He heard footsteps, then Mrs. Pringle strode into the room. The sight of her disapproving, pinched face did nothing for his disposition.

"What is it, Mrs. Pringle?" John said, already losing patience with her.

"Mr. Pringle told me I was to set a place at table for Miss Campbell. I didn't believe him."

"Why not?"

Mrs. Pringle grabbed the ends of her shawl and clutched it over her large bosom, then shot him a censorious glance. "Excuse me for saying this, my lord, but I must voice my opinion on this. She is nothing but a servant in this house." The jealousy rose in her voice. "She should be taking her meals with the rest of the staff in the kitchen. If Lady Matilda learns of this . . ."

"Lady Matilda is not the lady of the house. This is my house, and I'll eat with whomever I wish. When I want your opinion, Mrs. Pringle, I'll ask for it." John shot her his best quelling glance.

Pringle entered the room and bowed quickly, looking upset.

"What now?" John said, eyeing him.

"It's Miss Campbell, my lord. She's not feeling well and begs to be forgiven, but she will not be able to join you for dinner."

"Is that so?" John raised a brow at Pringle.

"Yes, my lord."

"At least she knows her place," Mrs. Pringle said.

John leveled a look at her that made her curtsey. "Excuse

me, my lord," she said, "but I'd better go and see to dinner. Mr. Pringle, I'll need your help after you are done here. The table needs setting and Lady Ann needs a tray taken up to her."

Pringle nodded, his shoulders rounding as if he'd been struck hard in the back.

John watched Mrs. Pringle leave, then shot Pringle a sympathizing glance. Having a shrew for a wife must have made his life an unending torment for the past thirty years.

Pringle glanced up at him, wearing a hangdog look. "I'm sorry about my wife, my lord. She doesn't know when to hold her tongue."

"Since I owe her half a year of back wages, she probably feels as if she can speak to me any way she damn well pleases."

"That's not it, my lord."

"No need to make excuses for her. I doubt I could fire her. She may be insolent, but she's loyal. Now, about Miss Campbell. What exactly is wrong with her, besides her fear of me?"

"I wouldn't know, but she was holding her head."

John rubbed his thumb along the snifter and stared at the amber liquid in it. "I suppose she needs a little time alone."

"Yes, my lord. Perhaps some rest."

"All the rest in the world will not cure what ails her. What is your opinion of our Miss Campbell, Pringle?"

"I wouldn't know, my lord. Seems like she's running away from something monstrous bad. But she's a good sort. Wonderful with the children. Miss Ann is a different child since she's come. I hope she'll be a permanent part of the staff."

"Yes, I don't want to lose her."

Pringle nodded. "I'd better go and help Mrs. Pringle,

my lord." He bowed, then left the room, his long, storklike legs plodding lightly on the carpet.

John downed the rest of the brandy, then made a face. He thought of Holly again. He'd give her some time alone, then he'd get the truth out of her. He'd waited long enough.

That evening, Holly lay in her bed, staring up at the ceiling, wishing she were home. She would give anything for just one glimpse of the whitewashed walls at Kimbly. They had always sheltered her from every kind of storm and trouble . . . until Kent came that horrible night and forced his way into the house, knowing she was alone. Then he'd thrown a bag over her head and carried her to Richmond and left her in that attic. He had been cruel and evil all right. A long-forgotten memory of him rose up in her mind . . .

She put her foot on another branch and glanced up at the white, glistening berries on the mistletoe. A few more limbs and she'd have it. It was a week before Christmas, and she had to get the mistletoe for the decorations. It was the first time Grandmother had let her come alone to get it, but she was twelve now, practically a grown woman.

Something scared a flock of sparrows in a tree behind her. Holly's hands froze. She listened to the flutter of their wings muted by the falling snow. They flew up through the snow, small brown spots in a sea of white. What had spooked them?

"Well, well, if it ain't Miss Priss up a tree."

Holly glanced the twenty feet below to the ground and saw Kent, his blond hair stark against his black coat.

"What do you want?" she said through her teeth, hating the sight of him.

"Thought I'd help you get the mistletoe for that old batty grandmother of yours. I know how she does the house up for Christmas."

Holly saw a vicious gleam in his eye and knew he had no intentions of helping her. "I don't need your help," she said, feeling her stomach churning, as it always did when Kent was about to do something nasty.

"I said I'd help you. Girls can't climb trees."

"I can climb better than you." She saw him grab the first limb and cried, "Stay down there. I mean it! I know what you want to do. You're going to push me out of this tree."

"I wouldn't do that." He grinned and looked like the worst kind of sinner swearing to a preacher that he'd never broken a commandment in his whole life.

"Stay down there, I mean it!" Holly clamped her hands around a limb, feeling the bark digging into her finger-nails.

"I tried to be nice, but now you've made me mad." Without warning, he reached into his pocket and threw a rock.

Holly ducked, but the rock hit her in the back. The pain paralyzed her for a moment. She sucked in her breath and lost her footing. Teetering on the limb, she groped at air, her heart leaping up into her throat. She saw herself sprawled at the bottom of the tree, her limbs twisted at odd angles, dead. Abruptly, her fingers connected with a thick limb. She hung suspended from the bough, her feet dangling.

"You're a lucky one . . ." Another rock flew past Holly, missing its mark. Kent cursed.

"Leave me alone!" Holly cried, and swung her legs back up on the limb, then pulled herself up and grabbed the trunk of the tree, strangling it, the bark cutting into her hands and face. She glanced down and saw Kent taking up a stance below her, getting ready to throw another rock. She ducked and took cover behind the trunk.

"I'll get you."

"I'm going to tell your father on you!"

He laughed and walked around the tree in an attempt to get a better aim at her. "Go ahead. He doesn't give a damn what I do."

"He does, too. He'll take the whip to you like he does to his horses." She crawled onto a branch that blocked her from Kent's view.

"If you open your mouth to my father, I'll cut your tongue out."

"Not if I can help it!" Holly yelled at him.

Another rock hit Holly's side this time. She grabbed her ribs, then stepped onto another branch, moving higher, trying again to hide behind the tree trunk.

"How's that for mean?" Another rock hit Holly, this time in the back of her knee.

Her leg buckled and pain shot up to her hip. She stumbled to the side and grabbed a branch, gaining her balance.

Frantic now, she climbed higher. In her haste, she hadn't noticed the branches were getting thinner until it was too late.

Crack.

The limb gave way. Then she was falling backward. Holly groped at air. Fear gripped her. A momentary vision of her body sprawled at the bottom of the tree, her limbs twisted at odd angles, flashed before her eyes. She could feel the tips of the branches splinter as she fell through them. By some miracle, her fingers closed around a thin limb.

A moment of relief flooded her. Suspended in the air by one hand, she dangled fifteen feet off the ground, her fingers gripping the bark like a lifeline, her arm trembling. Her heart hammered in her chest. She was afraid to move, to breathe, afraid the thin wood would crack. She glanced at the ground. It was a long way down. All she could hear was Kent's vicious laughter.

The limb held for a moment, then the wood gave way beneath her weight.

Crack.

The wood crumbled in her hand. She screamed and fell . . .

Holly felt someone in the room and turned to see Brock staring down at her. "I'm sorry, Miss Campbell, but you didn't answer my knock."

"I must not have heard you," Holly said, still trembling all over from the memory, her heart hammering. Inadvertently, she reached down and touched her ankle. She had sprained it in that fall and couldn't walk for a week.

"Let me help you up." Brock grabbed her hand. "Papa has retired for the night. We can go to the Christmas lodge now."

"What time is it?" Holly asked, still feeling shaky.

"Nine o'clock."

"I guess we should get ready. Is Dryden going with us?"

"He won't come. He's being stubborn about it."

"I see. I hope he doesn't tell your father what we're doing."

"He might be a lot of things, but he isn't a tattler."

"Let's hurry and be quiet. We mustn't let your father see us sneaking out of the house."

"I spoke to Pringle. He said he would make sure Papa stayed in bed."

"Pringle knows about the lodge?" Holly asked, grabbing her cape, gloves, and hat from the wardrobe in her room.

"Sure he does, he's a servant. All the servants know now,

save for Mrs. P. I'm sure she doesn't know anything."
Brock pointed at her legs. "You're wearing trousers."

"Yes, I borrowed them from Dunn. Wearing them will
make it easier to walk through the woods at night."

"I'm already wearing my coat." Brock pointed to the
garment.

"You came prepared, a very good idea." Holly pulled
on her cape, put on her gloves, then closed the door. She
turned to Brock and buttoned the top button of his coat
and drew the muffler around his neck. "You don't want
to get cold," she whispered, then took his hand and they
tiptoed down the hallway . . .

The hall door opened just as they reached it. Holly
jumped back from the tall, lanky figure blocking their way.
She grabbed her chest. "Land sakes! Pringle, you almost
scared the life out of me."

"Sorry, miss," Pringle whispered. "I just came to tell
you the coast was clear. Dunn is bringing Miss Ann. He's
to meet you down at the bottom of the stairs."

"Is his lordship in bed?"

"Yes, miss, all nice and tight."

"Good," Holly said, relieved. "We wouldn't want him
following us."

By the time they reached the bottom of the steps, Dunn
and Ann were waiting for them. Holly looked at Dunn,
who was wearing his coat. "Are you going, too, Dunn?"

He nodded. "Yes, miss, I thought perhaps I could help
with the decorating."

She noticed Pringle had on his coat, too. "You, too?"
she asked him.

"Yes, miss." He cast Dunn an anything-he-can-do-I-can-
do better look. "I thought I could help, too."

"What about Mrs. Pringle? Forgive me, but I don't want
her to know."

"She's sound asleep, miss. Snores like a bear. She'll never miss me," Pringle said with a brusqueness that bespoke of just what he thought of his wife.

"Well, I suppose we should go then," Holly said.

"Goody, isn't this the greatest fun." Ann rubbed her hands together, excitement brimming over in her eyes.

"Come, then, let's keep quiet."

Pringle pushed Ann out the door first, then Dunn and Brock followed. Holly was the last one to go out the door. Light footsteps in the stairwell brought her to a standstill. The footsteps paused, as if the person knew she was there. Holly grinned up the stairs and knew Dryden was following them. Her instincts told her he wouldn't be able to resist the temptation. Still grinning, she strode out the door.

On the second floor, John sat up in bed, then turned and pulled Holly's black dress out from beneath his pillow. He rubbed the stiff silk between his fingers. He would use the dress as an excuse to speak to her, then he'd finally get the truth out of her. She wouldn't run from him this time. He'd make sure of it.

He threw back the covers, pulled on his dressing gown, then picked up the dress and the candle by the bed and carried it with him out the door.

When everyone was abed, a particular silence settled over the house—that silence blanketed the hallway now. Confident he could go to Holly's room unnoticed, he strode to the stairwell. He opened the door. Cold air hit his bare chest, and he pulled his robe tighter, taking the steps two at a time.

The anticipation of seeing her again knocked his heart against his ribs. All sorts of ways he would seduce the truth out of her rose up in his mind. He could all but taste her lips. When he reached her door, his breathing was ragged and his hands trembled slightly.

"Holly." He rapped softly at the door.

No answer.

When he tried the door, he found it unlocked. He stepped into the room, then held the candlestick aloft. Candlelight danced dim shadows over the room. The coverlet on her bed was rumpled, but not turned down.

She might be in the boys' room for some reason. He threw the dress on her bed, then crossed the hall to their room. He eased the chamber door open so as not to disturb her if she were reading to them. The sight of the empty beds made his brows snap together. What if that bastard with the gun had returned? What if he'd taken Holly and the children to get to him? He ran down the hall to check on Ann.

"It doesn't look good there," Dunn said, jerking the Christmas tree back to the center of the room.

"It's perfectly fine in the corner." Pringle picked up the five-foot cedar and shoved it back into the corner.

Holly wondered if the poor tree would survive. She and Ann had found it growing near the lodge earlier in the day. Hoping Pringle and Dunn could work together and get over their petty rivalries, she asked them to cut it down. But they were like oil and water.

"It looks nice in the corner," Ann said, then stared helplessly at Holly.

"Yes, very nice," Holly agreed.

"Just leave it somewhere so we can decorate it," Brock said, losing his patience.

Brock's reproach made Dunn and Pringle look at each other. They appeared to realize how childish they were behaving, but neither would turn the tree loose. Finally, Pringle dropped his hands, then Dunn did the same.

"It looks lovely there," Holly said, breaking the tense moment. She walked over to the tree. Out of the corner of her eye she saw something move behind the wooden shutters. Through a crack, she caught a flash of Dryden's face, then it disappeared. She smiled to herself, then raised her voice loud enough for Dryden to hear her. He'd been standing out in the cold for an hour spying on them. "It will be lovely once we put the decorations on it."

"I've never seen a Christmas tree before, but I can't wait to decorate it," Ann said, staring at the tree. "What did you say they put on them in Germany?"

"My grandmother said her mother put candles on the tree, until she brought the custom to Virginia, then she and my grandmother decorated it any way they liked. I think we can do that with this tree."

"I wish Papa could see it," Ann said.

Ann got her wish. A second later the door swung back, hitting the hall and vibrating on its hinges as John stood in the doorway.

Chapter 14

John's gaze swept the pine roping over the windows and the Christmas tree, then landed on Holly. "Do you know I was mad with worry? I've been looking everywhere for you. I thought something had happened to you and the children. What the devil is going on out here?"

"Don't be mad, Papa," Ann pleaded.

"It's my fault. I wanted to give the children a little Christmas joy." Holly stepped in front of Ann, blocking John's furious face from her view. "Please, you can reproach me all you like, but in private."

John glared at Holly a moment, then looked at Pringle and Dunn. "Are you two involved in this?"

Pringle hung his head.

Dunn spoke up, "M-my lord, we just wanted to help."

"Where is Dryden?"

"He's probably back at the house by now," Holly said.

"He's been watching us through the windows, but wouldn't join us."

John turned and spoke to Pringle and Dunn. "See that the children get back to the house."

"Y-yes, my lord," Pringle stammered, moving faster than Holly had ever seen. He grabbed Ann's coat, wrestled her into it, then pushed her out the door.

Dunn already had Brock's coat on and shoving him out behind Ann. He shot Holly a sympathetic look, then slammed the door behind him.

"Why did you go behind my back when you knew how I felt about Christmas?" John asked Holly.

"I didn't think you'd approve."

"You were right." In two long strides, John paused and towered over her.

Holly didn't back away; she was ready to do battle for something she believed was right. "Just because you are against Christmas doesn't mean the poor children should suffer. Haven't you seen how horribly depressing it is for them in that house? They need laughter, they need cheer in their lives. You spend so much time working that you don't know what they need. They're still hurting from your wife's death. You can't be so unreasonable as to deny them these things."

"If you felt this way, why didn't you tell me sooner?" Some of the anger left John's face.

"Would it have done me any good? I know how stubborn you can be about your pride. One of these days you'll just have to swallow it. Money isn't everything, and it won't buy happiness. I'm sure your servants and tenants know that you can't afford to give them anything for Christmas, but would it hurt to invite them to your house and spend a little time with them? They would probably like that better than anything."

"I believe you are better at giving me a dressing down than my grandmother," he said, frowning at her.

"I hope I changed your mind about Christmas." Holly arched a brow at him and asked sheepishly, "Did I?"

"I'm not a monster, Holly. I'd certainly seem like one if I said no. If it will make you and the children happy, I suppose it couldn't hurt to decorate the house. Perhaps it will keep you from traipsing out here in the dark when there's a killer on the loose."

"Thank you." Overcome with joy, Holly flung her arms around him and kissed him.

When their lips met, Holly realized what she'd done. But it was too late to pull back. She was lost in the clean masculine scent of him, the heat of his mouth, the feel of his hard chest against her. His tongue slid into her mouth, while his hand moved to the small of her back and pulled her close against his hard thighs. She melted against him and wrapped her arms around his neck, tangling her hands in the thick crisp hair on his nape.

His hands went to her breasts. Holly arched her back and groaned, feeling a flame building in her. He jerked on her shirt, and the shirttail easily slipped out of the too-large breeches she had borrowed from Dunn. His hands slipped beneath the shirt and her chemise. His rough palms moved over the flesh on her soft belly, then upward, drawing the chemise and shirt up as he went. The feel of his wide hands caressing her naked flesh made her shudder and sway against him. He kissed a line down her throat, then in one quick motion he pulled the shirt over her arms and she was bare from the waist up.

Caught up in the need to feel his naked skin against her, she pulled at his shirt, jerking at the buttons until it fell from his arms, landing in a heap near his feet. For a moment they gazed at each other; he at her peach-tipped

breasts quivering with each ragged breath, and she at the
black patch of hair on his chest, tapering down past waves
of hard stomach muscles to disappear below his breeches.
His skin glistened like gold from the firelight, the soft light
playing over the granite contours of his body. He was
golden hardness all over, matching his eyes.

"You're beautiful," she said, mesmerized by the hard,
powerful sight of him.

"I pale compared to you, my sweet." He pulled her
close.

Their bodies touched and the jolt of heat from his body
burned her. A fine sheen of sweat broke out on her as she
spread her fingers across his broad back, then down past
the waistband of his breeches. She cupped his buttock as
he had done to her. He stiffened and sucked in his breath.
She smiled, feeling a little wicked at what her touch could
do to him.

Instantly, he was kissing her again, wild, drugging kisses
that sent Holly's senses spinning. He trailed kisses down
her neck, then his lips paused at the hollow of her throat.
His tongue flicked against the pulsing there before his lips
moved lower to her breast. His mouth captured one nipple,
then he ran his tongue over the sensitive flesh and nipped
it with his teeth, teasing it into a hard nub. Holly arched
against him, digging her hand in his hair and pushing his
mouth closer to her. She could feel the hard stubble on
his chin, abrasive against her soft skin.

His hands were trembling now as he pulled at the belt
holding up her breeches. They fell off her and mounded
around her ankles. His hands went to her back, then lower
to massage her bottom, his long fingers moving just the
right way to make her feel weak all over.

"You don't know how many times I've wanted to touch

you like this." The deep, silken edge in his voice seeped over her like warm honey.

"You can touch me now," Holly moaned, aware of his tongue rubbing across her nipple while he suckled her other breast, sending a swirling current through her.

His hand moved around her hip, then found the auburn mat of hair between her legs. He opened the delicate folds and touched the center of her heat.

"You are ready for me," he said, stroking her.

"Please . . . John." Holly didn't know what she was pleading for as her head lulled against his shoulder. Her heart slammed against her chest. She was panting and shaking all over. The searing warmth building inside her was consuming her. Her knees grew weak.

"All right, my sweet." John lowered her to the rug before the hearth, still stroking her. Then he settled down on top of her, kissing her wildly and pulling at his breeches. He freed his swollen flesh, then thrust into her.

A sharp pain made her cry out and dig her nails into his back.

He froze, every muscle tensed from the self-control he used to remain still. "Are you all right?" he asked, his voice ragged.

"It hurts."

"Only for a moment, my sweet. It's your maidenhead. We're through it now. It'll only hurt this one time . . ." He began moving inside her.

Holly felt her flesh closing in around his hardness, widening to accommodate him. Deeper now, he filled her totally. Her eyes widened in surprise that they fit so well together. He moved now, slowly at first, then faster. The pain melted away. All she could feel was him inside her, the friction and heat of him. Her eyes lulled closed, while her hips arched against each deep thrust.

All too soon, he cried out her name, then spilled his seed.

"Damnation," he said, then collapsed down on top of her.

"What is it?" Holly ran her hands over his back, wondering if she'd done something wrong and hurt him.

He raised up on his elbows, then kissed her. "I had meant to take my time making love to you, but you feel so incredible, you make me lose all control. I'll make it up to you . . ."

He grinned down at her, looking like a handsome satyr with the firelight reflecting off his tanned face and glowing in his soft golden eyes. The tension that seemed a permanent part of his face was gone. It was the first time Holly had seen him truly relaxed. He touched a long lock of her auburn hair, rubbing it between his fingers.

"You're so beautiful."

"I'm really not. I've always been plain." Holly entwined her fingers in the dark hair on his chest, feeling the rapid beats of his heart against her hand.

"There is nothing plain about you." He traced the side of her cheek and jaw with a finger. "You bewitch me with your beauty. You make me forget everything. I could live in poverty for the rest of my life if I have you. I'll never get enough of you." The golden hue in his eyes darkened as if to seal his possession of her, then he bent down and kissed her again.

His erection pulsed to life inside her. He began moving again and she wondered if it wasn't the other way around. Would she ever get enough of him?

When Holly awoke the next morning, she felt beside her for John, but cold sheets met her hand. She stretched, aware of the soreness between her legs and the lingering musky smell of their lovemaking. After they had made love twice in the lodge, he brought her to her room and slept beside her, then sometime early this morning, she'd awakened to find him touching her breasts, murmuring endearments in her ear, and he'd made love to her again.

The memory made a slow, lazy grin spread across her lips. She leaned over and sniffed the pillow, getting a deep whiff of his masculine scent still lingering there. She brought the pillow to her chest, hugging it, then stared up at a crack in the plastered ceiling. She should feel guilty about letting him make love to her, but she did not. They had shared a closeness last night that she'd always treasure when she was forced to leave him. He hadn't questioned her about her past last night, but she felt sure it was coming. She could never tell him the truth. The thought of leaving him made Holly dig her fingers into the newly replaced feather pillow and hug it tighter.

She blinked back tears, then decided crying over something that hadn't happened yet wouldn't do anything but make her miserable. And there was Christmas to see to. She tossed the pillow aside, threw back the covers, and rolled out of bed. The cold air hit her naked skin. She shivered and went to the wardrobe to find something to put on.

A knock on her door made her jump.

She realized she was naked and jerked the counterpane off the bed. "Yes?"

" 'Tis me, miss." Dunn's voice was muffled behind the door.

"Be right there." Holly stumbled over something near the bed, then glanced down and saw the black, tattered, ready-made dress Lady Matilda had bought her heaped around her feet.

How did that get back in her room? Frowning, she snatched up the ugly dress and ran to the window. When she opened the sash, a blast of frigid air blew back the strands of hair hanging in her face. She pushed her hair out of her eyes and felt her cheeks stinging from the cold. Quickly, she balled up the material and tossed it out the window, giving it a good heave, putting all her strength behind it. The wind caught it. The ugly frayed material billowed high into the air before it disappeared over the side the roof.

She brushed her hands together, glad to be rid of it, then slammed the window shut. Pulling the counterpane around her, she hurried to the door. The hinges creaked as she opened it a crack.

Dunn was grinning. "Morning, miss." He held up a beautiful bottle-green morning dress he'd made for her. "I have this ready. I thought perhaps you'd like to try it on."

"Thank you, Dunn." Holly took the proffered dress.

Dunn's keen eyes did not miss the fact her arm was bare. His grin broadened. "Was the master too hard on you after we left?"

"He was very understanding." She remembered how understanding he'd been and blood rushed to her cheeks. "He even agreed to let us decorate the hall. Can you believe that?"

"That will be lovely for the children, miss. It sounds as if we have a lot of work cut out for us."

"Yes, we do. I thought we could have a Christmas gathering here. And invite all his lordship's tenants."

"I don't know, miss," Dunn said, frowning. "His lordship may put the dampers on that."

"Perhaps we should surprise him. That way, if he doesn't

approve, he'll just have to look like he does with all those people around him.''

"That could work, miss. I'll just go and tell that old fool Pringle.'' Dunn turned to leave, but paused. "By the bye, the master is waiting on you in the aviary. He looks anxious about something, so you'd better hurry.'' Dunn grinned at her, then turned and strode down the hall.

Holly stared at Dunn for a moment, watching his coattails slapping around his short legs, then closed the door. The thought of seeing John again made her hurry and dress.

John stood in the aviary and glanced around him. It was a dome-shaped greenhouse he'd converted for the birds. Small trees and shrubbery lined the walls and a circular area in the center. He didn't like caging birds and the natural environment encouraged reproduction.

The aviary was a place to relax and forget about his money troubles. Normally it was a cheerful place, with bright sunshine coming in through the tall glass dome overhead, but today the sun was hidden by thick gray clouds that looked ready to burst with precipitation. The gloom overhead could not affect his mood today, though. He felt contented, really happy for the first time in years, as if he'd been floundering in a dark tunnel and finally found his way out. Holly was his way out, his bright light.

Bending over a nestbox, he stroked a Dutch frilled hen, a delicate yellow creature with undulating wavy feathers over the head, breast, and crest. The soft feathers beneath his fingertips made him think of Holly again, naked, her soft brown eyes staring up at him as she climaxed with him.

He heard light footsteps behind him. He stood and

glanced over the thick branches of an English hawthorn, a shrub with red bullet-shaped berries that the birds liked to eat. Holly's large brown eyes met his, and his grin broadened.

She looked lovely in a deep green dress that complemented the color of her skin and auburn hair. Her hair was down and swept back by a small braid in the back. Strands of curly hair fell around her face, making her appear more lovely than he'd ever seen her. Her huge brown eyes glowed with such giving, soft emotion that he felt an instant need to take her in his arms. She looked at him a moment, then gazed at the ten birds perched on his shoulders and the one standing on top of his head.

"You must have a way with them," she said, smiling at the birds. "Pringle tried to catch one of your birds, but it flew away from him."

"The hens like me." He cocked a teasing brow at her.

"Yes, I can see why. You do resemble a strutting cock." She grinned impishly at him. The dozens of birds perched in the trees drew her attention. For a moment, she listened to their songs, melding together into a pleasant, relaxing melody, then she said, "I can see why you raise them, it is lovely in here."

"Yes, I like being with the birds."

"Do you make much profit off them?"

"Enough to cover some of the expenses of running Brookhollow. Would you like to hold one?"

"Could I?"

John nudged the buff-colored one on top of his head on to his finger, then strode over to her. "Hold out your finger."

She did as he asked, then he urged the canary onto her finger. "It is so beautiful and delicate." She brought the bird up to her face and stared at it, gently stroking it.

"Yes, just like you." The sight of her stroking the bird aroused all sorts of erotic images in his mind. He needed to feel her hands on him again and drew her into his arms.

The abrupt movement made the birds take flight. He kissed her amidst a mass of fluttering feathers. They stayed that way until he felt a shudder go through her. He raised his head and peered down at her. "Have I told you how much I want you this morning?"

"Not really, but your lips told me. And I prefer those to words any day." She grinned, her dimples coming alive.

"Be careful for what you wish, I may have to make love to you here in the aviary, and the birds wouldn't like it." His gaze dropped to her full, proud breasts.

"Only the old hens." She smiled at him, then wrapped her arms around his neck and pulled him close, kissing him with sweet ardor.

Her passion and the taste of her lips aroused him instantly. When his hands moved to her breasts, she broke the kiss and grinned up at him. Her huge brown eyes glistened mischievously as she said, "We wouldn't want to upset the birds."

"You're teasing me on purpose, aren't you? Now I'm going to ache for you all day."

"I hope your pain doesn't bring back that scowl of yours. You are so very handsome without it." She winked, then ran her finger along the dimple in his chin. "Did you order me down here to cause you pain, or did you wish to see me?"

"I have been thinking about what we did last night and have come to the conclusion that the only alternative left to us is to set a date."

"A date?" She blinked in confusion.

"A date to have the wedding."

"What wedding?"

"Our wedding."

She remained silent for a moment, then made a pretense of straightening his cravat while she spoke. "Must we discuss that now?"

"I think it is wise." He grabbed her hands and held them. "I took your maidenhead. I intend to do the right thing by you."

"Why can't we go on like this? We needn't complicate things by marriage." Sudden aloofness covered her eyes, and she pulled back her hands.

"What's the matter? Is it my lack of wealth you object to? I know I can't give you much, but I'm sure it's more than you are used to."

"How do you know what I'm used to?" She turned her back on him and clasped her arms tight around her waist.

"So it *is* the money?" he said, disgust and pain coming through in his voice.

She turned to look at him again. "I should hope you know me better than to think my marrying you would hinge on your wealth."

"What is it then?" He grabbed her shoulders.

"I can't tell you."

"Are you already married?" He tightened his hold on her shoulders. "Did you run away on your wedding night? Do you have a husband back in Virginia?"

She flinched. "You're hurting me."

He loosened his grip, but didn't drop his hold on her. "Tell me the truth, Holly, you owe me that much."

"I'm not married, nor have I ever been married."

"What is it then?"

"Please leave me alone." She knocked his hands away, tears glistening in her eyes. She steadily backed toward the door as she spoke. "I can't tell you, and I won't. The less you know about me the better. Don't bring marriage up to me again. It is out of the question . . ." She turned, flung open the door and ran out, the swish of the silk gown going with her.

John took a step to go after her, but paused in consternation. Why wouldn't she trust him with the truth about her past? After taking her maidenhead, he knew she was telling the truth about not being married. It must be something else. It hurt knowing she didn't trust him. He'd make her trust him. Now that he'd found her, he wasn't about to let the only woman he'd ever loved in his life get away.

Her life with him wouldn't be easy, but she wasn't a spoiled, pampered lady like Elise. If she'd been a wealthy heiress, he would never have swallowed his pride and proposed to her, but she could adapt easily to poverty. Nothing about her hinted at wealth. She must have grown up in an impoverished household, or something close to it. She would never miss what she'd never had. And they *would* be living in penury, for he had nothing to give her but his love. It would have to be enough for both of them.

Chapter 15

Holly ran down the hall toward the servants' stairs. Tears blurred her vision, the damask wallpaper running together into dark burgundy splotches. She wasn't paying attention and collided with Lady Upton.

"Madam, I'm sorry." Holly grabbed the elderly woman before she fell.

"My word, gal, what is the matter?" She pulled out a handkerchief from her sleeve and dabbed at Holly's tears.

"Nothing . . . really."

"Stuff and nonsense! Something is the matter."

Holly tried to change the subject. "I hope I didn't hurt you when I bumped into you."

"It would take more than a little bump to hurt me. We St. Johns are made of sturdy stuff. I'll have you know, my stamina could undo my husband. He never could keep up with me on a walk, or . . ." Lady Upton lowered her voice, "in bed. He died in my bed, you know. The doctor said his heart played out. I believe I killed him, but he died happy." A grin widened her thin lips, then it faded and her gaze took on a faraway look. She stared at Holly, not really seeing her.

After a long, pensive moment, Lady Upton's eyes glazed over as she said, "Funny the little things I remember about my Alistair. Every morning he would sneak into my room and tickle my feet to wake me up. And when we kissed, he always smacked his lips and made me laugh. The thing I miss most is watching him read the paper in the morning and hearing him hum. It was an annoying habit of his. It used to grate on me at the time, but I would give anything to hear him humming again." She paused, her bottom lip trembling. "The sad truth is, I took him for granted. I never knew how much until he died. Once you find a man to love, they become a part of you, more a part of you than yourself. You remember that, gal."

"I will." Holly chewed on her lip and glanced back toward the aviary.

"Let me see your face." Lady Upton looked into Holly's eyes. "Uh, huh! Just as I suspected. That is what made you cry."

"What has?" Holly asked warily.

"You have the glow."

"Glow?"

"Yes, the glow. Didn't your mother ever tell you of the glow?"

"My mother died when I was but a baby. My grandmother raised me, but she never spoke of glowing."

"Some women find it embarrassing to speak of it, but it's a part of nature, and as natural as bringing children into the world. I've never understood some ladies' reticence in discussing such things. I told my Anoria about it. I think every young woman should know these things. It's damned silly to send them into marriage knowing nothing about what goes on. Damned silly." Lady Upton paused, and stared ahead, as if she had finished a thought and was lost now.

"What about the glow?" Holly prompted her. "What is it?"

"What glow?" Lady Upton looked confused.

"You know . . . *the* glow."

Recognition dawned in her faded brown eyes. "The glow." She opened her eyes wide and grinned at Holly. "Yes, well, women have a certain worldly glow after they lose their maidenhead—do not think you can hide it from a crafty keen-eyed old prune like me." Lady Upton drew close to Holly, staring in her eyes the way John did, looking directly into her soul. "You have that look about you, all right."

A blush flooded her cheeks.

"It's John John, isn't it?"

Holly was too embarrassed to answer her.

"No need to hide it from me. I can go and look at him. Gentlemen have a wolfish look after they make a woman theirs. No need to blush, gal. I know John John. Virile men like him cannot help but seduce the women they love. His grandfather seduced me before we were married." Lady Upton smiled wickedly. "My father caught us in the garden and made us marry before we had a proper engagement. We didn't mind, I believe Alistair told my father we were in the garden so he could find us—the wretch. I never forgave him for that." Her smile broadened.

"I'm sure you did, ma'am. You loved him too much not to forgive him."

"Perhaps I did." The smile slowly faded. Lady Upton's expression grew pensive, then her slender lips moved one over the other and tears glistened in her faded eyes again. "In the forty years we were married I never told him I loved him. I always thought if I showed any weakness, it would give him the upper hand. Of course, he must have sensed I loved him, but I regret never telling him so." She blinked, holding back tears. "Do not make the same mistake I made, tell John John you love him." She grabbed Holly's arm and squeezed it. "You have told him you love him, haven't you?" Lady Upton said with desperation in her voice.

"I don't know if I love him."

"Of course you do, gal, he's a St. John. All women fall in love with St. John men. Perhaps you are not sure now, but you will be once you marry him."

"I can't marry him," Holly said in a choked whisper.

A disoriented look slipped back into Lady Upton's eyes. She remained silent a moment, then said, "There now, Anoria. No need to cry, child. You'll feel better after the wedding." Lady Upton wrapped her frail arms around Holly.

Memories of how her grandmother used to comfort her flashed in Holly's mind. If only her grandmother were still alive. She needed her desperately. Holly's tears turned to sobs.

"It will all be all right." Lady Upton patted her back.

Holly sobbed louder. It would never be all right. She could never marry John.

Back in London, Teddy sat in the shipping office, took aim at a trash can in the corner, then threw a balled-up piece of newspaper at it. The paper sailed through the air and landed in a heap, joining the other misplaced tries.

The door to the shipping office opened. Cold air gusted

through the room, sending the papers swirling around the can. A footman opened the door wider, then Matilda strolled past him, wearing a red dress and a spenser that matched. The mink was so thick around her neck that she had to keep her jaw tilted upward. She waved the footman away with a nod of her head, then pulled off her gloves.

When she glanced up and noticed Teddy sitting at the desk, she shot him a cursory glance. "Where is your brother?"

"In the country." He must have hit a sore spot, for a frown marred her beautiful face. "But I'm here," he added, then leveled his most charming smile at her.

"What's he doing in the country?" Matilda's prim composure melted beneath her annoyance. "I just left the country yesterday. I didn't think he'd go there, not with all this going on with the shipping company."

"If you want my true opinion, I think he left London to escape the gossip. You know the bank foreclosed on the townhouse. Damned business, that. Lost all my clothes." Teddy moved his shoulders in the tight crimson blazer he had borrowed from Harry Renwick, the friend with whom he was staying.

"He could have come to me."

"You know he'd never do that. I believe he'd go to debtors' prison before he'd take money from another woman. Damned pride of his will have us all there. I should go and marry an heiress and be done with it, but John refuses to allow it. Though I have long since been of age. Do you know of an heiress? As long as she doesn't squint and have a mustache, I believe I could be happy."

"I think you had better not go against Lord Upton's wishes."

"He probably wouldn't take my wife's money anyway." Teddy frowned and stared at the red feather on Matilda's bonnet. It curled seductively over the left side of her face. "It is a shame Miss Campbell does not have money. I believe John is in love with her, and her fortune could get us out the River Tick." Teddy sighed loudly and propped his elbows on the desk.

"In love with Miss Campbell—that penniless waif? Why, her skin is as dark as a sailor's. She is not even attractive. Your brother couldn't be in love with her," Matilda said, more to herself.

"I wouldn't be so sure. Miss Campbell has a charming way about her. She's the most enticing young woman I've ever met. I'm sure John is as smitten by her as I was." He grew pensive, remembering the feel of Holly's behind next to his when he'd jumped into bed with her, then the sight of her, the thick waves of auburn hair cascading around her waist, the way her big brown eyes lit up when she smiled.

"I'm sure you are wrong," Matilda said adamantly.

Teddy took her measure for a long moment, then a wicked grin turned up the corners of his lips. "Well, something attracted him. You must have seen him kissing Miss Campbell on the sidewalk as I did."

"I did not see it," she said with too much emphasis in her voice, as if she were trying to convince herself it was true.

"What? Surely you saw them! It was your gasp that made me look out the window to begin with. I admit my jealousy flared when I saw them together. I'm still irritated with him, but I suppose he can't help it that every woman who comes in contact with him is attracted to him. Damned if I know why. I should have expected as much from Miss Campbell."

"She may be attracted to him, but I doubt he feels anything for her."

Teddy remained silent and watched Matilda twist her gloves in her hand. She turned and paced in front of the desk, her rounded hips swaying. "You love John, don't you?" he asked. "You've no need to deny it. It will remain our little secret."

She paused and looked at him with something akin to respect, then, as if he were the most ignorant bloke alive, she said, "For heaven's sake, where did you get such an idea?"

Teddy grinned. "I can't imagine. I suppose it's the fact you visit him almost every day and try to make yourself indispensable to him. Why, you even made a special trip down here today to find him."

"I needed to tell him something I found out about a certain person," she said, her eyes gleaming. "It was very important."

"You could tell me." He stared at her coat, cut perfectly to show off her full breasts.

She paused, strangling her gloves in a white-knuckled grip. "I suppose it wouldn't hurt, but you mustn't breathe a word of it to anyone before Lord Upton has a chance to investigate."

"Investigate what?"

"I happened to be riding my filly in Hyde Park this morning, early. As I slowed from a vigorous run, I overheard voices behind a thick stand of brushes. I recognized Lord Waterton's voice right away. He was very angry, and I couldn't help but overhear him. He was bellowing at a man whom he called Jarvis, berating the fellow for coming back to London so soon after Lord Waterton paid him to sink Lord Upton's ships."

"Good God!" Teddy's jaw opened and hit the sharp, starched points of his collar. He grimaced and rubbed his chin. It took him a moment before he could speak. "And you actually heard this?"

"Yes, every word," Matilda said, her tone slightly miffed that Teddy questioned what she had heard. "After I over-heard them talking, I came here right away to tell John."

"You did the right thing. John should know of this as soon as possible."

"I intend to tell him straightaway." She pulled on her gloves.

"Then you are going to the country?"

"Yes. I cannot trust this information with a messenger. I shall travel there on the morrow." Her eyes hardened, masking the soft blue in them. The tight edge in her voice softened as she said, "Forgive me if I have been short with you. I was just worried about your brother. If you are in need of lodgings, my townhouse will be at your disposal."

"That is very kind, but I'm staying with Harry," Teddy said absently, his mind preoccupied with the news he'd just heard.

"I'll be taking my leave of you. I have a long list of things to do before I go to the country. Good day."

Teddy watched the footman, who'd been waiting patiently outside the door, open it. She floated past him, the rustle of her red taffeta dress following her out the door.

Teddy frowned at the closed door. Suddenly, he recalled where he'd heard the name Jarvis. Just the other day, a sailor named Jarvis came to see John. Waterton had planted him on *Sea Challenger* to destroy it, and *Sin's Revenge!*

Teddy wasn't surprised by what Matilda told him. Waterton had disliked John for as long as Teddy could remember. Waterton's enmity didn't stop with John, either. Even in the clubs Teddy visited with his friends, Waterton snubbed him and went out of his way to make cutting remarks about him behind his back. John had never allowed him to take responsibility for anything, but Teddy would deal with Waterton on this matter. And he'd bloody well enjoy it!

He grabbed his greatcoat, hat, and cane off the coat rack, then hurried out of the office, locking the door behind him. John would be proud of him for once.

Twenty minutes later, Teddy strode into White's. Several men were sprawled out in the sitting area, their heads buried behind a paper. Teddy passed them, hearing the din from the gaming room. He paused at the doorway and scanned the many card tables. Most all the tables were full. Waterton's blond hair was easy to spot; he was also one of the tallest men in the room.

Waterton glanced up, and his cruel eyes bored into Teddy for a moment. He said something low that made everyone at the table laugh, then they turned and glanced at Teddy.

The muscles tightened in Teddy's gut. His fists clenched and unclenched at his sides. He kept his gaze locked on his prey and strode toward the table.

A tight silence settled over the room.

Teddy made it halfway to Waterton's table, then someone grabbed his arm. He looked down into the freckled face of Harry Renwick. Harry had wiry hair the color of a carrot. He tried to crimp it in the latest style, but instead it stuck out all over his head.

"Hey, English, I hadn't expected to see you in here. I thought you were minding the shipping office."

"I was, but now I'm here to call Waterton out," Teddy said, his gaze locked on Waterton.

Harry threw in his cards. "Count me out on this hand,

gents." Harry jumped up from his chair and left the other three card players staring after him as he dragged Teddy to a corner of the room. "Are you out of your mind?"

"Would I be here if I were?"

"I can't let you do this. Waterton has killed twelve men. And since your brother broke his nose at Gentleman Jim's, he's not likely to let you live."

"John broke Waterton's nose?" Teddy said with awe and pride in his voice. He glanced over Harry's shoulder at Waterton's nose. It did, indeed, look swollen and crooked. The sides of Teddy's mouth twisted in a sneer. He made sure Waterton saw it.

"Yes, and it's all anyone can talk about. You picked a hell of a time to call him out. What did he do?"

"He sabotaged one of our ships."

"I don't believe it," Harry said, drawing out the words in his slow American drawl.

"Well, it's true. I have a very reliable witness. I hope I can count on you to be my second. Now, if you'll step aside, I can get on with it."

Harry stayed stubbornly in his way for a moment. When he saw that Teddy wasn't budging, he said, "Damn English, stubborn as rusty nails." He cursed and stepped aside.

Teddy strode past Harry. All eyes were on him now, except Waterton's. He was pretending to look enthralled with his cards. When Teddy reached the table, he paused and watched Waterton continue to play his hand.

Teddy crossed his arms over his chest, then waited for his quarry to condescend and notice him, a game the marquis liked to play.

Waterton flicked an ace of clubs across the table with lazy disinterest, then sipped his drink and eyed the other card players. They had stopped playing to stare at Teddy.

"Are we playing or not?" He set his glass down on the table with deliberate slowness.

Teddy lost his patience and knocked the cards out of Waterton's hands. They flew up into the air, then rained down on the table and floor.

Waterton turned and narrowed his eyes at Teddy. With bored disdain, he said, "Forgive me. Did you want something?"

He knew Waterton was doing his best to intimidate him. Like a fool, he had allowed his temper to get the better of him. John would never have let that happen. Assuming the same bored tone as Waterton, he said, "I'm calling you out."

"For what, dear boy?" He lifted his quizzing glass and eyed Teddy through it as if he were an annoying fly.

"For destroying two of our ships and trying to ruin my brother."

"Really?" Waterton didn't look at all surprised by the accusations. "Why did your brother send a diapered fop to besmirch my name? Could he not do it to my face?"

The other men at the table snickered.

Teddy drew his fist back and was about to use it, but he saw the mocking grin on Waterton's face. He had played right into Waterton's hands. It took every ounce of self-control to drop his fist. "My second will be in touch with you," he said.

"It'll be my pleasure to send you home in a box in time for Christmas. I'll make sure the mortician puts all the Christmas trimmings on your casket so it will please your brother when he opens it." Waterton dropped his monocle, evidently done with the conversation.

The men snickered again.

"Dawn, then. Wrigley's Field." With that, Teddy stormed

out of White's, his guts in knots. What had he just done? He had made John seem like a coward.

Now John wouldn't be proud of him.

Later that evening, John left the aviary and walked down a hallway, noticing the garland over the doorways and the stark red bows. It was as if Holly had zapped a magic wand and the whole house had blossomed with Christmas greenery. How did she do it so quickly and without him ever seeing her? She was doing a good job of avoiding him. All day he had looked for her, but every time he'd gone into a room, one of the children or the servants had said she'd just left. He had a nagging feeling that she would suddenly disappear and he'd never find her again. He had to make sure that never happened.

He really should leave for London. Teddy wasn't very competent when it came to business. And perhaps the man with the gun would show himself again and John could confront him. But he had to deal with Holly first. Every male instinct he possessed told him she cared for him, so why wouldn't she trust him enough to marry him and let him help her. Whatever she'd done they could see it through together. Somehow he had to make her believe that.

The aroma of burning cookies wafted down the hallway from the kitchen, a sure sign Holly was there. At least he'd finally found her. He tried not to breathe too deeply and shoved open the door.

Ann and Brock were putting raisins and nuts on a batch of gingerbread men about to go into the oven.

"Papa!" Ann's eyes lit up when she saw him. "Did you come to help us?"

John smiled at her. "No, but I did come to taste them."

As he spoke, he glanced over at Holly's breasts, displayed to advantage in a green dress.

She saw him staring at her and a blush broke out on her cheeks. Trying her best to ignore him, she picked up a rolling pin and attacked a wad of gingerbread dough. She looked abundantly more edible than the burned cookies. Her hair was braided and pulled back in a prim bun, but strands of it hung down around her face. A white patch of flour dusted the end of her nose, adding a touch of disarrayed charm he found irresistible. She blew aside several strands of hair in her face while she proceeded to bludgeon the dough.

"Here, taste this one." Ann handed him a cookie from a pan that was cooling.

John bit into the cookie and noticed Holly watching him for a reaction. He smacked his lips and lied worthy of any young gallant swain. "Hmmm! Very good."

"Really?" Ann raised an incredulous brow.

"I've eaten ten." Brock frowned and grabbed his stomach.

Why would Brock put himself through such torture? What was there about little boys that made them eat any sweet put before them, no matter how unpalatable it was? John swallowed the cookie, took a sip of milk from a cup beside Holly, then, in a teasing tone, said, "What are you about letting my children eat cookies until they are sick?"

"I'm afraid that's all the fun of baking cookies."

He smiled at Holly, set the cup down, then turned toward Brock. "I think you should stop baking before you need a dose of Dunn's stomach tonic."

Ann and Brock shared a glance as if they'd rather be tortured on a rack.

John grinned. "Brock, take your sister into the parlor. Pringle is there, and he can carry her up the stairs."

"Yes, Papa," Brock said, the mention of Dunn's stomach tonic making him move faster than John had ever seen his youngest son move.

Brock jumped up and grabbed the back of Ann's chair.

"Wait." Holly set three cookies on a plate. They sounded like rocks hitting the stoneware. She handed them to Ann. "Would you take these to Dryden? I know he won't eat them if he knows I sent them, but he might eat them if you tell him you made them especially for him."

"Yes, we'll do that. And I bet he makes a pig of himself and stuffs all of them in his mouth at once."

"He'd choke," Brock said, pushing Ann out of the kitchen.

"I've seen him stuff a whole apple tart in his mouth at one time," Ann added.

Brock lowered his voice, but it still carried. "Yes, but Holly didn't make it."

John turned to see if Holly heard the comment. She was grinning and didn't look hurt by the remark.

"The cookies are only a little burned . . ." Ann whispered.

Ann's voice trailed off as John closed the door behind them and locked it.

"What are you doing?"

"I'm merely seeing we have a little privacy."

"Why?" Holly's large doe-like eyes widened.

"Because I've wanted to get you alone all day." He smiled, then his gaze devoured her as he strolled around the counter.

She saw him come toward her and backed up. "Don't look at me like that. Something always happens when you look at me like that. You didn't come in here to sample the cookies, did you?"

"Only yours," he said, wiggling his brows at her.

She grabbed a tin of flour near her. The top was off and she held it upright in her hand. "Don't start this. Last night was a mistake."

"It didn't feel like a mistake to me." He took two steps toward her.

"But it was. I can never marry you." She backed up two steps and clutched the tin tighter.

"You're mine, Holly. I won't let you go so easily."

Her spine hit the kitchen wall and she glanced around. "Stop right there, or I swear I'll throw this."

"You know that is only a threat." He reached out to grab her.

She let the flour tin fly. John ducked, but wasn't fast enough. The tin hit his shoulder. Flour flew up into his face and down the inside of his cravat, then . . .

Bang! The tin hit the floor behind him.

He paused a moment, blinking the flour from his eyes, surprised at what she had done, then found himself smiling. "You realize this means war." He picked up a nearby crock off the counter and dumped the contents over her head.

Black molasses streamed down over her hair, her neck, in her eyes. She wiped the molasses out of her eyes. "Ohhh! That was despicable!"

"Yes, but it felt good." A grin tugged at the corners of his mouth.

"See how this feels." She stuck her hand in a crock of butter, pulled out a wad, and slapped it down the center of his face, down his neck, and didn't stop until her palm reached his cravat. She wiped her hand on the lapel of his coat, then said, "There now. We can make dough on your face with a little water."

Enjoying this more than anything he'd ever done in his life, he tasted the greasy butter on his lips. "You need something to go with your new coiffure." He grabbed a bowl of eggs off the counter and dumped it on her head.

He pushed the bowl down, grinding the eggshells against her head. The broken yokes ran down over her face and hair and dripped onto her dress.

He removed the bowl. "Much better," he said and set the bowl down.

An eggshell slid down her nose. She picked it off, then looked on the counter for something else to throw on him. But every bowl was empty.

"All out of ammunition?" He wiggled a teasing brow at her.

"It's probably a good thing." She looked at his face, and her dimples came alive as she grinned.

He knew he must have looked comical with the flour covering his face, only his eyes peeking out at her. He could feel the butter hanging from his lashes and the smear of it along his nose and cheeks.

"I don't know. I would have liked to throw something else on you," she said, running her tongue across her full red lips.

That wet, sensual sight aroused him instantly. "Perhaps we should make a truce." He pulled her close, then lowered his head and captured those luscious lips.

John felt his mouth sliding against hers. He tasted molasses on her mouth. A shiver went through her as he deepened the kiss, slipping his tongue deep into her mouth.

He had never kissed a woman with molasses on her lips, but it definitely made the experience incredibly erotic! The sticky warmth enhanced the suppleness of her lips, making them feel like slick satin.

"You taste luscious," he said against her mouth, then moved his hands to her breasts, fondling them, feeling them fill his palms. He slipped his thigh between her legs and rubbed his hips against her. The feel of her soft belly against him made him groan.

"We shouldn't be doing this . . ." she said, even as her back arched and she gave in to her passion. She clung to his neck and wrapped her legs around his thighs, then her hips moved with his.

He could feel the hot heat of her through his breeches. Her hands slipped beneath his coat and rubbed his back. The feel of her hands on him drove him mad.

His hands trembled as he jerked up the hem of her gown.

She grabbed his buttock now, then ran her tongue along the dimple in his chin. "Make love to me again," she whispered against his chin.

Her softly spoken supplication made John jerk down her drawers. Then he tore at his breeches, freeing his hard flesh. He felt Holly's fingers close around him.

He sucked in his breath. "Oh, God, my sweet, I won't last long if you touch me like that."

She ran her fingers over the tip of his erection. "But you're so soft and hard at the same time. I love feeling you."

John grinned, then he couldn't stand another moment of torture. He lifted her hips and drove into her. She moaned and grabbed handfuls of his waistcoat and shirt.

John pressed her back against the wall and thrust into her, again and again, so deep into her hot, tight shaft he could feel her womb. He kissed her, his tongue matching the rhythm of his thrusts.

"Oh, no . . ." she moaned softly. Her thighs tightened around his legs, her hips moving to match his thrusts.

"I know, my sweet. Come with me." John felt her shudder, then he took her scream into his mouth as they both found their release together.

John rested his forehead against hers, his chest heaving like he'd run twenty miles. His knees still trembled from the power of their lovemaking. Both times he'd made love to her, he felt totally spent, as if he'd lost a part of himself to her. When he started to pull out of her, she tightened her thighs around his hips and clutched his neck as if she couldn't let go.

There was desperation in her voice as she said, "Hold me . . ."

John crushed her to him and looked down into her enormous brown eyes, hooded by long dark lashes. The glow of passion still burned brightly in them, and something else. Fear.

"I'll never leave you, Holly," John reassured her with a kiss.

For a long moment, they were lost in each other. He sensed Holly's total surrender to him. She had let down her guard and her past wasn't keeping her away from him. He basked in the feeling, then came to his senses. He leaned back and gazed down at her. "I think if we want to continue this, my sweet, we should do it in my bed."

She glanced around as if realizing where they were. "Oh, dear."

He laughed, then stared down at her hair sticking to the sides of her face, the yellow egg yokes glistening in her hair. Patches of flour covered her nose and cheeks.

"You look a delightful mess," he said, grinning down at her.

"You don't look so handsome yourself." She answered his grin with one of her own, then pushed back the stray hair that had fallen over his forehead. "What a mess you are." She glanced down at the flour and butter smeared on her hand, then wiped her hand off on his coat, grinning like an imp.

"You really are asking for it again, but I'll save my revenge for when we take a bath together."

"Do you think it will be as much fun as throwing cooking ingredients at each other?"

"I don't know, but I'm willing to experiment." He placed a soft kiss on her lips.

The doorknob turned, then the scrape of the key in the lock made John and Holly look at each other. He had never moved so quickly. He pulled out of Holly, set her on the ground, then fumbled with his breeches, trying to get them closed. Holly was shaking down the hem of her dress and petticoat.

Abruptly, the door opened.

Chapter 16

Mrs. Pringle breezed through the door, mumbling under her breath, "Whoever locked the kitchen door will deal with me." When she saw Holly and John, she gasped and took a step back. She stared at them as if they'd grown long ears and buck teeth.

"Don't stand there gawking." John took a step toward the sink to wash his face, but stepped on Holly's drawers. He stared down at them and held back a grin, then noticed Holly saw them, too.

The mortification grew in her eyes, while her cheeks looked as if someone had put a hot iron on them.

Mrs. Pringle found her voice. It came out shrill. "When she asked if she could come into my kitchen and cook, I had a feeling I should have said no. Against my better judgment, I let her in here with the children. Now look what she's done. Just look at her! Look at you, my lord!

Where are the children?'' She glared at Holly as if she'd thrown the children in the oven and cooked them.

"You need not worry about the children, they're safe in their rooms," John said flatly. "Now, if you wish to keep your position here, you will leave us."

"Well, I never," she huffed under her breath, then slammed the door and left the kitchen.

"This will be all over the household now," Holly said with asperity, bending down to pick up her drawers. "I should never have let you get near me."

"I care not a whit what the servants think. We are going to marry anyway."

"I told you I couldn't marry you. Didn't you hear me? You think because you order it that I will change my mind. Well, I won't."

John grinned at her back, then the grin faded as he grabbed her and forced her to turn and look at him. "You're mine, Holly. You could be carrying my child. We will marry, that is all there is to it."

She bit her lip and tears glazed her enormous brown eyes. "Why can't you understand? I must have my freedom." She paused, tears trickling down her cheeks. "I'm going to have to go one day soon, so you'd might as well get used to the idea."

He pulled her into his embrace. She struggled, but he held her tightly. "If you leave me, I'll find you and bring you back. I don't know what kind of trouble you are in, but we'll deal with it together."

She gulped, then the fight went out of her and she collapsed against him. "You can't deal with it. No one can."

"We will, and shall. You are mine, Holly, and I'll move heaven and earth to keep you." He touched her chin and tipped her face up for a kiss.

She didn't protest, only moved her mouth closer to his. Their lips were about to meet when someone rapped on the door.

"My lord, are you in there?"

"Damnation!" John growled at the sound of Pringle's voice. "Can I not have a moment's privacy in my own home?" Holly was seconds away from telling him this dark secret of hers, he was certain of it. She pulled back from him now. He cursed inwardly, then glowered at the door. "What is it?"

"A missive just arrived, my lord."

"I'm busy, Pringle." John stared down at Holly's full red lips.

"But it looks urgent, my lord. It's from London."

"Who the devil sent it?" He glanced toward the door.

"A Mr. Scibner."

John turned and locked gazes with Holly.

Holly's eyes widened in surprise, then her brows met with worry. "Do you think he's found the person trying to ruin your shipping company?"

"One can only hope." Louder, over his shoulder, he said, "I'll be out to read it in a moment."

"Very good, my lord."

He'd have to seduce the secret out of her later. Grimacing, he turned and stepped up to the sink.

"Promise me you won't do anything rash," she said, following him.

"I'll do what I have to do."

He left Holly in the kitchen, her face marred with worry.

Holly opened the door a crack and watched as Pringle shoved a silver tray at John with the letter in the center. "Here it is, my lord."

"Thank you, Pringle." John broke the seal and read the note. After a moment, he cursed, then crumbled the parchment in his hand.

"What is it, my lord?" Pringle clenched and unclenched his hands in front of him.

"I have to go to London. I'll be leaving within the hour." John turned, then strode down the hall, his fist strangling the parchment as he shoved it in his pocket.

Holly had been listening through a crack in the door. She waited until John neared the end of the hallway before she stepped out of the kitchen and whispered, "Where can I rent a hack, Pringle?"

Pringle had been watching John, and he jumped at Holly's voice, a likely reflex at having lived with Mrs. Pringle too long. He stared at her, taking in her appearance, then whispered, "What happened, miss?"

"Just having a little food war with his lordship."

"If you don't mind me saying so, it looks like he won."

"Yes, well, I should have been more selective in what I threw at him. I've learned a valuable lesson." Holly moved back on track. "Anyway, I was wondering about a hack?"

"The smithy in the village is the place to go. But are you leaving us?" Pringle asked, his voice anxious.

"No, Pringle. I have to follow his lordship."

"Why, miss?"

"He may be in trouble. I think Mr. Scibner might have found out who is trying to ruin his lordship, and he's keeping it a secret. I do not want him to get hurt. I'm sure he means to do something reckless." Pringle looked confused, and Holly waved her hand through the air. "Never mind, I just have to follow him. You'll watch the children for me. I hope to be back later tomorrow."

"Yes, miss, I'll do my best."

"Perhaps you can keep Mrs. Pringle happy as well and

not let her know I'm gone. I'm afraid she's not very happy with me at the moment. She caught me and his lordship fighting. We sort of messed up her kitchen.''

"I can handle her." Pringle didn't sound very sure of himself, but he nodded with confidence.

"Thank you." She patted his arm. "Would you mind terribly sending up a bath for me?"

"I'd say you were in need of one." Pringle leaned over and studied her hair and face. "Is that an eggshell in your hair?"

"I wouldn't look too closely, or you'll find more," Holly said in a flat tone.

"I'll get that bath." Pringle shook his head and grinned. He was about to turn, when . . .

"Mr. Pringle." Mrs. Pringle's screech echoed from the servants' quarters.

"My beloved calls," Pringle mumbled. The grin faded from his face. "I suppose I should go and see what she wants." Rolling his eyes, he turned and strode down the hall, his shoulders slumped, making him look ten years older.

Holly shot a pitying look at his back, then hurried to the servants' stairs. Somehow she had to follow John without him knowing about it, but as yet she didn't know how she would do it.

Half an hour later, Holly leaned over and pulled the covers up around Ann's shoulders, then bent and pecked her on the cheek. "Good night."

Ann kissed Holly back. "Must you go away to London?"

"Yes, but you can't tell your father."

"I shan't breathe a word."

"I knew I could count on you." Holly patted Ann's

shoulder, then stood. A bottle of laudanum sitting on the nightstand caught her eye. She stared at it as an idea formed in her mind. "Could I borrow some of this?"

"Of course. I used to take it sometimes when I couldn't sleep, but since I've seen the fairy, I don't need it at all. I think she must have cast a spell over me."

"I'm sure she did." Holly grinned down at Ann.

"You will be home tomorrow so we can put candles on the Christmas tree?"

"I couldn't miss that."

"I can't imagine what they will look like."

"It's the most exquisite thing you've ever seen." Holly added as an afterthought, "Though it might pall compared to seeing a fairy."

"I'm sure it won't."

The animation in Ann's eyes warmed Holly all over. Ann was getting excited about Christmas. It was what Holly had hoped for her. Then she remembered Dryden. "Perhaps you can convince Dryden to stop skulking around and help us decorate the tree."

"I'll try, but you know how he is." Ann rolled her eyes.

"Yes, well, I think he needs a little nudge. I'll leave that in your capable hands. I had better go now. And remember to have Dunn or Pringle find your stocking so you can hang it over the mantel."

"I don't believe in that nonsense," Ann said with an air of bored maturity. "I know Mama and Papa put gifts in my stocking and not Saint Nicholas. You know how I found out?"

"How?" Holly asked, frowning.

"One year, the tenants came on Boxing Day to get their presents from Papa. The children didn't look very happy, and I asked a little girl why she looked so glum after Saint Nicholas had come. I had just gotten my dolly . . ." Her doll was sitting beside her. She pulled it into her arms and embraced it.

Ann twirled the doll's thin strands of hair around her finger and continued. "I showed it to her and told her Saint Nicholas had brought it to me." Ann grimaced as if the memory were unpleasant. "She threw my dolly down and said there was no such thing as Saint Nicholas. She said if you were rich, your parents could afford to give you presents and say Saint Nicholas brought them. I asked Mama about it, and she said that was true, but I shouldn't let it upset me, that peasant children didn't know the difference whether or not they got something for Christmas."

Ann's frown deepened. "I didn't think that was right. I wanted to give my doll to the little girl. Mama got very angry with me and sent me to my room." As if to explain her mother's behavior away, she added, "She was sick and cross."

"Well, I think wanting to give away your doll was very admirable of you."

"You would. You are nothing like my mama." Ann hugged her doll tightly.

"Let me tell you something, and I want you to remember this always." Holly stroked the blond hair back from Ann's face. "Some people stop believing in fairies, angels, saints, and even God, then their hearts shrivel up and they grow into bitter people. Saint Nicholas exists to remind us of the giving spirit and love that should be within all of us, not only on Christmas but throughout the whole year. That is why I'll always believe in Saint Nicholas whether he visits me or not."

"Have you ever seen him?"

"No, but I always thought if I did see him, I'd know

him. I'm sure the little girl you spoke of needs to meet
him and so does her parents.''

"Her parents?"

"Yes, sometimes when adults' hearts grow bitter, it wears
off on their children. And they need something to wake
up their faith again."

"I hope I do not have a bitter heart."

"You have a giving, kind heart." Holly smiled at her.

"I'm going to believe in Saint Nicholas again. I hope
he doesn't mind I haven't believed in him for a while."

"I'm sure he knows the reason why. I think we should
make a point to invite this little girl to our secret Christmas
party. Can you be in charge of that?"

Ann nodded. "I'll even make her a gift."

"That is very kind of you. I'll help you when I return."

"I would like to do it myself, but thank you," Ann said
with an air of mature confidence way beyond her seven
years.

"All right. I'll see you tomorrow then."

"You'll hurry back from London, won't you?" Ann
stared up at her with large, imploring eyes.

"Yes, of course." Holly kissed her on the forehead again,
took the bottle of laudanum from the stand, then blew
out the candle and tiptoed from the room.

She only had a few minutes to execute her plan. She
hoped it worked.

Holly hurried down the hall to John's chamber and
rapped lightly on the door.

Dunn poked out his head. His eyes brightened when he
saw her. "Hello, miss."

"Dunn, I'm so glad you answered the door." Holly

touched his shoulder, then leaned past him and peered into the room. "He's not here, is he?"

"No, miss."

"Good, because I need to see his lordship's clothes."

"Whatever for?" Dunn looked dismayed by the idea.

"A missive he received. I need to read it. I hoped—"

"I threw it away when he changed for dinner."

"I hope you read it." Holly couldn't keep the desperation from her voice.

"Of course." Dunn didn't look at all ashamed by his snooping.

"What did it say?"

"It said Lord Theodore was to engage in a duel with Lord Waterton early in the morning near Wrigley's Field."

Holly breathed a sigh of relief. "Well, I'm so glad Mr. Scibner hasn't found that horrible person trying to destroy Lord Upton's shipping company." Holly held up the bottle of laudanum. "I came prepared to stop him if he had thoughts of getting himself killed."

"I believe he means to take Lord Theodore's place."

Holly remembered the cruelty in Lord Waterton's face and her fingers tightened around the bottle of laudanum. "Thank you for the information, Dunn."

"But what are you planning to do?"

"Stop him if I can." She hurried down the hallway to the stairs, leaving Dunn with a curious, nonplussed look on his face.

She reached John's office and picked up a decanter and two glasses. When she was about to leave, she heard heavy footsteps in the hall and darted back behind the door. Through a crack, she watched Mrs. Pringle lumber past, the keys around her neck jingling like Christmas bells.

Holly waited until her footsteps died away, glanced up and down the hall, then hurried up the three flights of stairs to her room. Her heart pounded at the thought of what she was about to do. But it was for John's own good. She poured two drinks, dosing one with enough laudanum to knock out a horse, then hurried from the room in search of him.

She heard his deep voice coming from the boys' room. She paused at their chamber door. It was open six inches, and she peeked at him through the crack.

John paused before he blew the candle out and looked at Dryden. "How would you like to come to the shipping office with me? Perhaps in a month."

Dryden's eyes glowed with excitement. "Do you mean it, Papa?"

"Can I come, too?" Brock asked, sitting up in his bed.

"Both of you can come as long as it doesn't interfere with your schoolwork. Which reminds me, I'll have to see about getting a male tutor for you. I think you both have outgrown a governess."

The boys' faces fell.

"Can you wait a week or two, Papa?" Brock asked.

"I suppose it couldn't hurt." John smiled at them, tousled Dryden's hair, then Brock's. He blew out the candle. "Now, good night."

"Good night, Papa," the boys said in unison.

Smiling, Holly hurried back to her room before she was caught eavesdropping. John had done something wonderful for Dryden. Perhaps he wouldn't brood so much now. Perhaps he wouldn't see Holly as such a threat and maybe they could be friends.

Like she was sure the sun would rise in the morning, she was sure John would come to her room to say good-bye before he left. She kicked off her shoes, pulled the pins out of her hair, then hurriedly tossed them in the wardrobe. Shaking her hair loose, she flopped down on her bed and rolled on her side, facing the door. She threw her thick hair down over her shoulder, letting it fall to the mattress, then pinched her cheeks and stared at the door.

The knock came, then he entered her room, unbidden. His eyes sought her as he closed the door behind him. His gaze roamed slowly over every inch of her. "What are you doing?"

"Waiting for you," she said, trying a seductive smile on him.

"I thought you'd send me away from your room."

"I could never do that." Holly sat up and made sure she picked up the glass without the laudanum in it. "I hope you don't mind, but I thought we could share a drink together before you leave."

"We shall do more than that." In spite of his obvious desire for her, he looked worried, his brows heavy over his eyes. He took the glass out of her hand and set it down on the table.

She strained to see around him so she could tell which glass held the laudanum. But he set the glass down before she could tell which one was hers. She groaned inwardly.

He bent down and kissed her, stealing her breath, then began stripping off his shirt.

She broke the kiss. "Shouldn't we drink our wine first?"

"I don't want wine. I want you."

"But I would like to drink my wine."

"What is this fetish over cheap wine?" He eyed her suspiciously.

"Nothing, I just thought it would help me to relax. I'm going to be worried about you all night."

"You needn't worry." He nuzzled her neck.

Praying hard, she leaned past him and reached for a glass. Her trembling hand hesitated a moment, then she squeezed her eyes closed and chose a glass. "Here you are," she said, handing it to him.

As if the wine annoyed him, he took the proffered glass and downed the contents in one gulp.

She raised her brows at him. Would so much laudanum at once make him sick? Worse yet, what if he didn't get the right glass?

"Now for you," he said, eyeing her.

Holly gulped past the tightness in her throat, looked at the glass, then downed it. The bitter liquid seared her throat, until it hit her stomach. A bitter taste lingered in her mouth, and she swallowed hard. She couldn't help but wonder if it was the laudanum.

"There, now. Can I make love to you now?" he asked, taking her glass and setting it down on the table, then continued to disrobe.

Mesmerized by the sight of his body, she watched him finish undressing. She stared at his broad chest and at the well-defined muscles rippling across his chest. Her fingers itched to twine in the dark brown patch of hair there. His corded stomach muscles flexed as he pulled off his breeches, then his long, muscular thighs were exposed. And it was hard to miss that dark thatch of hair between his legs and his arousal jutting out, so proud, so massive.

He eased her back and pulled up the hem of her dress. With maddening slowness, he peeled down her woolen stockings. "You have lovely legs," he said, kissing each of her thighs.

The feeling of his warm lips on her legs made her tremble. He slid his hands along her thighs, pushing the hem of her dress and petticoat up to her hips. He touched her through the opening in her drawers, rubbing the sensitive spot between her legs.

Her hips arched. In the candlelight, she saw his eyes

brighten to a bright golden yellow, then he pulled her drawers down and threw them on the floor. "Those things are always getting in the way." He grinned at her now, the strain momentarily leaving his face.

He ran his hands through the thick triangle of hair between her thighs. "You are lovely, my sweet."

Before Holly knew it, he opened her thighs, then his mouth touched her. Holly gasped and tried to push him away, but he raised his head. "Let me taste you, my sweet. I promise you'll enjoy it."

Her face burned as she said, "I don't think—"

He bent and separated the soft folds, his tongue running over her nub of pleasure. Holly *couldn't* think. Her thighs melted into jelly, falling open and lulling against the mattress. She arched her hips, an ache growing deep within her. She ran her hands through his hair and pulled his head closer to her. His tongue moved inside her hot canal, while his finger stroked her. When she thought she would die, he moved on top of her, then kissed her.

Holly tasted her own sweet dew on his lips as he thrust his tongue in her mouth, then, with deft, precise movements, he opened the hooks and eyes at the back of her dress. It didn't take him long until she was naked, then he bent and took one of her nipples in his mouth, while he rubbed his swollen manhood against her.

Holly needed to feel him inside her or she would burst. She wrapped her legs around him, then pulled him down to her. When their bodies touched, the heat of his skin burned her as no fire had ever done. A fine film of perspiration broke out all over her. She pressed her hips beneath his erection, guiding him inside her.

"I had hoped to take my time loving you this time, but you make me burn for you." He pulled her down for a kiss, tangling his hands in her thick hair.

He grabbed her hips, then thrust deeply into her again and again. She clung to his back and cried out when she found her release. He came with her, kissing her.

He paused, his arms trembling as he tried to hold himself up. "I don't feel well," he said in a groggy voice.

"You don't?" Holly said, hiding a relieved grin.

He opened his mouth to speak, but couldn't. As if the laudanum had turned off the energy in his body, he collapsed on top of her.

His dead weight knocked the breath out of her. It took all of her strength, but she managed to roll him off her. Sucking in a deep breath, she turned on her side and smiled over at him. She pushed back the strand of dark hair on his brow. "I hope you forgive me in the morning." She kissed his lips, feeling the coarse stubble on his chin against her face, then left the bed.

It took several hard tugs to pull the covers from beneath his limp body, but she managed, then covered him. She turned and picked up her petticoat, then slipped her hand through the secret front. Her fingers connected with a bracelet. She carefully tore it free. The diamonds glistened in the candlelight as she tossed it on the side of the bed, then searched for the earrings and necklace that went with the bracelet.

She held all three pieces in her hands for a moment. It was the last of her grandmother's jewels. They had belonged to her mother before she died, then on Holly's sixteenth birthday, her grandmother had given them to her and told her to take good care of them. For so very long, she had cherished them. Now this was the last of them, but she wanted to get the townhouse back for John. It would be the last thing she did for him before she left.

She gulped past the lump forming in her throat at the thought of leaving John and the children, then moved to her wardrobe and found the breeches and shirt Dunn had lent her. Since she didn't have a riding habit, she supposed it would be better than a dress. She donned the clothes, then stuffed the jewels in the pockets of the breeches and stared one last time at John. A sensuous smile turned up the corners of his lips. Was he dreaming about their love-making? Perhaps his pleasant dreams would help curb his ire when he found she was gone.

Holly entered the stable, the lantern in her hand dancing flickering shadows on the walls. The smell of hay, leather, and horse lingered in the air. She raised the lantern and scanned the stable. Eight stalls lined both sides of a paved walkway. John's black stallion stood in a stall near the back, his black eyes gleaming. The unexpected light must have bothered him, for he bobbed his head up and down and snorted.

"Hello there, my beauty," she said in a low, even voice, striding toward him. She had decided it would save time to borrow John's horse rather than rent one from town, but after looking at the huge stallion, she was having second thoughts.

A door creaked open, then Lawrence stepped out of a small room in the stable. His shirt was open, his breeches barely together as if he'd pulled them on in a hurry. He was a huge man with a tree stump-size neck and a large square face. When he brought her bath water up to her, she had met him. He was taking her measure, grimacing at Dunn's trousers poking out beneath her cape.

"Miss, what are you doing here?" His cheeks colored up as he turned and finished buttoning up his breeches.

"I've come to borrow his lordship's horse," she said, staring at the light gleaming off the animal's black coat.

"Ah, miss," Lawrence said, not sounding happy with the idea. He turned now and strode toward her, barefoot, the cold not seeming to bother him. "His lordship is particular about Whisper. He sold off all the other horses but old Whisp. He's real crazy over that horse. Had him for ten years. His lordship would eat me alive if I let you take him out."

"Would it help to tell you I've ridden horses since I was a child. And I wouldn't let anything happen to him. But I really need to get to London and quickly." Holly set the lantern down on the corner of a stall.

"I don't know." Lawrence scratched the dark stubble on his chin.

"It's for Lord Theodore. He's in trouble and I have to go and help him."

"Where's his lordship?"

"He's asleep." Holly hoped he stayed that way. She saw the reticence on his face and added, "To be honest, I sort of gave him a dose of laudanum to help him sleep."

"Well, that puts a new light on things." His wide face grew wider with a smile. "You think you can have Whisper back 'fore he wakes?"

"I'll try my best. And if I don't, you can play dumb and tell him I took the horse and you didn't know it."

"I couldn't do that."

"Well, it will absolve you of all blame."

He was silent a moment, scratched the thick stubble on his chin, then said, "I'll saddle him for you. He's a might particular about who he lets on his back. If he don't like you, you won't get as far as the stable doors 'fore he throws you."

"I can handle him," Holly said, trying to sound confident. She had never ridden stallions on the plantation back home, only Bessie, her grandmother's mare. Besides the anatomy, what could be different about it?

He went into the tack room and came out with a bridle and saddle, then eased into Whisper's stall, speaking softly while he saddled the stallion. "I was thinking, miss, if you don't mind, I'd like to help with the Christmas party," Lawrence said, keeping his voice low and even while he put the bit in Whisper's mouth. "We ain't had a Christmas here for two years. It will be nice to celebrate this year."

"If you like, you could get the word out to all the tenants. Please make sure they know it's a surprise."

"Yes, miss, but what about his lordship. He won't be liking it, will he?"

"I'm hoping he'll get into the spirit and enjoy it."

Lawrence cinched up the saddle, then led Whisper out of the stall.

Holly glanced up at the horse, her eyes leery. "Whew! He's a tall one."

"Sixteen hands, miss. You'll be needin' this." Lawrence handed her a riding crop.

She took the crop and said to the horse, "Now, don't act up and make me use this on you."

Whisper rolled his eyes at her.

The look in those dark, glistening eyes boded ill. She frowned back at the animal, aware of a battle of wills ahead of her.

"Here, I'll give you a leg up." Lawrence cupped his hands.

"Thank you." She climbed up into the saddle.

Whisper stepped to the side and bucked. She clamped her thighs tightly against his sides and hung on.

"Whoo now, Old Whisp," he said, holding the reins tight. "I know it ain't your master, but you'll get used to her." He held the reins up to Holly. "Sure you want to try it?"

"Yes," she said, her voice wavering as she eyed Whisper's laid-back ears. She took the reins and patted the animal's sleek neck, feeling the taut muscles ripple beneath her fingertips. "We'll be good friends."

"He might be a bit frisky with the cold weather and all . . ."

She made the mistake of nudging Whisper's sides. He shot out of the stable like a bullet. Lawrence's voice quickly faded away beneath the pounding of Whisper's hooves as she dug her knees in and hung on for dear life.

Chapter 17

Holly didn't gain complete control of Whisper until she was halfway to London. By the time she found her way to Wrigley's Field, Whisper was maintaining a sedate canter. Dawn was slow in emerging from behind the gray-white clouds that had been thickening since yesterday. The first few drops of snow hit her face. Her teeth chattered. An hour ago she had lost the feeling in her fingers and toes.

She scanned the field. Pencil cedars lined the sides like tall green walls. For a moment, she wondered if she were in the wrong place, then a coach and four, with bright yellow dragon crests on the doors, rolled to a stop near a line of trees. Two gentlemen on horseback reined in fifty yards from the carriage. One of them was Teddy; she could tell by the bright pink stripes of his wool muffler.

She barely tapped Whisper in the sides, not making the same mistake she had made back in the stable. His hooves ate up the ground, kicking clods of dirt high into the air. She reined in just as Teddy dismounted.

He glanced up at her, his eyes wide with surprise. "Holly, what are you doing here?"

"I came to stop this nonsense." Holly dismounted.

He noticed John's horse. "What the devil are you doing riding Whisper?"

"I borrowed him."

Teddy grabbed her arm. "He could have killed you!"

"He only threw me once, but I showed him I was as determined to ride him as he was determined that I shouldn't."

As if Whisper knew she was speaking about him, he nudged her in the behind. Holly stumbled forward a step, then turned and shot the horse a look.

A young gentleman strode up to Teddy and cleared his voice.

Teddy glanced at him. "Forgive me, this is my friend, Harry Renwick. He's the gentleman I was telling you about from Charleston. Harry, this is Miss Campbell."

"Pleased to meet you, madam." Harry tipped his hat. A thick thatch of bright orange hair sprung out about his head.

"Hello, Mr. Renwick." Holly saw Waterton get out of his carriage. "I'm sorry I don't have time to chat about Charleston." She turned and saw Teddy's gaze clamped on Waterton, the veiled terror growing in his eyes the closer Waterton came to them. She grabbed his arm. "You must stop this."

"I cannot. He is the one who sunk our ships. I called him out, and I mean to see the bastard pays."

"Are you sure of this?" Holly asked, incredulous.

"I have it from a good source."

"Do they have proof?" Holly asked, watching Waterton

getting closer, his greatcoat flapping around his long legs, his beaver hat sitting as straight as a stovepipe.

"He was bragging openly about it."

Holly could tell by the determination in Teddy's voice that all the reasoning in the world couldn't sway him. Before she'd left the house, she'd gone to John's chamber and borrowed one of his dueling pistols for the journey. She reached inside her cape for it now and pulled it from the waistband of her breeches. Quicker than spitting hot grease, she slammed the handle of it against the side of Teddy's head, surprising even herself at her swiftness.

He stared at her, wide-eyed and incredulous that the blow had come from her, then his knees crumbled beneath him.

Harry caught Teddy before he hit the ground. He shot her a look of chagrin. "Miss Campbell, you shouldn't have done that. You don't know how damn stubborn the English can be about their pride and honor."

"I've met his brother. Believe me, I know very well." Holly shoved the pistol back inside the waistband of her breeches and heard footsteps.

Waterton paused in front of them. He took one look at Harry holding Teddy's prostrate form, then glanced at Holly. His eyes gleamed with a sardonic blue hue. "Well, well, Miss Campbell, you've saved us all from a dreadfully cold morning." Waterton brushed off a fleck of snow that had landed on the sleeve of his gray greatcoat.

"I don't know about that, Lord Waterton. If what Teddy says is true, the whole morning won't be a total loss. I believe we should make a stop at the nearest constable's office."

A lazy smile spread across his lips. He pulled out his snuff box, flicked it open with his thumb, then snorted a pinch up each nostril. He flipped it closed with a precise snap. "I would be glad to accompany you anywhere, Miss Campbell."

Two men strolled up behind Waterton. One was medium height with black hair and a mustache, holding a flat, long box. The other was a balding man with fat cheeks. He carried a black bag.

Waterton waved to them. "There won't be a duel this morning. Miss Campbell has seen fit to interfere." He turned to Holly. "Allow me to introduce my friend, Mr. Benton, and Dr. Rathbone. Gentlemen, Miss Campbell."

Both gentlemen glared at her for meddling.

To illuminate her part in all of this, she said, "Well, I couldn't let Lord Waterton hurt Lord Theodore." She flicked her gaze at Waterton. "Why do men think it honorable to handle everything with a gun? It is beyond me. Anyway, I think this is a matter for a constable."

Waterton extended his arm. "Allow me to escort you. I would like to see the proof St. John has against me. I doubt he has any at all."

"I don't know about that," Harry said, laying Teddy down on the ground. "Teddy told me Lady Matilda overheard you speaking to someone named Jarvis about destroying St. John's ships."

"Lady Matilda has a keen dislike for me." Waterton's lips twisted in a tight smirk. "I believe she'd say just about anything to cause trouble for me."

"I don't know about that. I've met her, and I'd say her word was as good as yours." Harry stared at Waterton, and his bushy red brows came together.

"Did he speak to this Jarvis fellow?"

"Knowing English here, I doubt it." Harry glanced down at Teddy's limp form with something akin to disgust.

"You can tell your friend when he wakes up that until he finds proof of these accusations, I'll consider the matter closed," Waterton said, contemptuous amusement in his voice.

"I have a practice to run," the doctor grumbled, then turned and stomped toward his carriage.

"Damn nuisance. What's the world coming to when gentlemen can't settle a matter on the field?" Mr. Benton remarked, casting Holly a narrow-eyed glance, then turning and following the doctor.

"I'm going to take English back to my townhouse," Harry said.

"I'll go with you," Holly said.

"No, Miss Campbell. I don't think that's such a good idea. St. John will want to murder you when he wakes up. Better he calms down before he sees you. I have three sisters. They'll nurse him."

"If you insist." Holly felt terrible about what she had done to Teddy, but she had no choice.

Waterton surveyed Holly. "As a gentleman, Miss Campbell, I cannot allow you to travel in this weather on horseback." Some of the caustic cynicism left his voice. "Allow me the honor of escorting you wherever you need to go. It will be much warmer in my carriage. I only travel in luxury. I have one of the few carriages with a stove built into it."

The ache in her frozen fingers and toes felt worse. She stared at Waterton's carriage, then at the man. The cruel light was still in his eyes, but she was freezing, and she might be able to ply the truth out of him.

"Come, come. It should not take you this long to decide." His grin broadened. "I vow on my honor, Miss Campbell, you shall remain safe in my hands. In spite of what you may think, I do not molest damsels—unless, of course, they ask it of me, then I'm more than happy to oblige."

Holly wanted very much to slap his face, but she supposed Lord Waterton prided himself on his ability to manipulate and bedevil those around him. She paused, then said, "Since the extent of your honor is still in doubt, I don't know if I should trust anything you say."

He laughed. "Well done. With your witty quips, I can tell I shan't be bored on the journey. Please say you will amuse me and take my offer." He graciously extended his arm to escort her.

"Very well, since we understand each other." She didn't want to take his arm and said, "After you, my lord."

His smile broadened, then he turned and strode toward his carriage.

"Miss Campbell! Miss Campbell!"

She turned and saw Mr. Scibner pull up in a gig. He peered at her through his glasses, surprise and dismay on his face.

"Mr. Scibner," Holly said. "I didn't expect you to be here."

"I came to speak to Lord Upton. Where is he?" Mr. Scibner glanced around him, distracted.

"He's at Brookhollow Hall . . . a little under the weather," Holly said, unable to hide the guilt in her voice. "I came to stop the duel in his stead."

He stared at Waterton for a moment, then said, "May I speak to you privately?"

"Of course."

"I'll await you in the warmth of my carriage." Waterton ignored Mr. Scibner's grimace, then strode toward his carriage.

Mr. Scibner hopped down from the gig, his feet making a solid thud on the frozen ground. "I came here to see that Lord Upton did not kill Waterton, but I see now it was a futile exercise. But it's fortuitous I'm here. I must warn you to stay away from Lord Waterton.''

"Why?"

"He is not a nice gentleman. I believe he may be involved in the sinking of Lord Upton's ships.''

"I hope you've not formed your opinion from the rumor that made Lord Theodore call him out. Lady Matilda said she heard him speaking to a man about sinking the ships, but Lord Waterton swears she said it because she doesn't like him. I have seen them together, and she really does have a strong dislike for him.''

"Everyone has a strong dislike for the gentleman—but no, my suspicions are founded on much more damning evidence, about which I must speak to Lord Upton.''

"Have you forgotten it was I who hired you, sir?'' Holly jammed her fists on her hips. "I believe that information should come to me.''

"I have felt the brunt of Lord Upton's wrath.'' Mr. Scibner inadvertently touched the brown muffler around his neck. "I still have the bruises to prove it. I do not wish to feel it again. I'm sorry, but I must voice my suspicions only to him.''

"I don't blame you for being afraid of Lord Upton. He can be intimidating at times. At least I know it is Waterton now.''

"I'm not sure it is him. There are two others whom I suspect also. It is just I saw Lord Waterton speaking to my other two suspects. Far as I know, they could all be in this together.''

"I have an opportunity to find out if Waterton is involved. He has agreed to drive me wherever I wish to go. I was coming to see you. It's fortuitous that we met here.'' She reached in her pocket and handed Mr. Scibner the jewels. "Here. Please sell these and buy back Lord

Upton's townhouse, then mail the deed to him. Say it is
a Christmas present from a friend. And I wanted to make
sure you have invested my money in St. John Shipping."
A frigid breeze blew snowflakes at her. Her teeth chattered.
She rubbed her hands together and hopped on her feet
to stay warm.

"I have done that, miss." Mr. Scibner drew his muffler
tighter around his neck. "And I mailed the stock certifi-
cates to you."

"How very efficient." Holly blinked the snowflakes out
of her eyes. "With that business taken care of, it only leaves
Lord Waterton." Holly turned and glanced at Waterton.

He was watching her. Their gazes locked for a moment,
then he stepped up into the carriage. A groom in bright
yellow livery paused near the door, while Waterton said
something to him.

"Take my advice, Miss Campbell, and stay well away from
him."

"I must try to get the truth out of him."

"You won't succeed there. Waterton is shrewd and cunning. I insist you let me drive you back home."

"It is very considerate of you, but I must decline your
offer. Waterton may be shrewd and cunning, but there are
ways to get a person like him to see reason. Sometimes all
it takes is a few kind words. And I'm not too afraid of him,
I have this . . ." Holly raised her cape and showed Mr.
Scibner the pistol in her breeches.

"Miss Campbell, you mustn't use that." He stared at the
gun as if she'd pointed it at him.

She grinned confidently. "Don't worry, I don't know
how to use this. I thought it would help me look fierce
just in case trouble should come knocking. I'll be fine. It
will take a while to get home, so that will give me time
enough to encourage him to admit his guilt. Good-bye,

Mr. Scibner. And thank you." Holly left Mr. Scibner wringing his hands and staring at her as if she were going to the chopping block.

She strode toward Whisper, nibbling oak leaves on a nearby tree. She snatched up the reins and led him toward the carriage. The closer she came to it, the more she wondered at her hasty decision. But she could take care of herself. It was John whom she was worried about.

Two hours later, Holly sat on the opposite seat from Waterton. He was stretched out, legs crossed, sipping brandy. A small portable coal stove sat in the middle of the carriage. She could feel the delectable warmth seeping through Dunn's thin coat. The little heater really was remarkable. It kept the inside of the carriage toasty warm. The opulence of the carriage was almost comical. The seats were covered by royal-red velvet damask, and the ceiling was gilded and painted with a mural of angels. It was like a miniature drawing room in a mansion.

Holly might have smiled had she not felt nervous under his scrutiny. She wiggled in the seat and tried to ignore him. After they had exhausted the extent of the weather, and she had evaded all of his questions about her home, he had remained silent, just staring at her over the rim of his glass, his vivid blue eyes looking through her.

With a slight nervous tremor in her hand, she lifted the leather curtain over the window, then peered out. The sky poured thick flakes of snow, the wind whipping them in all directions like a blizzard.

"I see why we are moving at such a snail's pace," she said anxiously. "It will take two days to reach Brookhollow in this snowstorm. It really is terrible out there."

"I believe my driver is going as fast as he dares." He

eyed her over the top of his glass, looking not at all concerned about the snow. As a matter of fact, he almost looked pleased by it. "You should perhaps relax and have a brandy." He motioned to a little shelf on one side of the coach. It held two decanters and six glasses.

"No, thank you." She frowned at the thick snow falling. It was the second time he'd asked her to have a drink. She dropped the curtain and leaned back in her seat.

"Perhaps we should talk about St. John. That is the reason you allowed me to escort you, is it not?"

She saw the perceptive gleam in his eyes. "Since you put it so bluntly, yes. I must admit, I thought only of Lord Upton when I accepted your offer to escort me. So let me speak plainly. Are you the one trying to ruin his business?"

Waterton sipped his brandy, then stared at it. "I never do anything that will not benefit me. If I really wanted to hurt St. John, I could find better ways of doing it." At the mention of John, hatred passed over Waterton's eyes, then quickly melted away behind an impenetrable facade.

"Why do you dislike Lord Upton so much?"

He ran his finger around the goblet, making the crystal sing. "Let's just say, he has always had what I couldn't have. That makes me dislike him."

"He has nothing. He's lost everything. You must mean he has a family. You could have children who love you."

He laughed, but there was no mirth in it. "This may shock you, but I have children."

"You do?" Holly raised her brows in surprise.

"They are my natural children. Two girls and a boy." He said his next words sounding pleased with himself. "Each has a different mother."

Holly blushed. "I don't know if congratulations are in order in a case like this."

He threw back his head and laughed, then sobered.

"You really are a rare bit of sunshine, Miss Campbell. I see why St. John is attracted to you."

"Since you have a family, what is it exactly that makes you hate Lord Upton?" Holly asked, her voice growing impatient.

"I believe it's the sight of him."

"You can't hate someone for their looks. I admit he is much more handsome than you."

Waterton shot her a look.

"Not that you aren't handsome," she quickly amended.

"Thank you for the concession." His expression turned amused, a slow lazy smile spreading across his mouth.

"Stop looking at me like that, you know exactly what I mean."

"No, what *do* you mean?"

She fidgeted in her seat under his direct gaze. "I mean, you shouldn't judge someone because you're jealous of them. You know what's wrong with you, my lord? You suffer from having too much money and time on your hands. Ennui can cause unhappiness."

He smiled, but it didn't touch his eyes. "Perhaps you're right. Would you like to run away with me and help me spend my wealth? I doubt I'd be bored."

"I'll pretend I didn't hear that," Holly said, the blush on her face belying her words.

His smile faded. "You love St. John, do you not?"

"I won't answer that question. It really is none of your business."

"There's no need to answer it. It's written all over your face. That pretty face of yours says you'd sell your soul to the devil to help St. John," he said, his voice dripping with sarcasm.

Holly wasn't so sure she had a soul left with which to bargain. She probably lost it to the devil when she'd killed

Kent. Keeping the nervous edge out of her voice, she said, "I do want to help him, but I want to help you, too. Won't you admit your guilt to me?"

"You don't look like a priest to me." His gaze swept her body, then slowly crept up again to meet her eyes. "Even if you were—and I happened to be Catholic, which I'm not—I would sorely disappoint you. I'm not the one who sabotaged St. John's ships."

She narrowed her brows at him. He would never tell her the truth. "Would you do something for me?" she asked, desperate now.

He nodded. "I'm at your service, madam."

"I must beg you not to face Lord Upton in a duel should he call you out."

"What advantage is in it for me to play the coward?" He continued rubbing his finger around the top of the glass, the noise growing louder and shrill.

Holly grimaced, then leaned over and grabbed his hand. The shrill hiss of the glass ended abruptly. "Because you might find out you have a heart."

"I should tell you now, Miss Campbell, I have no expectations of ever finding any goodness in me." To prove his point, he rubbed the top of her hand.

Holly jerked her hand back, glad she had on wool gloves. "I believe everyone has some ultimate good in them. They just need to look for it." Holly clasped her hands in her lap and leaned back against the plush squab.

The carriage came to an abrupt halt. Muffled voices came from outside, then one of the footmen opened the door. A gush of freezing air hit Holly's face. She shivered and rubbed her arms beneath her cape.

A thick layer of snow sat on top the footman's hat. He rubbed his red, chafed cheeks. "I'm sorry, my lord, but we can't go on. The road is getting treacherous. We have to put up. There's an inn just half a mile ahead.''

"Very good, Jones." Waterton looked amused about something, then glanced over at Holly. "I suppose we will be spending more time together than we thought. Perhaps you can find the innate goodness in me yet."

Holly swallowed hard. "That is something only you can do. I'm going to ride ahead."

"My conscience cannot allow that, Miss Campbell. I've grown very fond of you. I wouldn't want you to suffer frostbite. Then there is St. John's horse to think about. You wouldn't want it to break a leg in the snow." Waterton began running his finger around the top of the crystal glass again.

The piercing sound went through Holly like needles. She wanted to toss the glass out the window, but she sat back and glowered at him. He was right about the snow and she had promised Lawrence nothing would happen to Whisper.

She was stuck.

Back at Brookhollow, John woke. His head throbbed as if someone had driven a spike through his temples. Grabbing his brow, he opened his eyes and glanced down at his naked chest. He grinned, remembering making love to Holly, the sweet taste of her, the way it felt to be deep inside her hot heat. The scent of her still lingered on the sheets. He brought the sheet up and sniffed it. But where was she?

Out of the corner of his eye, he saw the dull light coming through the window. He turned on his side to get a better view outside. Snow fell from the sky like a thick blanket. It was morning, but what time was it? He leaned over and fumbled through his waistcoat and looked at his pocket watch. Eleven o'clock?

"My God, Teddy," he groaned aloud, and sat up on one elbow. His gaze landed on the two glasses sitting on the nightstand. He recalled feeling dizzy, then everything had gone black. She must have put something in his drink.

He threw back the covers. The cold air in the room made gooseflesh break out all over him. He made a mental note to tell Pringle to bring more coal to her room. Shivering, he donned his clothes and boots, then ran from the room and down the servants' stairs.

When he reached the bottom, he flung open the door. He didn't see Mrs. Pringle until he ran into her. He grabbed her arm before she fell. "You shouldn't skulk behind doors."

"I wasn't skulking, my lord," she gasped, making a pretense of straightening her cap that hadn't moved.

"Where is Miss Campbell?"

"I wouldn't know. Even if I did know, I try to stay out of her way, since I usually find you with her, my lord." Mrs. Pringle looked down her nose at him.

"I don't need a damn lecture from you, Mrs. Pringle. The woman is going to be my wife. Where the hell is she?"

Mrs. Pringle took a step back at the loud bark, her eyes wide with incredulity. She thrust out her breast and said, "I truly don't know. Everyone has vanished. I can't find anyone in the house."

Some of the tension left his chest. He was worried Holly had gone to the duel herself and tried to stop it, but he was sure now she couldn't have drugged him and left Brookhollow. The cheap wine he was forced to buy was stronger than it tasted.

The front door swung open with a bang.

Teddy stood in the doorway, snow-covered from head

to foot. A whirl of snowflakes followed him inside. He slammed the door, and they billowed into a dotted cloud around him.

"Teddy!" John strode toward his brother, the frown melting from his face.

Mrs. Pringle followed on John's heels.

"Yes, it's me. No need to sound surprised that I'm still alive." Teddy stomped the ice off his boots, then took off his hat, gloves, muffler, and shook the snow off them.

"You must be frozen through," Mrs. Pringle said, taking his wet articles of clothing.

"Almost. What a bloody mess it is outside." Teddy took off his coat, then handed it to Mrs. Pringle.

"I'll fetch a pot of tea."

"Thank you. I could use something hot to drink."

"I'll get it right away." Mrs. Pringle hurried out the hall.

"How about a glass of brandy first?" John asked, heading toward his office.

"I suppose it couldn't hurt. My head feels like it's been flattened by a carriage."

John's hand went to his throbbing temple and thought a carriage flattening aptly described the pain in his own head. He walked over to the small table near his desk and poured Teddy four fingers of brandy, then handed it to him. "Now tell me why the hell you got into a duel with Waterton, and why you're still alive."

"Waterton is the person trying to ruin the company."

"How do you know this?" Every muscle tightened in his body.

"Lady Matilda told me she overheard him speaking to Jarvis in the park."

"That son of a bitch!"

"Yes, well, my thoughts exactly. So I called him out. But Holly showed up and hit me with some damn thing, and by the time I woke up, Waterton was gone." Teddy tipped back the glass and downed the contents.

John was pouring himself a glass of brandy. When he heard Holly's name, he almost dropped the decanter. He caught the side before it hit the table. With trembling hands, he plopped the heavy crystal bottle down and strode over to Teddy, grabbing his lapel. "Where is she now?"

"I thought she'd be here. Renwick said she left in Waterton's carriage."

Chapter 18

"Good God!" Inadvertently, John picked Teddy up out of his seat. He realized what he was doing and dropped him.

Teddy fell back down in the leather chair. With an indignant jerk of his hand, he straightened his crimson coat. "If you don't mind, could you watch the clothes? They are Renwick's. And it's not my damn fault she's not back yet. I was dead out."

"We've got to find her. He'll use her to get to me." John stormed out the office and bumped into Mr. Scibner coming down the hall.

"No one answered my knock," Scibner said, shaking the snow off his coat. "I let myself in. Hope you don't mind, my lord." He peered at John through the frosty condensation on his glasses.

"I haven't time to speak to you. Miss Campbell's with Lord Waterton." John strode past him.

Scibner grabbed John's arm. "I know where they are. I followed them." Squinting, Scibner took off his glasses, cleaned the thick glass with his scarf, then put them back on.

"How do you figure into all of this?"

"I went to the field this morning in hopes of stopping you from killing Waterton. I really needed to tell you what I've found out so far. When Miss Campbell came in your stead, I thought it prudent to follow her. Then I came here to tell you her whereabouts."

"Where is she?"

"I left her turning into Thorn Inn but twenty miles from here. You must speak to me, my lord, before you go there. I wouldn't want an altercation between you and Lord Waterton to end in a tragedy. The inn is full. I'm sure Miss Campbell will be safe a few more moments."

"All right, you have my ear, but be quick about it."

"As you know, I have my men on Mr. Jarvis's trail. Well, it has paid off. They have seen him with three people. I believe one of them must be our suspect, or perhaps they are all in this together."

"Who were they?"

"Well, one was Sir Joseph Romely."

John raised surprised brows.

At his reaction, Scibner went on. "I checked into his background. Romely has ruined companies before. He buys the stock cheap, then takes over the business. That is how he acquired the bank."

"I hadn't thought of him, but he could be the one." John gritted his teeth, feeling the pain in his head worsening.

"Jarvis was also seen speaking to Henry Thomas."

"Henry would never—"

"Forgive me, my lord, but you can trust no one. He

managed the shipping office in the West Indies alone. He could have been in league with the captains and making a nice profit on the side. The captains might have grown disgruntled by their cut and wanted to inform you of it. Thomas could have hired Mr. Jarvis to sink the ships and get rid of his accomplices. I have a man investigating his financial status as we speak.''

"Who is the third?''

Scibner paused, then said, "Waterton.''

"I have no doubts he's the most likely of the three,'' John said.

Scibner took a step back and held up his hands. "Please do not do anything rash, my lord. You must let me continue my investigation. We cannot convict Waterton for just speaking to Jarvis.''

"Matilda said she heard him berating Jarvis for showing up in town so soon after he hired him to destroy the ships,'' Teddy said, striding toward John.

Scibner turned to him. "I'm afraid some women enjoy seeking revenge on those they hate by causing such rumors. I would wait and let me investigate the allegations.''

"Have you found out anything about Miss Campbell's background yet?''

"No, but I've written a letter to a friend of mine who lives in Maryland. I've also been watching the docks for ships coming from Richmond's port. Someone on board is bound to know our Miss Campbell.''

John turned and strode toward the door.

"Wait, my lord!'' Scibner called to John's back.

"I'm through waiting. I'm going to get Miss Campbell back.''

"But you must not interfere in my investigation. Please do not do anything rash where Lord Waterton is concerned. I need him alive to investigate him further. You want to find proof that he is behind the shipwrecks, don't you?"

"I have no doubt Waterton is our man," John said. "He has always hated me."

"I'll go with you," Teddy said, following John.

"No, you have caused more than enough trouble. Stay here and find out where everyone has gone."

"No need to head for the stable." Teddy paused, smiled ironically, then slowly tossed out his next words as if they were daggers he was throwing at a target. "Holly has Whisper."

"She took my horse?"

"I saw her on Whisper this morning."

John looked accusingly at Teddy. "And you didn't do anything about it? You just let her ride a horse that could kill her?"

"Damn it, John. It's not my bloody fault she has your horse. You needn't look at me like that. I would have stopped her, but she knocked me out. What the hell was I supposed to do? It's partly your fault. How did she take Whisper without you knowing about it?"

John rubbed his throbbing temple, aware he couldn't admit to Teddy that Holly had drugged him. He ignored the damning question as he asked, "How did you get here?"

"I borrowed Renwick's gelding." Teddy saw the determined look in John's eye. "You can't take Renwick's cattle in this snow. It's his favorite horse. I promised to get the animal back to him in one piece."

"You shall have it back in one piece, but it will be the only thing that stays in one piece. If I have my way, Waterton will be in pieces." John turned and left the room, leaving Teddy and Scibner staring after him.

* * *

Holly glanced around the taproom. As inns went, Thorn Inn was small but quaint, with a thatched roof and thick oak beams that spanned the ceiling. Years of smoke had darkened the beams to coal black. Pine garlands hung from the beams, giving them a splash of stark green color. The fireplace was also decorated with garlands and a wreath of holly leaves, and pinecones hung in the center. The chimney smoked and filled the room with a thin, dark haze, which mingled with the acrid odor of a cigar a gentleman was smoking.

Holly wrinkled her nose and watched two young girls hurry around to the seven tables, serving hot tea. She guessed they were the innkeeper's daughters. A posting coach had pulled into the inn not thirty minutes before Holly and Waterton arrived, depositing ten freezing, hungry passengers.

The loud chatter in the taproom made Holly yell at Lord Waterton. "I believe the inn is full to capacity. You are lucky to have gotten the last two empty tables."

"Damned shame we couldn't get a private apartment." Waterton raised his quizzing glass and, with irritation, studied the people filling the tables.

"I don't think this inn has a private apartment. You really are a snob." Holly grinned at him, remembering the way he had tried to bribe the innkeeper with money. But the innkeeper wouldn't be swayed. Waterton was still sulking from not getting his own way and having to sit in the same room with the lower classes.

"Do you really think I'm a snob?" Waterton looked genuinely surprised by her remark.

"Yes, but at least you're a kind one. I'm glad you brought your footmen and driver inside."

"Only at your insistence." Waterton leveled his quizzing glass at her. In a snide tone, he said, "My generosity knows no bounds when I'm in your society."

"I know you didn't want them to stay out in the cold, while you were warm and cozy in here." She pursed her lips at him, then glanced over at the table occupied by the driver and the two footmen.

They smiled and nodded at her.

Abruptly, the door swung open.

Lady Matilda breezed past a footman, lovely as usual, shaking the snow off her blue mantle and matching dress. She pulled off her bonnet. Long, dark curls fell down to her shoulders. She patted the snow from her hat, then yanked off her gloves and thrust them at her footman. Finally, she glanced up. When she noticed Holly and Lord Waterton sitting at a table, her eyes widened as if she'd caught them in each other's arms.

Everyone in the taproom turned to look at her. She had the type of beauty and demeanor that wasn't easily ignored.

Waterton lifted his quizzing glass with a taunting smile. "Well, well, well," he said loud enough for Lady Matilda to hear him. "What an unexpected pleasure."

Lady Matilda flashed her beautiful blue eyes at him, then strode toward them.

Waterton's smile broadened as he followed Lady Matilda's progress through the taproom with his quizzing glass.

"Now try to be nice," Holly whispered to him.

"Nice?" Waterton echoed, then lowered his quizzing glass. There was nothing nice in his expression. "If Lady Matilda were a man, the undertaker would be measuring her for a casket."

"But she is a lady, you mustn't forget that."

"Yes, one can't forget that." He raised his quizzing glass

again and peered at his prey squeezing past the gentleman smoking the cigar.

Lady Matilda paused in front of Holly and ignored Lord Waterton. "Hello, Miss Campbell." She lowered her voice so the other patrons in the inn couldn't hear her. "May I ask what you are doing here with *this* person?" She didn't bother looking at Waterton. "It is highly improper, especially with someone of his reputation."

"Well, it is a long story. Won't you join us, Lady Matilda?" Holly wanted to see if she could stir things up a bit and find out which of them was lying.

"I'd rather stand than sit at a table with *that.*" Lady Matilda wagged her limp wrist toward Waterton.

"I would do the gentlemanly thing and give you my seat, but I'm sure someone who has perfected lying down to an art can certainly find a seat at another table," Waterton said, his voice barbed with derision.

Lady Matilda rounded on him now. She shoved her hands down on her curvaceous hips. "It is too bad Lord Theodore didn't put a hole in you, for you truly need to pay for what you did," she hissed. "I heard you speaking to Jarvis, and I won't take it back. You're a despicable reprobate with no conscience."

Lord Waterton lost the curtain of boredom over his expression and grabbed her arm. He stood, then locked his arm in hers. She struggled, but he growled near her ear, "You don't want to make a scene, now do you? You and I need to have a chat. I prefer to do it in private, unless you want to do it here. Either way, I'm going to teach you a lesson about lying."

"You're so proficient at it yourself, I'm sure you could teach a class on the subject. Unfortunately, it would sicken me to listen to you drone on that long." Lady Matilda jerked on her arm.

He clamped down on her elbow, his face flushed with furious determination. Lady Matilda winced, then glared at him.

Holly had never seen Lord Waterton lose his impenetrable sangfroid. She sat back in her chair, sipped her tea, and smiled behind the cup, enjoying every minute of the scene unfolding before her.

"Unhand me this instant."

"Not until we have our little chat . . ." Lord Waterton jerked on her arm and pulled her through the taproom.

Suddenly, the door burst open, banging against the wall. John stood in the threshold, his brows a thick dark line hooding his eyes, his mouth set in a grim line.

His gaze landed on Holly. His eyes had never glowed such a fiery gold before. She gulped down the tea in her mouth and choked on it.

Silence settled over the room, the only sound Holly's coughing. Every eye turned in John's direction. She watched John and Waterton lock gazes, the tension between them potent enough to knock down a bull.

Lady Matilda smacked Lord Waterton's arm. "Take your hands off me, you lout."

"Unhand her," John said, advancing toward Waterton.

"Stay out of this, St. John. This is between the lady and myself."

"I'm making it my business." John knocked Waterton's hand away and shoved Lady Matilda aside.

Holly saw the shrewd smile on Lady Matilda's face. It was blatantly plain she enjoyed being fought over.

"I do not know why you bother now," Waterton said snidely. "You were such a coward you sent your brother to defend your honor, then Miss Campbell—"

John struck, his fist darting faster than leaping fire.

Waterton never saw it coming. John's knuckles caught

him on the jaw. Waterton stumbled back, wiping blood from the corner of his mouth.

Holly leaped out of her seat and ran toward them.

"Your right is getting better, but it needs work on the follow-through," Waterton said, his lips straining to maintain a derisive smile, while he crouched, ready to pounce on John.

Holly jumped in between them. "Don't, Lord Waterton. Remember. Nice."

"I'm afraid nice has no place in this, Miss Campbell. He struck first." Waterton narrowed his eyes at John, while he maintained that irritating smile. "Perhaps you should speak to him about being nice."

"Stay out of this, Holly. You've caused enough trouble for one day." John's fingers dug into her shoulders, then he thrust her aside with one long sweep of his arm. He took up a boxing stance. "Well, Waterton, come on. I know you want a piece of me."

"You're right, I do. I owe you two, old boy. One for breaking my nose and one for just now." Waterton held up his fists, then lunged, punching with his left.

John dove to the right. His fist connected with Waterton's ribs. Waterton absorbed the punch without a flinch, then slammed his fist into John's jaw.

The din rose in the room, people cheering John and Waterton on. Some of the men were taking bets on the fight.

Holly noticed Lady Matilda's ladylike demeanor had melted. The frenzy of the violence held her captive, her eyes gleaming with a thirst for Waterton's blood. She was shaking her fist and yelling at John, "Hit him! Get him good!"

John and Waterton were punching each other with savage fury now.

Was Holly the only sane one in the room? She had to do something or they'd kill each other. She withdrew the pistol from beneath her cloak, pointed it at the ceiling, squeezed her eyes closed, and . . .

Bang.

The loud report reverberated through the small inn, silencing everyone in the room. Tiny pieces of plaster fell in her face from the hole in the ceiling. She rubbed it out of her eyes, then looked at John and Lord Waterton.

John dropped the fist he was going to swing. Lord Waterton stopped punching John. They glanced in her direction, chests heaving, fists still clenched. Blood trickled from Lord Waterton's mouth, an unruffled, amused grin on his face. On the other hand, John looked furious and his left cheekbone was turning bright purple.

"Don't look at me like that. How else was I to get your attention? Please, you must stop fighting." Holly lowered the pistol.

With an angry swipe, John grabbed the gun out of her hand. "You stole my pistol, I see," he said, his face a mask of fury.

Holly backed away. "Only for instances such as this one."

"I thought I told you to stay out of this."

"Well, I'm not going to let you two kill each other because you don't have the sense God gave a turnip. So Waterton insulted you. He insults everyone. You need not take it personally."

"He most certainly should." Lord Waterton crossed his arms over his chest and looked pleased with himself, the cynical grin, so much a part of him, etched in his expression.

John turned and shot him a baleful glance. "We'll settle this at dawn." He moved aside his cape and jammed the pistol down the back of his breeches.

Holly scrambled to her feet so she could peer past John's broad shoulder at Lord Waterton. Her gaze locked with his. Lord Waterton opened his mouth to speak, looked torn for a moment, struggling with something inside him. Finally, he clamped his mouth closed and gazed at Holly as he said, "So sorry, St. John, can't make it in the morning."

"Then name the day."

Lord Waterton stared at Holly again, her eyes beseeching him. "I'm afraid I can't do that." He looked down at his manicured nails and in a bored tone said, "More than likely, Miss Campbell would probably show up again and knock you unconscious, then I would have wasted a perfectly good morning again out in the cold. No, I must decline. Dueling with the St. Johns no longer holds any amusement for me." He cocked a derisive brow at John and added, "Of course, we could wait until summer when the weather is a bit more bearable and we could try sabers. Feeling my sword pierce your flesh might give me more pleasure."

"No, no. I think you should forget it," Holly said, rewarding Lord Waterton with a wide smile for his gallant gesture. There might be hope for him yet.

John saw Waterton staring at Holly, then turned, catching her smiling back at him. He grabbed her arm. "What is between you and him?"

"Nothing."

"I found them sitting together when I came in here," Lady Matilda said as she stepped toward them. "They made quite a cozy pair."

Holly frowned at Lady Matilda for trying to make trouble. The growing fierceness of John's expression prompted Holly to say, "Nothing happened. You can ask any of the people in this room." She glanced around and saw they had everyone's attention. "Lord Waterton was nothing but a gentleman—as surprising as it might seem." Holly's gaze flicked back to Waterton.

He tried to look insulted. In a poor charade of a wounded voice, he said, "Would you have St. John believe I made no passes at you at all, Miss Campbell?"

"Be quiet, please," Holly said. "You are just trying to cause trouble."

"If you laid one hand on my intended—"

"He didn't," Holly assured John. "And I'm not your intended."

"Intended?" Lady Matilda gasped. The blood drained from her face as she grabbed John's arm. "You can't mean to marry her."

"Yes, I mean just that," John said, his tone razor sharp.

"But she's penniless. You have to marry an heiress, someone of your own rank."

"I'm glad she's penniless. At least she will not miss the things I cannot give her."

Holly stared down at the floor, thinking of her deception in that quarter.

"But . . . but . . . you can't marry her." Tears glistened in Lady Matilda's eyes.

John's voice softened the slightest bit. "I'm sorry, Matilda, but I've made up my mind."

"You don't know what you're saying. She's bewitched you. Don't you see she's an upstart? She'll do anything to have your wealth and title. I suppose she threw herself at you."

"I resent that remark," Holly said, staring hard at Lady Matilda.

Lady Matilda ignored her completely. "Good Lord, John! Use the wench for a mistress, but don't marry her. You know nothing about her family or connections. She might come from a family of idiots for all you know."

"That is quite enough." John leveled a quelling gaze at Lady Matilda. "I won't have you speaking of my future bride in that manner."

"Does anyone care what *I* have to say about the matter?" Holly shook her finger at John. "I'm not marrying you."

"Marry him," the gentleman with the cigar said, then blew a smoke ring up to the ceiling.

"Stay out of this," John and Lady Matilda said at once.

"I would be honored if you would marry *me* then, Miss Campbell." Waterton bowed, his expression mocking.

"Stay away from her." John grabbed Holly's arm. "We'll discuss this later. You're coming home with me."

"I resent your high-handed ways. I have no intentions of marrying you and you know it . . ." John dragged her through the taproom and out the door.

Lord Waterton glanced over at Lady Matilda. "Well, madam, it looks like you've lost."

For a long moment, Lady Matilda just glared at him, then her expression grew absent, as though she wasn't really seeing him. She glanced at the door through which Holly and John had just exited and said more to herself, "The race is never over until the prize is claimed."

"Unfortunately, you have fallen out of the race. Miss Campbell has already won." Amused by her stubbornness and the glance she shot him, Lord Waterton's lips lifted in a slow smirk. "You had much better forget about this obsession you have with St. John. He doesn't give a damn about you and never has. I, on the other hand, am prepared to share a room with you for the night."

"You insufferable, lecherous knave!" Lady Matilda drew back to smack him.

He caught her wrist. "If I were truly lecherous, I'd carry you up those stairs on my shoulder and teach you not to tell lies."

"I hate you." Lady Matilda jerked her hand free, then stomped off to sulk in front of the hearth.

Lord Waterton stared at the sway of her hips and a slow, contemptuous grin spread across his lips.

The cold wind bit through Holly's cape and gloves. Fat snowflakes swirled around her face and made it impossible to see more than several feet in front of her. Ice stuck to her lashes and she constantly blinked it away. She huddled into the saddle, and looked at John's back. She could hardly see him for the thick snow, though he was riding in front of her and leading her horse. That was all right with her. They hadn't spoken for two hours, not since they had argued about her marrying him and he'd plopped her in the saddle. She didn't want to see him or speak to him when he was this angry.

She listened to the heavy tread of Whisper's hooves crunching in the snow, matching the big bay's she was riding. The white stone columns of Brookhollow's drive came into view, looming like tall polar bears in the snow.

John turned up the drive. Holly could feel the big bay's hooves slipping in the ruts. She gasped and half expected the horse to lose his footing.

"Are you all right?" John turned in the saddle and scowled at her.

"I don't think this horse is used to the unexpected holes in the drive."

Without a word, John backed Whisper up a step. Before Holly could protest, he pulled her across the saddle in front of him. "There now, you needn't be afraid the horse will fall with you on his back."

"I wasn't afraid," Holly said, her clipped tone matching his. "I was just making a comment."

"You could have fooled me."

Holly opened her mouth with a retort, but decided against it. Instead, she stared at him. An inch of snow covered the top of his beaver hat. Snowflakes stuck to the heavy brows hooding his eyes, turning them white. The stubborn strand of hair on his forehead was wet and clung to his skin, just touching the top of his brows. His jaw was tightly clamped, his lips in a tight line. He looked like a teapot ready to whistle or explode.

He did explode. Holly winced at the sharp edge in his voice. "If you ever put a sleeping potion in my drink again, and take my horse, and interfere in a duel that is none of your concern, I will turn you over my knee and beat you soundly."

"I had to do it. I know you wouldn't have let Teddy get killed. You would have knocked him out as I did, then you would have taken his place and probably been shot. I had the good sense to speak to Lord Waterton, who I'm beginning to believe is not guilty of the accusation Lady Matilda made against him."

"You know him so bloody well you can defend his character?" John ground his teeth together, forcing the veins in his neck to pop.

"No, but he seems nice to me, though he does like to insult you. And you play into his hands. If you could just ignore him."

"I'll ignore him when he's in jail, or six feet under."

"You mustn't duel with him," Holly said, her voice anxious. "He isn't as bad as you paint him, or he would have accepted your challenge."

"I suppose that is some more of your meddling."

"I only asked him not to because I don't want you to get hurt."

"He would be the one getting hurt. In spite of what you think, I'm considered a fair shot."

"I'm sure you are. I didn't mean to imply you're not." Holly rolled her eyes at him. "Why do men measure their manliness by their ability to shoot a gun or use their fists? I have never understood that. They have to settle everything with some sort of violence. It really took mettle for Lord Waterton to back down from your challenge. I think it showed great courage and sensibility on his part."

John laughed bitterly. "Do not think it was a noble gesture on that bastard's part. He had a reason for doing it. I'm sure we'll find out what that reason is."

"You are wrong about him. You are just saying that because you are jealous he did something I asked him to do. You need not be—though I'm flattered by it." Holly saw the jealous expression on John's face and couldn't help but grin at him.

"I'll strangle him with my bare hands if I ever find you with him again. And I won't let you stop me so easily next time. Stay away from him. Do I make myself clear?"

"I don't understand why you hate him so."

"It is not I who have hated him all these years, but he who hates me. For years it has been that way. And when Elise died and I was left virtually penniless, he took every opportunity to cast aspersions on my reputation. And he is not above using you to get to me. Until Scibner concludes his investigation, stay away from him."

"Has he found any other suspects?" Holly shivered and snuggled deeper into her cape.

"Two others." Some of the anger left John's voice.

"Who are they?" Holly tried to sound disinterested, while she held her breath waiting for an answer.

"I'm not going to tell you so you can interfere again."

John noticed her shivering. "Come here." He pulled Holly back against his chest.

Holly snuggled next to his warmth. "I won't interfere."

"I know you won't, not if you don't know who the other suspects are."

"I was just curious is all."

"Save your curiosity for my body." John looked down at her, his anger veiled by the burning desire in his eyes. "And if you ever leave me in bed like you did last night, I promise you'll regret it."

His gaze warmed her all the way to her toes. She didn't feel so cold anymore. "You looked quite happy when I left you."

"You know exactly what I mean."

"If I could stop you from getting hurt, I'd do it again." Holly reached up and flicked the snow from his eyebrows.

"You do and you'll regret every moment of your meddling." His words were uttered in a threatening tone, but his eyes held a golden softness in them. He bent and kissed her hard on the mouth.

When he raised his head, Holly realized they were reining in near the stable. She heard laughter and voices and glanced up. Pringle, Dunn, the boys, Ann, Sarah, Lawrence, and Lady Upton were striding through the snow toward them.

"Where have all of you been?" John cast them a dubious glance, then dismounted.

No one answered him. They looked at one another, waiting for someone in the group to speak.

Finally Ann said, "We've been playing in the snow, Papa. Great-grandmama taught me how to catch snowflakes on my tongue." Ann stuck out her tongue and showed him how it was done.

"Not like that, child," Lady Upton said. "You have to

stick out your tongue until it touches the bottom of your chin. Like this . . ." Lady Upton demonstrated, looking like a baby bird waiting to be fed.

Then the boys stuck out their tongues and joined in the fun.

Holly laughed and tried it herself.

"We do have a house to run." John shot Lawrence, Pringle, and Dunn a look that made Lawrence run to grab Whisper and the bay's reins. Pringle and Dunn looked at each other with dread on their faces.

"Sorry, my lord," Lawrence said.

John turned and stared at him. "I would like to know how Miss Campbell pilfered my horse without your knowledge."

"Well, I—I . . ."

Lady Upton stopped catching snowflakes. "Stop being so beastly, John John. If the gal did take your horse, how can you blame the help for it? That is solely your fault for not gaining control of her." Lady Upton turned and touched the boys on the shoulders. "Come along children, I think some hot chocolate is in order."

The look John leveled at his grandmother made Holly chuckle. "She's right, you know," Holly said. "You are beastly."

"You are asking for it, my sweet," John said, lifting her down from Whisper's back.

"I was just pointing out the obvious." A saucy smile stretched across her lips.

"I'll show you obvious." He grinned wickedly, then bent and grabbed a handful of snow and tried to shove it down her back.

"No you don't . . ." Holly took off running.

"Run, Holly! Run!" Ann yelled encouragement.

John's strides were longer than hers. He easily caught her, then shoved the ice down the back of her collar.

The frigid feel of snow trickling down her back paralyzed her for a moment. She saw the smug smile on his face. "So you want to play dirty." She reached down, grabbed a handful of snow and formed a snowball.

He ran in the opposite direction, his cape billowing out around his legs.

"Hit him! Hit him!" This from Lady Upton, who then cackled.

Holly took aim and let it fly. He ducked, but not fast enough. It hit his hat and knocked it off his head.

He looked surprised, then reloaded. "Take this, Miss Trifling Wench," he said, throwing the snowball at her.

Holly ducked, but the snowball caught her on the thigh, then exploded. The ice stuck to her wool cape in little balls.

Abruptly, a projectile was fired from a different direction. It hit Holly on the arm. She glanced over and saw Dryden holding back a guilty smirk. At least he wasn't ignoring her. Holly was about to get him back, but John came to her defense and pelted Dryden with a snowball. It hit his shoulder. He smiled, the dour expression momentarily leaving his face.

Brock joined the fun and hit his father in the side.

Pringle bent down, packed the snow, and handed Ann a snowball. She threw it at John. It barely reached his boot. He feigned being hit and staggered back several steps, making her giggle.

Snowballs catapulted through the air in chaos. Everyone was laughing. The boys ganged up on John and wrestled with him in the snow.

Holly stood back, grinning at John. He looked so carefree. He was not the severe, harsh, unhappy man she had first met. She didn't have long to ponder over him, for he and the boys charged her.

John tackled her first. She stumbled back and fell on her back, then he landed on top of her. The boys shouted a loud war cry and dived on top of John. He took the brunt of their weight so it didn't crush her. She laughed, looking up into John's eyes, thinking she had never been so happy in her life.

Chapter 19

A little while later they were all walking back to the house. Holly hung back and spoke to Pringle, while John walked ahead with the others.

"Did you invite everyone?" Holly whispered.

"Yes, miss," Pringle said in a conspiratorial tone, while he pushed Ann's chair.

Ann glanced up at Holly. "You should have seen the little girl's face when I invited her."

"She's coming, isn't she?"

"Yes, I told her Papa had ordered it." Ann grinned, pleased with the deception.

"Very good." Holly smiled at her. "We should do some more baking for our party." Holly beat her cape with her hand, trying to knock off the ice balls sticking to the wool.

"We must make plum pudding," Ann said, excited.

"Yes, and mincemeat pies, and more cookies."

"You should see the yule log we made."

"I'm sure it's lovely. Did Dryden help you? I was surprised to see he went with you to invite the tenants."

"He said he would come if you weren't along." Ann stared at Dryden's back, her annoyance with her brother showing through in her expression.

"Give him time, miss," Pringle said.

"Yes, I'll give him all the time he needs." Holly sighed and wondered if Dryden would ever warm to her.

John helped Lady Upton up the slippery terrace steps in spite of her protests. When they disappeared through the French doors, Mrs. Pringle emerged, fists on hips. Her small, beady eyes fell on Holly, then she stomped toward her, her full breasts bouncing.

"Well, there you are," Mrs. Pringle said. "It's about time you got home and saw to your job. Mr. Pringle here has been taking care of the children for you. I hope you realize all the inconvenience you put everyone to."

"I'm sorry," Holly said, not feeling very sincere.

Picking on Holly wasn't enough and she turned on her husband. "Where have you been all day in this weather?"

"Out." Pringle met her gaze, not cowering as he usually did.

"I know what you're doing." Mrs. Pringle shook her finger at Holly. "Sarah told me about the surprise Christmas party. The master won't like it, and I'm going to inform him so he can put a stop to it."

Pringle straightened his shoulders like a soldier finally finding the courage for battle. He pursed his lips, air filling his cheeks, then he marched around Ann's chair, past Holly and up the steps.

He grabbed Mrs. Pringle's plump arms and shook her. His voice turned vicious. "You hate to see anyone happy. Well, I'm sick of it. Do you hear? You could try to help us, instead of ruining everyone's Christmas. If you breathe one word of this to his lordship," Pringle shook his fist in his wife's face, "you'll regret it."

Holly stood there watching, amazed, wanting to cheer Pringle on.

At Pringle's aggressive behavior, Mrs. Pringle's eyes widened with surprise and her jaw fell open.

"And I'll tell you another thing. We're through if you don't change that fishwife tongue of yours. I've lived with it for five and thirty years. If you can't speak civilly, then don't speak. And I don't intend to hear one more word of your bossing and harping. I'm the butler here and over the housekeeper. Remember that? I'm not above firing you and getting a divorce."

"You wouldn't." Mrs. Pringle clasped her throat.

"I would. And no one who knows you would think the worse of me."

"But—"

"Not another word." Pringle leveled his gaze at his wife.

She closed her mouth, then stretched her long neck as if it hurt her to keep silent.

"Now get into the kitchen and fix hot chocolate for everyone."

She stared at Pringle, then stomped across the terrace, her wide hips swaying beneath the gray shawl hanging off her shoulders.

Pringle stared after her and brushed his hands together, looking pleased with himself. He strode back down the steps. "Well, I should have done that thirty-five years ago." He bent and picked Ann up. "Come on, child, we'll get you into the house."

"Pringle, you were marvelous." Ann looked at him with awe and respect in her eyes.

Pringle just smiled at her, then said to Holly, "Could you manage the chair, miss?"

Holly didn't dare say no. She smiled at him, then grabbed the arms of the chair and pulled it backward up the stairs.

Everyone was already in the kitchen when Pringle, Holly, and Ann arrived. Their wet cloaks hung on pegs by the massive hearth. John, the boys, Dunn, and Sarah stood near the fire, their hands stretched out toward the warmth. Holly took off her wet cape, while Pringle sat Ann in a chair.

Holly bent down to help Ann off with her coat.

"I'll help Mrs. Pringle serve. Will you be taking cocoa in the kitchen, my lord?" Pringle asked, turning to look at John.

John raised a brow at the new, confident tone in Pringle's voice. "I believe we'll take it in here by the hearth."

"Very good, sir." Pringle bowed, then strode over to the counter to help his wife, a strut in his step.

Holly smiled at Pringle, watching Mrs. Pringle pouting while she poured milk into a large pan.

The door to the kitchen swung open. Teddy stood in the door, scanning the room. His gaze narrowed on Holly. "Well, well, John found you."

"Now, don't be angry with me," Holly said, holding up her hands to ward him off.

"I hope John turned you over his knee."

"No," John said, smiling. "But I did punish her."

"Yeah, we got her good in the snow," Brock said. "You should have been there, Uncle Teddy."

"Well, I wish I could have seen it, but I can't do much of anything with this ache in my head." Teddy rubbed his temple.

"Where is Mr. Scibner?" John asked Teddy.

"Mr. Scibner was here?" Holly asked, raising a surprised brow.

"Yes," Teddy said, "and he had to leave before the roads got too bad. Poor fellow came all the way to inform us of your whereabouts. And I came all the way from town worried about you." He stared pointedly at Holly.

"I'm so sorry I caused so much trouble, Teddy," Holly said, moving toward him. "You'll forgive me for this morning, won't you? I just couldn't let you get hurt. I hope you can forgive me. Dunn can make you feel better."

Dunn was standing by the fire with his back to it. "Yes, I have just the thing for bruises, Lord Theodore. It won't take long to fix a poultice for you."

"I had hopes of making Miss Campbell nurse me, since she was responsible for my pain."

"Miss Campbell has the children to see to," John said, his voice tinged with jealousy.

"Stop your whining," Lady Upton said, then paused from warming her hands near the fire and gazed at Teddy. "If you let the gal knock you on the head, then you should be in pain. In my day, a gentleman of any caliber wouldn't stand for such nonsense. It's a good thing John John gave her the glow. She'd walk all over you if you were leg-shackled to her."

Teddy's face turned red. Holly knew her own face was blushing from embarrassment. She hoped no one else in the room knew what the glow was.

"Does giving her the glow mean Holly's going to be my new mama?" Ann looked at her father, thrilled by the news.

"When are you going to marry her?" Brock asked. "Can we come to the wedding?"

"Of course," John said. "I'm going to have banns posted

in tomorrow's paper." John eyed Holly, waiting for her to object.

She was too busy feeling humiliated to say anything. Out of the corner of her eye she saw Dryden stiffen at the news.

He picked up a poker by the hearth and jammed it into the fire. "I don't want her to be our mother. She'll never be a mother to me."

"Dryden, that is enough!" John stared at Dryden from behind narrowed brows.

"I don't want her here!" Dryden jabbed his finger at Holly. "You can't let her take Mama's place. You never loved Mama. You couldn't have and want to marry her so soon after Mama died."

"Go to your room." John pointed to the door, his voice low.

"I'll go all right, but I'll never let her take Mama's place." Dryden dropped the poker and ran out the kitchen.

The poker clattered to the floor.

Holly took a step to go after him, but John stopped her. "Leave him be. He needs to get used to the idea. I'll speak to him later."

"He need not get used to it. How could you just announce we are getting married, when I have never said I would marry you? Now you've hurt Dryden for nothing." Tears of frustration stung Holly's eyes.

"It's not for nothing. You're going to marry me. I'm posting the banns tomorrow."

"Did you not hear me? You can't do that."

"It will be all over town anyway."

"How do you figure that?"

"Waterton knows. When he gets back to town, everyone will know. He enjoys spreading rumors about me."

Holly pursed her lips at him. "You told him we were

getting married on purpose, didn't you? You knew he'd spread it around."

"I admit I did." An arrogant smile turned up one side of his lips.

"How many times must I tell you I won't marry you before it sinks into that hard skull of yours?"

"It will never sink in. Even if I have to drag you to the altar kicking and screaming, we are getting married."

"In case you haven't noticed, the Middle Ages have passed, my lord. You can't carry me off and force me to wed you. I am a free American and am bound by no man. You can't force me to marry you. Not now, not ever!" At that, Holly shoved past Teddy and stormed out the door.

Silence lingered in the kitchen, the only sound was Mrs. Pringle's spoon scraping against the bottom of the pan as she stirred the hot chocolate.

John took a step to go after Holly, but Teddy grabbed his arm. "You've buggered it up enough, big brother," Teddy said, his tone holding a note of satisfaction. "Let her have some time alone."

"Stay out of this," John said.

"John John, you must learn a little finesse—especially with those Yanks." Lady Upton waved her hand toward the empty doorway. "You know they do not take to being ordered about. A lot of nonsense. We should have won that war. Poor King George will never live that one down. Drove the poor man to Bedlam. I hope that gal doesn't drive you to Bedlam." She shook her head, a pensive look in her eyes, then glanced at Ann and Brock, as if just noticing them. She touched both their heads at the same time.

"Do not look so glum, children, you'll have a new mama. Shall we have that hot chocolate now? Come along, John John, and stop looking like you want to eat the wood off the stanchion. She'll come about. Yanks are a stubborn lot, but when it comes to matters of the heart, they are easily swayed. They're like the French in that respect. She'll wear down. Give her a little time, then ask her to marry you, not order it. That will get it done." Lady Upton escorted the children to the table.

"Thank you for your advice, madam." John strode over to the table and pulled the bench out for her.

"Well, shall we get you to the table?" Teddy picked Ann up in his arms.

"It isn't a very happy homecoming for you, Uncle Teddy," Ann said, smiling at him. "You have a bump on your head, and Holly and Papa are arguing."

"I'm always happy when I get to see you." Teddy bit her neck and made her squeal.

John was about to sit down when someone knocked on the kitchen door.

"I wonder who that could be out in this weather?" Pringle said, hurrying to get the door.

Dunn took a step toward the door, too, but Pringle turned and shot him such a look that Dunn froze in his tracks.

Pringle turned and walked to the door, his shoulders back, stiff with confidence. When he opened the door, a young boy, no more than ten and seven, stood in the doorway with a sack on his back. "Hello, Mr. Pringle. My ma said to bring this ham over. Thought it might help with the party and all."

John recognized the young man. He was Todd Winter, the son of Jason Winter, one of his tenants. Todd handed the sack over to Pringle.

"What party?" John asked.

"Oh! Me lord." Todd looked at him, his eyes widening in surprise. "I didn't see you."

"What is this about a party?" John asked suspiciously.

"Nothin'. I lost me head there for a moment. What my ma said was she sent it over in case you was thinkin' of havin' a Christmas party—oh, I found this hanging on a drainpipe when I was coming around to the door here. It's sorta torn up, but I didn't do it." He handed Pringle what was left of Holly's black dress. It was wet and frozen and stiff as a broomstick.

Pringle pursed his lips at it.

"I'll take that, Pringle," John said, holding out his hand.

"Yes, my lord." Pringle handed John the dress, appearing glad to be rid of it.

John was grateful for an excuse to see Holly. He wanted to make love to her again. Perhaps if he made love to her enough she'd realize they were meant to be together. She might even realize he could help with whatever it was that had her so frightened. He glanced down at the frozen dress. An odd premonition that Holly might be torn away from him plagued him.

"If you'll excuse me." John picked up the dress and left the room.

Holly hurried along the path toward the lodge, feeling her boots crunching in the snow. It was still snowing, the fat flakes drifting down through the air as silent as her breath. She shivered and rubbed her arms, cursing herself for leaving the house without a coat. But she had been so angry that she hadn't thought of anything but getting away from him.

She heard a twig crack behind her. She turned and saw Dryden duck behind a tree. "You needn't hide from me," Holly said loudly.

"I'm not hiding." Dryden stepped out into view, spread

his legs and crossed his hands over his chest, looking all the world like an arrogant miniature of his father.

"Perhaps we should settle this once and for all," she said, walking toward him.

"It will all be settled when you leave here."

"You needn't have any fear I'll take your mother's place." Holly paused several feet from him. "No one can ever do that. I know what it's like to lose someone you love. My mother, father, and my grandmother all died. No one will ever be able to fill the void in my heart from losing them, but it doesn't mean I can't care for other people. I know you resent your father liking me, and you feel he is betraying your mother. But something else is bothering you, too."

"How do you know what is bothering me?"

"I had the same feeling you had when my mother and father died, and my grandmother brought me to live with her. I pushed her away for a while. I was afraid if I let myself love my grandmother as I had loved my parents, then I would surely lose her. You see, I'd lost everyone dear to me. I didn't want to face that pain all over again if she died. Finally, I realized how precious my time with her was, and I couldn't let my fear keep me from loving her as I had loved my parents."

"I don't need to love anyone."

"Perhaps you think that now—"

"I don't want to hear this." Dryden covered his ears and started humming.

Holly grabbed his wrists and yanked them down. "Don't do this, Dryden. Can't you see? It won't be me who will marry your father, but he will eventually remarry." Dryden fought to pull his hands free, but Holly hung on to them. "You must get used to the idea. You will have another mother whether you like it or not. And she may even love you if you let her."

"I won't let her. Or you! I hate you!" Dryden put all his weight behind him and freed his arms. He took off running through the woods, his feet churning up snow.

Holly cupped her hands and called, "You may hate me all you like, but I don't hate you. I'll never hate you, Dryden." Holly shook her head. Would Dryden ever let her get close to him?

She continued toward the lodge. Something scared a flock of sparrows in a tree off to her right. Holly listened to the flutter of their wings muted by the falling snow. Dryden was back. Smiling, she watched the birds fly up through the snow, small brown spots in a sea of white.

"I'm glad you decided to come back," Holly said as she turned around.

A person darted out among the trees, then took off running through the forest. Holly gasped, watching the tall figure darting past the trees. It wasn't Dryden, but the man who had shot at John the other day! He wore the same hooded black cape. And he was getting away.

"Wait! Stop!" Without considering the danger, Holly ran after him. The snow was so thick, she could barely see his dark form.

She followed him, knocking bare limbs aside and stumbling over the uneven forest floor. She didn't see a large stump in the snow and tripped. He stopped running and turned to look at her. A mask didn't cover his face as before. As she fell, Holly caught a glimpse of Lord Waterton's face, then her head hit something hard and everything went black.

* * *

The same feeling of foreboding that had come over John earlier grew unbearable, gnawing at him, making his heart throb, his breath quicken. He ran harder, dodging limbs and hopping over fallen, snow-covered logs. Earlier, he had searched for her in the house, then he had gone looking for her outside. He stared down at her footprints and at the second set of footprints. Who was with her? The image of the man with the gun formed in his mind, and he ran harder.

Through the thick haze of falling snowflakes, John spotted Dryden bending over someone. Then he saw Holly's bright auburn hair stark against the white-covered ground.

"Oh my God!" John murmured, and ran to her side. He pushed Dryden aside, then fell to his knees. She was lying facedown, her arms twisted at odd angles out at her sides. Gingerly, he lifted her and saw the point of a sharp rock protruding out of the snow. A small amount of blood covered the tip. He cradled her upper body in his lap and brushed the snow from her forehead. His fingers moved over a lump near her temple, then he saw the blood on his hands.

"What happened?" John asked, examining the egg-size lump on Holly's head.

Dryden glanced up at him, his face as pale as the snow. "She fell. She was running after someone. I think it was the same man who shot at us the other day, but a cloak covered his head and face and I couldn't see it, so I couldn't tell for sure. After she fell, he ran away. I yelled at him to stop, but he got on his horse and rode off."

John felt her neck for a pulse. He knew a moment of relief when the slow, thready pulse beat beneath his fingertips. But her face was so pale, her lips so blue.

Tenderly, he scooped her up in his arms and stood. He looked at Dryden, the pain coming through in his voice.

"I know you dislike her. If you were responsible for this—"

"No, Papa," Dryden yelled back at him, his bottom lip trembling. "I didn't, I didn't. She was running and tripped."

"What were you doing out here?" John said, his voice raspy with emotion.

"I had spoken to Miss Campbell and headed back to the house, but then I heard someone. I saw the man with the cloak over his head dart away into the woods, then I saw her follow him. I ran after them." Dryden jammed his hands in his pockets and bit his trembling lip.

John made his way carefully through the woods with Holly in his arms, feeling her limp head bumping against her forearm. "Listen to me carefully. Run ahead and send Lawrence for the doctor, then tell him to go to the magistrate and relay what happened. If the masked man came back, I want him found."

"Yes, Papa." Relief covered his face. He took off running, obviously glad to be gone from John's presence.

He watched Dryden disappear through the trees, the crunching of his footsteps growing softer and softer. In the silence John could hear his own pulse throbbing in his ears.

"No . . . doctor."

The barely audible words made John stop and look down at Holly. Her eyes fluttered for a moment.

"Holly, are you all right?"

She raised her hand to touch his face, then it dropped against his chest and her eyes closed tightly again.

"Holly . . ." He shook her, but her body was limp. "Oh, God!" He clasped her against his chest, hardly able to swallow past the growing tightness in his throat.

*   *   *

John watched Dr. Collins bending over Holly, the silence in the chamber throbbing in his ears. The doctor, a middle-aged man with dark balding hair, ran his hands over the lump near Holly's temple. Candlelight gleamed off his shiny pate as he gently laid Holly's head down and pulled the covers back up around her shoulders. He stared down at her a moment, shaking his head.

"Why doesn't she wake up?"

"She has a nasty contusion. A few more inches and the blow would have killed her instantly. It could be a concussion, or there could be bleeding inside her skull. I just can't tell. You did say she regained consciousness for a moment?"

"Yes, for a moment." John gazed at Holly, remembering the last words she had spoken to him. "No doctor." He swallowed past the lump in his throat that hadn't left him since he'd found her.

"I'll be honest with you, she might never wake up. I'd like to bleed her, just to keep the blood off her brain if she is bleeding internally." He turned and opened his black bag.

"No." John raised his hand, remembering Holly saying a doctor had bled her grandmother to death and that is why she had such a fear of doctors.

Collins's hand paused over the bag. "You could be doing her a harm not allowing—"

"No. She wouldn't let you do it if she were awake. I can't give you permission now."

"Very well, but if she does die, you have only yourself to blame." Collins slammed his bag shut, then picked it up. "The only advice I can offer in a situation such as this is to watch her closely. The next few days," he glanced down at Holly with no hope in his expression, "will be crucial."

"Pringle will show you out," John said, staring down at Holly, the doctor's last words stabbing him to the quick.

Collins cleared his throat and looked uncomfortable about something. Finally, he said, "The fee is half a crown."

John narrowed his brows at the doctor. "You used to bill me for your services."

"Yes, but, you know, your . . . um, financial troubles and all that. And you haven't yet settled Lady Ann's account." To further his cause, he added, "It's Christmas and I do have a family to support." He held out his hand.

John reached in his pocket and pulled out his last crown. In a tone filled with contempt, he said, "Here, keep the change. We might need your services again before this is all over."

Collins stared down at the coin in his hand to see if it was genuine, then said, "Thank you, my lord. Good night and a merry Christmas to you."

John shot Collins such a dark look, he hurried out the door, slamming it as he went.

The noise sounded like thunder in the room. John sat on the side of the bed, then picked up Holly's hand. He touched his lips to her soft skin and felt the clammy warmth against his mouth as he whispered, "I sent him away. I didn't let him touch you. You can rest easy now, then you can come back to me." He squeezed her fingers, then bent and kissed her.

Her lips were cold, unresponsive. For a moment, he couldn't hear her breathing. He bent and laid his ear against her breast. Her heartbeat was steady, but faint. He could barely feel her breath on his face. He stayed there for a long while, listening, relieved with each beat, then someone knocked softly on the door.

John sat up quickly and straightened his shoulders. "Come."

Pringle opened the door, then Brock, Dunn, Mrs. Pringle, Teddy, and Lady Upton entered the room. Dryden was absent from the party. Sarah pushed Ann in last. They circled the bed.

"Will she be all right?" Teddy's voice cracked with emotion.

"The doctor thought perhaps it might be a concussion." John couldn't mention what the doctor had said about the possibility of her never waking up with the children in the room. He stared pointedly at Teddy, John's eyes expressing what he couldn't say aloud. He forced an upbeat tone in his voice. "Things could be a lot worse, but the doctor is sure she will recover."

Teddy understood the silent communication and so did Dunn and Pringle, John noticed. Their expressions turned desolate.

Ann hugged her doll to her breast, twisting the hair in her fingers. As if afraid to look at Holly, her gaze stayed on her doll.

"Can I sit with her?" Brock asked.

"Yes, I think she'd like that." John motioned him over to sit on the bed beside him.

"Sarah, I want to go to my room now," Ann said in a somber voice without looking up at Holly.

"Are you all right?" John stood, walked over to Ann, then bent and lifted her chin, looking into her eyes. With a confidence he didn't feel, he said, "Miss Campbell will get better."

Ann looked up at him. The spark that had shone so brightly in her eyes since Holly had come was gone. Nothing was left in them but hollowness, the same look she'd had when her mother had died. She swallowed hard. With a forced evenness that made her voice sound too mature for her age, she said, "I'm all right, Papa. I just want to go to my room now."

John stood and nodded to Sarah to push her out.

Lady Upton stepped up to the bed, tears gleaming in her faded eyes. She stared down at Holly. "Oh, Anoria." She shook her head.

Teddy put his arm over his grandmother's shoulder. " 'Tis not Anoria, Grandmama. Your daughter died forty years ago from consumption."

Lady Upton looked at him with bewilderment in her eyes, then got a stubborn look on her face. "No, no, this is Anoria."

"No, this is Miss Campbell."

Lady Upton remained silent, deep in muddled thoughts.

"Perhaps I should escort you to your room," Teddy offered.

"Yes. Will you play casino with me? It always helps to keep busy. We must keep busy."

"I'd like to play cards with you." Teddy smiled wanly at her, then escorted her from the room.

"We'll go, too, my lord," Pringle said.

They filed out the room. Ann and Sarah were the last to leave. Ann kept her head bowed. John watched her leave, certain if something should happen to Holly, it would devastate Ann like the death of her mother had done. He hoped for Ann's sake—and his own—that Holly woke up.

Brock picked up Holly's hand. "She'll be all right, won't she, Papa?"

"Of course," John said, forcing a confident tone in his voice that he in no way felt.

Chapter 20

At midnight, John took one look at Holly's listless form and pale face and found it almost impossible to breathe without pacing. He rose from a chair, crossed the room, and stepped out into the hallway. A pall of silence had fallen over the house since Holly's injury.

He passed Ann's chamber door and heard soft, muffled sobbing. Carefully, he opened the door. Ann lay in her bed, her hands over her face, sobbing.

John strode into her room and sat on her bed.

"Go away. I want to be alone," she said between sobs.

"Not until you tell me what's wrong." John gathered her up in his arms.

She buried her face against his chest, her sobs wracking her body. He held her and rocked her. They stayed this way a long time, before she said in between sobs, "It's almost Christmas Eve, Papa."

"That is no reason to cry."

"Yes, it is—it is. Holly will die like Mama did. I know it. I didn't want to celebrate Christmas. It's all my fault. I should never have helped with the Christmas party. I just know she'll die. Everyone I love dies on Christmas. I hate Christmas, and I don't care if Father Christmas knows it or not. I hate it . . ." She went back to sobbing.

"First of all, this was not your fault." John stroked the back of her head. "And what is this about a Christmas party?"

"It was supposed to be a surprise." Ann glanced up at him. Long streams of tears ran down her cheeks.

"A secret, huh?" John pulled a handkerchief from his pocket and wiped her face.

"Yes, I guess I've spoiled it now. But it's all spoiled now anyway. Holly wanted to surprise you. Now she won't even be able to come. We've invited all the tenants. Don't be angry."

John stared down into the tears glistening in her blue eyes. "I am not angry, just disappointed everyone kept it from me."

"Well, Holly didn't think you'd approve."

"She was right."

"I wish I'd never helped with Christmas. She wouldn't be hurt now if I had said no. We shouldn't have the party. We don't have to have it, do we, Papa?"

"Certainly not. I'll tell Pringle to get the word out."

"I never want to celebrate Christmas again. Ever."

"No one will make you." John hugged her tightly. "Now you should go back to sleep."

"All right, Papa."

John tucked her back into bed, then kissed her on the forehead. "I'll see you in the morning." John blew out the candle burning in her room, then smelled the lingering odor of tallow. He wished he had the money for wax candles.

"Good night, Papa."

"Good night, puss."

The next morning, John heard a knock on his chamber door and opened his eyes. He had fallen asleep on the bed beside Holly. He glanced at her to see if she had moved, but she lay there in the same spot he had left her, still as a corpse.

Dunn stuck his head in the door and whispered, "You have a visitor, my lord."

"Who is it?" John's brows furrowed.

"Sir Joseph Romley, my lord. He said it was urgent." The dread came through in Pringle's words.

John's gut tightened. He wondered what bad news Romley brought with him. Then he remembered Scibner telling him Romley might be one of the men trying to destroy him. John's frown deepened. "Where did Pringle put him?" John asked, rising from the bed.

"In your study, my lord." Dunn came into the room and eyed him with disapproval, then snatched up the cravat John had thrown on the floor by the bed. "You slept in your clothes all night, my lord. I'll get you a new shirt and coat."

"Don't bother." John looked at his reflection in the mirror. His shirt was open down to the top of his chest. Thick shadows of stubble sat on his chin, lending a dirty appearance to his face. Dark circles made his eyes look sunken. His hair was mussed from where he'd slept on it. He ran his hands through his hair. "What is the point of dressing for bad news? I'll go like this." John bent over and pulled on one of his boots where he'd dropped it by the bed.

"I hope it's not bad news, my lord." Dunn helped him on with the second boot.

"The way my luck has been running, how could it be anything else? Stay with her, Dunn."

"Yes, my lord." Dunn looked reverently over at Holly.

John left his chamber. It took only moments before he entered the study. Every muscle in his body tensed when he saw Romley's ruddy face.

"St. John." Romley heaved his large frame out of a chair and bowed.

John smelled the smoke from a recently smoked cigar lingering on Romley's clothes. "What brings you out in this snow, Romley? I know this isn't a social call." John sat behind his desk, clasped the arms of his chair, and eyed Romley with rueful impatience.

Romley plopped down in his chair. The brown leather creaked, protesting so much weight. "Extraordinary news, St. John. Bloody extraordinary!"

"What is it?"

"Someone—and I do not know whom—has bought every share of stock in your shipping company."

"Really?" John leaned back in his chair.

"You should have seen the frenzy it caused among the investors. When they found out someone was buying all the stock, they wanted more—fickle lot. The shares went up to the roof. You'll have more than enough money to replace your ships and the goods you lost, but you still won't be able to get your townhouse back. I'm sorry about that, but at least you'll be able to stay afloat." Romley rapped his cane on the edge of John's desk and looked pleased with himself. "How's that for a Christmas present?"

"I wonder who would take such a chance on me?"

"I do not know, my lord. Just be glad that person was willing to gamble a large sum of money on you. I wanted to tell you the good news. It will surely be in all the papers soon."

"I suppose you bought a hefty share of the stocks." John narrowed his eyes at Romley.

"Well, I admit I did. Couldn't pass up the opportunity."

"And how did you like making money from my misfortune?"

"You don't think I had anything to do with ruining your company?" Romley fidgeted under John's sharp stare.

"Someone did."

"Upon my honor, it certainly wasn't me. I found the investors for you. I helped you get started. Why would I do something like that?"

"Money. I believe it is the root of all evil." John watched Romley's fingers tighten around the end of his cane until his knuckles protruded from his plump hand. They looked ready to burst out of his skin at any moment. John watched Romley's hands and continued. "When I needed the investors to stay, you were all for talking them out of it. Now there's this strange investor driving up the price of the stock."

"My word. You cannot think that I—that it could be me."

"Why not? You stand to earn a great deal. One thing has come from all this, I've learned the true nature of your character. You're a two-faced maggot who preys on the misfortunes of others. I'll be finding another banker in the future."

"No matter what you think, I'm innocent and you'll find it out. This insult is the thanks I get for coming all this way in the snow to inform you of your good fortune."

"Merry Christmas," John drawled, the corner of his mouth lifting in a sneer.

"Well, I never . . ." Without another word, Romley slammed the study door and left.

John sat back in his seat and wondered if Romley was the one who tried to ruin his company. But why would Romley send someone to try and kill him? Unless he thought to take over the shipping company at his death. That could be, but what if it wasn't Romley? Then who was this wealthy investor willing to gamble a fortune on him? Lady Matilda came to mind again. John wondered if she had tried to save the company without his knowledge. He would definitely have to confront her.

John thought of Holly again. In his mind, he could see her large brown eyes light up when he shared the good news with her. He longed to see her red lips parting in a smile, to see her dimples come alive. The image faded, in its place appeared the sight of her lying on his bed, inanimate, her face ashen. None of his good fortune would mean anything without Holly to share it with him. He rose from his desk, feeling the tightness come back in his chest.

A knock made John glance toward the door. "Come in."

Pringle opened the door. "I showed Sir Romley to the door, my lord."

"Good, don't let that bastard grace these walls again."

"Yes, my lord. The post has just come, my lord. It's a bit late. The snow kept it from coming on time."

"Thank you, Pringle." John accepted the letters.

"Will you be taking breakfast, my lord?"

"No, I have no appetite."

"Yes, my lord." Pringle was about to close the door, but John's voice stopped him.

"Pringle."

"Yes, my lord."

"You need to visit all the tenants and tell them the Christmas party has been canceled. . . . No need to look so surprised, Ann told me everything."

"I—I did want to tell you, but Miss Campbell persuaded us to keep it a secret. She wanted to surprise you."

"I'm not blaming you, Pringle. I know how persuasive Miss Campbell can be. Just see the party is called off."

"Yes, my lord." Pringle's expression fell as he turned and left the study.

John frowned at the mail in his hands. A large important-looking envelope caught his eye. He picked up a letter opener and carefully broke the seal, then pulled out the paper inside. Attached to it was a note. Scribbled across the page, as though the person wanted to disguise his or her handwriting, were the simple words:

Merry Christmas from a friend.

He laid the note aside, then opened the document. It was the deed to his townhouse. He cursed under his breath. When he could think and not worry about Holly, he would see Lady Matilda and put a stop to her meddling in his affairs. Now that he had the money, he could pay her back and not feel obligated to her. She was to be pitied in a way. Getting the townhouse back and investing in his company were desperate attempts to gain his affections away from Holly. He would explain to Lady Matilda there would never be anything between them. Holly was the only woman he could ever love.

His thoughts drifted back to what had happened to Holly. He wasn't totally convinced Dryden hadn't pushed Holly and caused her to fall. A part of him didn't want to believe Dryden capable of such cruelty, but he hadn't come to see Holly when everyone else was so worried about her. John was sure if Dryden had hurt Holly, then the boy must be suffering from a guilty conscience. He decided to speak to Dryden. Perhaps the boy would tell the truth. John headed for the door.

John walked down the steps from the top floor, shaking his head. Where could Dryden be? Brock said he hadn't seen him that morning. John had combed the house, but couldn't find him. He'd given up and headed back to check on Holly. Now, he strolled down the hall toward his chamber. He saw Dunn standing out in the hall, his head bowed. John slowed his pace, going through the motions of putting one foot in front of the other, while a sinking feeling swallowed him with each step he took.

Dunn must have heard his approach, for he glanced up and stared at John. He frowned. "No need to look so stricken, my lord. She's still the same."

John felt a moment of relief wash over him, then asked, "Why are you standing out in the hall? Why aren't you watching Miss Campbell?"

"Master Dryden's in there." Dunn motioned toward the door with his head. "I've never seen him looking so blue-deviled. I thought he needed some time alone with her."

"I see. You may go. I'll stay with her now." John opened the door carefully, trying not to make any noise.

Dryden was sitting in a chair by the bed, shoulders slumped, elbows resting on his knees, hands covering his face. His dark hair needed cutting, and it fell around the edge of his hands. It had finally stopped snowing and the sun was shining. A shaft of morning sunlight cut through the window and across the bed. It just touched the top of

Dryden's bent head, bringing the dark highlights of his hair to life.

John noticed Holly hadn't moved. Dust motes floated listlessly over her, forming a misty cloud of light around her prostrate body. He couldn't bear to look at her for long. He walked into the room, then closed the door behind him.

Dryden raised his head and looked at John, his golden eyes gleaming with unshed tears. Their gaze held a moment, then, embarrassed by his tears, he turned away and buried his face in his hands again.

John laid his hand on his shoulder. "Shall we talk about it?"

Dryden kept his face buried in his hands for a moment longer, then raised his head. Tears streamed down his cheeks now. He wiped them away with the back of his hand. "I've been cruel to her, and all she's ever been to me is nice."

John reined in his temper and asked, "Did you push her?"

"No," Dryden bawled. "I didn't, I didn't. I swear it!"

"Tell me the truth."

"I am telling you the truth."

"He is . . ."

The barely audible words made John and Dryden look at each other for a moment, then they glanced at Holly. John saw her large brown eyes staring back at him.

"My God . . ." In one long stride he was at the bed, crushing her to him, burying his fingers in the thick hair streaming down her back. "You had me so worried. Are you all right?"

"I believe I'd feel . . . better if I could breathe." Holly smiled wanly at him.

John eased her back down on the bed. "I'm sorry, did I hurt you?"

"No . . ." Holly blinked up at him, her long-lashed lids drooping over her eyes, giving her a sleepy-eyed coy beauty like Da Vinci's "Mona Lisa."

"I'm glad you're awake." John smoothed back the hair from her face, then gently kissed her on the lips. He didn't let his lips linger.

"You should apologize to Dryden . . . not me." Holly grinned feebly at Dryden, a hint of her dimples visible. "He didn't push me, I tripped."

"Did you get a look at the masked man?"

"No."

Holly looked as if she were hiding something, but John didn't press her. He turned to Dryden, who stood at the end of the bed, his expression grave. "Come here, Son." He motioned him forward with his hand.

Dryden stepped around the bed , looking sheepish now that Holly was awake.

John put his arm around his shoulder. "I'm sorry. I wanted to believe you were innocent, but when I found you standing over her and knowing the way you have acted toward her—"

Dryden looked down at Holly and spoke. "I'm sorry."

"I know." Holly held out a trembling hand to him, tears glistening in her eyes.

Dryden hesitated a moment, looked at her outstretched fingers, then bit on his bottom lip to keep it from trembling. He fought some war deep inside him, then, finally, reached over and grasped her hand.

"Are you too big for a hug?" Holly asked, blinking back tears.

Dryden shook his head and bent down, hugging her tightly, burying his face in her shoulder. John saw Dryden's shoulders shaking and heard his muffled sobs. He rose and left the room quietly, leaving the two of them alone. It pleased him that Dryden had finally warmed to Holly. He felt his conscience stab him. He had spent far too much time away from the boy. From now on, it would be different. He headed for Ann's chamber.

The door was ajar and he paused, listening to Brock read Defoe's *Robinson Crusoe* to Ann. John pushed the door open a little wider and saw Ann lying on her bed, withdrawn, despondency personified, her features lacking even a spark of spirit. Brock was lying across the foot of the bed, on his back, with the book above his head.

He paused in his reading, then said, "Now listen, this is the good part."

"Please, I do not wish to hear anymore. I want to be alone."

Brock slapped the book closed and rolled on his stomach. "Holly wouldn't want you to lie here like you were dying . . ." He paused on his last word and watched tears stream down Ann's cheeks. "I'm sorry, I didn't mean—"

John opened the door. "I think some cheering up is needed in here."

"Oh, Papa . . ." She burst out crying, burying her face in her hands.

Brock had tears in his own eyes. He shrugged. "I only tried cheering her up."

"I know." John tousled Brock's hair, then bent and put his hand on Ann's shoulder. "You've no need to cry any longer. Holly is awake. I believe she is going to be all right."

"Is that really true, Papa?" Ann looked up at him, tears streaming down her cheeks, her shoulders shaking. She hiccupped. "She didn't die? I thought for sure she would die like Mama did. But she's all right, you say?'' Ann could hardly talk for trying to hold back her sobs.

"Yes, she is awake. I believe the worst has passed." John took out a handkerchief from his pocket and handed it to Ann.

"Can we go see her?" Brock sat up and leaped off the bed.

"Yes, I'm sure she'd like that."

Brock ran out of the room, smiling.

Ann wiped her eyes. "We've been given a Christmas blessing. After so many years without one, we've been given one. It is a miracle, isn't it?"

"Yes, I believe it is."

"I'm so glad she's well, Papa. So very glad." A slow, timid smile turned up the corners of Ann's little rosebud mouth, even as tears still streamed down her face.

John kissed the top of Ann's head. "I'm glad, too, puss."

Hours later, Holly glanced at all the people standing around John's chamber, all talking at once. For as long as she could remember, it had been only her and her grandmother. She had always wanted brothers and sisters. Large families were incredible, and there was so much love to be had in them. And the proof of it was before her. Never had so many people cared about her.

"I want to sit by her," Brock said, shoving Dryden aside.

"No, I'm going to." Dryden shoved his brother back.

Holly smiled at Dryden. After he had cried in her arms, he had been so attentive, like a different child altogether. She knew once he let down the walls he'd erected around his heart that he would be a loving little boy. And he was special. She watched him shoving Brock up against the wall. In a lot of ways he was just like his father—arrogant, aggressive, overbearing. He'd make a proper heir for John.

"What is the meaning of this?" Teddy asked in a feigned prim voice, then he joined the boys and began roughhousing with them.

"They'll bring the house down." Mrs. Pringle glanced at Teddy as he grabbed a pillow off the bed and hit the boys with it. She fluffed up Holly's pillow and actually smiled down at her. "How's that?"

"Very nice, thank you." Holly wondered at this new transformation in Mrs. Pringle. Pringle's new authority over her must have something to do with it.

"I'll stoke up her fire."

Holly glanced toward the fireplace and watched Pringle grab the poker from Dunn's hand.

"You did it last time. I'll do it this time." Dunn grabbed it back.

"Someone stoke the fire," Lady Upton said, shaking her cane at Dunn and Pringle.

They looked at each other, then Dunn slapped the poker in Pringle's hand. A smug smile spread across Pringle's face. "Here, I suppose it's your turn."

"I was so worried about you," Ann said, from where she sat on the edge of the bed. She leaned over and touched Holly's hand. "I'm so glad you are better."

"Me, too," Teddy said, taking time out from hitting the boys to wink at Holly. Then Dryden hit him in the head with a pillow. He fell back on the floor, moaning in the throes of pretended death.

Holly grinned at them, then glanced at John, who stood at the foot of her bed, looking anxious for the family visit to be over. Their gazes locked for a moment. John rolled his eyes with impatience. She almost burst out laughing. Ann spoke, drawing Holly's attention again.

"I was so worried Christmas had caused you to be hurt. Do you think Father Christmas will be angry with me?" Ann stared down at her hands. "I was very bad and said I hated Christmas."

"I think he understood." Holly had to raise her voice, over the growling and grunting between the boys and Teddy. "You don't hate it any longer, do you?"

Ann shook her head, then stared down at her hands. "But I told Papa about our Christmas party and that I didn't want it."

"Oh!" Holly glanced over at John.

His brows drew together. "Are there any other schemes that you've hidden from me?" Even though he was scowling at her, his voice held a teasing note.

Holly thought of the money she had invested in his company and the townhouse, then lied with an ease that surprised even her. "No, I believe that is it. Can we still have our party?"

Everyone in the room grew silent. Even Dryden and Brock stopped mauling Teddy on the floor and grew still, waiting for his answer.

John waited, letting the moment drag, then finally said, "Yes, if I don't have to hear any more about it. Pringle, you will have to invite the tenants again." John glanced at Pringle, who was poking the fire.

Pringle paused, then looked conscience-stricken about something. He clutched the poker, his knuckles turning white. "Well, my lord, I didn't get around to uninviting them yet. I was worried about leaving the house with Miss Holly still ill."

"Thank you for caring," Holly said.

"Well, if we are to have this party, we'd better get busy," Mrs. Pringle said, then looked over at Pringle and added, "if that is all right with you, Mr. Pringle." She smiled amiably at him.

"Yes, we'll have to get busy." A grin tugged at the corners of Pringle's mouth, but he managed to maintain a stern mien.

"I can play the pianoforte, if these old fingers can still move." Lady Upton moved her fingers to check.

"What fun. A Christmas party. I hope you two whirling dervishes will behave yourselves." Teddy poked the boys again.

They laughed and dived on him.

Holly saw Ann glance down at them, a wistful look in her eyes as if she would like to join them. Holly touched her arm. "Would you like to help Mrs. Pringle? I'm sure she could use it."

"Yes." Ann smiled, but it didn't light up her eyes.

Holly felt John's gaze on her. She glanced toward him. Their gazes locked. The heat and longing in his eyes made her body warm all over.

"All right, everyone out," John said impatiently. "You're disturbing the patient."

"Aw," Brock complained, crawling off Teddy and Dryden, then he and Dryden helped Teddy get to his feet.

"Come on, we'll put you to work on the party. That will get rid of some of your energy." Lady Upton cast Dryden and Brock a look of reproach, then she straightened her spine and glided out of the room.

Teddy scooped Ann up into his arms. "Come on, cute face. You'll have to show us where to put the decorations." He looked at Holly. "I'm glad you're better. I hope the first dance at the party will be mine."

"If I'm dancing, you'll be the first." Holly smiled at him.

"I doubt that," John said. "The first dance is mine."

With feigned haughtiness, Holly said, "I'm sorry. I don't believe you have asked me for the first dance."

"You are right." John matched Holly's teasing tone, his eyes glistening at her.

Ann and Teddy were the last to leave the room. "Aren't you coming, Papa?" Ann asked.

"I'll be down in a minute. I have something important to ask Miss Campbell."

"She'll give you the first dance," Ann said. "Won't you, Holly?"

"If he asks nicely." Holly grinned at John.

"Come on, before we miss all the fun." Teddy closed the door behind them.

"I thought I'd never get you alone." John's frustration came through in his deep voice as he walked around the bed.

Holly laughed at him. "You are terrible."

"Can I help it if I want you all to myself?" He sat, the mattress dipping under his weight. He took her in his arms. "Now what is all this nonsense about asking nicely for the first dance?" He placed tiny kisses on her forehead, working his way down her nose.

"You just naturally assume I will do your bidding. It doesn't hurt you to learn to ask."

"I suppose not." He stopped kissing her, then stared into her eyes, all the teasing leaving his handsome face. His eyes shone like two pieces of bright amber. "I am asking you now to spend the rest of your life with me and to grant me every dance. I love you to distraction. Say you will be my wife."

She hesitated a moment and stared at the long, dark lashes shading his eyes, then at the possessive gleam that burned in their golden depths. The look was so intense she felt it warm her all over. She clasped her arms around his neck. "I'll marry you."

"It took you long enough to decide. Are you sure? Once you say yes, there'll be no changing your mind." He ran his finger along her bottom lip.

"I won't change my mind. Before my head struck that rock, I realized how much I loved you. I'm afraid you are stuck with me." Holly ran her finger down the dimple in his chin, feeling the stubble beneath her finger. "I won't waste the few precious moments of happiness we have together."

"You talk as if we won't be together." John gently grasped her chin. "Nothing will ever part us. Do you hear? I won't let it. Perhaps you will trust me enough to tell me what has you so afraid."

"I can't." Tears stung her eyes and she glanced down at his coat sleeve. "I just want to forget it."

"I can help you now. My company has capital again. I have the money to replace the ships I lost and to help you fight this thing. What is it?"

Holly tried to change the subject. "How did you get the money to save the company?"

"I didn't do a thing. Someone invested a large amount in the company. It caused the other investors to buy more stock. My company is healthier now than it's ever been."

"Do you know who the investor was?" Holly asked innocently.

"I believe it was Lady Matilda."

Holly forced a straight face and remained silent.

"Enough about that. We have digressed. I want to know what you are hiding."

"Don't ask me, John. I'll tell you one day, but don't ask me now."

He opened his mouth to speak, but Holly kissed him.

His fingers threaded through the thick hair at her nape, then he pulled her close, his tongue slipping into her mouth. He groaned deeply in his throat. Holly clung to him, consumed by his passion.

After a moment, John broke the kiss. His chest heaving from desire, he looked into her eyes. "If we keep this up, I'll want you. And you're not well enough for that."

"All I have is an ache in my head. You won't hurt me. If you do, I'll throw you out of the bed." Holly grinned impishly at him, then pulled his head down to her for another kiss.

"My little vixen," John said against her mouth, then his hands went to her breasts, kneading them through her nightgown.

The sensation of his hands sent tiny shudders through her. Her fingers tangled in the lapel of his coat as she tried to yank it down over his broad shoulders.

He helped and made quick work of his clothes, while he never broke their kiss. When he was naked, he slid beneath the covers. He gently eased up her nightgown, moving his large, warm hands up her thighs.

The feel of his hands sent tingles of heat up her legs and pooled in her loins. He eased on top of her, then slid into her. Holly clung to him, trying to commit to memory the extraordinary feel of him on top of her, the way he felt deep inside her, the closeness they shared at this moment. Moments were all she had with him, and each one was precious. One day they would have to say good-bye. She hoped it wouldn't be soon. And she would have to tell him it was Lord Waterton who had hit her, but she would wait until after Christmas. She wouldn't spoil their happiness now.

Chapter 21

Later that evening, Holly felt almost well, save for a slight ache in her head. Laughter from guests drifted up the stairs. She listened to the voices, mixing with the melody "The Holly and the Ivy." Every now and then Lady Upton hit an off-key note, but she was doing her best.

Holly grinned and took in the beautiful greenery roped along the stairs and the red bows placed in just the right spots. The air, redolent of pine and cedar and the luscious scent of food, filled her senses as she entered the parlor.

People dallied in front of the many tables that were laden with food. A colorful array of mincemeat pies, plum puddings, canapes, jellies, even a roasted goose, filled the tables. Pringle stood behind the table directing Dunn and Mrs. Pringle, who were carrying in platters of sweets from the kitchen.

Out the corner of her eye, she saw a Christmas tree, not the small one from the cottage, but a huge cedar at least twenty feet tall, filling one whole corner of the room. The candles were lit, the light throwing dancing shadows on the walls. Her face brightened as she recalled all those Christmases with her grandmother and the magical moment when they had finished lighting the candles and they had stepped back and got their first view of the tree. She had always hugged her grandmother and wished her a merry Christmas. Tightness clenched the spot over her heart and she blinked back tears.

John's footsteps echoed behind her. Quickly, she dashed the old memories from her mind.

"Papa, look at the tree. Isn't it marvelous? Didn't we do a good job picking it out?" Ann's voice sounded full of reverence and awe.

"Yes, and it took all of us to get it in the house," John said tonelessly, then added, "It was worth all the effort. I've never seen anything to equal it."

"It was Holly's idea. Her grandmother was German and they always had a Christmas tree. I wonder why we have never thought to have one."

"From now on, I promise you we will have one." John glanced over at Holly.

She smiled back at him, then turned toward Ann. "Is your little girl here?"

Ann scanned the people and children in the room. "There she is. Over there with her parents, Mr. and Mrs. Wheatly. Her name is Amanda." She nodded to a girl who appeared the same age as Ann. She had long, dark hair and a somber, pensive look in her dark eyes. She gripped her mother's hand.

"She doesn't look very happy to be here," Holly said. "Perhaps you should speak to her."

"I'd like that very much. Do you think it will change her attitude about Christmas?"

"I don't know, but it's a start. And if anyone can do it, you can, now that you have the Christmas spirit. It's contagious, you know." Holly smiled at Ann and touched the end of her nose.

"Shall I put you on the sofa near her?" John asked Ann.

"Yes, Papa."

"You'll excuse us," John said to Holly, then walked across the room with Ann in his arms.

Holly watched John place her on the couch, before he went to speak to Amanda's parents. Amanda eyed Ann warily for a moment, then her mother nudged her and she walked over to sit near Ann. Amanda stared shyly down at her hands. Ann spoke first, drawing Amanda out of her bashfulness. Soon they were chatting away like old friends.

Bang. The French doors opened, grabbing everyone's attention.

A tall man appeared in the doorway. A long white beard covered the lower half of his face. Long silver shimmering hair fell past his shoulders. He laughed and knocked the snow off his brown hooded cloak. The velvet of his cloak was worn and thin in spots. His brown leather breeches and laced tunic were old and threadbare, and looked like the raiment of someone from the Middle Ages. The brown wool gloves on his hands had the fingers cut out. A huge burlap sack was slung on his back. He hefted it off his shoulder and plopped it down on the floor.

Holly saw Ann's eyes light up. Then Holly watched all the other children stop what they were doing and stare. Dryden had his usual skeptical expression. Brock stared, his jaw open. Amanda looked the most surprised out of all the thirty or so children in the room. She blinked, mesmerized with disbelief.

"Well, now," the man said in a thick Scottish brogue.

"Are ya goin' to be starin' at Saint Nicholas, or comin' to get your presents?"

Holly smiled, watching the children clamber to get near him.

"Whoa, now! Lads on one side. Lasses on the other. Let's not shove," Saint Nicholas said.

Ann looked longingly at Saint Nicholas, as if she wanted to get in line, too.

He noticed her right away and walked over to her, leaving the other children while they scrambled to get in line. "Well, now, Miss Ann. You'll be first in line." He handed Ann a small package.

"Thank you." Ann didn't bother looking at the package in her hands, but continued to stare up into his twinkling eyes. "You really are Saint Nicholas, aren't you?"

"Yes, I have to own it." He bowed to her.

She smiled and looked too amazed to speak.

"Now, if you'll excuse me, I'll be gettin' back to me job." He touched her head with a gloved hand.

Dunn laid down the tray in his arms and went to join Holly. She dragged her gaze away from Saint Nicholas and looked at him.

"How do you like our Saint Nicholas, miss?"

"Wherever did you find such an enchanting man."

"He found me. He came to the back door today and said he heard we were having a Christmas party and could he come."

"What a kind man." Holly glanced at him, watching him hand Amanda a wrapped box.

He glanced up at Holly and winked, his blue eyes twinkling. Did he know what she'd just said? Holly had the oddest sensation that he did.

When Lady Upton hit a wrong key, Holly and Dunn

looked at each other. Dunn made a face. In a pleading voice, he said, "Do you know how to play, miss?"

Holly grinned. "A little, but I can't promise I'll be any better than Lady Upton."

"You couldn't be any worse."

Lady Upton played another sour note, and Dunn hunched his shoulders in protest.

Dunn saw Pringle motioning him back toward the kitchen. He frowned. "The taskmaster will get out his whip if I don't keep at the tables. If you'll excuse me." Dunn bowed, then hurried across the room.

Holly heard Pringle berating Dunn for dallying and smiled at them, then they walked toward the kitchen, nipping verbally at each other.

Holly strolled over to the pianoforte and sat beside Lady Upton on the bench. "Are you getting tired, my lady?"

Lady Upton finished the final notes to the song, then looked at Holly and sipped her drink, a cranberry-colored liquid that smelled more of spirits than punch. "I am feeling a bit giddy. I'm afraid my fingers are feeling it, too."

Holly felt John's gaze on her. She glanced up and saw him moving across the room toward her. He acknowledged his grandmother with a bow, which sent the stubborn piece of hair falling down on his forehead.

He didn't seem to notice as he stared at Saint Nicholas. "Who is that man?"

"He came to our door earlier and asked to be invited," Holly said, itching to twirl the stray lock on his forehead around her finger.

"He is singular in the extreme. When he strode past me, he said for me not to worry, that I'd get what I wanted for Christmas."

"Isn't it odd? I feel like I know him, but I've never seen

the man before in my life. Did you see the way he lit up the room when he entered it? There's a wonderful aura about him.''

''Yes, he's probably had too much to drink.'' John shot her a skeptical look that made her grin.

She watched Saint Nicholas hand out all the presents to the children, then make his way around the room, giving presents to all the adults.

He paused near Holly. ''I don't have a present for you. You'll be gettin' yours later.'' He winked at her, then at John. His white beard stretched across his face in a broad, knowing smile.

Holly stared at him, astonished this stranger had spoken to her as if they were old friends. It was odd, but she felt as if she'd known him all her life.

''Would you be knowin' a waltz, Miss Holly? I'd love to dance a waltz with this lovely lady.'' Saint Nicholas bowed in front of Lady Upton, who was still sitting on the piano bench.

Lady Upton eyed him with open astonishment. ''Bless me, I will accept, sir.'' She stood and took his arm.

Holly began playing Weber's ''Invitation'' and watched Saint Nicholas escort Lady Upton out to the middle of the dance floor. Everyone turned and glanced at Saint Nicholas and Lady Upton gliding around the room to the fast-paced melody, then the men began to single out partners. Pringle found Mrs. Pringle and whisked her out onto the floor.

John sat next to Holly on the bench. ''So you play also. What other hidden talents do you have that I know nothing about?''

''I believe you know them all.'' Holly grinned at him, teasing, then she looked at the man playing Saint Nicholas and her grin faded. ''I can't help this odd feeling I keep

having that he is a real saint," she whispered. "There is
something extraordinary about him. Look at the way his
beard shines just like it was real silver."

"I think if you believe that, then we should cart you off
to Bedlam directly." He grinned at her, then glanced over
to Saint Nicholas and studied him.

Holly watched him, too, surprised with what grace and
style he whirled Lady Upton about the room. Their feet
hardly touched the ground.

Holly let her fingers glide along the keys, the melancholy
and fear she'd felt earlier gone. This was her home and
family now. She was safe and loved. It would be a lovely
Christmas. But still there was a small nagging voice in the
back of her mind, saying, "You're too happy. This will
never last."

Two hours later, everyone had gone home after much
dancing. Holly had played until her fingers were sore. Saint
Nicholas had made a quick exit after he had danced with
Lady Upton. The grand lady wore the smile Saint Nicholas
had left on her face until she became too tipsy from the
spiked punch and staggered to bed.

Holly stood near the Christmas tree, looking at Dryden,
Brock, and Ann playing with their toys. She didn't have
the heart to put them to bed yet. They looked too excited
to sleep anyway. Teddy was sprawled on a sofa, next to
John, watching the children while he sipped punch, his
eyes heavily glazed.

Holly was pleased with how the evening had gone, but
she kept seeing Saint Nicholas winking at her and saying,
"You'll get your Christmas present later." What did he
mean by that? John would think her mad if he knew she
secretly believed that man was indeed the real Saint Nicho-

las. Of course, it didn't help that he had lived in the fourth century and was long dead. He was the patron saint of schoolchildren and sailors, wasn't he? He could appear wherever he was needed.

John must have read her thoughts. He glanced at her and smiled. With his gaze locked on her, he stood and walked to the mistletoe, which hung from the dome in the middle of the room. He paused beneath it, then crooked his finger at her. His grin turned sensual, and a little wicked.

She walked toward him, feeling the warmth of his smile pulling her toward him like a magnet, heating every nerve in her body. She paused before him.

He grinned down at her and whispered, "Merry Christmas," then enfolded her in his strong arms and kissed her. His kiss was long, lingering, stealing Holly's breath. John finally broke the kiss and smiled down at her, his eyes glowing with such unbridled emotion it made her heart skip a beat.

She glanced back at him, and whispered, "I love you."

John opened his mouth to speak, but Brock said, "Look! Papa is kissing Holly under the mistletoe. I want to kiss her, too." Brock scrambled to his feet and ran toward them.

"She doesn't want to kiss you, but she'll kiss me," Dryden chided his brother and ran after him.

The two boys fell in line behind John.

"I believe she wouldn't mind if we all kiss her, since she is to be part of the family," Teddy said in his teasing tone, then rose and stood behind Dryden.

"What about me?" Ann asked from her spot on the couch. "I want to kiss Holly under the mistletoe, too."

Holly and John turned at the sound of Ann's voice. They watched Ann grasp the arm of the sofa and pull herself up. Holly gasped, then heard John suck in his breath. Ann bit her bottom lip, her gaze never wavering from Holly's face. She took two wobbly steps toward her, then her legs gave way and she crumpled to the floor.

Holly heard her own pulse throbbing in her ears as joy burst inside her, the power of it warming her from the inside out.

"Oh my God . . ." John said under his breath. In two long strides he was at Ann's side and squatted beside her.

He helped Ann sit up. "Are you all right?"

"Of course, Papa," Ann said with a sureness in her voice.

"Can you stand up again?" John asked, his voice sounding husky with emotion.

"I'll try, Papa."

"You can do it," Holly said, holding out her arms.

John held on to Ann's arm, until she brushed his hand aside. "I can do it alone, Papa."

Ann took a step and wobbled. Holly held her breath, thinking Ann might fall again, but she groped at the air and kept her balance.

"You're doing it, Ann. You're doing it . . ." Holly motioned her over with her hands.

John walked beside Ann in case she fell. Each slow step Ann took brought elation and wonder to John's face.

Teddy, Brock, and Dryden looked frozen to the floor, watching Ann's progress.

Ann bit her lip, her expression a mask of concentration. After four more wobbly steps, she grinned proudly and fell into Holly's waiting arms.

Holly hugged her tightly. "You've given me the best Christmas present I'll ever receive in my life. Thank you." Ann's face blurred behind Holly's tears. She knew now this was her present from Saint Nicholas.

John grabbed Holly and Ann, embracing them, looking too overcome by emotion to speak.

Dryden and Brock were not to be left out and they ran forward, hugging John, Holly, and Ann.

"I'm glad you can walk," Dryden said, smiling.

"Have you been pretending all this time?" Brock asked, sounding put out.

Ann raised her brows at him. "Of course I haven't."

Teddy stepped forward and kissed Ann, his eyes magnified by unshed tears. "I'm proud of you, Miss Priss. Now maybe I'll get that first dance at your come-out ball you promised me when you were three."

"Oh, Uncle Teddy," Ann said, "you still remember that."

"Of course I do," Teddy said, sounding offended.

Pringle cleared his throat from the threshold. He saw Ann standing, and the blood drained from his face. He looked unable to speak for a moment, then he regained his aplomb. "You have visitors, my lord."

Abruptly, Lady Matilda appeared behind Pringle, wearing a bright red dress and a smug smile. Lord Waterton was beside her and . . .

Holly stared into the frigid gaze of Mortimer Scott, Kent's father. A visceral grin screwed up one corner of his mouth. Her knees grew weak, and she fell against John.

He supported her, all the joy gone from his eyes. "What is the matter? Are you unwell?"

Holly felt too light-headed to speak. All she could do was stare at Mortimer Scott.

When she didn't answer him, John followed Holly's gaze toward the door. "Who is that man, Holly?"

She kept her voice low so the children wouldn't hear her, her words sounding oddly controlled. So calm, in fact, they frightened even her as she said, "He is the father of the man I killed."

John flinched as if her words had hit him. The color drained from his face. "So that is what you've been hiding from me? You killed someone?" he said, his voice so ragged and soft it was barely audible.

Holly nodded.

John looked surprised she had agreed with him, then his eyes filled with torment and despair. She sensed his pain, and it stabbed her chest like a dagger. He had every right to despise her. She had dreaded this moment, feared it, the second she knew she loved him. What could she say to ease the blow for him? She tried to find the words to tell him she loved him, that she'd always love him no matter what she'd done in the past. But somehow telling him seemed inane at the moment, just empty words to cover a horrible act. No amount of heartfelt words could soothe the fact she had murdered Kent. Somehow, words only made it seem worse.

Lord Waterton strode toward them, his usual bored mien veiled behind the distress in his eyes. He deliberately avoided looking at Holly. When he stood opposite John, he said, "I don't think you want Mr. Scott to say what he has to say in front of the children. Is there somewhere private we can go?"

"What are you doing with this man?" John glowered suspiciously at Lord Waterton.

"He found Lady Matilda and me at the inn. After I heard his story, I thought I should accompany him here."

"I'm sure you wouldn't want to miss the excitement," John said snidely. Waterton opened his mouth to speak, but John ignored him and turned to Teddy. "See that the children get to their beds."

Worry masked Teddy's eyes, and he didn't protest as

he gathered the children around him. "Come on, you monkeys, to bed with you."

"What is wrong?" Ann asked anxiously.

"Who is that man?" Dryden glanced at Mortimer Scott.

"Why is he here with Lady Matilda?" Brock asked.

"Nothing for you to worry over . . ."

Holly followed John out the room and listened to Teddy's voice fade away. What would the children think of her? What must John think? He would never forgive her from keeping the truth from him. Never. Knowing that hurt worse than having to leave him. The tightness grew in her throat until she couldn't swallow. She wanted to cry, but she knew she'd lose all self-control if she allowed herself one tear. No, she'd cry much later, when she was alone and could let out the pain.

John paced the length of the library and listened to the hiss of the fire in the grate, whispering over and over, "You fool, you fool, you fool."

He looked at Waterton, who leaned indolently against the mantel, his monocle leveled at Mr. Scott. Lady Matilda sat on a chair wearing a satisfied grin and an all-too delighted expression. Mr. Scott stood near Holly. He was tall, gray-haired, with shifting blue eyes. An aura of arrogance pervaded his countenance and the tight line of his mouth. He clutched a cane with a fat ruby embedded in the end and stared down at Holly.

She hadn't moved since she sat down in a wing chair. She was gazing down at her hands folded in her lap, her expression grave, her face whiter than the cliffs of Dover. All the red had left her lips and they looked a faded bluish-pink. Her lashes cast long half-moons on downcast cheeks. Why did she sit there and not say one word in her own defense? John's frown deepened, his brows so low they touched his eyelashes.

"I believe I've said all there is to say." Mr. Scott reached for Holly's arm and John stepped in front of him.

"I won't let you take her until I investigate this further," John said.

"If you need proof—here." Mr. Scott pulled a newspaper clipping from his pocket and another piece of paper, then thrust it at John. "It's all in there, how she killed my son. She stabbed him, then fled on a ship. I've tracked her all the way from America. I doubt I would have found her if she hadn't caused a stir in London by kissing you on the sidewalk." Scott grinned deviously. "I showed a miniature portrait of her around and it was easy tracking her here, until I got lost on these godforsaken back roads you people have here and I came across Lady Matilda and Lord Waterton. They were kind enough to show me the way here."

"She's not going with you." John stared at the man, daring him to disagree.

"I have a writ for her extradition from the Chief Justice of the King's Bench, and she's going back to Richmond to hang for her crimes, whether you like it or not, Lord Upton."

"You cannot go against the law. You have to see reason, my lord," Lady Matilda said. "If it were up to me—"

"This is not up to you." John cast her a quelling glance that immediately made her clamp her mouth closed. "What are you doing in the middle of this anyway?"

"I came to see what I could do to console you once you found out about her." Lady Matilda pointed to Holly as if she were on trial for using witchcraft.

"I do not need to be consoled by you. Haven't you done

enough by investing in my company without telling me, and paying the lien on my townhouse?''

"I don't know what you're talking about," Lady Matilda said, then stretched her lips tight across her mouth. "I did no such thing."

"If you didn't do it, who else could have done it?"

"I did." Holly finally spoke.

"You did it?'' John stared at her, feeling like she'd just driven an axe in his chest. He could get used to the idea she had murdered a man, but this?

"She's a very wealthy woman, our Miss Kimbel," Mr. Scott spoke up, answering for Holly, his eyes gleaming.

"My lord!" Lady Matilda's face turned ashen, then she leveled her gaze on Holly. "Pray, how could you pretend to be a pauper? And all those things I said to you. You're a lying, deceptive little wretch! A wretch, I tell you!"

Holly stared blankly back at her, flinching from each one of the words Lady Matilda flung her.

Mr. Scott laughed aloud, cutting off Lady Matilda's tirade. "Her grandmother was one of the wealthiest women in Virginia, but she chose to live like a pauper, pinching pennies until they squealed. The old eccentric bat could have bought half the state if she had wanted. She left everything to Miss Kimbel here when she died." He shot Holly a reproachful look. "Have you been keeping that a secret, too, Miss Kimbel?"

Holly grimaced at Mr. Scott, the first sign that she felt any emotion since she'd walked into the room.

John approached Holly and grabbed her shoulders. "How could you lie to *me?* I thought I knew you better," he said, searching her large brown eyes. They were blank and impassive. "My God! Did you think I wouldn't find out? How you must have laughed behind my back, playing the poor servant all the while you were so wealthy you could bail out a poor sinking fool like me! Damn your meddling!" He stared at her, his heart tortured by the lovely deceiving sight of her.

She blinked up at him, her eyes glistening with torment now. In a barely audible voice, she said, "I'm sorry . . ."

"All you can say is you are bloody sorry?" As if her touch scalded him, John dropped his hands and stepped back.

"I wanted to be honest with you, but I couldn't tell you," she said, chewing on her bottom lip, tears gleaming in her eyes. "I had to keep my wealth and identity a secret."

"You could have told me," John cried.

"I couldn't involve you. Don't you see that?"

"No! You had rather lie to me. You didn't trust me enough to tell me the truth. Have I misjudged you so completely?" John turned away and stared into the fire, unable to look at her any longer.

There was a quick rap on the door, then Mr. Scibner entered the house carrying a canvas sack. "Forgive my intrusion, but I must speak to you, my lord."

The magistrate, Silas Denton, came in behind Scibner. He was a large man with a face like a bull dog and an inherent tenacious look in his eyes.

"Good evening, my lords," Denton said, bowing to John, then Lord Waterton.

"If you will spare me a moment, my lord, I know who has been trying to ruin you." Scibner glanced over at John.

John's gaze flicked to Waterton, who dropped his looking glass and stood up straight now. The deliberate indifference that seemed so much a part of his mien disappeared. Waterton stared at Holly and shared a knowing glance with her, his expression guilty enough to be condemned by a jury. Waterton was guilty. Another lie she had been keeping from him.

"You bastard!" John cried, leaping at Waterton.

Chapter 22

Holly held her breath and watched Mr. Scibner leap between the two men. "It's not Lord Waterton," he said, shoving against John's chest.

"Who the devil is it then?" John paused and glared at Lord Waterton over the top of Mr. Scibner's head.

"It's her." Mr. Scibner pointed a finger at Lady Matilda.

Lady Matilda straightened uneasily in her chair and met Mr. Scibner's gaze. "It was not I, sir, you are mistaken."

Holly gazed at Lord Waterton. "But I saw you skulking out in the woods."

"Yes, you did, and I'm sorry you fell and hit your head." An icy smile spread across his lips as he glanced over at Lady Matilda. "I was following you to make sure Lady Matilda didn't harm you. I would have stopped when you fell, but St. John's boy was with you."

"That is a lie!" Lady Matilda cried.

"He's telling the truth." Mr. Scibner spoke up. "You

are a cunning foe, my lady." He swept an exaggerated bow in her direction. "You wanted Miss Campbell dead and that's why you put on a mask and shot at her."

"I didn't."

"But you did. Jealousy was eating away at your soul, wasn't it?"

"Why should I be jealous of her?"

"Not of her, but of Lord Upton. You wanted him, so you masterminded a plan to get him."

"I did no such thing," she said, trying to sound indignant, but there was a nervous edge in her voice now.

"Yes, you did. One of my men heard Mr. Jarvis in a pub, bragging about having been hired by a lady to do a little dirty work. He didn't say whom, but the only likely lady in this case was you. I wasn't sure of your guilt yet, so I had my men question Mr. Romley and Mr. Thomas, my other two suspects. They said Mr. Jarvis sent them a note asking to see them. It wasn't Mr. Jarvis, was it, Lady Matilda? It was you trying to steer me off your trail. And it worked for a while."

"You're lying," Matilda said, her blue eyes blazing.

"Am I? It worked until you spread that lie about Lord Waterton speaking to Jarvis in the park. Then I grew more suspicious and started following you. When I knew you were out of your room at the inn, I searched it and found this." He opened the sack and held up a mask that had the eyes cut out of it, a pair of men's breeches, and a black cloak. "You brought them to the inn and planned to make another attack on Miss Campbell. You made sure the cloak matched Lord Waterton's so it would look like he was doing it. You wanted to finish the job you had started. Lord Waterton knew this and that's why he was following Miss Campbell."

Lady Matilda glared at Holly now, a malignant glow in

her eyes. "You should have died the first time, but he got in the way." Lady Matilda nodded toward John. "I came close to shooting him for that. He was making me quite angry, trying to follow me."

"Why, Matilda?" John stared hard at her.

Lady Matilda lost all the self-control she was trying desperately to master. Her face turned ugly with bitterness. "Why not? I've loved you since before you married my cousin, but you were too blind to see it. What was left to me but to ruin you and have you come to me for help? I was willing to marry you and give you all the money you needed. All you had to do was ask, but no, you lavished your affections on *that*." She jabbed her finger in Holly's direction, then turned on her.

"And you, with your sniveling niceness. You were supposed to leave after you encountered those brats of his, but no, you stayed on to annoy me."

"Then Lord Upton came to the country. That must have made you very angry," Holly said.

"Yes, it was not in my plan. I thought he would surely stay in town and mind the shipping office, but no, he had to run here after you. I had to figure out a way to get you away from him, so I tried to kill you."

John looked at Lady Matilda, anger and pity in his eyes.

"I hope you're happy now," Lady Matilda said to John. "You've fallen in love with a murderess. You could have had me for the asking, but no, you chose her. It's too bad she didn't die." Lady Matilda smiled maliciously. "She'll hang. I'm going to make sure I know the day and the hour so I can laugh the whole time." Lady Matilda's laughter filled the air.

"Who'll hang?" the magistrate asked, confusion on his face.

"She will." Mr. Scott pointed to Holly. "She killed my

son and is wanted for murder in Virginia. I have a writ to carry her back and stand trial.''

"We know nothing of the circumstances.'' John stared pointedly at Holly. "Why did you kill him?''

"It was an accident. I never meant to kill him. He held me prisoner for a week. I escaped. There was a struggle.'' Holly wrung her hands in her lap.

"Why did he hold you prisoner?'' John asked.

Holly opened her mouth to say something, but Mr. Scott blurted, "You can tell your story to a court of law. All I know is, you killed my son and there was no good reason for it.'' Mr. Scott pulled out his pocket watch and looked at it. "This is all very intriguing, but I have to get her back aboard ship. It is due to sail soon. Mr. Denton, you will please escort my prisoner, and put her in chains. I don't want her escaping.''

"If you put her in chains, I'll wrap them around your neck.'' John glowered at Denton.

"Sorry, my lord, but it'll have to be done.'' The magistrate looked at Holly. "Come along, young lady.''

Holly's gaze locked with John's for a fleeting moment. She couldn't bear to see the hurt in his eyes and glanced down at her hands. "I'm sorry,'' she said. "Please try to forgive me. I never meant to lie to you. I only wanted to help you. Don't tell the children where I've gone. Just tell them I had to go home.''

She turned then, knowing he was lost to her forever. She strode through the door without looking back.

John stood, frozen to the floor, watching the magistrate grab Lady Matilda. Lady Matilda shot John a look of hatred mixed with regret, then he shoved her out the door and she was gone. Mr. Scott followed in their wake, his cane swinging over his arm. He looked delighted he'd finally caught his son's killer—a little too delighted for having recently lost a son, John thought, scowling at his back.

Mr. Scibner waited until Scott left, then turned to John. "Do not worry, my lord. I believe with a good lawyer she will get off."

John stared ruefully at the empty doorway. "I hope she does."

"Since this case is closed, I'd better get back to my wife. It is Christmas Eve. Good night." Scibner bowed to John and Waterton, then left the room, his white hair gleaming in the candlelight.

At the mention of a wife, John turned and glanced back at the doorway. Where was Holly now? They were probably putting chains on her.

Waterton stood near a table, pouring two drinks. "Here." He handed the glass to John. "You might need this."

John stared at Waterton, surprised by his kindness, then accepted the wine. He clutched the glass. "I suppose this ties all the loose ends up but you. What were you doing speaking to Jarvis?"

"I, dear boy, have been in love with Lady Matilda since I went to her come-out ball fourteen years ago. But the silly wench wouldn't give me the time of day. She thought herself in love with you."

"That is why you've hated me all these years?"

"To be absolutely blunt, yes. She's the one thing I've wanted and my wealth couldn't buy her. I usually get what I want, and I didn't take it well." Waterton downed his glass of wine in one gulp. He made a face. "Love. It's a bloody nasty business."

"So you knew about Lady Matilda's scheme to ruin me."

"I had my suspicions, so I went to Jarvis. He told me everything." Waterton set down his glass and filled it again.

"I was going to invest in your company anonymously and clean up the muddle she'd made of your life, but Miss Campbell beat me to it. I wanted to persuade Lady Matilda to confess and throw herself on your mercy, but I didn't realize how obsessed she'd become. She really is ready for Bedlam."

"Yes." John downed his wine, then stared at the door, seeing Holly leaving through it again, without so much as a glance in his direction.

"Mooning at the door won't get her back, dear boy."

John's gaze flicked back to Waterton. "Nothing will bring her back to me. The woman I knew—the woman I fell in love with—is gone. I don't know that person who just walked out that door. All I know is she's a good little liar."

John's hand inadvertently tightened around the stem of the glass. It cracked in his hand. The pieces crashed to the floor and shattered near his boots. John stared down at the blood dripping from his hand.

Waterton threw John a handkerchief. "She's the same woman you fell in love with, but more intriguing, don't you think?" He didn't wait for John's answer, but continued on. "She's proven she'd do just about anything for those she loves. Ah, to have a woman love me like that . . ." Waterton's voice trailed off and he looked pensive.

"I'm sure you'd like to be made a fool of by a woman paying your bloody debts."

"Where would you be without her help?" Waterton said with exasperation. "You're too damned proud and hurt to see logic. You've got your priorities all wrong. Every nobleman in England has been bailed out by a woman's wealth. It's an accepted norm among our class."

"I know, I married for wealth once. Elise never let me forget that it was her money that had saved my family's name. After that I swore I would never marry a rich woman again.''

"Pride is all well and good, but it doesn't warm your bed on a cold night, nor does it keep you from debtors' prison. I understand completely why she went behind your back and helped you. You're too damned stubborn to have accepted help otherwise.''

John knew Waterton spoke the truth, but said, "She could have told me she was wealthy.''

"Would you have believed her, with that charming, unaffected air of hers?'' Waterton ran his finger around the top of his glass. "I'm usually a good judge of character, but she even fooled me. I would never have guessed she was wealthy.''

Waterton was right, but John wasn't about to tell him so. He remained silent and thought of Holly. He clenched his cut fist, feeling the bandage tightening around the wound, the tightness traveling up his arm and swelling deep in his chest.

At John's silence, Waterton continued. "I understand completely why she couldn't tell you about her wealth, or the murder. If you were she, would you have told the truth?'' He didn't wait for a response. "Not damned likely. You're lucky to have found her. I've wasted my life loving a woman who'll never return my love. Until I met Miss Kimbel, I didn't realize how futile my pursuit had been,'' Waterton said, a hint of regret coming through in his voice. "You have a chance for real happiness with Miss Kimbel, seize it while you can. I can help you get her back, then we can smuggle her to France. I have a chateau near Nice. You can change your identity and set up housekeeping with her and the children. No one will ever find her.''

"You would do that for me?'' John raised a brow of disbelief at Waterton.

"Not for you, but for her." The dry tone was back in Waterton's voice. "She really is a marvelous creature. And if she wasn't so in love with you, I'd court her myself."

John shot him such a jealous leer that Waterton burst out laughing.

Teddy appeared in the door. He saw Waterton laughing, then narrowed his eyes at him. "What is so damn funny?"

"We were just discussing love in all its asinine absurdity." Waterton raised his glass at Teddy, then downed the contents.

Teddy looked at John in disbelief. "Why the devil are you talking to him like he is a long-lost friend? He tried to ruin our company. You should take the man out and shoot him." Teddy glared at Waterton, then back at John.

John proceeded to inform Teddy of Matilda's scheme and how she had made Waterton look guilty, but he couldn't bring himself to speak of Holly.

"And what about Holly?" Teddy asked, looking worried. "Where is she?"

"She's been arrested for murder," Waterton said.

The words struck Teddy and he stumbled back, clutching the stanchion. "Murder?"

"Most foul," Waterton said, a touch of the dramatic in his voice. "But we're not going to let her hang." He turned and looked at John. "Should I ask him along, or is he more trouble than he's worth?"

"I'll have you know, I'm quite a good shot. You would have found it out had not Holly—"

"That's enough." John eyed both of them. "We do not have time for arguing. If we're going to get her back, we had better make a plan and quickly."

* * *

The moon hung low over London, a swirling mass of vivid blue, its spherical shape shifting behind thick clouds that scudded across the sky. Dim lights from the docked ships winked at Holly through the frigid night air. She strode up the gangway toward a ship, listening to the wind pounding the riggings against the aft mast.

Mortimer Scott prodded her shoulder with his hand. "Hurry up."

She turned and stared at him, the chains on her wrists rattling. "I'm going as fast as I can."

"It's not fast enough." Mortimer shoved her again.

She stumbled down onto the deck and saw the captain, a one-eyed man with scraggly long hair. He leered at her and said, "Well, well, you found the mademoiselle." He spoke with a thick French accent.

"Yes, I did. When can we set sail?" Mr. Scott asked, pulling Holly toward a set of steps.

"It must be soon. I've just got word the Thames is about to freeze over."

"Very good. Perhaps when you are out of the harbor, we can get on with what we planned for Miss Kimbel here."

"What is that?" Holly asked, turning to Mortimer.

"You'll find out soon enough, my dear," he said, emphasizing the word dear.

A shudder went through her as she wondered what he was planning to do to her. Out the corner of her eye she saw three scraggly, long-haired, bearded sailors striding up the gangway. They staggered against each other, their intoxicated voices bellowing out a vulgar song. The captain was cursing at them in French. One of them, a tall, broad man, had a dirty bandage wrapped around his hand.

"Let's get you below. Wouldn't want you escaping again." Mortimer grabbed her arm.

This *was* her chance to escape. She pulled back from

Mortimer and dove down the companionway, taking the stairs two at a time. His shouts for her to stop rang in her ears as she ran through a small hallway. Before she reached the end, a pair of huge hands grabbed her from behind, then lifted her up like a tiny doll. She glanced over her shoulder and looked into the face of a huge, burly man.

"Where you think you're going?" He smiled, showing his rotten teeth.

"I know you," Holly said, her legs hanging in midair. "You attacked me those months ago on the dock!"

"Aye. The governor what was looking for you hired me."

"That doesn't speak well of his character."

"Snippy bitch, ain't you?"

Holly thought Rotten Teeth was about to throw her against the wall, but Mortimer appeared and said, "Lock our little murderess in the cargo hold. Let her have a taste of the rats, it might make her a little more biddable."

Rotten Teeth appeared unhappy about the order. He looked as if he'd much rather bash in her skull. He plopped her down on the floor so hard her teeth ground together, then his fingers dug into her arm. She grimaced at the pain as he forced her down a ladder. Finally, he paused in front of a door.

"Get a little taste of the darkness, wench. You'll be sin-gin' another tune when ye get out." With a grin that flashed his rotten teeth, he opened the door and shoved her inside.

Darkness and the damp odor of mildew filled the cargo hold. Rats scurried past her feet, then the key scraped against the lock, a sound much like the rusty hinges of a casket closing. The wind caught the sails and the ship lurched. She could hear the water rushing past the planking of the hull. Soon, they'd be out to sea.

Trembling now in the frigid cold, she pulled her cape around her and leaned back against the door. All the tears she'd held at bay rushed out of her. She thought of John. She'd lost him forever. Soon she would hang and she'd die aware that he hated her for lying to him. But didn't she deserve this hell. God was punishing her for taking Kent's life.

For a moment, Holly was back home at Kimbly. It was Christmas Eve night. Her grandmother had gone to church for midnight service. She hated the lonely feel of the house when Grandmother was gone. Holly sneezed for the umpteenth time, then brought her handkerchief up to her nose. Why did she have to get a cold, and on Christmas Eve.

She nestled back against the pillows on her bed and picked up a book of Byron's poems. She kept it under her mattress and only brought it out when she was sure her grandmother wouldn't walk in and find it. Grandmother didn't approve of Byron's risqué ramblings of love, nor of his lifestyle.

She didn't hear the noise at first, but then it grew louder. She tensed and glanced toward the window, watching a knife slip beneath the sash.

Then someone's fingers pushed it up. She could see the top of the person's head and the bright blond hair. Before his face appeared, she knew it was Kent. He saw her and smiled. As bold as day, he slithered through the window. Not an easy feat since her room was on the second floor, but he must have climbed the rose trellis beneath her window.

Holly screamed and threw the book at him.

He easily dodged it, then his eyes twinkled in the candlelight as he stared at her breasts. He was only seventeen, but he ogled her body like a dirty old man. "Don't be frightened, Holly. It's me." He bent and picked up the book. "Mmm! Byron, huh? A young girl of fifteen shouldn't be reading this. Or are you craving a man's body now? One can only hope."

"Get out of here!" Holly jerked the covers up to her neck.

"Don't think so. You've been teasing me for years now. I'm here to collect. I've been waiting for that old bat to leave you alone. I knew my patience would be worth it." He tossed the book on the floor.

The loud thump sounded like a report from a gun. Holly jumped.

He enjoyed her discomfort and smiled, then ran his finger along the blade on his knife.

Incensed by him, she said, "I haven't been teasing you. You're the one that's been tormenting me all my life. And if you don't get out of my room this very instant, I'll hurt you."

"That is rich. You hurt me?" He threw back his head and laughed. His smile died as he came toward her bed.

Holly glanced frantically around her. He was getting closer, then he dove for her. Holly rolled out of bed, grabbing a heavy candlestick as she went. Before Kent could grab it, she slammed it across his head. It was the first time she'd wanted to really hurt Kent. She thought of all the mean things he'd done to her and she wanted to hit him again. But she dropped the lamp, then grew aware he'd always be alive to torture her . . .

The memory faded, and tears welled up in her eyes. She collapsed against the door, sobbing. No longer able to support her, her knees crumbled. She slid down the door and buried her face in her hands, the chains on her wrists rattling near her ears.

* * *

After what seemed like years, but in reality had only been a few minutes, Holly heard the scurrying patter of rats coming closer and was forced to regain her composure. Standing, she wiped the tears out of her eyes and kicked out blindly at the darkness. Oh, to be anywhere, rather than trapped in the cargo hold with these rats crawling everywhere.

As if St. Nicholas had heard her plea, she heard the muffled sound of two men arguing behind the door. One sounded like Mortimer Scott.

Then the key turned.

The door opened and a shaft of light cut through the darkness. The rats scattered behind the many barrels and crates stored in the hold, then someone grabbed her arm and yanked her through the door.

"There you are."

Holly blinked up into Mortimer's face, shaded by a lantern in the hallway. The dim light made his skin glow yellow and his deep-set eyes appear ghoulish. For a moment, he reminded her of his son, but Kent's eyes were a lot crueler.

"It appears someone is anxious to see you." Mortimer pulled her up a ladder and along the hallway.

"Who?"

"You'll find out soon enough."

Abruptly, he opened a door and shoved her inside a dimly lit cabin. She glanced around the cabin and heard the key turn in the lock. It was sparsely decorated with only a table, a sea chest, and a bed tucked in a dark corner.

"Well, well, what have we here."

Holly jumped, recognizing the softly spoken southern drawl. It had tortured her for most of her life. She turned toward the bed, scanning it closer this time. Vivid blue eyes stared back at her. She blinked, thinking she was seeing a ghost.

"You look like you're going to faint. Has England changed you so much? As I recall, you never swooned." Kent graced her with a smile, his face growing wickedly handsome. He was sprawled out across the bed, his arms behind his head, his ankles crossed.

"You?" Holly said, her bottom lip trembling. "You're alive."

"You sound disappointed."

"Only because I was accused of your murder."

He laughed. "Now that is the girl I knew." He swung his long legs down onto the floor and sat up. His blond hair had grown longer since she'd last seen him and hung down around his shoulders, gleaming in the candlelight.

"I don't know what you hope to accomplish by following me to England and having everyone believe I killed you." Holly heard a loud thump above deck. She glanced at the ceiling for a moment, then looked back at Kent.

"I would have thought it was obvious."

"I'll never marry you. You and your father will never get your hands on my plantation, or my money."

"Come, come, you know Father has always coveted your grandmother's land, since it borders our properties, but I'm at least innocent of wanting you for your land and money." His gaze slowly raked over her.

"No, you only want me because I wouldn't marry you." She shook her finger at him, the chains on her wrists rattling. "I'll never marry you. I'm sorry I stabbed you, but you shouldn't have tried to force me to marry you. That was wrong and you know it. I'm in love with someone else, and I mean to marry him—if I can win him back." Holly frowned, wondering if John could ever love her again.

"Go ahead, be stubborn, but the captain will marry us before we reach Virginia," Kent smiled, "or you'll go back down to the cargo hold. Which will it be?"

The thoughts of the rats made her skin crawl, but no more than marrying Kent and having him touch her. "I'll go back into the cargo hold," she said, forcing resolve into her voice.

The corners of his mouth twisted in a wider grin. "I would've thought a few minutes down there would cure your stubborn streak. I told Father he shouldn't have put you down there right away, but perhaps he was right. Maybe you need to stay down there for a day or two." He stood and started toward her. "Or maybe the quicker route would be to take you right now. That might settle the matter once and for all."

"If you touch me, I really will kill you." She took a step back toward the door. "You won't get away with this."

"I shall. I told no one that you stabbed me. And before we hopped on a ship to come here, I published our engagement. Everyone thinks I was coming to Europe to marry you, and we were to honeymoon here. So even if you protest, it will be too late. Everything you own will be mine, including your body." He reached out to grab her.

Holly jumped to the side, but she wasn't fast enough. His hand snaked out and caught the chain connecting her wrists, then he jerked her into his arms. He tried to kiss her, but Holly turned her face away and hit out at him with her fists.

Another crash sounded outside in the hallway, then the door burst open.

The drunken sailor with the bandaged hand stood in the threshold, his broad shoulders filling the doorway, his chest heaving. She looked into the man's golden eyes and knew it was John. He was wearing a black wig and false beard. A murderous scowl was etched into his brow. She was never so glad to see him scowling at her. He'd come for her. Tears stung her eyes.

"Take your hands off her," John ordered, his gaze cutting Kent into tiny pieces.

In one swift jerk, Kent pulled the chain up and twisted it around Holly's neck. "I don't think so. She's mine." He bent down and said in Holly's ear, "So this is the man you love. He's not much to look at."

"You must be the murder victim risen from the grave." John took a step forward.

"Yes, funny how that happened."

"I won't let you take her." John stepped closer.

Kent tightened the chain. The cold iron links cut into her windpipe. She coughed, trying to breathe, but only an airless croak come out of her mouth.

"Don't come any closer," he warned.

"Don't hurt her." John stepped back, never taking his eyes off Kent.

"I won't if you cooperate. We're going to leave now. Back away from the door or I'll strangle her." Kent shoved Holly forward, her arms still bent back behind her head. The chain was wrapped around her neck in such a way that if she dropped her hands she'd strangle herself.

"I'll never let you take her." John backed slowly out into the hallway, keeping his gaze locked on Kent.

"I don't think you have a choice." Kent shoved her forward through the threshold, then stepped out, keeping enough tension on the chains to allow her to breathe, just barely. Her lungs ached for want of air.

Holly would have missed what happened next had she blinked. John stuck out his booted foot and tripped Kent. Taken off guard, Kent let go of the chain and tumbled forward, careening into Holly. Holly fell and her arms jerked forward. Instantly, the chain clamped around her neck, crushing her windpipe . . .

Chapter 23

Large, strong hands caught her, then John pulled her upright. Kent scrambled to get up, but John kicked him in the chin. His head lolled to the side, then his eyes crossed and he collapsed against the floor.

"Are you all right?" John unwound the chain and crushed Holly to him.

She listened to his heart beating against her ear, felt his strong arms around her, then sobbed. In between gasps, she said, "I didn't think you'd . . . ever be able to forgive me. I hated the thought of dying . . . knowing you hated me. Can you forgive me for lying to you?"

"It might take some convincing."

He wrapped his arms around her, then bent her back over his arm in a deep kiss that made her knees weak and her insides melt. His imitation beard tickled her chin, and she smiled inwardly. It felt like heaven to have him kiss her again. She wrapped her arms around his neck and heard the chains rattle against the manacles on her wrists.

Someone cleared his throat and drawled, "There is a time and place for this kind of thing."

John broke the kiss and mumbled a curse under his breath.

Lord Waterton stood staring at them. He, too, was in disguise, looking like a scrubby sailor who'd been out at sea too long, wearing a red bandanna wrapped around his head and an earring in his ear. He'd blackened his two front teeth and smeared something black over his face to make it look like he hadn't shaved in a week.

Holly stared at Lord Waterton. Her eyes widened at the sight of him, then she glanced back at John. "I see you brought reinforcements."

"Yes, well, Waterton insisted he be allowed to come along."

"How nice of you, Lord Waterton." Holly smiled at him. "And may I add, you look very handsome in your disguise."

He bowed graciously. "At your service, madam. I hope it's an improvement." He grinned, showing the faux gap between his teeth, which added an absurdity to his appearance that was endearing and made Holly grin at him. "I'd do anything to see you smile at me. I've already turned over a new leaf."

John cocked a brow at him. "No one believes that tripe, Waterton."

Lord Waterton threw back his head and laughed.

Teddy came striding down the hall, wearing a dirty cap and a long pointy imitation beard. He shoved a groggy Mortimer Scott in front of him. Blood dripped from Mortimer's nose and lip. "What are we to do with him? It's the last of them," Teddy said, pointing at Mortimer.

"I believe there's a deportation ship leaving for Australia. I'll see if we can't get passage for him. We'll take this, too." Waterton picked Kent up by the front of his coat, hefted his limp form up on his shoulder, then carried him up the steps. His sagging arms swayed over Waterton's back.

Holly watched them leave, then said, "Can we get these chains off me and go home? It will be Christmas soon and I want to be with the children when they wake up."

"Yes, my sweet. My thoughts exactly." John swept her up into his arms.

"Where did you get your disguise?" Holly straightened his wig that had fallen down over his forehead.

"Scibner was kind enough to lend them to us."

"I was fooled when I first saw you, but when I looked closely in your eyes I knew who you were."

"Unfortunately, he didn't have anything to change the color of my eyes."

"I'm glad. I like them that color. I hope our children will have your eyes and my disposition. I couldn't bear to have a house full of scowling children." She snuggled her face next to his neck, breathing in the clean familiar male scent of him.

"Hah! They would be running off, doing God knows what behind my back," he said with an endearing softness, then smiled and kissed the top of her head. "They will wreak havoc on me."

"You know you wouldn't want it any other way." Holly smiled impishly up at him.

"You're right," he grumbled under his breath, belying the grin on his face.

Christmas morning, John sat in the parlor next to Holly. She was nestled against him, with her head on his shoulder, her hair spilling down over his arm that was around her. He was watching the children playing with their presents, rubbing his fingers through Holly's hair, marveling at the softness, a sated grin on his face from having made love to her that morning.

"Don't they look happy?" Holly whispered to him, not taking her eyes off the children, their happiness reflecting in her face.

"Yes," John said, watching Dryden move a toy soldier from a mock battle that involved a battalion of men presided over by Ann, Brock, Teddy, and even Lady Upton, who was down on her hands and knees, too. "But there are too many generals." John grinned at her.

"Don't move him there, child. Always keep your general in the rear of the ranks," Lady Upton chided.

"Yes, Grands." Dryden took her advice and moved his general back.

"I'd put him over here," Teddy said, surveying the battlefield.

Dryden frowned at Teddy. "Whose present is this anyway?"

"Perhaps I should have gotten everyone toy soldiers." Holly looked worried that she hadn't pleased them for Christmas.

John's shoulders shook while he held back a laugh. "Don't worry, the former Miss *Kimbel,* we'll buy everyone toy soldiers next year."

Holly saw the amusement on his face. "Oh, you . . ." She hit his chest playfully.

He grabbed her hand, flattening it against his chest. His shirt was open, and he felt her fingers tangling in the dark mat of hair there.

Her expression grew lusty and she whispered to him,

"You look like a handsome, bedraggled rake in need of sleep."

"If you hadn't kept me up this morning, I might have gotten some sleep," he said, teasing.

"I couldn't allow you to sleep on our honeymoon morning." She ran her finger along the dimple in his chin. "Wasn't it kind of Lord Waterton to procure a special license so we could marry?"

"You should have seen him. I thought he was going to strangle the clerk when he said he could not be bothered on Christmas Eve."

Holly smiled. "Lord Waterton is truly a noble man." At John's unconvinced grunt, Holly laughed.

This brought a reluctant grin to John's face. "That reminds me," he said absently, then pulled a small box out of his pocket. "Merry Christmas."

"But I didn't get you anything." She looked stricken.

"I got what I wanted . . . you." He placed a soft kiss on her neck and felt a shudder go through her.

Holly opened the small box. Her eyes grew wide as she stared down at the ring he'd bought her. As if it were the most precious thing in the world, she picked it up and studied the gold band. Holly entwined with mistletoe covered it. Five small diamond berries scattered through the leaves winked as she turned the ring.

"It's a Christmas ring. How lovely." She put it on and admired it.

"I ordered it some time ago as a Christmas gift, but considering our wedding day, I thought it would make an appropriate wedding ring."

"It's perfect," she said in a husky whisper, her large brown eyes glowing up at him with tender emotion.

Every time she looked at him with love in her eyes, he wanted to draw her close and kiss her just to prove to

himself she was real. He gave in to that need now, tilting
her face up to his for a kiss. Their lips touched, a gentle,
warm melding that made a fierce, possessive feeling rise
up inside him. She was finally his. He could hardly believe
his good fortune.

"Listen!" Ann said. "It's the Christmas bells."

John broke the kiss and listened to the muffled din of
bells ringing.

Ann grabbed hold of the sofa and slowly pulled herself
up, then reached out to hold Holly and John's hands.
"Come. Let's go listen to them. We'll miss it if we don't
hurry."

Ann pulled them toward the foyer. John still marveled
when he saw Ann walking. He still had trouble believing
it, and here she was dragging him down the foyer. John
smiled and allowed her to lead him.

Ann flung open the front door and stepped out onto
the porch. A burst of frigid wind whipped back the strand
of hair on John's brow.

"Come on," Ann said, pulling them through the door.

John felt the sting of cold against his cheeks, then Dryden, Brock, Teddy, and Lady Upton joined them on the
porch. Holly snuggled next to him. They stood out on the
porch, the air reverberating with the din of thousands of
church bells, echoing from all directions, ringing in the
joy of Christmas.

"Look." Ann pointed to a group of carolers trudging
through the snow toward the house. The notes of "Here
We Come a Wassailing" lifted up in a harmonious chorus
of voices, melding with the drifting melody of the bells.

"Saint Nicholas is in the chorus," Brock said.

The man who had played Saint Nicholas was standing
on the back row with the gentlemen, his mouth open in
a large O as he sang, his beard glistening like soft, polished

silver. John stared into the twinkling, starlit eyes of the elderly bearded man.

Their gazes locked.

The man winked at him. John couldn't help but wonder if he truly was Saint Nicholas. It was a silly notion, but no more foolish than believing in miracles. And he did believe in them now. Every time he saw Ann walking, and the complete change in Dryden—not to mention having escaped debtors' prison, he was convinced Holly was a miracle. His miracle.

As if she had read his mind, she turned and looked up at him with those long-lashed brown eyes. Then her dimples beamed in a smile, a miracle of a smile that held all his happiness. He'd never again think of Christmas in the same dismal way, not after being given Holly, the most immeasurable gift of all.

Dear Reader,

If you are a history buff as I am, I thought you would be interested in the custom of the Christmas tree. Symbols of survival, evergreens have a long association with Christmas festivities, probably dating back to the eighth century, when St. Boniface completed the Christianization of Germany. He dedicated the fir tree to the Holy Child, which replaced the sacred oak of Odin.

Christmas trees became popular in England during Queen Victoria's reign. The tradition of the Christmas tree started in 1841 with German Prince Albert, the Queen's husband. But it was not the first tree known in England. In 1832, when Victoria was but thirteen, she recorded in her diary an account of a Christmas tree decorated by her aunt Sophia. Sophia's German mother had always planned the family celebration around the tree, and the tradition stuck with Sophia. The popularity of the tree was assured, when, in 1848, the *Illustrated London News* carried a description of the royal tree.

In America, trees had been decorated since the 1700's, but smaller parlor-type trees were used until the 1800's. Christmas trees were popular for decorations because of the sheer abundance of them.

I hope you enjoyed reading Holly and John's story as much as I enjoyed writing it. Please let me know what you thought of the story. I would love to hear from you. My address is:

Constance Hall
PO Box 25664
Richmond, VA 23260-5664

Merry Christmas and Happy New Year! May all your Christmas wishes come true.